JOSHUA GAYOU
COMMUNE

BOOK TWO

ACKNOWLEDGMENTS

I am indebted to my wife, Jennifer, and my friends, Dusty Sharp and Scott Brandt. Anything that I got right in here, I lay it at their feet.

A NOTE ON THE LANGUAGE

A great deal of the research I conducted leading up to writing this book had to do specifically with the character of Blake Gibson. Namely, it was critical to me that I got him right. Owing to an intense and abiding gratitude that I personally feel to the men and women serving in all branches of the United States military, it was a key mission that I set for myself in this story that Gibs not feel like a cartoon. For better or worse, I wanted to do what I could to get as close as I could to a real life Marine. I wanted SSgt Gibs to feel like someone any real veteran might recognize.

Being a civilian, I had a lot of work to do in order to get him authentic, not the least of which had to do with his speech. For better or worse, Marines curse up a blue streak. Not only that, they do so in some of the most creatively poetic ways I've ever encountered. If you, kind reader, are the type who might take exception to such language, I feel it's only right to warn you right now: Gibs is a bit of a hayride. I'm accepting no complaints on the matter as well; Marines curse, people. This is just the reality of their nature.

I feel it is also necessary to state here that Marines have

several common curses and sayings that are universal to the culture. They all know who Jody is, that bastard; they know how to skate; they've all broken it down Barney-style; they all know that field days suck ass. There is a whole language unto itself within their group that has evolved from simply existing in their common family. The act of service in the Corps can be and often is punctuated with misery, and Devil Dogs since the beginning have used this shared condition as a means of bonding. The rest of us are just outsiders looking in.

I wish I could say that all of the dialog written for Gibs is one hundred percent unique but that would be a lie. The simple fact is that even Marine profanity has evolved and normalized over time; had I written all of Gibs's lines on my own, he would have sounded like a foul-mouthed civilian… and he needs to sound like a foul-mouthed Marine. Because of this, some of his expressions and stories are lifted directly from the stories of real Marines who served; those who I have spoken with one-on-one as well as those who have published their stories on line, either in blogs or in simple forum posts.

It is my humble hope that my readers forgive me this minor bit of cheating; I considered accuracy to be far more important than ego in this regard.

Josh Gayou

PROLOGUE

T his document comprises the second book of the history of the Jackson Commune, covering its growth from a small homestead to a collective of survivors occupying an increasing footprint in the mile-diameter valley that we have unofficially named "The Bowl."

As in the first book, these stories have been collected through interviews with the people who live here and are presented in narrative form for the sake of readability (for my original, unfiltered interview notes, see Jacob Martin's library—all notes utilize a basic key script shorthand, which should be readable with little effort).

—B.C.

1

GIBSON'S FIELD TRIP

My understanding is that Blake Gibson's (who everybody just calls "Gibs") arrival was something of an unsettling experience for everyone involved. I was not present for this event; I showed up sometime later. From his perspective, he was shepherding a collection of diverse people across the country in a school bus searching for a safe haven, or at least someplace they could make into a safe haven. From the perspectives of Jacob "Jake" Martin, Amanda Contreras, and Elizabeth Contreras, they had only recently defended their home from the incursion of a large group of squatters, losing their good friend Billy in the process.

It is fair to say that relations were tense in those early days. Gibs and many of the people who came with him (such as George, Barbara, and Oscar) have since become integral members of the community, of course, but this was a state that had to be actively pursued by the constituent members (against their own instincts in many cases). There were some key decision points along the way that would play a major role in defining the intra-social relationships of our members as well as what I would personally define as the "karmic balance" of the whole. As is typically the case in life, the answers were rarely black and white.

Gibs has found a niche for himself in the group as the head of security with a secondary function as liaison between us and the United States Military Remnant under Commander Warren (being a Marine veteran, he speaks their language a lot better than any of the rest of us). In his mid-forties, he stands at six foot two, is fair complexioned, and what hair remains to him is a trim, sandy brown. He maintains a clean boxed beard, some of it grey, and has the physical build of the perpetually thin—meaning that any dietary struggles on his part would have been along the lines of putting weight on rather than trying to work it off.

He is consumed by an inner, frenetic energy that seeks expression in various ways. The man simply cannot sit still. If he is in a chair, one of his legs must be bouncing. If he is standing, he is shifting from foot to foot or continually walking forward and back for a few steps. When backing up, he tends to run into things that are behind him (often more than once on the same occasion). It takes a directed effort of will for him to put his hands in his pockets (I've seen him do it—he jams his balled-up fists in and grimaces).

Gibs is an eloquent man for the most part, well-spoken and well-read. Even so, it is clear that he has devoted a significant portion of his life to learning how to swear in the most creative (often times surprising) manner, elevating the practice to his own personal art form. An old world chivalry has been programmed into his psyche, both from his time in the Marine Corps and from his mother, who he dearly loves and idolizes (referring to her alternately as "Mom," "The Kraken," and "Queen Killjoy.") Because of this, his usual brand of profane eloquence is reduced to stuttering sentence fragments when he is in the company of women or children; half of his vocabulary is rendered off limits. In such company, he often lapses into official military-speak—the kind of procedural dialect one used to encounter when speaking with active duty service members or police officers on the clock.

Gibs lives in a fifth wheel, a forty foot Forest River Sandpiper, which is positioned fifty yards northeast of Jake's cabin (to the right of the cabin, essentially, if you stand in front of it facing the entrance). The fifth wheel was a special project executed between Gibs and Jake; Gibs discovered it on a particular excursion into Jackson and was unable to forget it once he saw it. Jake was happy enough to go out with him in the Ford and bring it back. He parked it fifty yards out from the main property and embedded back into the tree line. He stated that he preferred the arrangement, noting that it would, "keep the riff-raff off the front lawn." He refers to his trailer as Casa de Redneck.

Sitting with him at the dinette inside the impressively appointed camper (it has no less than five pop-outs, two bedrooms, two entertainment centers, two full bathrooms, and an interior and exterior kitchen), I arrange my notebook, pens, and a delicious cup of coffee that Gibs has provided from his personal stores. A self-professed coffee addict, he regularly uses his clout to get the product bumped to the top of any scavenging list, whether it be ground or unground beans, instant, or any of the paraphernalia necessary to brew the beverage. He never has to push very hard to ensure that coffee is looked for on our excursions; he is well loved, and we are happy to make the effort.

Gibs takes a sip from his own mug, leans back in his chair, and says, "Well, what would you like me to talk about?"

"Anything, really," I answer. "I've found that people often only need to pick a place to start. Once they've found that, everything else flows naturally. Just start with how you arrived here."

"Okay, then."

Gibs

I want to say we came rolling through here just under two years ago. I'm not certain exactly how long it's been now… maybe a year and a half. I don't spend much time looking at calendars anymore. But let's call it a year and a half for shits. And "rolling" is probably too charitable a word. We were essentially limping along on fumes in a last-ditch desperation effort. Things were pretty bad when we ran into Jake.

We had been driving around in one of those big, yellow Laidlaw school buses; me and fifteen other people. We punched into Wyoming by way of Colorado looking for somewhere safe to settle. Initially, we had looked into Denver to see what we could find, but things didn't go well there. I lost some people.

We were in the area on George's (that's George Oliver) advice. He had been with me since Texas along with Tom David-son. In a discussion we'd had very early on, he explained how the entire United States east of Abilene as well as Arizona, the coast of California, and up into Washington and Oregon were basically pockmarked with nuclear-goddamned power plants. Now, we had never heard any news about a meltdown in those early days, and I guess the emergency shutdown systems in the American plants were pretty good, but I'm old enough to remember Chernobyl. In fact, Fukushima was our most recent demonstration of just how nasty things get when a nuke plant goes Tango-Uniform; we had no way to know if an area we were living in or driving into was contaminated with radiation. We wouldn't know until we started getting sick and by then it would be too late. Old Georgie made a compelling argument: avoid nuclear power plants.

States like New Mexico, Colorado, and Utah were all free of nuke plants and, according to George, Wyoming was in the dead center of a nuke-free oasis. We started heading in that general direction while keeping our eyes open for a good place to settle.

We picked up others along the way. We ran into Barbara in Oklahoma. Rebecca, Oscar, and his daughter Maria joined us just outside of Pueblo, Colorado. It was like that—just running into people in two's and three's along the way. We'd stop to talk with them, trade news and such. I was always looking to trade supplies, but nothing ever came of that. We always just ended up pulling people into our little caravan. Everybody just looked so fucking lost; I wasn't about to stop, shoot the shit with them, and then leave them behind with a wave and a smile.

It was in Colorado Springs where we finally had to stop and adjust our tactics. Davidson ran into a big group of eight people living in a King Soopers grocery store while he was out on a scavenging run during a refueling stop. I had a little siphoning tool that I was taking from car to car to fill the gas cans we had with us; nothing sophisticated—just a couple of stiff hoses and a hand pump. It was a pain in the ass to use and took forever, but if you were patient, you could snake the hose down past the gas cap and carefully rotate it until it wedged past the rollover valve. You couldn't get all of the gas out of the tank because there was no way to control where the hose ended up once it was past the valve, so we left a lot of gas behind, but what we lacked in efficiency we made up for in volume.

We were all standing out there together while I cursed up a blue streak trying to get the hose into a Subaru. It was maddening —you can't rush the technique at all. You twist slowly while you carefully insert the thing and you know if you've got it or not; there's slight resistance, but the hose will eventually push through. If you fuck it up you'll also know because the hose will bind up and go no further; it's stiff enough that you can tell you need to back it out and try again. I had fucked it up three times already, and I could feel Davidson's eyes resting on my back by that point, which only served to agitate me, which caused me to fuck the job up a fourth time…

I finally straightened up and took a deep breath, rolling my shoulders. "Hey, Davidson. Why don't you push out a bit while I'm doing this? See if you can find some water, maybe."

"I can do that," he said. The kid was nothing if not enthusiastic. He reminded me of that little runt dog in the old Looney Tunes cartoons ("Hey, Spike, you want I should pick up some bones for yah, huh?")

"Keep within a klick," I advised.

He slung the rifle I had given him, a civilian M4 with a Vortex dot optic (he had accepted the thing like I was handing him a Hatori Hanzo samurai sword for chrissakes), and headed out. The M4 was one of two rifles I had brought along with me for the apocalypse. The other rifle (the one I still have and which nobody gets to touch… well, for the most part, anyway) is my baby: a Heckler and Koch MR556A1 loaded up with a 4x32 Trijicon ACOG optic and a Surefire light. This rifle was everything that the M4 I carried in the Corps should have been. If there had been any way for me to get my hands on the 416, I damned well would have, but you can't do much better than the civilian MR556 in my learned (and correct) opinion.

"You're really very good with him," Barbara said. I like Barbara Dennings. She's a sweet little old lady. I'm not sure exactly how old; you never ask a lady that—Mom would have broken her foot off in my ass if she ever heard of me doing such a thing. Even so, I'm going to guess late fifties to early sixties. I'm willing to bet she was and is a wildcat behind closed doors as she can flirt right alongside the best of the Spring Break college crowd. Better, in fact, because she has a lifetime of education and experience backing her play. No ditzy co-ed, our Barbara. My kind of lady.

"He's a good kid," I told her. "Once he gets a few accomplishments under his belt he'll calm down a bit. Oh, thank you, Jesus!" I had finally managed to get the hose inserted. I heaved a sigh and began to work the little hand pump.

"We should see about finding some more of those," Oscar said to my left, indicating the pump. "I could help you do this."

"You are helping," I told him. "Soon as I have enough in this gas can, you can take it over and fill up our ride while I go get another tank started."

"Come on, man, you know what I mean."

"Yeah, I do," I agreed. "But for now, I'm happy with you keeping your head on a swivel while I'm bent over this thing. You just keep that M9 handy."

Don't ask me how this had come about but not a one of these damned people that I picked up along the way had a firearm of any kind. I originally thought at the outset of this whole thing that bringing two rifles and a pistol was just being dumb, but I couldn't bring myself to leave them behind. If I had known I would eventually be traveling with the 1st Battalion Snowflakes, I would have brought a lot more.

Davidson returned twenty minutes later with a wide-eyed expression on his face. "Uh, Gibs? I think you'd better come have a look at this."

I straightened up from the hand pump and rolled my eyes. The kid could be a walking movie cliché sometimes.

"Really? You can't just tell me? Use your words, man."

"Sorry. I ran into a ton of people living in a grocery store. They seem okay, but I figured I'd better come get you."

I was not excited to hear this news. The seven of us were already piled into three cars; keeping them all fueled had grown into an operation that could take at least a couple of hours depending on how lucky we got while moving from vehicle to vehicle.

"Define 'ton,'" I said.

"Eight people. All kinds, like our group."

"Oh, Jesus bacon-eating Christ," I groaned. I looked at Rebecca, a knock-out of a redhead that was both too damned young and too damned hot for my aged ass (a fact which deterred me not a bit from stealing the odd glance at her turd cutter—I am only a man after all) and said, "Okay, Rebecca, you come take this over, please. Davidson, trade weapons with Oscar and come show me this group. Oscar, you good with that rifle?"

"Yeah, I remember how it goes."

"Good deal," I nodded. "Lead the way, Davidson."

He led me a few blocks away from where we had parked, the both of us weaving around or climbing over the various vehicles that had been pulled up onto the sidewalks. I hated walking through the area like that; hated everything about being in cities. They all felt too much like Fallujah now, with all the damage and all the shit everywhere. Every bit of conspicuous garbage lying on the side of the road made the hairs on the back of my neck stand up, and I just about gave myself whiplash walking down the streets trying to clock every window and rooftop. I just couldn't help myself. I mean, I knew intellectually that there were no Muj waiting to jump out at us but "old habits," you know?

He finally brought me to a grocery store where, I swear to God, every square inch of glass in the storefront had been busted out. To compensate for this, the people inside had apparently piled up everything that wasn't nailed down in front of the wreck-age. And I mean everything—whole sections of aisle shelf, every shopping cart they could get their hands on, even a goddamned ATM was all stacked up in a big old barricade along the entire storefront. Wedged in front of the door in the center of it all was one of those refrigerator-sized Coke machines.

Davidson walked up to the thing like he was planning on inserting a dollar and slapped the plastic front panel with his open hand. "Hey, guys!" he called out. "We're back. You can let us in."

The sound of men grunting came from behind the machine, and it began to slide back slowly over the floor, creating a bit of a squeal and dragging a shopping cart along with it. As the gap between the machine and the door frame increased, I could see at least one man pulling from behind. He reached out and moved the stowaway shopping cart over with his hand.

Davidson looked back at me and indicated my rifle. "These people are skittish, but they're okay. Go ahead and let that hang."

I had my doubts and decided to compromise; I lowered the rifle across my body but kept my hands wrapped on grip and handguard. I did not engage the safety.

The Coke machine was pulled back only far enough that we could get past it and into the store by stepping to the left or right around it, so I couldn't see in. A grubby, shell-shocked head poked out from the right of the opening and stared out at us. His face was dirty enough that I couldn't tell he was Asian at first; I had to really stare at the guy to place his ethnicity.

"I brought him," Davidson said. "This is Gibs."

"It's just you two?" said the man. His accent was just barely noticeable; you had to really listen for it to detect it at all.

"Sure. I said it would be."

"Okay. Come on in." The head pulled back and disappeared around the corner.

Davidson looked back to me and smiled nervously. "Hey, I know this looks fucknuts, but these people really seem okay. They're mostly just scared."

I nodded while grimacing internally at his use of the word "fucknuts." There's no nice way to say this: Davidson was a fanboy. He was in college when everything came flying apart, his plan being to join the Marines as an officer. Unfortunately for him (or perhaps fortunately, depending on how you look at it), the Marines stopped existing before he had a chance to sign up. It still bugs the shit out of him now but back then he was overcompensating. I remember regretting telling the kid that I was a Marine; as soon as he heard that, he was busting out the lingo at every opportunity. I swear, I think he knew more Jarhead jargon than I did and I left the Corps as a Staff Sergeant. Davidson was that one motarded kid who would have shown up at the Island with a high-and-tight and a Semper Fi t-shirt. The drill instructors would have murdered his poor, dumb ass.

"That's fine, but let me go in first anyway," I said and shouldered past before he could say anything.

I poked my head around the Coke machine to see a group of eight people huddled together at the front of the store, clearly waiting for me. Squeezing the grip of my rifle and really not wanting to kill anyone, I took a breath before stepping in.

The interior of the store looked as though a bomb had been detonated right in the middle of it. The light level was very low; there was some illumination creeping in through the tops of the front windows in the gap between the ceiling and the shit-pile the inhabitants had stacked up—there were also some lanterns set up throughout the place. All of the aisles were in disarray, having been pulled out of alignment and repositioned along the outside walls of the store. Many of them were stacked up against the front windows, as I had mentioned before, but there were so many in the store that a lot of them were just shoved to the side. There appeared to be some kind of common area in the center of the floor space beyond the checkout stands—I could see some boxes and a few office chairs (probably hauled over from the manager's office). There appeared to be a dwindling supply of food and water stacked up in this area. Along the outer perimeter of the floor were places to sleep (a few mattresses, some blankets, and even a couple of yoga mats).

I looked back at the people in front of me. There were males and females, but they were so damned filthy it was hard to guess their ages. I thought I saw the angular shape of a teenage body on two of them. There were no children.

"How long have you people been in here?" I asked. I screwed up my face and tried to breathe shallowly. The whole place smelled like a rhino had taken a shit in a moldy old sock.

"Weeks," said the Asian kid.

"Jesus," I responded. "Name's Gibson. Call me Gibs."

"Wang," he offered back. "Where are you folks coming from?"

Before I could answer, one of the others pushed forward. Again, I couldn't tell much about him regarding his appearance, outside of the fact that he was tall and skinny. He said: "Yes, it's all very nice to meet you but can you help us? We need food and water. We're starving."

I looked past him back to the pile of supplies. From what I could see, they weren't starving yet, but they appeared to be on their way. Water looked like more of a problem than food, certainly.

"Hang on a second," I said and turned back to Davidson. I whispered, "Head back to the cars and grab a couple jugs of water. Have Barbara come back with you and tell her to grab a couple of packs of wet wipes. We gotta sanitize these people before they get ass-to-mouth disease."

He nodded and bounded back through the store entrance. I'd half expected him to say "Yut!" before he went.

I turned back to the others and tried to think of something to say next. It was hard—that whole place was foul and oppressive. "Look, can we step outside?" I asked. "The air in here is kind of close."

A few of them looked nervously at each other, and I saw one or two hands reach out to grab other peoples' arms. Finally, Wang said, "I'll go out with you. We don't all need to come." The tall, skinny guy got indignant and said, "I'll be coming along too."

Right away, I had a feeling about that guy. You know how some people just telegraph "asshole" wherever they go? This guy had it coming off him in waves. Even through all the dirt and grime I could see it in his posture, hear it in his voice… fuck, I could see it in his eyes. Second Lieutenant material all the way.

I thanked Wang, ignored the asshat, and backed out of the store. Once outside, I took a deep, cleansing breath and let it out slowly, trying to get all the funk out of my lungs. When I no longer felt like I had the creepy crawlies all over me, I slung my rifle down on my shoulder and said, "Okay, Wang, read me in." I saw the skinny asshole bristle at being ignored, which I would have enjoyed if I wasn't as mature as I am.

Okay, fuck it, I enjoyed it.

Wang crossed his arms over his chest and said, "We've been here a few weeks. There isn't much to tell besides that. We got into the store and made a little home. There was enough food at first, but it didn't take long for it to run low. We've been collecting more from around the area, but that's all getting scarce now too."

"Yes, this is all very nice," the skinny guy broke in. He held out his hand to shake and said, "My name is Edgar. Were you going to be able to help us? Your friend Tom indicated that you could."

I didn't take Edgar's hand. "I need to understand the situation here so that I can determine the best way to help."

"Don't mind him," Wang said. "He just gets pissy when people don't bow to his obvious authority."

This statement was delivered so effortlessly and without inflection that it surprised a snort out of me. I had no idea what the history between these two was at that point but I was glad to see that I wasn't being unreasonable in my assessment of Edgar— he clearly bugged some other folks as well.

Edgar's face went red as his mouth clicked shut. He breathed out the word "bastard," turned, and walked back towards the store entrance. I swear to Christ, he almost said, "I never!"

"Thought he'd never leave," Wang said as Edgar disappeared behind the Coke machine.

I smiled and said, "You seem to have a way with people. 'Wang,' right?"

His eyebrows rose as he smiled back at me. "Oh, are you setting up a dick joke? I promise to act as though I'm hearing it for the first time if you are."

This got a genuine laugh out of me. "I wasn't, but I can make up a few new ones on the spot if you're feeling frisky."

He walked over to lean against a concrete pylon. "Oh, let's not do that right now. You want to dole them out slowly over time. I don't want you to shoot your wad all at once."

"Ha!" I laughed. I was going to get along with this guy just fine. I went over to stand by him. "Okay, fella. No one's here to interrupt now. Let's have it."

"It's like I said," Wang shrugged. "Our short term plan is close to finished now. We've picked the immediate area over pretty well."

"What about picking up and moving on to a new area?" I asked.

"I've been trying to talk them into that. I have maybe half of them convinced but that asshole Edgar opens his mouth and screws it up whenever I start making some real progress."

I began to understand the source of the friction between the two of them. "Why so resistant to moving?"

"A group of bikers came through here not too long ago. They made a lot of noise, broke things up."

"A… group of bikers? Like, a no-shit apocalypse biker gang?" I had been wondering how long it would take for the Mad Max wannabes to band together and start tooling along the countryside like their own little douchebag posse.

"Don't think of it like that," said Wang. "They weren't on Harleys or anything. They were just riding a bunch of bikes. A lot of them were on dirt bikes, some had BMW's. I even saw a couple on scooters. We could tell they were no good, though. They were making all kinds of noise, shooting out windows. A bunch of jerks."

"Yeah, what happened when they saw you?"

"They didn't," said Wang, shaking his head. "We ducked out the back of the store like a bunch of cowards and hid out behind some of the other buildings. They came through the store, helped themselves to our supplies, and left."

"You wanted to fight them?" I asked.

"Maybe. I don't know. I didn't want to just let them take our food and water. Maybe they would have killed us, or maybe they weren't really bad people—just a bunch of loud dickheads. I just didn't see the point of hiding to survive if we were going to end up starving anyway later on. You can guess who it was who talked everyone into hiding."

I nodded. "Yeah, well, he was probably right though. It sounds like they were armed and I didn't see any weapons on you guys. 'Guns versus Fists' is never a thing you want to get into unless you're the one with the guns."

"Maybe," he said. "Or maybe we could have ambushed a few in the dark, taken some of their guns, and evened things up."

"Maybe," I said, but I wasn't buying it. In my experience, it's pretty hard to take a gun away from someone who doesn't want to give it to you. Typically, you need to shoot them a lot to pull it off.

"So, anyway," he continued, "since then Edgar's gone roach and complains at anyone else who doesn't do the same."

"Roach?"

"Yeah, it's what some of us call it when you hide out like

Anne Frank: absolutely quiet at all times, venture out only at night, hide like your own shadow is trying to kill you. It sucks."

I nodded agreement. It did, in fact, sound like a shitty way to be.

Davidson and Barbara popped into view down the street ten minutes later; with him lugging the jugs of water and her clutching the wet nap packages. He was wearing his usual goof-ball grin, and Barbara had a concerned, purposeful expression on her face.

"Here they come," I said to Wang. "C'mon, let's go inside and get your guys cleaned up a bit and hydrated. We'll figure out what's next after that."

It turned out that what came next was the whole goddamned crew joined up with mine for a cross country field trip.

"Brace yourself," I advised Barbara. "They smell like they've been swimming... well, they've been swimming through it." She nodded at me and followed us in.

Everyone was where I'd left them, more or less. I noticed Edgar was a little off to the side talking quietly to a smaller group, not that I really cared. "Uh, hey guys," I said, waving with a hand. "We've got some water for you and Barbara, here, will come around and hand out some wipes for you to clean yourselves up with. We gotta get your sanitation under control before you get sick. You don't want to get dysentery right now; it's likely to kill you."

Barbara started making the rounds among the group as I talked. I noticed she was handing out only one or two wipes at a time and said, "Fistfuls, hon. Their hands and faces need a total rub down." She nodded to me and returned back to the beginning of the line. "The rest of you take the used wipes and just throw them in a pile on the floor. No sense cleaning up, we gotta get you outta here."

Davidson glanced my way with raised eyebrows. I knew what he was thinking. I was a little shocked myself. I hadn't realized I was going to say that last part until it came out of my mouth. I knew it was the right thing as soon as I said it, though. These people were going to die here if I left them.

"Just a minute," Edgar said from his little cluster of people. "Exactly where do you propose to take us?"

I ground my teeth and took a deep breath through my nose. "For now, just out of here. Back to the others. We have some cars that we're traveling in; we can get a few more and bring you with us, I guess."

There were some uncertain glances around the room from everybody when I said this. I could see that some people were ready to pick up and go right then, but others weren't so certain. They had been living in fear for a while now. I wondered how much of that fear was earned and how much of it had been implanted by Edgar's attitude.

"And where is it that you're traveling to?" he asked.

"Uh, well, we don't know."

"You don't… know?"

"Yeah, I said that, didn't I? We're going towards Denver. It's a big city, probably a lot of things we can scavenge. We were thinking we might find a little patch out in the suburbs; maybe find a place worth setting up a camp."

"Does anyone else think this is a bad idea?" Edgar said to the rest of the group. "These people, of whom we know nothing, propose to take us into their little group to go to a new area which may or may not be more secure than this?"

"What, you call this secure?" I said. "Couple of Molotovs busted over all the crap piled up in the windows, and you guys are looking at a Soylent Green barbecue."

"This has worked out for us so far," Edgar said, overriding me. "We know it's safe here because we've been here and it has worked. Even if someone gets curious and pushes their way in, we know we can get away from them. We know this because we've done it. We know this area..."

"Hey, listen, you dipshit..." began Davidson. I cut him off.

"Davidson, watch how you talk in front of my girl." Barbara smiled at me and winked. The ladies never could resist my animal charms.

"Sorry, Top."

I rolled my eyes. *Top.* I was gonna need to have a talk with him at some point. Top is what you call the Master Sergeant. I was a Staff Sergeant when I left the Corps, and I hadn't even been one of those for twelve years now.

I looked back at the group of survivors. "Look, how much food have you got left in that little pile back there? How long is that going to feed eight people? How well is scavenging going right now? Are you still finding what you need or are things starting to thin out?" I looked over all their faces, hoping mostly that someone (anyone) other than Edgar would answer. Thankfully, my man Wang didn't leave me hanging.

"It's getting tight," he said. "We can still find things to eat, but we're going to bed hungry most nights now."

"I cooked a rat a few nights ago," one of them said; a young, slender looking man who I later learned was named Jeff.

"A *rat*?" I asked, disgusted. I looked back over at Edgar. "And you want to stay here?"

"You don't even know where you're going," Edgar reiterated. "You can't promise us that where you're going will be any better or safer than what we've carved out right here."

I was dumbstruck. Clearly, he and I saw the palatial digs of the King Soopers in an entirely different light.

"Guys, you're overlooking something really important,"

Wang cut in. "These people have guns. We have a much better chance going with them. They can defend themselves. What do we have besides a couple of sharpened mop handles?"

"How many guns have you guys got?" asked a large black man in the rear of the group. His voice was Darth Vader deep.

"Hey," I nodded to him, glad that more of them were willing to speak to me rather than let others speak for them. "What's your name, man?"

"Fred."

"What's your last name, Fred?"

"Moses."

"Nice. Okay, Fred, we have two rifles and a pistol, all semi-automatic," I said.

Edgar jumped back in all over that, the little twat. "Three guns between us and… how many did you say were in your group?"

I sighed: "Seven."

"Seven?" he scoffed. "So three guns between fifteen people? That hardly sounds like enough."

A black lady who had so far been quiet as a mouse spoke up and said, "I don't know if we can go out there on the road again. Nevermind the people who have come through this area shooting guns and whatever else. There are bad people out on the road." She hugged a young girl to herself (her daughter, I guessed) and shivered.

"The more of us that travel together, the stronger we'll be," said Barbara to the woman. The woman looked down at the back of her daughter's head, uncertain.

"Three guns are not exactly what I would define as 'strong,'" Edgar replied.

I couldn't take any more. I finally lost my shit and said, "For fuck's sake, I can't believe I'm standing in the middle of a goddamned King Soopers trying to convince a bunch of starving people into lifting a single finger to rescue their own miserable, broke-dick lives." Everyone had shut up at that point, but I didn't care. I was on a roll now. Without even realizing what I was doing, my right hand had extended out in front of me, opened flat with the edge pointed down toward the floor, thumb tucked into the palm, with the elbow bent hard at ninety degrees and pulled into my ribs. Yeah. I was giving a bunch of starving civilians the "Knife Hand." Not my finest moment, I know.

"You wouldn't think that I'd have to twist arms and 'pretty-please' a crowd of desperate people into climbing out of a shit pit for the purposes of getting a hot meal and unfucking themselves in general, but I guess we're all just celebrating Opposite Day! Outstanding!"

I grabbed the gallon jugs of water out of Davidson's hands and threw them across the floor at the crowd of people, some of whom had to skip out of the way to avoid impact.

"Now hear this: I have officially expended my daily allotment of fucks on all of you. I have a group of people who are awaiting my return to safeguard their way to some territory that is not a complete and total shit show. If you would like to join our merry band on this grand adventure, I advise you to move your goddamned asses! Or, you can stay here for all I care. I hereby resign from trying to talk you jokers into saving yourselves!"

The area was dead silent after my little tantrum. As was always the case after such an explosion, I felt like a shit heel for yelling at them all. These people were all terrified. I didn't have any idea what they'd been through, but I could easily see that it had been rough. Regardless, you can't reel back an ass chewing once it's been deployed. You just have to let it hang out there and hope some of it sinks in. I slung my rifle over my shoulder, turned and walked toward the Coke machine exit. I stopped next to Barbara on my way out and said, "Sorry, sweetie," under my breath.

"Oh, I don't mind," she whispered back. "They needed a wake-up. Plus, that was kind of hot."

I smiled at her. Man, if only she was twenty years younger. Hell with that, I would have settled for ten. I nodded my head towards the exit in a "let's go" gesture and walked out of the store.

Once outside, I made a beeline back for our cars. They had to be fully refueled by now, and our group had been made to wait long enough for this stupidity. I heard the sound of footsteps trotting up behind me, but I didn't turn to see who it was—even Davidson's footfalls sounded eager.

"Man, that was *so* badass!" he said when he caught me up.

"It was not," I shot back. "It was a failure. If I had been able to make my case better instead of blowing my stack, those people back there might have half a chance."

"Uh, well, I think they're following us," he said.

"The fuck?" I said and looked back over my shoulder. There was Barbara, followed by that giant of a man (Fred Moses), Wang, and a trail of other people behind them. I even saw Edgar coming out at the tail. I faced back in the direction I was walking.

"Well, shit," I said. "Now I gotta figure out what I'm gonna do with all these fucking people."

2

PICKING UP STRAYS

Gibs

"What the hell?"

Oscar came over from where our cars were parked to meet me as I approached, looking past me at the filthy pack of strays that had followed me back. He looked over at me (well, okay, he looked up at me—he is pretty short) and said, "Uh, so I guess we better find some more cars, eh?"

"Yeah. Sorry," was all I could come up with.

He looked back at them as they approached and sucked air through his teeth. Finally, he said, "Nah, man. You guys took me and Maria in. I'm not gonna start being an asshole when someone else needs help. What's up with these people? They look like they haven't eaten in forever."

Wang had reached us by then. He shook hands with Oscar and introduced himself. Our group had come together behind us, and Wang's group had stopped just a few feet back from where Oscar, Wang, and I were standing. I spoke up so everyone could hear me.

"These people are gonna be traveling with us now. This is a good thing. More bodies mean a wider distribution of work. It means more sets of eyeballs to apply to lookout. And, more importantly," I looked at each of my people for any signs of dissension as I spoke, "it's a good thing because these people need our help and we're in a position to provide it. If anyone has a problem with that, this is the time to sound off."

It was a bit of a dick tactic, I'll admit. Nobody wants to be the asshole that says, "Hey, no, fuck these guys," while the guys in question are standing right there in front of them. It was probably unnecessary too; I had a good lock on the people I was traveling with by this time. None of them were one-way types. I knew I could rely on them to do the right thing.

"Well, okay then," said George. He was positioned a little behind our group so that he could lean on a car bumper (he had a bad knee and used a cane to get around). "What's the plan for provisions?"

I nodded. "I've been thinking about that. We had enough food and water for our group to keep us moving at least a few more days. These people are going to need some of that right now so we can get some strength back into them and get them pulling their own weight." I wanted to keep presenting the idea that we were coming out ahead by bringing Wang's group in, even if my guys were showing good attitudes. As I said this, Rebecca walked back to the Taurus (one of the cars we'd been driving) and opened the trunk, which is where we were keeping our rations.

I continued to lay out the plan: "We'll get them squared away right now. This is going to put a significant dent in our supply, so we'll need to address that soon but not today. The bit of logistics we need to handle right now is transportation. Two cars don't cut it for..." I knocked out a quick headcount, "fifteen people. We'll need two more cars at least plus we'll need to spend the time to refuel them now." I rolled my eyes as I thought about what it was going to take to keep four cars fueled. I felt a light tap on my shoulder and turned to see Wang standing behind me on my right side.

"I may have an idea for transportation, if you're interested," he said.

"I'm all ears, man," I told him. I was excited to hear any ideas. The more initiative I could get people to take, the better off we were going to be.

"There's a school bus off the side of the road just on the outskirts; about a twenty or thirty-minute walk from here. I'm pretty sure it was being used to transport people to emergency facilities. I don't know how it's set for fuel but it isn't totally boxed in by other cars and traffic is light where I saw it. It might be easier managing one big vehicle rather than four little ones, don't you think?"

I thought about it for a moment, weighing the obvious drawbacks (size and lack of maneuverability) against the positives. It was a simple, utilitarian approach. We would have all of our people and supplies in a single vehicle. Communication would be instantaneous; we could just talk to each other without having to pull over to the side of the road. If we felt a need to keep moving, we could continue to drive in shifts while others ate or slept. The only thing we'd really need to stop for was head calls. On the other hand...

"You have any idea how much fuel those things hold?" I asked. "I don't, but I'll bet it's a lot. I'll bet they get lousy mileage, too."

Wang nodded and said, "Yeah, I don't know either, but I'm sure you're right. It still can't hurt to go check it out, though, right? Maybe we get lucky, and it has a lot of gas to start with."

"Eh, it's probably diesel. What do you know about this area? Did a lot of folks drive diesel?"

"I've lived in Colorado for several years now," said Wang.

"Yes, you can find a lot of trucks that run on diesel. You could say that outdoor activities are big around here."

I chuckled. "Yeah, probably," I agreed. "Okay, let's go check it out and see what we find." I eyeballed Wang for a moment, trying to decide if I should hand him the Beretta or not. I ultimately decided against it. I was reasonably confident in my ability to cover the both of us with a single rifle; an M4 and a pistol between the thirteen people remaining here was already incredibly stupid, and I didn't want to make it worse by taking that pistol to hand over to Wang. I turned to look for Davidson and Oscar—the two guys in our outfit who I had managed to brief on safety. I could at least trust them to handle a firearm without shooting their own dicks off. Probably.

They were both standing over by everyone else near the supply trunk (most of Wang's group had walked over for chow while I was talking to him). I approached and pulled both Davidson and Oscar aside.

"Wang thinks he has a solution for our transportation," I said. "It's in walking distance from here, so I'm going to head out with him and take a look. I want you guys to maintain position here until we get back."

I looked around at the buildings surrounding us on either side of the street. The place resembled your basic middle-America city street. A lot of the buildings were brick and mortar, went up two or three stories, and a lot of them had side alleys with fire escapes. The place actually looked like it was a nice little getaway town once upon a time.

I pointed to Oscar (more of that knife hand—it's a hard habit to break) and said, "I want you to take the rifle and get some overwatch on one of these buildings. You're limited to whatever has a fire escape but pick one of the taller ones, get to the roof, and keep your eyes open. Be close enough that you can call down to Davidson if you see anything. Be ready to lay down suppressing fire if shit gets stupid. *Do not* shoot anyone that belongs to us."

Oscar nodded, slapped Davidson's shoulder, and headed off with the rifle to find likely candidates. I grimaced to myself as he went, praying that nothing would happen. If a firefight actually did break out, I gave these guys even odds on shooting one of our own by mistake in all the confusion. They were untrained, unskilled civilians, which made them every bit as dangerous to themselves as they were to others.

To Davidson, I said, "You hang on to the M9. Keep everyone close and keep your eyes on these alleyways; they'll be a blind spot for Oscar. If Oscar calls down to you, I want you to lock up the cars, take the keys, and get everyone displaced into a building somewhere."

"What do I do after that?" he asked.

"Barricade and dig in. Get everyone under cover, including yourself. Shoot anyone that tries to come in without first identifying themselves."

He nodded and (Jesus Christ) saluted me. I suppressed an eye-roll and returned it, being a lot lazier than he was on the snap— hoping he would take the hint. I sincerely hoped I wasn't making a poor call.

I returned to Wang and advised him to grab some food that he could eat while walking as well as a bottle of water. We headed out after that. Once we made some distance away from the group, I took the opportunity to grill him.

"So what's the deal with this Edgar guy?"

"Deal?"

I elaborated: "Well, what I mean is how much trouble am I going to have with him?" I wasn't excited about every little decision turning into an argument.

"Oh, yes. He can take some patience. He's actually pretty smart in a lot of ways if you get to know him; unfortunately, a lot of those ways aren't very useful anymore. I guess he was a pretty successful accountant of some kind from before. Let's turn right up here…"

"Here, let me go ahead of you," I said. I edged up to the corner of the building and poked my head around. I spent several seconds in this position sweeping the area with my eyes, looking at nothing in particular and trying to detect any kind of motion. Halfway down the street, a knot of vehicles was stacked up almost on top of each other, completely choking off the way through. Several of them were little more than burned out hulks.

I looked back at Wang and said, "The street's blocked off by a pileup—we can get through on foot, but we'll never get the cars through. Is there another way?"

"Yeah," Wang said. "We'll just have to go another block up and circle back."

"Okay, let's do that. I want to find the route we'll have to take with the cars to get there if this works out. I don't want to hump everything over there."

The majority of Colorado Springs was laid out in a grid, so he just led me up the street another block and found us a way through. Wang took the opportunity to finish his thought regarding Edgar as we walked.

"Anyway, he can be a pain, but he can be pretty useful. He tends to argue about everything, but I've chosen to use this behavior as a way to reinforce our planning. Basically, if we can get him to shut up, we know we've covered all the angles."

I snorted while grimacing inwardly. Edgar sounded just like the type of guy who was going to tap-dance all over my last nerve. I decided to change the subject before I managed to piss myself off again just thinking about him.

"So what about yourself? It seems like a lot of those people tend to follow your lead."

"Well, I guess they do. What, that's a bad thing?"

"Oh, no," I said. "Well… I guess it's a bad thing if you're a dumbass, but you don't strike me as a dumbass—"

"We haven't known each other that long. Give me a little time."

"Anyway," I said laughing, "you seem okay."

"So what I can tell you is that from what I've seen, it doesn't take much more than speaking to get people to listen to you. The key thing is that you just can't say anything stupid. It's okay to appear ignorant as long as you show that you're aware of your ignorance, but nobody forgives stupid."

I compared what he said to my own life experiences and found that they agreed with what he said. I was impressed; he was a pretty young kid compared to me (I'd have to guess he was twenty-two or twenty-three) but he already knew more about basic leadership than most of the junior officers I had encountered in my military career. They always seemed to come to us with a chip on their shoulder; they knew they were young and inexperienced and always seemed to think that they had to compensate for this by knowing *everything*. The problem with that approach is that you can't actually know everything at that age. The ones that ended up being good officers (few and far fucking between, I might add) learned early on that ignorance wasn't actually a cardinal sin and that, by and large, you survive by listening to your NCOs. It seemed obvious to an old fart like me, but the quickest way to win confidence from people was usually to be open and honest about your weak points. Then again, I was an old fart with years' worth of leadership experience under my belt. Wang was a kid. I pointed this out to him and asked how he came about having such a seasoned understanding of human nature.

"How did I figure it out so quickly?" he asked, rephrasing my question. "Could it be that it just took you a long time to learn?" he asked while smiling.

I laughed and said, "I'm serious, asshole."

"You're right, I apologize," he said, nodding. "Basically, I was studying architecture in college and worked at this firm as an intern. They typically don't let you do anything as an intern outside of being involved in the proofing process—usually assisting a senior designer. You sit in on a lot of meetings, mostly taking notes for the senior guy, but I noticed early on that a lot of people were never willing to speak up or make decisions in meetings. It was like they all just sat around waiting for somebody else to stick their neck out."

"Sounds familiar," I grumbled.

"Yeah, I think it's universal human behavior. You can find it anywhere, really. So anyway, I've always had a bit of a mouth on me—"

"Oh, no shit? You don't say?"

"—and I would speak up in the meeting every so often to suggest a course of action, mostly because I just wanted to move things along. Those guys would waffle back and forth forever. I wasn't even saying anything brilliant; just stating the obvious in most cases. They were all a little shocked by an intern speaking out at first, but when it turned out that I was just saying stuff that they all basically knew anyway, they started to relax. After a while, they started asking my opinion in these meetings. I think a key part of all that was that I never opened my mouth if I didn't know what I was talking about and if they asked for my input, I made sure to tell them when I didn't know the answer. It helped to build trust in the relationship."

I nodded my agreement and walked on silently. He had made it sufficiently clear why the folks in his group were following his lead. He wasn't describing anything that an effective person in a leadership position didn't already know at a basic level, but then again, he was really damned young. I was duly impressed.

It took us over a half hour to get to the bus because of all the time we had to spend searching around and doubling back for passable streets. I was confident in my ability to find my way back to the cars from memory; a skill I had picked up in my previous deployments where I often found myself traipsing through unfamiliar cities populated by unreadable signs and markers (where there were signs and markers, that is). That's the bummer about being a Marine: outside of Okinawa and the Philippines (which I enjoyed the hell out of) you didn't get to go see the nice parts of the world when you were deployed. Any place that needed the attention of the United States military was, by definition, already a shit hole.

The bus had been abandoned in the middle of the street. We approached from the rear, swinging out wide to the right to get a good look down its length. There was nothing particularly note-worthy about the vehicle; it was your standard big goddamned yellow school bus. The only thing that made it stand out for me was the blue-green letters running along the top side saying "COOL SPRINGS DIST 11."

I traversed the length of the bus from back to front while trying and failing to get any kind of a glimpse through the windows; their tint job made it impossible. Past the front, there was a minor vehicle block that would prevent us from traveling forward. It didn't look like any of the cars in front of us had crashed; they were only crammed in bumper to bumper. The knot of vehicles ran four deep at its worst point, but beyond them, the street opened up enough that we would be able to navigate through if we used every square inch of it (along with a bit of the sidewalk).

"We'll have to move all that shit out of the way," I said to Wang, indicating the mess with a nod.

"Do you think it'll take long?" Wang asked glancing down at his watch. I looked down at my own watch on the inside of my wrist. It said 1412 (or 2:12 pm).

"It shouldn't be bad," I told him. "What are we looking at, six cars? No, seven. We can get them moved in twenty minutes if we hustle—the ground is nice and flat here. Why don't you go have a look at the next cross street and see if there's room enough to store them all? I'll check this bus out."

Wang trotted off in the direction I suggested. It made me a little twitchy to have him head out like that without any kind of a weapon, but we were never going to get anything done if I insisted on keeping him in my back pocket. I kept reminding myself that this wasn't Iraq, there weren't any Muj up in the buildings waiting to light us up, and that anyone we did run into were more likely to start with talking than they were with fighting. Regardless, it all felt very familiar.

I shoved open the accordion door of the bus, stepped on, and made a quick circuit of the aisles. The interior was blessedly abandoned—if there had been any dead things inside I would have given up on the whole project. I'd cleaned out corpses before. I wasn't interested in doing that shit again without a really good reason or, at the very least, the promise of bacon. I can be bribed with bacon.

Returning to the front, I checked the driver seat, visor, and the little compartments in the immediate area. There were no keys anywhere, but I wasn't terribly worried. I heard Wang approach from behind and step onto the bus.

"Damn, it looks even bigger on the inside," he said as he looked towards the rear. "Do you think you can drive this thing?"

"Me?" I said, mildly shocked. "How the hell did I get signed up for this?"

"Well, I can't drive it."

I looked down at the instrument panel on the dashboard. There were more buttons than I was used to seeing in any vehicle along with a big yellow push button for the parking brake next to the ignition.

"Son of a bitch," I said. Nothing like a little OJT (on the job training).

"Did you find a key anywhere," Wang asked.

"No, but it's not a problem. I think Oscar can hotwire it."

"Oscar—he was the guy with that little girl?"

"Maria, yeah," I said.

"Huh. He was a mechanic?"

"Nope, construction. He was a foreman. But, he was also a bad boy before his daughter came along," I said and smiled at him. I nudged past him to exit and called back to him over my shoulder. "Come on, let's head back and pick everyone else up. It will help to have everyone here; we'll be able to work in parallel. I'll need a tire iron to break out the windows on these cars, at least."

"We still don't know if there's any gas in it," he warned as he followed me.

"I know. It's a calculated risk," I told him. "The thing was in park and looked like it had the break set. Whoever drove it took the key when they left. There's a pretty good chance it didn't idle down to empty. How did those cross streets look?"

"We're good," he said. "There is at least enough room to get the worst of the cars moved out of the way."

"Outstanding," I said and looked at my watch again: 1418. "Okay, it's almost 2:20. Let's keep up a good pace and try to shave some time off that return trip. I want to be driving out of here before we lose our light."

3

SUPER DUPER FUN TIME SHIT BUS

Gibs

I really, really hated that cock sucking bus. Driving that fucking thing was like trying to steer a fat, drunk woman away from the last slice of cake—you'd better start turning her early and if your judgment is off, plan on running into things. It was basically a real-life version of one of those crappy, frustrating smartphone games that made you want to tear your hair out.

I imagine such an app would be called *Super Duper Fun Time Shit Bus*.

We had completed our transfer to the bus a little after four. Wang and I got back to the group, updated everyone as quick as we could, and then thirteen of our people all piled into two sedans like a circus clown act. We got an initial five into each vehicle in the usual fashion, then took the smaller people (there was our Maria, Oscar's nine-year-old daughter, and another girl with Wang's group named Rose Dempsey, who was fourteen) and put them on laps. Even Rebecca, that incredibly attractive redhead that was way too young for this leatherneck, ended up in David-son's lap—he looked like Christmas had come early and she kindly pretended not to notice. It was kind of touching, really. She was twenty-six to his twenty-two, but it was obvious that she was something more like forty-six in hottie years, experience-wise. I felt like I was watching a waitress at a Hooters restaurant patiently dealing with an adolescent boy who was having a hard time keeping his eyes on the menu. Oscar and I escorted the two vehicles on foot, each of us armed with a rifle.

Things went quick when we got back to the bus. The first thing we did was get our two eldest members, Barbara Dennings and George Oliver, installed safely on board. I passed Oscar some screwdrivers and a multi-tool, asked him to go to work on the bus ignition and had the rest of our crew transfer all of the baggage, gear, and provisions from the two cars to the center aisle of the bus all the way to the rear. I took a tire iron from one of the cars, trotted around to the front of the bus where the pileup was and began to move as quick as I could from vehicle to vehicle breaking out windows. When that was done, I had Davidson get into the driver seat of the first vehicle out in front, and Fred Moses came over to help me push the car out of the way. We had to shove each car about two hundred feet to get them all onto a cross street, and out of the way, but with Fred's help pushing, it was pretty easy work that went by fast. By the time we had the pileup cleared, everyone was set up on the bus and ready to go. Oscar had exposed the necessary ignition wires a long time ago and was just waiting for us to come back before sparking the bus to life.

I could see that he already had a couple of the wires twisted together and that the instrument panel was currently lit up, which was a good sign as far as the battery was concerned; however, the fuel gauge was all the way down to empty. He held two other stripped wires in each hand.

"This is really gonna suck if the tank is empty," he warned and touched the two wires together.

The starter began to chitter immediately, and the engine itself growled to life soon after. Oscar separated the two wires he was holding immediately and kept them apart. We both looked over at the instrument panel, where we saw the fuel needle positioned at just over three-quarters of a tank.

"Oralé pues!" Oscar said and smiled up at me. "You got any electrical tape in your bag, man? I don't want to leave these wires out; they'll shock the shit out of anyone that touches them."

"Wait one," I said and went to the rear to find my duffel. I dug around until I found my Universal Repair Kit (a roll of 100 mph tape) and took it back to give to Oscar. He wrapped the ends of the exposed wires and let them hang against the popped center console panel, which he'd had to remove to pull the ignition switch. He also wrapped the end of the two wires he had twisted together.

He got up out of the seat and pointed at a big yellow push button floating out in space next to the dangling ignition switch. "That's your e-brake there. Make sure you pop it before you try to drive."

"Hey, do you think you can drive this thing?" I asked.

Oscar hesitated, looking down at the wheel.

"I mean, don't take it personally, but you kind of have more experience driving all sorts of different vehicles than I do," I said in hushed tones.

He leaned in close and also lowered his voice. "I was jacking Toyotas, man. I never got into hijacking, like, shipping trucks and whatnot; there was too much danger of someone getting hurt. I'm as likely to roll this bitch as you are." He straightened up and gave me the satisfied smile of an asshole absolved of all responsibility. "Saddle up, cabron!"

"Hey, I know what that means, dick," I said to his back. "You think I didn't have any loudmouthed Mexican Marines in my outfit? They're so much of a stereotype that the Corps just gave up and started issuing at least two to every squad."

Oscar sat down in one of the bench seats towards the middle of the bus next to his daughter and smiled at me. "Okay, Mr. Bus Driver, move that bus!" he called out, earning some giggles from the others.

I turned back to look at the steering wheel, which waited passively as if to say, "We can sit here and waste fuel idling all day, buddy. I don't give a shit."

As previously mentioned, driving the thing was a challenge, to say the least. Managing a full-sized bus is one of those jobs they used to make you undergo training for, and that was just when we lived in a world where the roads weren't pockmarked with broken down and stalled vehicles. The apocalypse had significantly upped the difficulty of Super Duper Fun Time Shit Bus. Driving along the straight sections in the road wasn't too bad; as long as you stayed away from the most traveled areas, you could get around, although you sometimes had to sideswipe a car here and there. In some cases, I had to put the bus in park and take one or two guys along with me to go push another car out of the way. After a couple of instances of this, Fred, Davidson, and Oscar just stayed up at the very front of the bus with me, ready to deploy when needed.

No, the worst part of driving that bastard was making a right angle turn. The first time I tried to do so through an intersection, I heard a shout erupt from behind me followed immediately by the distressing sound of grinding. I hit the brake and looked back over my shoulder to see the right side of the bus pressed up against a pole on the street corner (I think it was a light or a street sign of some sort—I couldn't see the top of it through the window). I had to back up in order to get off of it, straightened out the wheel, and attempted the turn at a slower rate, stealing glances over my shoulder as I went. Again, the side of the bus came dangerously close to the pole, and I heard Kyle, an eighteen-year-old kid from Wang's group, say, "Nope. You gotta swing out way wide, bro."

"Oh, fuck me with a toaster, you think?" I growled through gritted teeth—I kept it under my breath, though. I didn't know him very well yet and wanted to avoid scaring him. I needed people to be able to come and tell me bad news without fear of my chewing their ass. I'd give him some time to get to know me before I introduced him to the more winning aspects of my personality.

We made it around the corner on the third try, swinging out so far that the front of the bus nearly hit the light pole on the opposing end. I got the hang of it after a while; the fact that there was no one else on the road helped. If I had to make a right turn, I could swerve over to the left side of the road first to give myself the greatest possible radius, and vice versa for left turns as well. This was one of the more dangerous aspects of driving the Super Duper Fun Time Shit Bus. It was like working with really dangerous woodshop tools; as soon as you got comfortable with what you were doing, your attention might wander, and *that* was when the malevolent intelligence hiding inside the machine would reach out and dick punch you.

We weren't on the road for very long before I was pulling over to stop again, this time for reasons that excited me. Down a side street, almost tucked out of the way, there was a tan humvee sitting next to the curb. A humvee meant two things: diesel fuel and gear. This had potential to pay huge dividends.

"Oscar," I called back. "How the hell do I turn this thing off?"

He came up to the front with me and said, "Pull those two red wires apart. Don't touch the ends, though."

I did as he said and the engine went to sleep. I slapped the parking brake, got out of my seat, and called back down the length of our ride. "Everything is okay. I've just seen potential fuel and supplies. Sit tight; this shouldn't take long."

To Oscar, I said: "Grab the fuel can and pump." Then, looking over to Davidson, "You grab the M4 and come keep an eye on us."

As Davidson was coming along to cover us, I left my rifle on the bus by the driver seat (I was going to need both hands anyway) but grabbed the tire iron. All three of us approached the humvee from the rear.

"You'll find the gas cap on the right side," I told Oscar. "Make sure you dump out whatever is left in that can before you pump any diesel into it."

"Uh, you wanna show me how to do this?" asked Oscar. "I've never actually done it before."

"Oh, sure, man," I said. It occurred to me that I hadn't shown anyone how to siphon out a tank from start to finish; I had just been doing everything for people. That was going to have to change—I wasn't doing anyone (especially myself) any favors by keeping people ignorant. It was time to put my SSgt hat back on again.

"Okay," I said, "take the donkey dick off that can and pour out whatever is in it."

"The what?" said Oscar, laughing.

I had said it without thinking and suppressed a grin. It wasn't the first time I had seen someone entertained by jarhead terminology. I reached out to take the can, unscrewed the cap, and pulled out the spout a few inches. "This thing. You unscrew and detach it from the can completely. Why, what do you call it?"

"Like, a pour spout?" Oscar was still chuckling.

I put on my best disappointed face. "Well, that just isn't any fun at all. 'Donkey Dick' it is."

Oscar removed the spout, upended the can, and shook it vigorously while I unscrewed the humvee's cap. I took the pump and unrolled the hoses. Handing it to Oscar, I said, "Okay, you take this end and feed it down to the gas tank. You want to go gently until you hit some resistance."

He did as instructed, finally saying, "Okay, I feel it hitting something right now."

"Good. Now, this part can be kind of a bitch. The end of that hose is cut at an angle so it can wedge past the roll valve and get down into the tank. You have to twist the hose in order to get that wedging action to work, so what you're trying to do is twist it slowly while applying enough downward force to get it to dig in. You can't use too much force, though, or you'll just bind up the hose against the inside of the tube, and it won't go anywhere."

Oscar paused a moment to take all of that on board and then nodded. He began to work the hose with his fingers and said, "How do I know when it's past?"

"I don't know how to describe it," I said. "You'll feel it—it'll grab for a bit and then you'll suddenly be able to push it forward again." I watched as he fought with the pump while trying to rotate the hose. "Why don't you go ahead and detach the pump for now? Once you get the hose set you can reconnect it."

"Yeah, that's a good idea," he said and did so.

I gave him a light slap on the shoulder and approached the passenger side door with the tire iron. Looking in through the window, I could discern the outline of a head and shoulders inside the vehicle. I grunted, "Yep. Shit." I half expected this.

I tried the handle and found that the door was unlocked, so I set the iron aside. I opened the door and found the remains of a soldier in a partial state of undress in the front seat. His plate carrier, chest rig, and fatigue jacket had all been stripped off and thrown into the driver seat. He had been there for a while; having no odor that I could detect. I looked at the name tape on his jacket. "Sorry, Adams," I said. "This was a shitty way to go. Rest in peace, buddy."

I glanced into the back seat and immediately experienced a

wave of intense sexual arousal. "Oh... oh hello... you big... beautiful bitch."

From my left, I heard Oscar bark happily. "Ha! I got it, homes! Finally!"

"That's good," I muttered in a daze. "That's really good, man." I couldn't tear my eyes off what I was seeing. It seemed as though Adams had been a Grenadier. I was looking at an obviously well-loved M4 with an underslung M203 grenade launcher. Wordlessly, I walked around the front of the vehicle to the other side and opened the rear door, grabbed the rifle, and began to inspect it. It all appeared to be in good working order. There were plenty of scuffs and scratches on the surface of the weapon, which is what you expected to see from a soldier that actually had to work for a living, but all was in place where I hoped to find it. The action functioned smoothly, the ACOG optic was good to go, and the magazine dropped out and reseated with no issue. Moving towards the front of the rifle, I confirmed that the grenade launcher leaf sight was undamaged and then slid the M203 barrel forward. A spent 40 mm shell extracted and clattered to the pavement.

"Holy shit," I whispered. "You had to fire this thing." I wondered about what must have happened that drove this man to fire off a grenade in a U.S. city. Hopefully, he had only gone as far as firing smoke or some sort of crowd control.

"Goddamn!" I heard Davidson call from behind me. I looked back over my shoulder and saw him staring openmouthed at the weapon in my hands. "I call dibs on that shit!" he said, pointing excitedly.

"Negative," I said. "Aiming and firing an M203 is not a straightforward operation. At best, you'll waste rounds. At worst, you'll fuck it up and kill a buddy."

"Awe, shit, come on, man..."

"No, Tom. I'm serious on this. When we get somewhere a

little more permanent, I'll square you away on this thing myself but not before then."

"Crap," he said. "Okay, I can live with that."

I set the rifle down on the pavement and leaned it against the rear wheel. "I'll be back with you in a second," I said to the rifle and walked around to the rear to pop the aft storage compartment hatch. I was rewarded with the sight of a couple of ammo crates, water, a case of MRES, and a ruck. "Fucking jackpot," I said.

I looked over to Oscar, "How's that going over there?"

"This can is almost full, but there's more in the tank."

"Outstanding. Transfer that to the bus and keep going. I'll start getting this equipment moved."

"Okay," he said and then started to giggle. "I'll just put that donkey dick back on."

"Okay, man," I said, "now you're just being childish."

He laughed harder as he lugged the can back towards the bus. I climbed onto the bus myself and called back to the people inside. "We've hit a little bonanza, guys. I need volunteers to offload this gear." Several people came up out of their seats, but I didn't need everyone at once. I saw two people from Wang's group stand up first (a younger female and very young male), so I pointed at them, thanking everyone else and advising them to relax.

They both followed me off the bus and out to the humvee. "Thanks, you guys," I said. "What are your names?"

"Jessica," said the woman. She appeared to be in her early thirties with dark brown hair, striking green eyes, and a few mismatched tattoos on each arm.

"I'm Kyle," said the teenage kid. He was blonde, good looking with fair skin, and appeared to be barely capable of shaving.

"Jessica and Kyle, outstanding," I said. "Here's what we need: I want you two to get everything on that humvee that isn't dead soldier or secured equipment and move it onto the bus. Throw it all back in the rear. Don't think about what you're grabbing or what it is; we'll inventory later on the road." They both nodded and began to move.

"Hang on…" I said, causing them to look back. "If you see any firearms, leave those and let me handle them."

Jessica nodded and moved to carry out her task, but Kyle griped. "I'm okay; I used to go shooting all the time with my dad."

"That's good but just humor me for now, okay? When I have things the way I want, most of us will be going armed but just bear with me for now. Just let the old fart have his safety brief, rah?" *Rah*. Old habits were easy to fall back into, it seemed.

"Yeah, okay. You got it, Gibs." He turned and started gathering up an armload from the aft compartment. Good kid.

I went back around to retrieve the grenadier's rifle (which I was beginning even then to think of as the Boomstick) and slung it over my shoulder. I then opened the driver's side door to inspect the dead soldier's fighting load carrier (what we typically called a "chest rig" or just a "rig.") Among several pouches stuffed full of thirty-round PMAGS and a twelve slot grenade belt loaded with 40mm grenades was the man's sidearm, a Sig Sauer P320 with a stack of 9mm magazines. Laying the grenade belt aside, I tapped the front and rear carriers of the rig, confirming that they were loaded with intact ballistic plates. Finally, I confirmed that the standard complement of utility gear was present, including a blowout kit, personal flex cuff restraints, some grenades (smoke as well as flashbang) and so on. I threw the grenade belt across my shoulder and lifted the whole chest rig out of the seat, remembering how goddamned heavy the things were (I hadn't needed to deal with one in years).

I traveled back to the bus encumbered with all of this gear, not really thinking about how I must have looked until I stepped up into the driving cab and heard various whistles and comments from the passenger area. I looked up to see several shocked faces staring at me.

An African American woman towards the front (I learned later her name is Monica) said, "How many soldiers were in that truck, anyway?"

"There was only the one," I answered. "You think this is bad? I haven't even grabbed his assault ruck yet. You'd be amazed how much junk a grunt has to hump around." I walked past her down to the rear and unloaded. Turning back to the others, I said, "Hands off the firearms unless I've instructed you personally in their use, is that understood?"

A few people voiced their agreement, but mostly I just saw a bunch of nodding heads. I wasn't worried about most of them; in my experience the average civilian tended to fear modern firearms, avoiding them wherever possible. For the ones that did concern me, I had just issued a directive—there wasn't much more that I could do without carrying all weapons on me at all times. Unlikely, that. I was just going to have to trust these people to police themselves.

I ran into Kyle entering the bus just as I was stepping off the platform. He was carrying a couple of flat-earth colored fuel cans that looked heavy. "Oh, fantastic, man!" I said. "You just stick those bad boys in the rear with the gear and crack some windows. They're supposed to be airtight, but you never can tell."

When I stepped outside, I saw Oscar with a now empty can. "Was there more gas in the humvee?" I asked.

"I think so. I'm gonna try to get more."

"Good," I nodded. "Keep taking as much as it has to offer. If and when the bus tank overflows, we'll top the can off as much as possible from whatever's left in the humvee and consider the goat completely fucked."

"Donkey dicks and goat fucking. You got some serious farm issues, eh?" Oscar laughed.

"Don't knock it 'till you try it, *homes*," I said, pronouncing the word "homes" with perhaps the single worst imitation of a Hispanic accent to have ever been perpetrated in the state of Colorado. Oscar continued to giggle as he carried on about his business. I returned to the rear compartment of the humvee where I found Jessica hauling on the aforementioned assault rucksack (I assumed it was the property of the deceased Adams).

"Have you got that or can I help?" I asked.

"I got it," she said in a strained voice. The tattooed muscles in her arms quivered under the strain. "I think the stupid thing is just hung up on something."

I shifted around her and hung my head over the side of the compartment and saw where one of the MOLLE loops of the ruck had hung up on a bolt head on the internal frame. "I see what it is," I said. "Stop yanking a minute, and I'll fix it."

I saw the ruck go slack and reached my hand in to free the loop. "Okay, try now."

The assault ruck (really just GI Joe's version of a backpack) came out easily, and Jessica sighed. "Thank fuck, that thing didn't want to let go."

I raised my eyebrows at this but said nothing. She caught my look and said, "Oh, what? You guys can talk about donkeys fucking goats but I drop one F-bomb, and you get your panties in a bunch?"

This surprised a sharp laugh out of me (I hadn't realized she overheard us). "Jessica," I said, "you and I are gonna get along just fine."

4

———

THE HORSE

Gibs

We burned off the rest of our daylight in the process of pillaging the humvee and, given that the distance from Colorado Springs to Denver was about seventy miles as the crow flies, we decided to end the day on the northern outskirts of the city just off the side of the 25. We finished off the meager provisions that had been added to our stores by Wang's group, which were nowhere near enough to satisfy everyone; we dipped into the canned goods that my group had been hauling along and further supplemented the meal by dividing the humvee MREs in half and handing them out to two people at a time. When everyone was finished eating, I went to the rear of the bus to go over what food and water we had left. With a crew of fifteen people, we had just enough food for everyone to get about one more twelve-hundred calorie meal, which we could stretch out over two days by cutting everyone down to one-meal-per-day half rations.

I shook my head in disbelief. These people were going to be harder to feed than a house full of teenage boys. We would have to get settled somewhere very soon, dig in, and start socking away some serious provisions or we were all going to end up being a bunch of Starvin' Marvins. I heard the alternating step-thump of George Oliver's feet and cane as he moved down the aisles toward me. I zipped up the large duffel bag that carried all of our food, stood, and turned to face him.

"It must be bad," he said, "if you're actively trying to hide it before I get here."

Damn it.

I leaned close into him, glancing over his shoulder to see if we were being watched by others. It looked like we weren't, so I lowered my voice and said, "We're not in deep shit yet, but we will be tomorrow. We need to get some more of everything and look at setting up some sort of camp somewhere."

"Well why not here," he whispered back. "There appears to be plenty around."

"Naw, the original plan was Denver. It was a good plan. There's some stuff around here, sure, but a lot of it is picked over, and the surrounding area is primarily homes. Whatever we do find here is going to be small little caches; it'll take all day gathering just to keep everyone from starving."

I could see his leg was bothering him, so I motioned for him to sit down and joined him in the opposite seat across the aisle. Once he was settled, I continued, "If we stay here, we're going to get into a daily pattern of just barely outrunning starvation, and it'll happen sooner rather than later. Not only that, but whatever we do find will have a short shelf life. We need to get another jackpot like we had today, only with food this time. We know there is… or was… a tent city up by Denver. That means military supply pallets. There will be MREs. Sure, they taste like cafeteria food, but that's cafeteria food that'll last for seven years."

"That's assuming we find what we're looking for," he said.

"Yeah, I know, there's a lot of 'if' involved," I told him. "But even if we don't find MREs or other goodies up there, we'll be in the same boat there as we are here; only Denver is just a touch bigger. It's just another seventy miles or so. I think it's worth a try."

He nodded and leaned back against the window in his bench seat. "Okay, Gibs. Denver, then."

I didn't tell him the other half of my reasons. Driving to Denver gave everyone a goal—gave them that next task on the list that they had to look forward to. It gave them some green grass on the other side of the fence to stretch their necks out for. Morale was very much on my mind back then, specifically the ways in which it could be preserved. Everyone was working well together so far, but all it was going to take was a slight shortage of food and a few setbacks before they all started eating each other alive. It was bad enough when I only had a crew of six people to worry about along with myself. Now with fifteen, I had to worry about getting up to speed on the personalities of Wang's group and how they would work alongside mine, not to mention managing Edgar's bouts of self-important assholery. Keeping a carrot dangled out on a stick for them to chase after was my main secret weapon; the trick was making sure none of them noticed. This would be a problem in the long run—plenty of them were probably smarter than me (George was for sure, and I suspected Wang was, too). They'd be calling me on my bullshit soon enough.

Getting a permanent establishment with reliable food and water was critical.

The Denver tent city had not been what I'd hoped for.

The best information we had on its location had it positioned right next to the airport out in the surrounding fields. None of us actually had any clue where the airport was located, so the first thing we did on arrival was pull over to a gas station to burn an hour sifting through a riot of garbage until we found a local map. Davidson eventually got lucky and we brought his find back to the bus to get out of the smell of the market area (the food had stopped being offensively ripe long ago, but a general odor of corruption still hung about the place; it made me want to limit my breathing to my nose and take an alcohol bath).

Looking over the map, we learned that the 470 essentially made a giant, sloppy loop around the entire city; we could take that road due east to the 70, hang a right, and be by the airport in no time. This had the additional benefit of keeping us on the outskirts of the city. After the shit show we had been through in getting the bus out of Colorado Springs the day before, none of us were in a hurry to drive into the heart of Denver.

As the airport came into view, I suffered a moment of confusion, thinking I was actually looking at the tent city. The main "building" looked like an enormous row of white circus tents with tall, sharp peaks stabbing up into the sky—more than I could count at a glance. I'm serious; there must have been something like thirty or forty individual spires. They were arranged in a long row and were dwarfed on one side by a gigantic, glass building that reminded me of a shiny "W." Once I came to my senses and saw the parking lots surrounding the area I figured out that I was looking at the main terminal of the airport. Having been a Marine, I've done some traveling in my life but I'd never had occasion to come to Colorado in all that time, and I'd never seen anything like this airport.

I felt a presence over my shoulder and looked to see who it was. Wang stood next to me, holding onto my seat back for balance with his eyes locked on the airport. I made the mistake of asking him what was up—he must have spent the next fifteen minutes pissing in my ear about the history of the airport's design. He just went on and on about the original designer of the place

(I'll be goddamned if I can remember the guy's name now) and how he had this whole artistic vision of a profile that was suggestive of the snowy tops of the Rockies while paying homage to the teepees of the Native American Indians, blah, blah, blah. He really went on forever; I tried to get a word in to calm him the hell down, but he transitioned from discussing the artistic aspects of the joint straight into the internal structural design without even taking a breath. I guess the inside of the building was based on some sort of bridge design or something, which didn't make any sense to me at all. Why would you base an airport on a bridge? Just base it on a goddamned airport.

I didn't have the heart to tell him that the whole mess looked like a big-ass circus tent to me.

As we got closer, we realized that what had been the actual emergency tent city that the Army set up was on the outskirts past the southeast runway. It made sense to me from a logistical standpoint; that airport would have been a major supply hub for the forces encamped in Denver, and they would have used it for emergency supplies as well. The place was well positioned in the middle of a wide-open flat area where it would have been relatively easy for our pilots to take off and land using Visual Flight Rules (VFR), which was a necessity back then due to the loss of GPS and ground-based radio beacons. Placing the tent city right next to the runway would have effectively turned resupply into a simple unloading op. Smart dogfaces.

We rolled slowly by the main terminal roads, taking the smaller streets in an ever more zig-zagging pattern towards the east runway (which appeared to have also serviced all of the shipping aircraft back in the airport's heyday; I saw some FedEx aircraft still parked out by the smaller hangars). As we approached the turn off that would lead us to the runway security gate, Wang leaned in and said, "Can we stop here for a minute?"

"Uh, yeah," I said. "What's up?"

"I have to see the horse at least once."

"The… horse?"

"Yeah," Wang nodded. "Come on with me, and I'll show you."

"Well, okay, I guess." I put the bus in park, not bothering to pull over to the side of the road, opened the door, and separated the power wires like Oscar had shown me to kill the engine. I looked back down the length of the vehicle to see some very curious faces. "Uh, rest break, guys. Take a minute to refresh yourselves—maybe smoke if you got 'em."

Wang bounded off the bus like he was hurrying to be first in line at the ice cream parlor. I slung my rifle and followed.

We didn't have to walk very far to get to "the horse." Now, I call this thing "the horse" but that really doesn't do it justice. A more accurate description would be "Giant Soul Devouring Hell Demon." First of all, it was huge—it had to stand thirty feet at its highest point. Second, the goddamned thing was blue. It was a giant, Smurf-blue horse rearing up on its hind legs like it was setting up to kill something.

I'm really not getting my point across. I mean, this thing was obscene. The mane stood up from the neck like a punk mohawk, and its whole stomach was crisscrossed in a web of dark blue (almost black) veins. The veins across the stomach and the stylized, elongated body reminded me of a big blue dick; yet for those people with a less active imagination, the artist had chosen to include an actual dick complete with a set of dark blue balls just hanging out in front of God and everybody. The damned thing looked like a cock slapped on top of a cock.

The kicker to this whole mess was around the back end. This was something you wouldn't see at all unless you walked up to the thing and really got in there among the sheer animal glory of this monstrosity. In the back, the tail was lifted well up and out of the way to expose an intricately (nay lovingly) sculpted anus pushed out to the point of near prolapse in expression of the animal's fury. More dark veins originated from the base of the creature's scrotum to wrap out symmetrically around the bottom of the ass cheeks; a vascular cradle for the inflamed shit pipe.

This horse made The Elephant Man look like Angelina Jolie.

"Wang," I said, unable to tear my eyes away, "what in the hell did you bring me out to see?"

Fred Moses's voice erupted from behind me in his characteristic rumble, "Now that is just the ugliest motherfucking thing that ever existed. Who the hell is responsible for this?"

"I don't remember his name anymore," Wang said. "I had seen pictures when we studied this airport in college. I always told myself if I ever came this way I'd have to stop and get a picture of myself next to it." His voice sounded almost reverent.

"Well… why?" Fred asked. "I wish I could un-see the damned thing."

"Jesus wept!" said Jessica as she walked over to join us.

"I mean, is it a joke or something?" Fred continued. "Did the artist get screwed by the city government and this is his revenge?"

"Why would you go to the trouble to give it an asshole?" Jessica asked in dismay.

"That's not even the best part," said Wang. His voice was shaking on the verge of laughter. "In the evening when it was dark? The eyes would glow bright red."

I erupted into laughter at that point. I couldn't help myself; the whole thing was so preposterous. The blue color, hideous veins, genitalia, and inflamed asshole were insane but could be explained away with artistic eccentricity. Glowing red eyes was just an obvious troll. This horse was a giant middle finger extended right at Denver; there was nothing anyone could have said at that point to convince me otherwise. I laughed so hard that I started coughing uncontrollably; huge, wracking hacks that came from the center of my windpipe and burned like fire. I felt a shaking hand on my shoulder and realized that Fred was leaning on me, laughing as well. Wiping tears from my eyes, I looked up and saw that all of us were doubled over in various states of duress.

We carried on for several minutes before we began to regain control of ourselves, the intense laughter giving way to roiling aftershocks. Through choking hiccups, Wang stopped laughing just long enough to gasp, "The locals used to call it 'Blucifer…'"

And just like that, we were off again. I ended up on my knees clutching my side, genuinely afraid that I was about to crack a rib.

"You're a fuckin' asshole, Wang," Fred said in a panicked voice a few moments later, still laughing. All of us were panting desperately.

When I was capable, I stood up and said, "Very well, can we get the hell out of here now, please? Before Wang takes us around the side of the building to have a look at the Goatse exhibit?"

Wang giggled at this, but Jessica asked, "Goatse?"

I rolled my eyes, wanting to kick myself for running my mouth. "Yeah, look, don't ask me to explain it, okay? You don't want to know anyway. I'll just say that a bored Marine is a dangerous Marine and the advent of the internet only magnified the problem."

"I'm not following," she said.

"One of the ways a bored Marine will typically pass the time is to try to gross out his buddies and, well, you could find some pretty disturbing imagery on the Internet. Do you have any idea how depraved you have to get to gross out a Marine?"

"Oh…" she replied.

"Yeah," I agreed. "I'm not entirely convinced that the Internet going 'poof' was such a bad thing." I slung my rifle over my shoulder and nodded at Wang. "Are you good now?"

"Yeah, thanks," he said, shaking out one last chuckle.

I turned on my heel and walked back toward the bus, eager to put distance between myself and Blucifer.

We had to wait a while longer for everyone to get back onto the bus (they were out either stretching legs or watering the sides of buildings). I sat up in the driver seat trying to keep from fidgeting while I waited. Once everyone was back in their seats, I started her back up again and drove down a street that emptied out directly on the tarmac. There was a guard shack with a security gate barring our access to the field, so I parked the bus, retrieved the hooligan bar from the back (which had been part of the soldier's gear from the day before), and stepped off to go to work on the gate. Fifteen minutes of grunting and cursing saw the gate opened with us on the other side.

We had to drive across the two runways and park on a road on the opposing side. I saw a C130 sitting abandoned up by the northern end of the runway and made a mental note to check on it when we came back. Having parked the bus, I exited to have a look at the tent city spread out before us.

The whole thing appeared to go on for several kilometers, but it was hard for me to tell; after a certain distance, I just lost all ability to estimate. It may have been five klicks across, but that's really only a wild-ass guess. In the distance, it just looked like a sea of different sized white, brown, and olive squares laid out in a grid. The tents that were closest to us had clearly seen better days.

Many of them were either knocked down or blown over; whatever had been inside of them had been strewn out all across the field. Whole patches of the encampment, some as large as a football field, were blackened from a fire that must have raged through the area. There was no rhyme or reason to the pattern— you'd see a cluster of tents that looked totally intact right next to a gutted area that had been charred to the ground.

Concerning me the most was the lack of support vehicles. With an encampment of that size, I had expected to see a wide variety of trucks lined up throughout the field, from 7-tons all the way down to Growlers. There was none of that. I saw a couple of burnt out chassis in a few areas next to tents that had seen significant fire damage, but outside of that, there was nothing. I stood there with my hands on my hips staring out at the wreckage, trying to figure out what came next.

Straining my eyes, I looked closer at the garbage scattered between the tents and saw the occasional human body at odd intervals.

I heard the old familiar thump-step approach from behind.

"Do you think there's anything left out there?" asked George. Other people from our group manifested in my peripheral vision to either side of me.

"I don't know," I finally said, sighing. "It looks like a battle took place here."

"It makes sense, doesn't it?" asked Rebecca. I glanced over at her and then had to look away to the field again; I had a serious weakness for Irish girls (well, being fair, I had a serious weakness for anything with a pulse and appropriate plumbing) but looking at Rebecca was dangerous. She'd make you forget what you were talking about; make you say stupid shit if you weren't careful.

Oblivious to (or perhaps used to) my reaction, she said, "Whoever was left alive in the city would have come here for food and supplies, the same way we did, right? There would have also been survivors in the tent city itself. Most of us came from a tent city, didn't we?"

"I did," agreed Fred.

"Us too," said Monica Dempsey, her hand draped over her daughter's shoulder.

"Yeah, so survivors living here were trying to protect what they had from survivors coming in from the city. It probably got super brutal," Rebecca concluded. I turned my head toward her again, getting a good look this time and not allowing myself to be distracted by her eyes, full lips, chest, or those big, fat, red curls coming out of her head in every direction (Jesus, that hair was something else, though). I had always thought of Rebecca Wheeler as your typical, selfie-addicted bundle of bad decisions. Outside of the fact that she was nice to look at, I had her categorized as just another person to look out for and keep fed; never really expecting much back from her on the return angle. Looking at her then, I could see some genuine street intelligence at work in those eyes. I took it as a data point to adjust my expectations for her. Not just another pretty face.

"That actually makes *all* of the sense," Wang agreed.

"Okay, well, we're out here now," I said. "We might as well make the full effort and have a look. You all know what MRES look like, right?"

I received several nods and verbal confirmations; everyone had become very familiar with the little brown bags over the last year.

"Okay, keep your eyes open for other stuff as well; don't get tunnel vision. If you *do* get lucky and find MRES, inspect the packaging. Don't take anything that's sweating or has been punctured. You don't want to take in any food that's been compromised. Also remember to keep your eyes open for water, ammunition, or anything else that looks useful."

I looked to my right and left to see who was out there with me, trying to decide who to send out and who to keep back by the bus. This quickly became a frustrating exercise, compounded by the fact that people were looking at me and beginning to fidget.

The main problem was that I wanted to be in two places at once. I trusted Davidson with a rifle the most because I had spent the most time discussing fire team tactics with him in our downtime (he ate that kind of thing up; always had another question to ask on the subject). That being said, this trust didn't go terribly far. I wasn't sure what Davidson actually had or hadn't done in his life. I knew he had plenty of range time, but the guy didn't have any experience moving through a dynamic situation within a small team of people, not even to play paintball. As far as I was concerned, his ability with a rifle in relation to the rest of our group was comparable to a cat that had learned how to bury its shit in the litter box among siblings that just left their little care packages exposed on top of the sand to air out. I knew I could trust him not to flag anyone in a calm, relaxed situation because I had spent so much time chewing on his ass the first time I saw him do it; he had learned and corrected. I had no idea what I could expect if he was thrown into a firefight, but I had a good idea—he needed training and practice, which required time we hadn't yet discovered.

Consequently, it should have been me pushing out into the field with everyone to keep a close watch on their asses. I'm not Rambo or anything, but I have actually been in firefights and know what to expect (honestly, they even got boring sometimes). Proximity and repetition are critical training tools. I would be able to keep my head screwed on, maintain good situational awareness, and not shoot my buddies.

On the other hand, I needed someone back here on overwatch to keep an eye out while everyone was digging through the field with their heads in the garbage. Again, the only person I knew I could rely on to carry out this role was me. Marines qualify at five hundred yards (we were the only branch to do so), and I've personally made groupings good enough for center mass at a thousand yards out on the range with a friend's American Predator. I'd been out of the Corps for twelve years by then, but I kept my rifle skills current and even picked up a few tricks that they don't teach you in the Marines. While I had never been a sniper (I was a rifleman before promoting to Staff Sergeant), I knew I could make the longer than average shots. As far as everyone else was concerned in that regard, I again had no freaking clue and no time to find out.

So, how can I be in two places at once? The simple answer was: I can't. goddamnit.

In the end, I decided that sending Davidson out into the field was the lesser of two evils.

"Okay, Barbara, George, Kyle, and the kids stay here. Everyone else heads out among the tents to look for food, water, ammo, or medical supplies. Davidson, take the rifle; you're not looking for anything on the ground. Keep your head on a swivel and watch everyone's back."

"What are you going to be doing?" Edgar asked.

I suppressed my annoyance at the question. I had already decided at that point that anything coming out of Edgar's mouth was borne on the worst possible intentions. Because of this, I knew I had to pay extra attention to anything he said. I couldn't allow a good idea to slip by because I didn't like the source; doing so could mean someone's life. I had to pay extra attention to Edgar, the prick, to keep from developing a blind spot.

"I'm going to the bus roof to watch you guys from as much elevation as I can get." I looked at everyone else and continued. "Everyone get a good look at that first DRASH tent out in front," I said while pointing.

"DRASH...?" Jessica asked from my right.

"Sorry: Deployable Rapid Assembly Shelter. It's the larger, longer tent down in front where I'm pointing."

"Okay, I get it," Jessica said.

"I make that a distance of about four hundred yards or at least close enough to four hundred that it doesn't matter. Nobody pass that tent."

"Why not?" asked Fred. "Food might be just on the other side."

"Because it will severely impact my ability to shoot anything that jumps out at you."

"Oh," Fred muttered. "Right on."

"Also," I continued, "try not to put anything between you and me; try to maintain a line of sight back to this bus at all times. If you can see me, I can see you. That's a good thing. Everyone clear?"

I got several nods and comments in the affirmative. "Good, let's get moving then. Davidson, come here."

Davidson had just stepped off the bus carrying the M4 (my M4, not the boomstick with the M203, thank God—I didn't want to have that argument again). I put my head close into his and whispered: "You make goddamned sure you know where your muzzle is every fucking second, do you get me? If you fuck up and shoot any of our people, you will *not* be forgiven. Clear?"

The color drained from his face, and he nodded. "Yeah, man. Crystal." He was taking it seriously. That was the best I could hope for.

I nodded and slapped him on the shoulder. "Get out there, then. Protect your people."

Kyle was waiting to piss in my ear as soon as Davidson was off with the others.

"I'm not a kid, dude. I could be going out there with the others."

"Negative," I said, walking past him to the bus. "I need you up top so you can spot for me." I retrieved my MR556, a couple of spare mags, some binoculars, and stepped back off to see him standing outside waiting for me.

"Oh," he said.

"Come on, follow me."

I walked up to the nose of the bus, which stuck out from the cab like you see on a Peterbilt truck. There were two side view mirrors on each side of the bus for a total of four; one was bolted high up on the roof above the accordion door, and the other was supported by a frame attached to the front of the fender over the headlight. I grabbed the frame of the mirror over the headlight with my right hand and with my left I grabbed the strap that was holding down the engine cowling. From this position, I put my foot on top of the front tire and boosted myself up to stand on the bus's hood. After that, it was easy to climb up onto the roof. I turned back to regard Kyle, who was still on the ground looking up at me.

"You coming?" I asked. I turned back to put eyes on our people moving out among the rubble. From below, I heard Kyle say, "Hey, you guys just hang out in the bus, okay?" He was talking to the children; Maria and Rose. That was good. The kids weren't just someone else's problem as far as he was concerned.

I could feel the bus rock minutely under my feet as Kyle grunted and heaved himself up to the roof. He came over to stand by me and look out at the field.

"Do you think they'll find anything out there?" he asked.

I sighed. "I don't know. Whatever hasn't been burned out looks pretty mangled. I can't see a field kitchen in there anywhere, but those might just have been positioned in the camp so far back that I can't see them from here. The big thing is that I don't see a lot of vehicles. It's like whatever military were here packed up and left at some point."

"Or, you know, they died like the rest of us and other people came through to take the trucks, right?" Kyle suggested.

"Yeah. There's that, too."

I handed him the binoculars. "I want you to keep an eye out while I'm busy watching everyone down there," I said. "Don't keep the binos glued to your face. Just keep on a constant swivel while looking back behind us to make sure that we're not being crept up on. If you see movement, use the binoculars to confirm."

He did as instructed but also griped, "I can handle a rifle, dude. Serious."

"Kyle… what's your last name?"

"Montgomery."

"Montgomery… okay, Gomer it is. How old are you?"

"Eighteen. And what do you mean 'Gomer'?"

"Guys on the fire team gotta have a nickname," I said. "I have determined that yours shall be Gomer."

"Awe, dude, fuck no. Can't you call me something else? Like, I don't know, 'Ace' or something?"

"Nope, you don't get to pick your own nickname. If it worked that way, everyone would walk around calling themselves stupid shit like 'Terminator' or 'Predator.' No one could take anybody seriously. It would be total chaos."

"Yeah, but Gomer? Bullshit, man."

I glanced at him and smiled. "You know what my nickname was in Boot Camp? Mr. Brown."

"Oh, well see? That's a cool name—"

"No, just hang on. They called me Mr. Brown because I have a bit of a sensitive stomach and it took me a long time to get used to military chow. It wasn't until I was approaching graduation day that I really started getting used to it. But before you get close to graduation, you have to get through The Crucible."

"Oh, dude. 'Mr. Brown'? Is this going to turn into a story where you shit yourself?"

"No, no. Almost, but no. But I *was* farting the whole time like a sick rhino." Kyle started laughing, which made me smile. "I couldn't help myself. It was like clockwork. Me and my buddies were out there, caked in mud and soaked through to the bone, going through the most demanding physical trial that we had yet experienced, and I was farting loud enough that guys were hearing it three columns over. And the smell was fucking putrid.

One of the DI's came as close as I ever saw to breaking character to comment on it."

"Holy crap, man," Kyle laughed.

"I ended up being one of the guys to get a nickname change halfway through boot camp. I'd started out as 'Chimp.'"

"Chimp? You mean chimpanzee? What the hell for?"

"My last name is Gibson. 'Gibbon,' 'monkey...' Chimp."

"That's... that's not even funny," Kyle said. "Like, you have to think too hard to get it."

"Yes, it is, in fact, like going around your elbow to get to your ass," I agreed. "But that was just like a place holder nickname... you're keeping your eyes open, right? Scanning the area and such?"

"Oh, yeah, man. No sweat."

"Good. So we had this one drill instructor in my platoon; Sergeant McGill, our kill hat. He was amazing. He rarely if ever referred to any of the recruits by their names. By the first day, he no-shit had a nickname assigned to every one of us and never forgot a single one, no matter how much we tried to float under the radar or how much we pissed him off."

"How many people were in your group-thing, or whatever?" he asked.

"Platoon. Fifty-four of us graduated; a couple washed out."

"Damn," Kyle muttered, impressed.

"I know. He had a gift. But in a lot of cases, those nicknames were just placeholders. They were there until we did something sufficiently stupid to get rebranded. There was one dude, Simmons, who made the mistake of asking another of the DI's to make an 'emergency head call' during our morning PT."

"You can do that?"

"Well, you can," I said. "The drill instructors don't want recruits pissing themselves any more than the recruits want to piss themselves. But you never call it an 'emergency head call.' The very microsecond the words left his mouth, he had three very large, very loud DI's running circles around him screaming 'emergency! We have an emergency!' and forced him to make siren noises. One of them followed poor Simmons all the way to the head making siren noises and screaming 'emergency!' as loud as he could, which is goddamned loud. From that day forward, Simmons was known as Potty Break."

Kyle began to laugh. Loud, honking explosions erupted from his throat; the kind of laugh a sick teenager makes after one of his buddies nuts himself on a skateboard. It surprised the hell out of me, and I almost considered changing his nickname on the spot.

We fell into silence for a little while. He scanned the area behind us and, to his credit, never expressed boredom in the activity. He seemed to grasp that the job was important if not glamorous. I appreciated that in a teenager. I would have been complaining nonstop at his age.

I looked out over the field and watched our people pick among the remains of the tent city. They made slow going but covered a broad area. Every so often I'd see one of them stop and bend over to examine something closer; sometimes they would pick something up and take it with them. It was a hopeful sign, but not enough of them were holding parcels in their arms and, even if all of them were carrying something, we needed more supplies than each person could carry in their hands. I decided we were going to have to push into the city and started planning; who was coming with me and who would stay behind to guard.

"So you mentioned that you used to go shooting with your dad," I prompted.

"Yeah," he said, sounding serious again. I never learned the circumstances of his separation from his family. "We'd go target shooting out at the range and stuff. We went deer hunting a couple of times too."

"Nice," I said to myself. "What did he teach you about shooting?"

"Mostly safety stuff. I mean, he showed me how to line up the sights and all; he never even let me have a scope until our first deer hunt. He said he wanted me to be comfortable on iron sights first. It used to piss me off at the time, but I think now that he was right. It made me a better shooter. Never got to tell him that… that he was right."

I kept my mouth shut, not wanting to interrupt. I suspected he'd speak again when he was ready, and it turned out I was correct.

He cleared his throat and said: "The only 'lesson' I really remember, if you want to call it that, was what he told me before he'd even let me hold his rifle… it was a Marlin. He said 'The only safe gun is a gun that isn't pointed at anyone.' Man, I remember this just about as well as I remember anything. I asked him about safety switches, and all that, and said 'Don't those make the gun safe?'"

"What did he say?" I asked.

"He said that any safety mechanism that could be disengaged isn't foolproof, so they can't be relied on. He told me that I needed to be the safety instead of some little switch."

I raised my eyebrows at that. I liked the sound of Kyle's dad. He had made it clear to his son that he needed to own responsibility for his weapon at all times. I could get behind that.

"How long and how often did you guys go shooting, Kyle?"

"He started taking me out when I was eight. We went out to the range all the time unless it was raining. He'd only started taking me hunting just before… you know. We only went out hunting a couple of times."

I nodded. I was starting to feel pretty good about this kid, so I made a decision on the spot.

"We're not finding what we need here," I said. From my right side, Kyle turned and looked back out at the people in the field.

"No luck, huh Mr. Brown?"

"Nope. We're gonna pack it up here pretty soon and move closer to the city; set up a staging area. I'm going to head out into the city looking for more stuff. We're good on fuel for now, but food and water are a big problem. I want you to come with me. I'll give you the rifle to carry."

"Oh, sweet! Can I get the grenade belt too?"

"No, you can't get the… what is it with everyone? I'm not handing you guys a grenade launcher. It's too dangerous if you fuck it up. I'm giving you my M4."

"Oh. Well, okay, I guess."

"'Okay, I guess.' Well, I'm so very grateful to have your consideration, good sir."

"No, it's cool, man," Kyle said. "I get it. You can count on me, Gibs. I won't fuck this up."

There was real sincerity in his voice, and it put me at ease.

"Your father taught you one of the major laws of firearm safety: muzzle awareness. Never put the muzzle on anything you're not ready to kill."

"Right on. What're the other laws?"

I held up my hand to start counting off fingers: "The gun is always loaded (therefore always clear any gun you pick up), muzzle awareness—as I already said—know what's behind your target, and trigger discipline."

"Trigger discipline?" he repeated.

"Trigger discipline," I answered. "There's no reason for you to have your finger on the trigger until it's time to shoot. You just lay your finger along the receiver, otherwise."

"Oh, okay. Got it. Always loaded, muzzle awareness, know what's behind the target, and trigger discipline," Kyle repeated to himself quietly.

He was a good kid.

5

PUSHING OUT

Gibs

The excursion out into the field wasn't a total waste of time, but it also wasn't the major payday I was hoping for. A few people who had been out looking managed to find the odd MRE and Jessica even found a filled water bladder insert from a camel-back but, by and large, what they encountered most was either trampled, burned, ripped open, or compromised in some way. As we spent more time on the site, I became convinced that whatever military presence that had been here had actively packed up to leave; either to consolidate forces elsewhere, travel to some agreed upon rally point, or just displace to a more defensible posi-tion. Whatever had actually happened, it was obvious they had combed through the area and packed up every useful item they could find.

The C130 was likewise a bust. I didn't have a great deal of hope as we approached, so I just put the bus in park and left it running. The airplane's cargo door was down (another bad sign), so I just ran up the platform, made a quick circuit around the interior, and poked my head into the flight deck. As suspected, the only thing the cavernous plane had to offer was a lot of empty space.

One of our ladies (I can't remember if it was Rebecca or Barbara anymore) asked if it made sense to try and get some fuel out of the aircraft. I thought about that suggestion a moment and realized that, yeah, that was a damned good point. Those old turboprop engines basically just ran on kerosene, which would burn fine in that bus's diesel engine. I ran over to the plane and started slapping all the fuel tanks, which were suspended under the wings, but they sadly all rang empty. Whoever it was that had lit out of there, it seemed as though they'd pulled everything off that plane but the skin.

We got back on the 470 and continued North around the perimeter of Denver, our plan being to take Washington Street due south, then push down into the city from the top. The idea was that we would penetrate in as far as we could without having to shove a bunch of cars out of the way and, when we could go no further, a small team would continue on foot towards the heart of the city.

The primary goal of this team was reconnaissance; confirm the existence or lack of other survivors, identify likely scavenging targets, and report back within a set timeframe (in this case we decided two hours was reasonable). On the chance that the team found something really good (defined here as a cache of provisions in one spot capable of sustaining the whole group for a substantial period), the search was to be called off, and they were to RTB (return to base) immediately.

Well, we were able to hold to this plan until we got to Washington Street before we had to abandon the whole damned thing. On our map, Washington just looked like any other street. Sure, it ran from the outskirts all the way into the heart of Denver, but I had kind of hoped that it would be a little open given how close it was to the 25 freeway; I figured people would have just skipped it altogether. Fat chance. Washington was a nice, thick artery running through the city with a total of four lanes and a wide, open median running down the center. Up by the 470, it was completely snarled with vehicles packed in bumper to bumper. We ended up driving around like a bunch of tourists before finding a way in through Quebec Street, and only then because we were able to come in on the soft shoulder. So from there, we were able to reach Riverdale, which got us to 104th, which got us back to Washington Street, only now it was deep enough into the city that we were past the pileup and could travel on the street. Once we were back on track, I resisted the urge to look at the fuel gauge, preferring to remain ignorant about how much diesel we had spent wandering around like a bunch of dickheads.

We pushed far enough south that the residential area gave way to actual city (or, at least what passes for city in Denver—a lot of it was wide open, it must have been a very lovely town at some point), which was what I was looking for. I didn't know how likely we were to find food or water within a place of business like a store, but I was banking on the hope that there were going to be outposts and distribution points in the heart of the city, set up either by FEMA or the military. I knew there was a better than average chance of these being picked over (anyone living in the city would have known exactly where they were), but it was a start. If we came up dry, we could just go back the way we came and take our time going house to house. This final option was a matter of last resort for me; I was still hoping we could hit it big somewhere.

When I decided we had gone far enough, I pulled over and executed something like an eight-point turn to get that goddamned bus reversed in the other direction (I wanted it going back the way we came mostly because I didn't want to hassle with it later). I parked it, opened the door, shut off the engine, and walked down the aisle to have a chat with the group.

"I'd like to accomplish a few different things at once with this," I said. "Yeah, we need to get food, but I also need to get you guys familiar with moving in teams, comfortable with carrying weapons, and everything that entails. The only way to do that is practice, and there's no time like the present. We have three rifles and two pistols. I'm leaving a rifle and two pistols here at the bus; I'll take two rifles and Kyle out with me."

I saw Kyle straighten up at this; Jessica also perked up. She waved at me and said, "I'd like to come too, if that's okay. We'll get up to speed a lot faster if you take two people out at a time… and also, I really don't want to just sit around on this bus."

As I considered this, more people started offering opinions. Suddenly everyone had a reason why they should be coming along as well, and before I knew it, we were looking a lot more like a squad than a team. I had to get control of this quickly.

"Alright, alright, knock it off. We're not all going at once. I'm sorry; I know sitting around on the bus sucks, but this is how it's gonna go until we have a better handle on the area. Jessica, you have a point. Since you were the first person to speak up, grab the Sig; you'll come with us.

Edgar chose this time to weigh in, of course. "You know, I'm sure we all appreciate your experience as a soldier," I inwardly cringed when he said this but didn't bother to correct him; Marines and Army soldiers like to have their little pissing contests from time to time but, truth be told, I was actually very positive on the Army… besides, the only people who actually care about the difference between Marines and soldiers are Marines and soldiers, "but I don't ever recall voting to put you in charge—"

"That's because you didn't vote. I just am."

That shut him up.

"Let's be perfectly clear, guys. The arrangement here is thus:

I've voluntarily agreed to be responsible for this group's well-being. This is nothing new to me; it was my job for twelve years as a United States Marine." I restrained myself from emphasizing the word "Marine" for Edgar's benefit—one must not be petty. "It may be a little more personal now; back then I was serving for a more abstract concept like Country whereas now I can see all the faces of the people I'm working for, but the concept is the same. The conditions of my service, now, are that I'm in charge. You all follow my lead; otherwise, I can't do my job and keep you safe. And frankly, if I'm unable to do this properly, I'm not going to kill myself trying to half-ass the job."

I let the unspoken threat hang in the air. I was absolutely serious, too. I wasn't about to hang around with a group of people if they were going to start engaging in a bunch of fuckery likely to get people killed.

"So," I concluded, "does anyone now care to hold a vote?"

No one spoke. I saw a few heads shake back and forth, some people had downcast eyes. It made me feel like a shitbag, but I still believe it was critical to get it out in the open. Clarity for the group was more important than my pangs of guilt over stomping puppy dog feelings. I locked eyes with Edgar, waiting to see what he would do. He breathed in, exhaled, and looked out his window.

"Outstanding," I said. "Davidson, you take the rifle we found at the humvee." Davidson lit up like a Christmas tree, no doubt thinking about the grenade launcher. I thought about taking the grenade belt along with me; the look on his face made me question whether I could trust him with ammo for the damned thing.

"Kyle, you'll take my M4, and Jessica gets the pistol. Oscar, hang on to that Beretta." I gestured to Kyle and Jessica, motioning them to the back of the bus. I followed them back and opened up the bag of provisions. I pulled out an MRE (Mac 'N' Cheese, I noted, the lucky bastards) and handed it up to Kyle with a bottle of water. "You guys get this heated up and divide it in half. I'm going to get everyone else fed and then I'll be right with you."

I took the duffel back up the aisle to the center of the bus and addressed the group. "Let's get some chow, people. One MRE for every two people; pair off and select your poison from the bag. If you run out of MRES, switch to canned foods and other items. I don't know if it will come to that because I haven't counted these out, but there are definitely less MRES than there are people. When it comes to the other, non-military food, make sure you get at least six hundred calories but take in no more than seven hundred. We need to ration this out until we get a resupply."

I grabbed a can of ravioli from the bag and took it back with me to the rear of the bus. Kyle and Jessica had their ration pack underway; it was on the floor of the bus leaning against a seat strut. I used my pocket knife to saw through the lid of my can, making the jankiest, most jagged opening in history and not caring. Thinking about how I was going to eat my food, something suddenly occurred to me. I pulled out a pack of wet wipes from our supplies and pulled out several sheets to share between Kyle, Jessica, and myself. "Wash your hands," I said.

I called out to the rest of the group towards the middle of the bus: "Hey! Everyone wash your hands! You do not want to get ass —" I cut myself off as I noted the women and children looking back at me. "That is… you don't want to make yourselves sick." I threw the wet wipe pack forward, where it was caught by Wang.

I spent the next fifteen minutes going over the operation and safety procedures of the M4 carbine and Sig Sauer P320 with my new team. I'm happy to report they never once rolled their eyes or fidgeted during the safety brief.

Within a half hour, everyone was fed, and the three of us were ready to hop off our ride to take a walk into town. As I was lifting my rifle to sling over my shoulder, African Carry style with the barrel down, Jessica said, "Shouldn't you be putting on that equipment that we took from the dead soldier?"

"Negative," I said. "There isn't enough armor to go around. I'm not about to see to my own protection if the other guys in my team are going out naked. In fact, here Kyle, you're the baby. You wear it."

I smiled at his grimace when I said "baby"; I began to dig through our gear to find the rig. From behind me, I heard Wang speak: "Hey, don't take this wrong, Gibs, but that's pretty dumb."

I straightened up to look back at him. "Excuse me?" I asked. I wasn't pissed off at him; just a little surprised.

Instead of answering me, he addressed the rest of the bus. "How many people on this bus have served in the military?"

George Oliver, Mr. Thump-Step himself, raised his hand. That surprised me. I hadn't known that about him. Either way, the guy looked older than the Pyramids and walked around on a cane; he probably served in World War One or something. Maybe I was being too optimistic. Spanish American War, probably.

Wang continued. "And how many of us have combat experience?"

Nobody raised a hand this time. Wang looked back at me along with everyone else.

"As you say," Wang said, "we need you to teach us how to fight effectively as a team. We need to learn from you so we can survive. You're kind of a VIP now. You're not going to be good to anyone if you do something stupid like get killed."

Jesus, I thought. *You morbid little asshole.*

I thought about it a minute and then shook my head. "Look, it's probably a moot point, anyway. We haven't seen a single person since we got here, and we've driven all over the place. I'm sure it's safe out there."

"If that's the case then leave the weapons behind," said Wang. "You'll be able to carry more back here when you return."

goddamnit, the cagey little bastard had me pinned. I was strongly considering just overriding everyone and forcing Kyle bodily into the gear if I had to. Edgar spoke up before I could.

"You do know that we're right, of course. You wouldn't look so uncertain otherwise."

I held back anger at his insufferable, know-it-all, little comment. Maybe they were right. Maybe the best way I could do my job was to start by ensuring that I stayed upright. It was a bitter damned pill to swallow, though.

"Fine," I growled. I pulled the whole works over my head and started strapping into it, adjusting the mag and grenade pouches as I went. Things were a little moved around from what I was used to when I wore one of these for a living, but I decided to not eat up the next several minutes repositioning pouches on the webbing. Instead, I started opening and inspecting each pouch to verify what I had. In addition to the usual stack of PMAGS wrapped around my belly, I located fragmentation, flashbang, and smoke grenades. There was all the other usual crap that I was used to seeing too; the flex cuffs, flashlight and chemlight, a blowout kit (I found that it was outfitted with the newer QuickClot gauze, which was a good thing; I'd never experienced this personally but the older pads used to burn the hell out of people)—I noted, however, that the standard CAT (combat application tourniquet) was missing. I also located some partially filled out casualty and witness cards, now rendered useless by the fact that there was no one to submit them to in the event that we took any casualties. I stuffed them back in their pocket, not wanting to explain them to anyone else for fear of spooking them.

I looked around. "Okay, I'm wearing the damned thing. Is everyone happy now?"

Barbara smiled at me. "I'm happy. You're looking yummy."

I restrained a laugh. "Later, Barbara. Not in front of the children." I turned back to the pile of gear on the aisle floor, crouched down to the food duffel, and pulled out the last of the food and water, which was distressingly little. I handed the empty bag up to Jessica and said, "Here, you can pack mule for us. If we luck out and find a large cache somewhere, we can come back for more people to help us carry it all out."

She took the bag and I nodded to both of them, confirming it was time to head out. I paused by Davidson as I went and said, "You stay away from those grenades, okay? Don't let me come back here and find that you've blown half your face off."

"Understood, boss. Not until I've been trained."

"Good," I said, feeling a little guilty. Davidson was eager, but he was no dummy; I'd ordered him to keep off already, and so that was very likely what he would do. I felt as though I needed to loosen up a little and stop expecting the worst possible performance out of everyone all the time. The fact that none of these people were Marines didn't make them five-year-olds. In fact, a lot of the guys in my platoon had demonstrated several times that they were perfectly comfortable operating at a five-year-old level —all they had to do was get a little bored, and the shenanigans would ensue.

"There isn't really any place to get elevated around here," I said to him. "At the same time, the buildings we do have around will limit your field of view. I recommend you just position yourself outside the bus, so you have good visibility running up and down the street. Keep everyone else close by."

He nodded and grabbed the grenadier's M4 to follow us off the bus. I walked up the aisle towards the exit, having to rotate around the people in the seats to keep from smacking them in the heads and shoulders with all the pouches hanging off my torso.

Outside of the bus, I looked at my two new teammates and said, "Let's just stick to Washington. We'll head south and keep our eyes open for anything good. Keep on the lookout for the standard stuff like grocery stores and the like, but also look for larger businesses or office buildings. Most of those places had employee rec rooms or cafeterias. They would have food and Coke dispensers we can break open."

We walked south together for several blocks, looking for things to jump out at us. Kyle gestured to several buildings as we went, but I shook my head to indicate we should keep moving. The businesses in the area were small; a lot of them were little Mom and Pop take-out joints that would have either been cleared out or stuffed with rotting food. There would be more hope for water in these places, but we had a good distance to go into the city; I didn't want to load down with bottles of water here only to have to carry them double the distance. Besides, I was still dreaming of an Army checkpoint.

Being younger and subject to less aches and pains (and perhaps also because he wasn't humping another forty pounds of combat load), Kyle began to drift out ahead of us as we walked. I appreciated his drive but called out to him anyway, advising that he not get too far ahead. He waved back to me and slowed his pace. Jessica stayed by my side as we walked, the tattoos on her bare arms standing out in the daylight. She had the long strap of the duffel bag crisscrossed over her body with both of her hands wound up in the strap at the center of her chest, keeping the bag up high on her back rather than slapping around at her hip.

I stole glances at her out of the corner of my left eye as we walked, trying to get some kind of read on her. I could tell she was younger than me, but she was a lot closer to my own age (forty-two at the time) than she was to Kyle's; I'd have to place her in the early-to-mid-thirty range. Her brown hair was pulled back in a ponytail, and she had a serious face; a face that described a certain familiarity with getting only slightly less than what was needed from life. It struck me, then, that she was an attractive woman in all of the ways that Rebecca was not. Rebecca had a lot going for her including an unlined, baby doll face and a body loaded down with curves in all the right places; but her attitude was basically still that of a kid. Taking into account her flash of insight at the tent city, I had begun to suspect that the whole "helpless bombshell" thing might be more of a performance on her part; a calculated persona designed to attract those of the White Knight mindset. I wasn't anywhere near certain if this was actually the case, but if it was, my estimation of her would be knocked down a rung or two; I am not an admirer of feigned incompetence.

Jessica's beauty, on the other hand, had its core in the competence she expressed. Her face carried life experience in the fine wrinkles at the corners of her eyes and mouth as well as the deeper wrinkles of her forehead, and yet these only added to her appeal. She looked like she had probably hit some rough patches along the way and had been blessed with the inner drive necessary to push through. On the road in a pair of dirty, stale jeans, a sweat stained shirt, greasy unwashed hair, and grime highlighting all the cracks of her skin she yet managed to be striking. I imagined that once she cleaned up, dressed nice, and applied a bit of makeup, she could turn some serious heads.

"Uh, you see anything you like?" she asked, shocking me out of my thoughts. I had been convinced I was being all stealthy, but apparently, I was staring like a dumbass.

Having enough experience to answer with neither "yes" nor "no," I said, "Sorry. Don't take it wrong; I was just curious about who I'm traveling with. I have a pretty good lock on Kyle since we had a chance to talk a bit up at the airport. I was just wondering about you, that's all."

Apparently not willing to let me off the hook, she said, "Ah… nice dodge but you still didn't answer my question."

I blew air out between my lips in an obvious stall for time. Rather than going for a gambit in either direction, I decided to hedge by calling attention to my position, hoping for a little pity.

"Okay, well if I say 'no,' I'm the rude prick that thinks you're not much worth looking at. If I say 'yes,' I'm that creepy old guy that likes to get the ladies separated off from the group so he can ogle them and start making propositions."

"I don't think you're old at all, Gibs." She didn't look at me, but the corner of her mouth pulled up in a smile.

Well... damn.

I decided to put a pin in that train of thought and see if I could press her for background. I'd be coming back to this, though. There was charming to be done here. Oh, yes.

"Okay," I said, scrambling to pick the main thread back up, "all that aside, I'm basically walking into an undefined situation right now with a couple of armed strangers and Kyle is slightly less strange than you. No offense; I just mean that you're unfamiliar. I don't know anything about you. For instance, have you ever fired a gun before?"

She tilted her head and nodded off into the distance, body language indicating that she considered this a worthy line of inquiry. "I have," she answered, "but I was not the best at it nor did I enjoy it."

"Oh, what happened?"

"Bad case of a shitty instructor," she said. "It was my ex-husband. He was dead set on having his 'woman learn how to handle a weapon.'" She said the last part of the sentence in a mock-basso voice while puffing out her chest and widening her elbows far enough to encroach into my space, which didn't bother me in the slightest. "Then he let me rattle my fillings loose with his .44 magnum."

I grimaced and said, "What a douche." Realizing what I had said out loud, I quickly added, "Uh, excuse me."

"It's no problem at all; he was, in fact, a massive douche."

I'd seen videos with people like this guy on the internet before. The pinnacle of humor for them was apparently to take a waif of a girl weighing in at about ninety pounds soaking wet, hand her a goddamned hand cannon loaded for bear, and then sit back and laugh their asses off when she'd inevitably shit herself in response to the concussive forces unleashed by the monster. More often than not, the subject of all the laughter ended up hurting herself in some way; either by falling down or smacking herself in the head with the barrel as it rotated violently back in her hand. As someone who strongly believes that a good citizen is a well-armed citizen, videos like that used to make me all stabby. You simply could not devise a better means to make the average person terrified of firearms nor find a way to better condition them to believe that guns are evil.

"Well, I won't pry," I continued, "but if that's an indicator of the man, I guess I can see why his title is 'ex'-husband."

"Oh, that's a small, small part of it. But in general, yes. He never laid a hand on me or anything like that. He was just a controlling prick. I spent more time than I care to admit being worn down by him, being told 'I couldn't,' believing I wasn't worth anything. You see these?" She held her arms out in front of her, indicating the various tattoos that wrapped all around them. They weren't quite sleeves, but if she managed to cram any more in there, they would qualify.

"I got these as a big F-you to my ex. I'd wanted a tattoo ever since I was in high school. It was nothing elaborate; just my father's name on the back of my neck… he died when I was fourteen. Whenever I dreamt about him, the back of my neck was where I could still feel his touch on waking. He always had his hand there. When I was a little girl, it was how he guided me through a crowded area. During dinner at the end of the day, he'd reach out to pull me over for a kiss on the cheek; he'd do it by gently pulling me over by the base of my neck. If I close my eyes right now, I can still feel it. I wanted his name inked right where I could feel his touch."

"Damn," was all I could think to say. It was a heavy thought.

"Anyway," she continued without acknowledging my interruption, "my ex forbade it. He said that no wife of his was going around with some bullshit trailer trash badge of honor stamped across her neck."

After hearing the deeply personal reason behind her desire to get the tattoo, this last statement made my blood boil. The thought that anyone should be roped into wasting time with such as him was galling. Keeping in mind, of course, that there are two sides to every story; I'm sure she had her moments when any sane man would favor jumping out of a window to dealing with the worst of her tirades… most women do in my experience. But still: that story about her dad was a heartbreaker, even for a salty old Marine. Reducing it down to "trailer trash shit" was indefensible in my view.

"It sounds to me, if you'll excuse me saying so, that you made the right choice for yourself. So all that ink was before or after you broke it off?"

"In the process of," she answered. "I actually wish I had left it until all the proceedings were done. It might have helped in the custody fight."

"Oh, no, there were kids tied up in it?"

"One: my daughter, Pinch."

"Pinch?" I asked. I was unable to keep amusement from my voice.

"Yeah," she smiled. "My baby girl. Her name is Emily, after the asshole's mother. I could never bring myself to call her that. I called her Pinch instead."

"Any particular reason?"

Jessica looked me over up and down, appraising. "You have any kids?"

"No, ma'am, thank God. I like kids just fine, you understand. I'm just lucky I never had any with the women I married."

"Plural, huh?" she said with an impressed air.

"Uh, yes. It takes a special woman to be married to a Marine and remain faithful, especially when you spend half your marriage deployed. Unfortunately, young Marines don't have a lot of luck at picking special women."

"Ah, none of it was your fault, of course."

"Oh, hell no! There were all kinds of fu- uh, things I could have done better. It's just that they weren't giving me a whole lot to work with either."

"Well, in either case, you're probably right to be thankful," she said. "An ugly divorce is a hard thing for a kid to go through. Anyway, I called her Pinch because that's all I wanted to do to her when she was born. Fat little arms, fat little legs, her fat little cheeks... I don't know what it is, but something about all that screams PINCH ME to a mom." She started to giggle, recalling some private memory.

I thought back to the holidays of my formative years and the outright beating my cheeks took at the hands of my sadistic Aunt Angie, deciding that Jessica's statement must be a true one.

A thought occurred to me during this lull in the conversation. From what all of us survivors had seen, immunity to the plague was a guaranteed deal through maternal heredity. "Jessica, where is Pinch now?"

She sighed. "Her father had her for a few months out of the year; it's why I made the comment about waiting until after the custody battle to get my tattoos—things may have gone better for me. She was with him when the plague hit."

"Oh, no," I said. Knowing what we all knew about the statistics behind the plague, there wasn't a lot of hope that the father was still alive. If her kid (Pinch not Emily, I reminded myself) was still alive, the chances were good that her father wasn't around to look out for her anymore. "How old is she?"

"Thirteen," she said.

"Goddamn. Well, where was she last?"

"He lived in North Platte, Nebraska. There was a FEMA camp up by Sioux City, so I imagine they must have ended up there."

"Well, why the hell didn't you say something sooner?" I asked, feeling agitated. "We could have been making plans to go that way!"

"You've been going my way so far," she answered. "I wasn't going to ask anyone to make the trip with me; Sioux City is a really good distance from here. I was going to help you get some supplies here in Denver, claim my share, and go my own way up the 76. It's why I wanted to come out with you guys. It gives me a better claim on taking some of the food and water with me."

"Damn, man," I said. "Just… damn." I looked out ahead to see Kyle still maintaining a good distance out in front. There wasn't a great deal of anything in the immediate area that looked like it was worth stopping for so I put my attention back on Jessica. "Well, crap," I said. "And here I was under the impression that you just came out for the company." I glanced at her sidelong.

"Oh," she laughed, "that was just a bonus. You can always break off from this group and come with me, you know."

"Well, yeah, what about *your* group?" I asked, coming back to reality for a moment. "I get why you're going for your kid but can you really just bounce on them like that? Why wouldn't you ask them to come? It's not like they're going to be dead set in going anywhere else."

"They're not my group," said Jessica without any malice. "I had only been with them a couple of days in Colorado Springs by the time you showed up. I was there to rest and hopefully resupply before heading out; I think they were getting ready to vote me off the island, honestly."

"Oh, why is that?"

"Because I wasn't planning on sticking around and they knew

it. Why should they invest time or resources into keeping me healthy if I was just going to bounce? There would be no reason to do that if they couldn't rely on me to stay and pitch in."

I chewed all this over in my head for the next hundred yards or so. Finally I said, "Well, let's get this food situation handled. After we get that under control, I might just tag along with you."

"Hey," she said, sounding genuinely excited, "no shit?"

"No shit," I agreed. "Who the hell else am I going to flirt with? Davidson's not my type. Too much ass hair for my taste."

Jessica laughed and, to my surprise, snorted. This shocked her as well as me, which caused her to laugh harder. When she calmed down a bit, she said, "What about that red head? She didn't look so bad. I've been into dudes for as long as I can remember, but she's enough to make me second guess my position."

"Sure, sure, she's a looker. There's no denying that," I agreed. "But as I've gotten a little older, I've found that youth and a perfect rack becomes a secondary concern."

"Oh, yeah? What's the primary concern."

"Backbone," I said without hesitating.

She was quiet for a while before she responded. "You'd come with me because of my backbone?"

"Well… among other things," I said, taking my turn to smile out of the corner of my mouth.

She aimed a devious smile in my direction, causing my heart to shift up a couple of gears. I hadn't flirted this successfully with a woman in I couldn't remember how long (well, one that I wasn't passing a couple of dollars to, anyway).

We had plunged fairly deep into Denver within an hour's time, often veering away from Washington but never getting more than a block away. Washington eventually passed under the 70 freeway and became 38th Street, which quickly passed under a railway overpass and dumped out onto a busy little intersection. The hour itself hadn't been consumed entirely by walking; a good portion of our time was spent in breaking into and casing buildings which looked like good candidates to contain food or water. In several instances, we found some good prospects in the form of vending machines, as I had mentioned earlier. We noted their locations and continued on, still holding out hope for that big score. The vending machine food was a good find; much of the food they contained would keep for months if not longer but I didn't want to bank our hopes on it. Most of that garbage is of low nutritional value. It's the crap that people eat when they're bored and not when they're hungry. Even if we managed to bring back several pounds of the stuff (Funyuns, crackers, cookies, and trail mix), the group would burn through it like fire through dried brush in an attempt to stay nourished. The Coke machines were a much better find in this regard—water is water regardless of the source, despite what any new age health guru may tell you. It just needs to be uncontaminated, and you can live on it.

We stood at the intersection looking down Walnut to our right and Marion just ahead of us. Walnut appeared to lead towards a business district with larger buildings of various shape, size, and intent, whereas Marion went into a residential area with single family homes.

Not wanting to dictate every little thing, I said, "Well, people, what do you think? Businesses one way or homes the other?"

They both looked in either direction. Presently, Kyle said: "We've been having some decent luck with the businesses and such. Those look like bigger buildings down Walnut than what we've hit so far."

"What do you guys think would be more likely for a military

checkpoint?" Jessica asked. "Would they set up in a business or residential area?"

"It would be more about how heavily traveled an area is," I said. "A checkpoint is set up for security; it's about limiting movement and violence. We're most likely to find them on major arteries. The soldiers manning them would have staged from those points and patrolled the immediate area."

"Well, let's stick with the businesses," Kyle suggested. "We're kind of just hoping to get lucky and stumble on some Army stuff, right? Well, we've totally been getting lucky with offices so far."

The logic was decent if you only gave it ten seconds of thought and we weren't feeling strongly either way, so we followed his suggestion. On Walnut, we spread out a bit as we traveled southwest to cover more ground. Jessica walked a block to the north down Blake, I stayed on Walnut, and Kyle was south of us on Larimer. We traveled on in this fashion for a few minutes, each of us stopping at cross streets and waiting for the others to come into view on the adjacent intersections before continuing for another block. I was in the middle of one such block when Kyle came running up my street from behind me. The sound of his feet pounding the sidewalk had me spun around with my rifle leveled before I realized what was happening. This brought him up short, his eyes wide and mouth opened in surprise. I didn't yell at him nor was I angry; the fact that I'm wound tight was not his fault.

"What's up?" I asked as I dropped the muzzle.

"I think I have something on my street," Kyle said in excitement. "Some trucks, a big sun shade of some kind, and a whole crap load of sandbags stacked up everywhere."

"That does sound good," I said. "How far?"

"Uh, I don't know."

"Did it look like more than a mile?"

He considered for a moment before saying, "I guess? I'm really not sure, dude."

Attempting to restrain frustration (and perhaps failing), I said, "How many intersections were between you and what you saw."

"I dunno. Something like five or eight? Definitely no more than ten."

I drew in a deep breath and blew it out slowly. Finally, I said, "Okay, good job. In the future when we're doing something like this again (and we will be), remember to count the number of blocks to your target. A guy like me is always gonna want to know the distance."

"Okay. You got it, man."

"Good deal. Let's grab Jessica and go see what you found."

We went a block over to Blake to flag down Jessica. She put her hand on her pistol, which was stuffed in her right hip pocket, and jogged over to us. I updated her on the situation, at which point she looked over to Kyle, smiled, and punched him lightly on the shoulder.

"Way to go, stud!" she said. Kyle blushed bright red and stood there grinning like a little idiot. I suppressed a laugh, not wanting to embarrass the poor kid, and said, "Come on. Let's go have a look at what you found."

We crossed the two blocks over to Larimer and turned southwest again. Our target came into view as soon as we rounded the building corner; more of an outpost than a checkpoint about three blocks away. As reported by Kyle, the outer perimeter was walled off with chest-high sandbags and covered with a large canvas shade. There appeared to be some razor wire wrapped around the whole thing; the outpost itself spanned all four lanes of the street, from building to building. There was a traffic gate on the north side of the street that narrowed vehicle passage down to a single lane; it was the only break in the sandbags that I could see. I could just make out a Jeep and a supply truck on the other side of the outpost enclosure. Thinking back to the bonanza we had encountered in the single soldier and his humvee down in Colorado Springs, I felt my heart beat harder in anticipation. There would be much here that we could make use of; I could taste it.

"goddamnit, Gomer," I called out, "you keep up this kind of performance, and I'm gonna have to start paying you! Well done!" To my left, Jessica began to clap as she laughed.

Kyle looked back at us over his shoulder and smiled; a genuine, unfiltered, unreserved smile that made him look five years younger, made him look far too young to be slinging a rifle around. He threw a lazy, two-fingered salute my way and then opened up into a light jog towards the little encampment.

As the distance between us increased, I detected movement behind the sandbags.

I immediately called out to Kyle to wait, to stop running away. At the same time, I took a knee and brought my rifle up to look at the site through my optic. Everything jumped into high detail under the 4x32 magnification, but I saw only sandbags. Through my other eye (you never close one eye when looking through an optic) I could see Kyle standing poised with all of his weight on one foot in mid-stride, straining his eyes to see into the enclosure. He was about fifty feet ahead of me. I can't say where Jessica was positioned exactly; she was on my left and behind me, outside of my field of view.

He looked back and said, "What is it?"

I shook my head but did not get up. I continued to scan over the bags looking for anything. Finally, I called out, "Whoever's back there, come out where I can see you."

Kyle's eyes widened when I said this. He spun around to face the outpost and pulled his own rifle up to cover the area.

Through my optic, I saw one of the sandbags under the shadow of the sunshade shift, and I realized at the last second that

I was actually looking at someone's head. I saw the puff-flash of a firearm discharge; heard the report of the weapon. Out of my left eye, I saw Kyle's head snap back. His knees buckled out from under him, and he fell backward—his body was rigid, so the first thing to hit the ground was the back of his skull followed by the collapse of his body. His legs remained folded back under him.

6

ESCAPE FROM DENVER

Gibs

I heard Jessica yell out as I opened fire, though I can't recall if she said anything specifically or just made inarticulate noise. She began to run towards Kyle. I increased my rate of fire, concentrating along the top line of the sandbags to suppress whoever was back there and called out to her to stop, which she ignored.

On the north side of the street, additional shots rang out from the buildings, and I realized in horror that we were outflanked, outnumbered, and out of cover. I heard a scream and saw Jessica topple to the ground only fifteen feet away from Kyle's body.

I may have been shouting words at this point, but I can't remember anymore. It could have been things that made sense, or it may have just been growling and cursing; I certainly wasn't shouting any commands out to my team—they were incapable of responding. Sacrificing accuracy for speed and volume, I began to alternate fire between the building's storefront and the sandbag enclosure—three shots to one then three shots to the other, back and forth. I did this while holding my rifle with only one hand;

with my other hand, I reached down to my rig and pawed at what I desperately hoped was a smoke grenade (assuming my memory was correct). My accuracy was for shit, hitting all over the storefront, bouncing off the street, the sidewalk, passing over the sandbags, and hitting the trucks behind. I wasn't trying to hit anything in particular—I just wanted to throw a bunch of fire downrange.

I pulled the grenade out and could tell by feel that I had gotten it right. I stopped firing for a brief second and, without taking my right hand off the grip of my rifle, I threaded the middle finger of my right hand through the ring on the grenade to pull the pin (Hollywood has done an outstanding job of perpetuating the belief that grenade pins are actuated with teeth; this is an excellent way to pull your teeth right out of your head). Letting the spoon pop, I underhanded the grenade down the street, just managing to split the distance between the sandbags and the building despite the fact that I had lobbed it with my off-hand. It began to produce red smoke almost instantly, but it would be a few seconds before it built up enough to effectively obscure the area.

I resumed alternating fire between the two positions while raising to my feet and moving to Jessica's location. She was still on the ground and groaning though I couldn't tell where she was hit. I shot my mag empty before I got to her and my hands performed the old routine on their own without me having to think about it; drop magazine, pull new magazine, slam it home, close the bolt, continue firing. I do recall that they were returning fire at this point, but it was not effective. I couldn't see anything inside the building by now due to the smoke, but I could still make out the odd rifle held over the top of the sandbag wall to be fired blindly up the street.

I reached Jessica and saw she had sustained a gunshot to the thigh, her hands clamped around it with blood everywhere. She had the look of a panicked animal but said nothing to me when I arrived.

I maintained my downrange fire as I bent to grab her by the collar of her shirt, but I could feel it begin to rip as soon as I started to pull. Pressed for time (a thirty round magazine will go dry a lot faster than you realize in these situations), I wound my left hand up in as much of her hair as I could dig my fingers into, barked out a "Sorry!" and dragged her bodily to the north side of the street towards the intersection. As we neared the building, I was saved from having to worry about the storefront since I had effectively rotated out of their range of fire; the sandbags were soon obscured from view as I pulled Jessica around the corner onto the cross street.

Now in temporary safety, I released her hair and said, "Can you walk on it?"

She reached a shaking hand out to me and said, "Help me!"

I hauled her up onto her feet, pulled her arm over my shoulders, and wrapped my left arm around her waist. She hopped alongside me for a few yards, nearly falling as I dragged her along. Shouts came from behind me; they had likely figured out that I was no longer on the other side of that smoke waiting to shoot them when they came out. "Fuck this," I growled. I stood her up straight just long enough to get my arm between her legs, jam a shoulder into her pelvis, and hoist her up into a fireman carry. Thus situated, I hoofed it double-time back to Walnut Street, turned northeast, and began to move as fast as I could up the street.

I could feel the hot wetness of her blood running down my back as we went and knew that I didn't have much time to work. I heard the voices of hollering men in pursuit behind me and began to scan buildings for possible entry points, needing to get under cover as quick as I could so we could make some kind of a stand. I clocked movement ahead on my left and, as I strained to bring my rifle up under Jessica's dead weight, I saw an arm and long, flowing, jet black hair peek out from behind a tinted glass door. Under the hair were very wide, very intense eyes. The arm started to wave and beckon at me furiously. Without stopping to wonder who it might be, I ran towards the door as quickly as I could manage.

I dove through the door and emerged into a musty environment with little to no light; the only illumination was the filtered sunlight coming in from the tinted glass door. We appeared to be in a reception area with several chairs wrapped around the outside perimeter and a high desk jutting out from the wall to take up most of the central floor space. The woman who waved us in hissed from behind me, her voice charged with anger.

"Idiot! What have you started? Didn't you know they were out there?"

She spoke in a flat, featureless American accent with no suggestion that she had ever spoken anything besides English in her life, but her appearance put me back on my heels. She was younger than me but no longer youthful; perhaps in her early thirties—young enough that you could still see the girl she had once been but old enough that you could see where the laugh lines and wrinkles were forming. Her features were unconventional in unexpected ways. Her face was wider than what TV had told us is desirable; her nose was just square enough that Cosmopolitan would have suggested makeup tips that she could employ to slim it back down to a petite line. None of that mattered. Her look worked for her.

Her eyes were really what stopped me. Seeing them now as they expressed aggravation in my direction, I could understand why they stood out to me as I was hobbling up the street. They were a grey so light that they nearly glowed, framed by dark black lashes in a field of olive brown skin. The corners pulled back like cat's eyes.

I took this all on board in rapid course, my inner lizard brain noting those features that were attractively exotic while my analytical mind advised me to unfuck myself and get moving in a hurry.

"Who the hell are 'they,' lady?"

She shook her head at me, oil black hair spilling around her face. "Scavengers. Strangers. Really dangerous people."

I heard shouts outside the building coming from far away. "Is there a back door?" I asked. "There'll be a blood trail; they'll find this—" I gestured at Jessica's leg.

The woman crouched down next to my elbow to look up into Jessica's face as it lolled off my shoulder. "Lay her down on the desk," she said. "Hurry!"

I did as instructed, grunting to get her onto the high surface. I straightened up after laying her down, looked at her face, and felt my guts go soft. She had gone bone white and fluttered her eyelids like she was punch drunk.

From behind me and to my right, I heard the woman say, "Greg, give me your flannel." I paid no attention to this; I had my knife out and was slitting the thigh of Jessica's jeans open. I ran the slit all the way down to her ankle, pulled the pant leg away from her like a cast-off banana peel, and cut the whole mess off her leg at the hip with the knife, completely exposing the leg from crotch to shoe. There was an entry wound on the inside of her thigh towards the top; I lifted her leg at the knee to look under it but could find no exit. The skin surrounding the area was covered in an angry, purple bruise extending down to her knee. More blood came oozing from the wound in slow pulses that were very weak.

On the other side of the counter, a young male approached with some wadded, checkered fabric in his hand. He moved to apply it to Jessica's leg, but I shoved his hand away, saying, "Hang on a minute."

I ripped open my blow out kit and pawed through it for a pack of QuickClot gauze and another package of standard sterile gauze. I looked up at the kid in front of me and indicated his flannel shirt, saying, "Stuff that in her mouth," which he did without hesitating.

I ripped open the QuickClot packaging, unrolled several inches, wadded it up, and packed it into the wound with my finger. Jessica barely responded to this, which distressed me; I started taking deep, shaking breaths to maintain my composure. I had no idea what I was going to do for her in the long term. Whatever she had been hit with, it had nicked or severed her femoral artery; that much was apparent from the way she was bleeding. I was praying that I could arrest the blood loss with the use of the hemostatic agent, but I couldn't tell if I had crammed it deep enough to make a difference. She had also lost far too much blood, and I had no way to get any back into her. I didn't even have a bag of plasma to give her.

I ripped open the standard gauze package and wrapped up the whole leg.

I looked up at the kid and was surprised to see another young male standing behind him. They were both teenaged boys with brown hair, rail thin, and looked so much alike that it would have been funny under different circumstances.

"What was your name again? Greg?"

The kid nodded his head, eyes frightened.

"Put your hand on that leg and push down hard," I commanded. He jumped to do so as though he had been goosed.

I turned and grabbed one of the chairs lining the wall. Laying it on its side, I proceeded to curb stomp the living hell out of one of the legs. When it had bent far enough that kicking wouldn't get me any further, I grabbed it and started wrenching it back and forth like I was trying to yank the horn off a rhino. It didn't take me very long to snap the cheap metal tubing. I could hear the shouts of pursuing men and women outside in the street. They were taking their time and being careful; I suspected I may have hit one or more of them with my wild shooting. Even so, they were getting closer.

I twisted and ripped some paracord out of a side pouch on my rig, cut off a six-foot length, and jammed the remainder back into the pouch. I doubled the severed length, wrapped it around Jessica's leg, and tied it off above the gunshot wound.

"Okay, move your hand, Greg," I urged. He did, and I could see that all the bandaging was on its way to being soaked through, despite the clotting agent. "Fu-uck," I growled under my breath.

I jammed the broken chair leg under the lash and started cranking it in circles like a windlass, clamping down savagely on her whole leg until it looked fit to pop off her body. "Hold!" I commanded Greg, who reached out and kept the improvised windlass positioned over her knee while I got another length of paracord going. I tied the bottom end of the metal tubing at her knee joint, securing the whole tourniquet in place. I jammed my fingers into her neck under the, bend of her jaw and held my breath. I failed to find a pulse but that didn't necessarily mean anything; I was frantic and moving fast. It may have just been so faint that I couldn't detect it under those conditions.

I looked up at the kids and said, "Alright, you two: get her on her feet, and each of you take an arm. You—" I gestured to the woman standing back in the corner, "name?"

"Alish," she said.

"Good. Alish, there's a trail of blood out there that's going to lead those people right into this room. Find us a rear exit; get us going north towards 38th."

"And what makes you think we're coming with you?" she said in a low voice. "We were fine until you brought all that along!" She threw a hand at the door as she said this.

I pinned her with my best no-shit stare. "Lady, you come with me, or you take your chances here. I appreciate you waving me in here, but I'm not in a 'pretty please' mood. Make a decision *now*." I swiveled back on the teenaged boys, who had not moved. "I said pick her... the fuck... up."

They did.

I looked back at Alish, who still appeared to be thinking about the best way to respond to me. "Move, goddamn you," I growled. "You can hurl insults and slap the shit out of me later."

This finally seemed to get the point across; she shook her head once, turned, and pushed past the boys as they were hoisting Jessica off the counter. She went through a door that led deeper into the building.

"You two keep up with her," I said. I wiped my bloody hands across my thighs, not wanting to spare the time to screw with my water carrier. I had baby wipes back at the bus. "I'll cover the rear and shoot anything that moves."

They reversed direction and heaved through the door, each of them with one of Jessica's arms braced over their shoulders. I dove through behind them, emerging into a much darker back office area filled with a little cubicle farm. I reached up with my thumb to turn on my weapon light; one of the boys in front of me (not Greg) hunched slightly at the sudden illumination throwing the room into high relief and looked back over his shoulder at me. I pulled the muzzle of my rifle around to the side to keep from blinding him with all one thousand of the little light's lumens and said, "Don't look directly at the light, man! You'll spend the next ten minutes walking into walls." Saying nothing, he turned his head back around to face forward and continued to negotiate the grid of walled-in desks.

We pushed through into an adjoining rear storage area that qualified as little more than a closet, all five of us stacking up on top of each other in the cramped space.

"This leads outside," Alish said.

"Okay, let me stick my head out first," I replied, and nudged through to the front of the line. I heard Jessica moan as I jostled past her and experienced a moment of simultaneous relief and panic; relief that she could still vocalize and panic that she was fast running out of time.

At the door, I pulled my rifle up tight and, without looking at Alish, said, "Pull that open." As her hand closed around the knob, I killed the weapon light. A brilliant, white point of illumination appeared floating out in space; immediately stretched into a needle-thin line spanning from floor to ceiling. Even after the brightness of the weapon light, I felt as though the image of that crack must be burning into my retina. I had just enough time to squint before the line widened and distorted, dimming from pure white to the muted drab of a back alley. The doorway framed the rear end of another small business building of some sort; there was trash built up outside on the ground, and I could make out the side of a dumpster from my position. I pushed forward to stick my head out.

The alley was clear in either direction, though I could hear shouts of pursuit now amplified due to the fact that I was no longer enclosed in a building. It sounded like whoever was after us were coming down on our heads, but I pulled a deep breath to calm myself. I knew and was counting on the fact that cities, with all of their hard, flat surfaces of different shapes and sizes pointing in multiple directions, did strange things to soundwaves. The people chasing after us could be right around the corner or a couple of blocks over. I stepped out into the alley and positioned myself across from the door, trying to be ready to shoot in either direction with a minimum of delay.

"Okay, let's go," I whispered. "Head to my left and keep to the alley. Wait for me to get in front of you before crossing the street and remember: if we can hear them they can hear us. No talking above a whisper."

Alish nodded and came out first, followed by the two boys (or young men, I guess; they looked an awful lot to me like some joker had glued baby heads onto teenage bodies), and I crowded in behind them. I divided my attention between looking back behind us and monitoring Jessica's leg to see if we were leaving a blood trail. So far, it appeared that my field dressing was doing its job; there was plenty of blood on her leg from before, which was drying up already, but nothing new was flowing down her leg or making a trail that could be followed. On the other hand, her whole thigh was now a vivid purple color and was noticeably swollen in size compared to the other. Thoughts of what that meant came before I could stop them and I shook my head angrily, trying to dispel them like they were some obnoxious swarm of gnats. This technique is equally effective for both thoughts and gnats, by the way; it is completely inadequate.

Before I expected it, I felt myself bump into the heels of Jessica and her bearers. I realized we must be at a cross street and tried to remember how deep into this area we had gotten from 38th and the Blake Street overpass, finding (with some measure of disgust at myself) that I could not. Because we were in an alleyway rather than an actual street, there were no signs within view to tell me where we were or how far we had to go. I rushed past everyone to the mouth of the alley to look up and down the street. It was empty; however our pursuers had also gone quiet, so it was even harder to place them on the mental map I had going in my head.

"Wait for my signal," I said, and then ran across the street to the alley on the opposing side. Once there, I turned back to face my little group of people and looked along the cross street, focusing primarily on the southeast direction; this had me looking back at Walnut as it ran parallel to our alleyway. There was no movement or other evidence of pursuit, so I beckoned at the others to follow. As they came, I braced my left shoulder up against a building corner and kept my eyes glued on Walnut. I could see my new friends coming out of my peripheral vision and was pleased to note that the boys, though young in appearance, were able to make some good speed even though they were lugging a nearly unresponsive casualty between them. Adrenaline or not, they were stronger than they looked.

I waited for them to pass me and then fell in behind them. As I turned to follow, I heard the sound of breaking glass and the sharp, multi-crack of small arms fire. It sounded like they were crawling right up into my colon.

I called up ahead of me while still trying to maintain some kind of a whisper (I guess you'd call it a stage whisper at that point), saying: "Hang a left up here as soon as you see a clear path to the next street over!" I couldn't be sure where our pursuers were, but if they were in the little office where we had packed Jessica's leg, it was a good bet they'd be spilling out into our alley very soon. I wanted them to have to guess which direction we were going rather than just be able to see us and start chasing. Alish and the boys were able to make the turn almost as soon as I finished speaking and we found ourselves trotting north east up Blake shortly after.

We soon approached a cross street, and I squinted to see the name printed out on the street sign: 31st. I groaned internally, realizing that made it about seven blocks to where I wanted to be, give or take. I put my head down and reminded myself that I didn't have to hump the distance while carrying Jessica; she wasn't a fatty by any means at all, but she was curvy and carried some good muscle besides. I had already been panting by the time I set her down earlier, and I hadn't carried her a great distance at all. If I had needed to make the trip to the bus without help, I'm pretty sure we would have been boned.

Not wanting to deal mentally with the total distance we needed to travel, I employed a little trick that just about every

Marine or soldier figures out at some point; I broke the trip down into smaller sections and focused only on completing the next little part that was directly in front of me. We talk about mental resilience or resolve all the time, but sometimes, the job is just too goddamned big to deal with; you just figure there's no way in hell you're getting it done. Running five more miles after you've just run ten might be mentally crushing, but there's a good chance you can always run another hundred yards. If a hundred yards gets too tough to handle, you can always run another fifty feet. In the end, no matter how far you've gone, you can always find the strength to take one more step. You think to yourself: *Five miles? Fuck you, I might as well just lie down and die. There's no way I'm getting five more miles out of these legs.*

But in the time it takes you to think that, you've taken ten more steps. It's all about chaining a series of little steps together in a sequence, one after the other, in a consistent direction; chipping away at the task until it's achieved. Amass a large pile of tiny victories. You can always take just one more step.

As we hugged the wall of buildings on our right, I turned to look behind us and saw nothing. No pursuers, no doors suddenly opening, no heads suddenly poking out. I heard nothing but our footfalls and our labored breathing. I faced forward and asked, "How we doing up there?"

Neither of the boys answered, but the one on the right (I think it was Greg) gave me a sharp nod of the head. The knuckles of both the boys' hands were white where they were wrapped around Jessica's wrists. For her part, Jessica was limp; her head lolled around uselessly, and her feet dragged behind her. I would have to rotate one of them out very soon. We passed another street, and I looked up at the sign as we went by: 34th.

Still no sign of pursuit. Good deal. I began to make plans for when we got to the bus; trying to figure out what I was going to do for Jessica's leg. I kept coming up against the same wall; the most training I got in field medicine took me just far enough to stop bleeding and stabilize a casualty long enough for real medics to arrive. I didn't know anything about dealing with a nicked or severed artery. Back when I was still working within a functional military, you typically shipped your wounded back to the forward surgical team (or FST) and let them handle treatment. I imagined that, in this case, such a team would have to open the leg up a bit and sew the artery shut to kill the bleeding. I hadn't the first clue how to do this. Maybe I could amputate and cauterize the leg, but that had its own set of problems. She had lost more blood than I cared to consider, most of it crusting up in a giant sheet down my back. There was simply no blood to pump into her to replace what she had lost; any supplies that were still available in blood banks or hospitals had long since died out when all the refrigeration failed. I had no idea what her blood type was and, even if I did, I still didn't have the tools or the knowledge necessary to take any out of a donor and pump it back into her. If she was going to live, she was going to have to replace whatever she lost the old fashioned way: metabolizing it naturally via nutrients and water.

Blood is manufactured in the body's bone marrow. Some of the largest bones in the body are found in the leg; precisely the part of her I was thinking about hacking off. Even assuming she survived the shock and trauma of a limb removal, never mind the amount of blood loss sustained, there was still the risk of probable infection to deal with. There was a small amount of broad-spectrum antibiotics in my blowout kit and probably a bit more in the ruck that I had taken off the deceased soldier (Adams, I reminded myself; his name was Adams) but I was certain there would only be enough to get me to a nonexistent FST. A partial course wasn't going to get the job done for Jessica. I was afraid that, in the end, Jessica's survival was going to come down to Jessica and her inherent inner strength; how stubborn she was naturally. Unfortunately, the kind of wound that she had sustained tends to take the fight right out of a person.

I looked up as we passed another street; 36th. The Blake overpass was in sight, thank you, Jesus.

"Alish, I need you to get in here and spell one of the kids," I called ahead.

"Take over for Alan," Greg grunted. "I'm still good for a while."

The two swapped places and the younger of the two boys got out ahead of us. I moved ahead to walk alongside of him and said, "We're going to 38th," I said. "If you don't know where that is, the street we're on right now goes over it. When we get there, we'll have to veer off at the last minute to get under the bridge, understand?"

The boy named Alan nodded and said, "Where are you taking us?"

"I have friends up Washington Street waiting for us. There's a bus—we can get the hell out of here."

"What if we don't want to get out of here?"

I took a deep breath, blew it out through my lips. "Fine. Once we get my friend back to the bus, you three are free to go."

"We should just leave her," Alish said from behind me. "She's not going to make it; I think she may have passed already."

Without turning around to look at her, I said, "Drop her at your own fucking peril, lady." She said nothing in response.

I glanced back at Alan and said, "Sorry, kid. You guys don't have any choice but to help me lug her back. If you try to cut and run, I swear to god I'll mow all three of you down, even if that means I bring our new friends down on top of my head. If you want to stick with us, I can promise that I'll do the same for you if the day ever comes when it's necessary. Failing that, you'll be free to scamper off once she's unloaded."

Alan glanced over at me, and I could see him working it over in his head. I wondered if I'd actually be able to shoot them if they just dropped Jessica and ran off. I mean, it was definitely within my skillset to tag all three of them without very much trouble; I just wondered if I'd be able to squeeze the trigger. I told myself '*Absolutely,*' but the deeper part of me (the honest part) suggested that I would only watch as they left me behind, mentally jammed between calling after them and just sitting down on the sidewalk next to Jessica to wait and fight it out with whoever happened by.

Finally, he said, "Okay. We'd probably do the same thing, anyway."

"Thank you," I said, and fell back to the rear.

Blake Street ran over 38th as a bridge overpass; as we approached our goal, we found our way barred by a waist-high metal fence protecting us from a ten-foot drop to 38th below us. We had to swing right about eighty feet to get around the fence and onto 38th to achieve a path that would take us underneath the bridge. I was just starting to breathe easy; I had built it up in my head that passing under Blake was our ticket to freedom. We just had to get on the other side of that, and we were well on our way to safety.

Before we could round the fence to 38th, I heard a shout, the sound of gunfire coming from much closer than I would have liked, and a ricochet from only a few yards away.

"Go, go, GO!" I barked at the others, turned, and dropped into a crouch. There were three people only a few hundred feet away that had taken up position under some trees a few streets over; they were almost directly south from my position. I dropped into a prone position to give them the smallest target possible and lined them up in my sight. I got good center mass hits on two of them; the third ran off down the street like trailer trash racing to Walmart on Black Friday. I got up and ran to catch up with the others.

"Let's pick the pace up, guys," I bawled. "We're getting some company real quick."

The three of them really started hoofing, and we made better time up the street, but it still felt agonizingly slow to me. I used to have nightmares about this kind of running gun fight when I was in Iraq, nightmares that continued long after I had left the Corps (when I wasn't having the standard "You've been reactivated, and we're deploying you tomorrow!" bad dream). Contrary to what TV and movies would have you believe, getting into a firefight isn't the end of the world. Many times, especially in the city, the people you were shooting at were so far out that you only ever hit them if you got lucky; maybe five or six hundred yards. They were just close enough to have us in range of their 7.62 (which wasn't that big a deal as their AKs weren't exactly sniper rifles, and they weren't exactly snipers) but just outside of the effective range of our 5.56, which meant guys like me didn't have a lot to do outside of barking out instructions to the radioman or walking our machine gunner onto a target. We'd be positioned behind some shitty dirt wall somewhere or stationed up on a rooftop and just take shots to keep them pinned down, blow the hell out of any vehicles that looked like they were coming our way, and either call in some air support or wait for the QRF to show up. Sometimes it even got boring enough that we'd start cracking jokes here and there just to keep entertained. It was pretty easy to stay calm and collected when you knew you had the whole of the Allied Forces backing your play and prepared to drop ordinance on all the *Allahu Snackbars* out there. If you *had* to be in a firefight, that was the way you wanted it to go.

This was entirely different. My closest support was probably a mile or more away, they were in a school bus instead of an MRAP, and they had a single rifle and a pistol between them. They had no idea what my situation was because I had no way to radio back to them. They could probably hear the gunfire and were more than likely tap dancing in place trying to figure out what they should do (I prayed to any god that would listen they were smart enough to stay put). I had a single rifle and whatever ammunition I was carrying. Kyle and his rifle (my M4) had simply been lost in the no man's land between our initial point of ambush and the military outpost; I hadn't even thought to check Jessica for the pistol until I had her stretched out on the counter, discovering that it was nowhere to be found. Our asses were hung out twisting in the wind, and our only chance was to simply outrun whoever was coming at us. We had however long it took for that runner to catch up to his buddies and tell them where we were before we had a serious running gunfight on our hands. I began to contemplate sending the three ahead of me to the bus while finding a strong position to make a stand.

We had just passed a narrow river and were rounding a bend to travel under another overpass (this time the freeway) when I heard a sound that made my bowels turn to water; way, way off in the distance of the city, I heard the shrill revving of motorcycle engines. The sound was muted and far away, no doubt baffled by all of the buildings and other structures between us. They knew where we were, though, and it would not take them long to reach us.

Now we were in some shit. Making a stand to buy Greg, Alan, Jessica, and Alish some time to get away was out of the question now. A single guy with a rifle wouldn't be able to stop a bunch of people on motorcycles. I might get two or three before they veered off my line of sight and, with their superior mobility, they would just blow right by me. By the time I caught up on foot, it would probably all be over with the better part of my group dead or dying. We could try getting off Washington and running up a side street, however this wouldn't gain us much. This area north of the freeway was a lot more wide open than the denser city we had just come from, with far greater visibility in all directions.

Additionally, the last thing I wanted was for our pursuers to pass us by, getting between me and my group waiting back at the bus. All they had to do was ride up the last street they'd seen me on, and they would run right into my people.

I ran up, slapped Greg on the shoulder, and said, "Out! Lemme carry her a bit. Alan, take Alish's spot. Move, move!" We jockeyed around for position, and then I really started to haul, man. I was dragging Jessica and Alan both up the street like they were overfilled bags of shit and I was terrified of flies. I heard Greg say, "Holy crap, dude!" as he struggled to keep up. Jessica's legs were still dragging behind us, slowing us down, so I shouted, "You two! Take a leg each and run out in front of us!" Alish and Greg both scrambled to their new positions and pulled Jessica's lower half off the pavement. Having each quarter of her body-weight supported by a person lightened the load considerably, and I started feeling pretty good about our chances again.

"Now run, goddamnit!" I bellowed. "Don't stop and don't you dare trip; I'll kick your ass all the way up the street! *Go*!"

They went. We hauled literal ass, running for the next several blocks at full tilt, breathing heavy and grunting like frothing horses. Alish and Greg both exhibited excellent endurance, keeping their arms curled under the weight of Jessica's legs so that they could stabilize her shifting mass as we ran. Alan and I didn't have it so easy; the whole of her dead, flopping weight was transferred right into our spines. We hadn't even gone a mile yet before the two bearers out in front had their elbows completely extended and were leaning out away from the center to counter the constant pull against their arms. Women are naturally stronger in their lower bodies than they are up top, so I called for Alish to swap places with Alan. The change in weight distributions appeared to help both of them because I was able to detect a momentary increase in speed. Unfortunately, the intensity of the screaming engines coming from behind us also increased.

Greg glanced back over his shoulder as we ran and I saw his eyes widen in panic. "Oh, shit, I see them back there! They're coming!"

I coughed and shouted back, "Don't look back that way, damn it! Watch where you're going!" I jammed my head over into Jessica's to knock it out of my way and look around Alan. In the distance, I could see the bus. Standing in front of it appeared to be Davidson and Oscar; there were other people milling around as well, but I was in too much of a scramble to identify them. Both Davidson and Oscar stood rooted in place; distance rendered their expressions unreadable, but their body language said they were in a state of either utter shock or complete confusion.

In the midst of running under load, awkwardly carrying a casualty, and resisting a magmatic burn in lungs that hadn't worked so hard in years, I pulled in enough air to physically hurt and bellowed: *"Start... the fucking... bus!"*

The desired effect was achieved; Oscar jumped to life, back-handed Davidson across the shoulder to get him moving as well, and ran around to the front entrance of the bus while fanning his hands out in front of him in an underhand motion. He looked like he was trying to direct a herd of scattering ducklings, which looked so ridiculous to me that I wanted to laugh. The scream of pursuing engines increased in volume behind us, feeling as though they were riding right up our spines. The skin on the back of my neck began to tingle in alarm as I angrily tamped down the anticipation of bullets ripping into our backs. There were one hundred yards between us and the bus if there was a foot.

"Make for that bus," I gasped. "Don't stop... until you're on it!"

No one responded to me. Alan and Greg dropped their heads down low like charging animals, hunched their backs, and began to pound pavement so hard that I began to wonder if they were trying to translate force of impact into speed. Alan began to growl on every exhalation, either in frustration, anger, or fear; he had Jessica's knee pulled up into his chest like a cradled football. On my left, I heard and felt the shrill wheeze of Alish's exertions; a short, frantic scream that sounded only on every alternating footstep.

Before I realized what was happening, the rear taillight of the bus was blurring by the five of us on the left side, and the two boys out in front were slowing down to match the speed of the vehicle, which was already rolling forward. The fact that whoever was driving had the bus rolling before we were safely on told me everything I needed to know about the proximity of our assailants. As if to punctuate this realization, the sound of gunfire erupted behind us.

I looked up at the entrance to see Fred Moses in all of his giant glory hanging out of the door with his arms extended to us. I reached down under Jessica's ass with my left hand and heaved her bodily up into Fred's general vicinity, praying that he would catch her. He did, grabbing her like a linebacker and pulling her back up the steps and down the aisle. I reached out, grabbed Alish by the arm, and shoved her into Greg and Alan. I was attempting to cram all three of them through the door at once and succeeding, despite the fact that I was probably shaving skin off any exposed parts coming into contact with hard, metal edges. They began to stumble up the stairs of the bus on legs turned to rubber; I chose to assist their efforts by slapping backs and asses indiscriminately while screaming, *"Go, go, go!"* like a madman.

Inside the vehicle, I heard more gunfire; this time right up on top of me. I realized it was coming from inside the bus and saw Davidson shooting through the windows all the way down at the tail. I looked over to the driver's seat, which happened to be populated by Oscar. "Do *not* crash this son of a bitch, do you read?"

He nodded hard enough to rattle his brains, not even looking up at me, hands white-knuckled on the oversized wheel.

"Good," I said. "You take us out the way we came in. Don't get lost!"

I turned and bounded down the bus to the rear. As I went, I screamed at all on board to either hit the deck or lay down in their seats. Halfway down the length of the center aisle, I planted my hands on seat backs to either side of me and vaulted over Jessica's body.

Davidson continued to fire out the windows as I approached; the closer I came to the rear of the vehicle, the more of our attackers I could see. There was a large group after us, perhaps twelve or thirteen people, on all manner of two-wheeled vehicle. Many were riding alone, attempting to manage throttle, clutch, and pistol all at the same time (which likely accounted for their failure to hit any of us as we ran); a few rode double and appeared to be making good use of their ability to focus on aiming. Despite Davidson's efforts to shoot everywhere at once, the rear of the bus was taking fire, and I saw pinpricks of light appear instantaneously on the areas of the back wall not obscured by seating. I could see all sorts of vehicles pursuing us, from some of the standard Harleys to a lot of Asian crotch rockets; I think I even clocked a Ducati out there and I know for certain I saw two scooters.

One of the Harley riders pulled up along the bus on our right side, a heavy man with a bandana obscuring his face like an old Western bandit. He held out a machine pistol in our direction with the clear intent to spray our broadside. Before he could do so, I screamed, "Swerve right!!!" to Oscar, who complied immediately, God bless him.

The "bandit" managed to squeeze off a few before the bus slammed into him. It was expertly done on Oscar's part; you typically want to oversteer in these situations and destabilize your vehicle, which would have been catastrophic in a bus with such a high center of gravity, but our man Oscar swung her over like a true artist. The biker was lost to view under the side windows, but I heard his shout along with the crunch of metal on metal as we first plowed into and then over him. The whole back end of the school bus launched up under my feet and ratcheted back down, slamming my head into the ceiling before driving me into the deck. The others of our group screamed or grunted depending on how hard of a shot they sustained; I came from my knees to my feet in a daze and shaking my head.

Davidson was firing out the window again with his M4, scoring good hits and dumping pursuers onto the pavement. I leaned forward to squint out a rear window almost completely devoid of any glass, save a few stubborn fragments, seeing a twisted Harley, a body, and a big red smear trailing behind us in our wake. As I looked, a red-hot line of pain bloomed across my right shoulder, and a side window exploded behind me, spilling safety glass all over Rose, who screamed in a voice that was only beginning to find womanhood.

It was at this point that I'd decided we were done putting up with the Denver Chapter of the Hell's Asshats.

I looked over at Davidson, specifically at the M4 with under-slung grenade launcher he was firing out the window. I growled, pulled the sling of my MR556 off my arm, and shouted, "Trade me!"

Davidson looked at my rifle in dismay, shook his head, and bawled, "But… you said—"

"Stick a dick in what I said!" I called back and held my rifle out at him. "Give, give, *give!*"

He scrambled to do so. I saw him pull my rifle into his shoulder and grin wide as he aimed it out the window. "Don't you *dare* get comfortable," I shouted as I rammed forward the barrel on the M203. "You do not get to keep her, and she damned well better come back unsullied!"

I pulled a 40mm frag grenade off the belt stashed in our sorry excuse of a weapons duffel, stuffed it into the pipe, and rammed it closed. I crab-walked up to the rear window and shouted, "Down!" at Davidson, who dropped below the window level instantly. I stood up like the world's most pissed off jack in the box and took aim out the back; they were so close it didn't even occur to me to raise the leaf sight at the front of the rail. I just took aim through the optic as though I was firing normal rounds, put the reticle on center mass and pulled the M203's trigger with my left index finger. A loud *POONT!* issued from the weapon and, out in front of me at a distance of no more than thirty feet, an explosion erupted right in a biker's lap.

Now, I feel as though I should pause here and dispel some Hollywood bullshit about our friend, the M203. The former artists in cinema (bless their hearts) like to show these things blowing up entire cars and throwing devastating fireballs up into the air, almost as though they were firing exploding gas cans instead of little exploding artillery rounds. In reality, you get a puff of grey smoke only a little larger than a man; the effective range on these things is really only within a five-yard diameter and, in most cases, they won't kill you unless you take a direct, unprotected hit to the chest or face. They'll just load you full of shrapnel and ruin your whole week.

Unless you're some jerk on a motorcycle hassling a tired, pissed off, salty old Marine and you're dumb enough to ride so close that said Marine doesn't even have to aim.

That first grenade fairly blew the motorcycle right out from under the man, plowing him all across the pavement. I heard the metallic patter-clank of shrapnel fragments as they struck the rear of our school bus and was thankful I had told Davidson to kiss the deck. I made a mental note to also duck on subsequent shots. The guy just behind the man I had blown up (one of those riding a scooter) was unable to avoid the wreckage and drove right into it, flipping over the handlebars and landing directly on his face, which was unprotected.

I dropped to my knees and fished out another grenade from the belt while, behind me, Davidson popped up to send more fire out the window over my head. He was doing well, anticipating my need and intent. I felt a tentative degree of pride in his performance but, of course, he still had a whole firefight to fuck it up, so…

I drove the launcher's barrel open, and the expended grenade shell popped out onto the floor; I snatched it before it could roll away. I had no desire to step on the thing, fall over, and fire off a grenade into the ceiling or inside wall. I threw the empty into the duffel bag and popped the fresh grenade into my weapon. Without needing to be told, Davidson again dove to the floor.

I sprang up, selected a new target, and fired. I missed this time, the round passing just over the intended mark and detonating in the street between two motorcycles riding side by side. Both men appeared to be peppered; they flinched and dumped their rides into the pavement, rolling off in different directions and hammering into vehicles lining the street.

Before I had any time to admire my two-for-the-price-of-one score, I heard Oscar yell, "Hang on!!" while the bus swerved alarmingly to one side. The entire length of the vehicle jolted, then shuddered violently as I heard the hollow, box-slam of metal on metal combined with the melody of shattering glass. The tires directly under me squealed across the pavement and were arrested as the back end blasted into a truck parked along the street's shoulder, driving myself, Davidson, and likely a few others into the seats and right wall of the bus.

"What the hell—" I began but was interrupted by a muted

bang sounding off just beneath me, followed by the *whop, whop, whop* of a blown tire. "goddamnit, blowout!" I shouted.

Davidson shook his head at me and replied, "It's okay. This bus has a dually rear axle! We can probably keep it moving."

I nodded, recalling the four wheels in the rear. It certainly wasn't optimal, but then, we left optimal behind a long time ago. I reloaded the M203 a third time, climbed to my feet, and fired it into another motorcycle, this time picking a couple of people riding double. My aim was good, and I just glimpsed them belly-flopping into asphalt as I ducked back down below the window line.

Without stopping to catch a breath, I was already digging into my pack for a fourth grenade. Before I could tug it out of the belt loop, Davidson said, "Hey, stand down. I think they're breaking off."

Ignoring him, I shoved another grenade home, climbed to a standing position, and looked out the window. A greatly reduced gang of bikers did, in fact, appear to be falling back, either to check on their dead and wounded or because they had lost the will to continue. I lifted the leaf sight on the rifle, braced the barrel against the bottom of the rear window frame, and began to line up my next shot. A couple of bikers were turned side-on to me, so I picked one of them as the broadest area at which to aim.

"Dude," Davidson said over my shoulder, "They're breaking off, man!"

"Hell with that," I muttered and fired. For a guy who had only played with the M203 during weapons training (never having carried one in combat), I have to say the skill comes back pretty fast. The grenade impacted into my target's broadside, knocking him off his bike and plastering a few others close by with frag-ments if their reactions were any indication. I pulled the rifle up to my shoulder, rammed the selector over to full auto, and sprayed in their direction as we drove away, even managing to hit a couple before the rest dove behind cover. I put the rifle back on safe, set it down in the seat next to me, and screamed, "*Fuck you!*" out the back window hard enough that I was afraid I might have torn my throat open.

I turned to see a horrified Davidson staring back at me. He was frozen in place and clutching his rifle (my rifle, damn it) to his chest. I was annoyed but did not resent his shock; he hadn't been out there with us nor did he see what happened to Kyle. I waved him out of my way and ran over to Jessica, who was contorted around in a new position owing to all the jostling punishment we had suffered in our escape.

I knelt in front of her to go over her vitals. As I did, Oscar called from up front, "Hey, someone clue me in on where I'm going up here! Please!"

"I don't care," I called back. "Just get us out of the city and onto some road leading away."

Jessica's skin was cool to the touch. Her lips were blue, and there was no pulse to be found anywhere. I looked up to her leg, which seemed to have sucked all of the color out of her body to condense into that one area of deep purple lividity. A set of brown, delicate hands were mashed down onto the bloody leg bandage. They were attached to Alish, who looked back at me with wide and haunted eyes.

"I'm sorry," she croaked and took her hands away.

7

BACKBONE

Gibs

I consider it to be my fault that we continued on to Wyoming rather than adjusting course to travel into Nebraska. As it is, I'll admit that I felt (and continue to feel) a bit of guilty relief that the decision was taken out of my hands. The deeper part of me, the part that likes to keep all accounts balanced, wanted to drill into Nebraska in search of Jessica's daughter, Pinch. It was Jessica's plan, after all, and I felt like I owed her. I still do in some respects.

At the same time, I had a certain degree of responsibility to the people who were still alive and with me. There were fifteen people with me when we came out of Denver, all of whom I had boldly declared to be my problem. None of them (not counting Alish, Greg, and Alan, who weren't there at the time) had spoken up to dispute the point when it was made; their acceptance of my position was implied in their silence. They had all agreed together that, yes, this man can be trusted with the safety of the group.

All I knew of Pinch's whereabouts was a half-guess her mother had made. Jessica herself wasn't willing to ask the group to come along with her because she knew how shaky her chances of finding her daughter were. Now with her and Kyle gone, we were left with a bus missing a wheel, enough food and water for one last partial-ration meal, and a tank of diesel that would get us an undetermined distance (I hadn't been paying enough attention to our consumption to get an idea of the bus's fuel economy). I had assigned so much hope to topping up our provisions in Denver that I was pretty well out of ideas and was having trouble mustering up enough give-a-shit to dream up any more. Asking everyone to embark on such a quest would have been unfair; they probably all would have said yes, whether they did so eagerly or reluctantly. Jessica viewed herself as a loner, but she was well liked in the group.

Our group was down to the red line on everything imaginable, from resources to morale. In opposition to that reality, I was responsible for the death of two people and owed their memory better than just packing up and moving on. Had I been forced to make a decision regarding our next steps, I would have just frozen up anyway.

I sat for a long time on the floor in the middle aisle of the bus with Jessica's head on my thigh. I kept my hand rested on her forehead, sometimes smoothing the hair away but mostly just holding it there, keeping the flesh warm, trying to keep at least some part of her warm. I don't know what the hell I thought I was doing; I had this sense that I could somehow hold a part of her spirit back inside her body if I could just keep a part of that body warm, like it was still alive. I felt that as soon as I let her go fully cold, I had to admit she was gone. Stupid shit; and it probably had a lot to do with the fact that Jessica was a "she" rather than a "he." I had lost three buddies in my career as a Marine, all men. It was brutal each time, and I still miss the hell out of them all, but it was somehow more manageable than this. I'd never lost a woman until that day in Denver. Whether you want to accept it or not, it's different losing a woman. The relationship is different. All discussion of equal rights aside; I don't have the words to explain why it should be like that, but there it is.

I'm not sure how long I sat like that on the floor, but at some point, I felt a hand on my right shoulder. From behind me, Barbara said, "Hey, are you alright?"

Unsure how to respond, I simply stated the fact: "I got them both killed."

"That's nonsense," she said softly. "You were trying to teach them. You still need to teach the rest of us. You certainly won't be able to protect all of us all the time. The only ones responsible for this are the people who attacked us. This is *not your fault*." She emphasized those last words in anger.

I reached up across my body with my left hand to clasp hers. I squeezed it, turned my head, and kissed the back of her soft, wrinkled knuckles in order to remove any sting from my next statement. "Lay off a while, Barbara, and let me process a bit, huh?"

She said nothing else but squeezed my shoulder before removing her hand.

In time I realized that I had to deal with the fact that rolling along with a dead body was going to make the survivors pretty uncomfortable, not to mention play some messed up games with their minds. I gently put Jessica's head aside, leaned forward, and put my right hand up onto the seat behind me to push myself up. This elicited a harsh burn at my shoulder, and I remembered the asshole that had grooved me during the gunfight. Sighing, I opened up the blow out kit on my rig and got out some antiseptic wipes, cream, and gauze. Rolling my shoulder, I could see that the damage wasn't horrible; it probably didn't even need stitches. I pulled some wipes out of a packet and began to clean the area, scraping out the valley of the wound with a wrapped finger and snarling at the stinging burn that I could feel all the way up in my neck. Completing this, I tossed the wipe aside, squirted some cream onto the area, smeared it in, and began to curse at myself under my breath as I tried and failed to wrap the area up in gauze with my clumsy left hand. Wang, who was across the aisle from me, looked back over his shoulder to see what I was up to. When he saw my predicament, he turned out into the aisle and said, "Let me help with that," while reaching out over Jessica's body to take the gauze from me. I grunted and let my hands drop. He started complaining that the wrap wasn't staying in place, so I pulled a small roll of tape out of the pouch and handed it up to him wordlessly.

He smiled and said, "Handy little kit."

"They're alright," I agreed.

With things finally secured in place, Wang handed the remainder of the material back to me, which I stuffed back into the pouch. I nodded my thanks and levered myself up to a standing position. Heads turned back to look at me, which I ignored as I walked up the length of the bus to speak with Oscar.

"How you doing, bro?" he asked as I approached.

"I'll get there," I said. "I'm not there yet, but I will be."

"Sure, of course," he nodded, sounding unsure.

"Pull us over when you get a chance," I said. "Something like a field. Try to find someplace nice."

"You got it," he said.

I went to the rear of the bus and shrugged out of my rig, feeling suddenly forty pounds lighter… mostly because I was suddenly forty pounds lighter. Nearly the whole rear of the thing, including the camelback and plate carrier, was colored a solid, dark brown from blood. Twisting awkwardly, I could see the same had happened to the right side of my back and the rear leg of my pants. Shaking my head, I set the rig aside and dug out the soldier's shovel (what we called an E-tool). The bus slowed and came to a stop alongside the road.

Looking out the side window, I saw that Oscar had stopped us next to a private farm surrounded by acres of grass fields with a large, attractive home out in the distance. The grass was peppered with small white flowers that looked to me like Baby's Breath in a teenaged girl's Prom corsage. It wasn't exactly a sacred shrine, but it was apt to be as good as we would find.

I moved for Jessica's body, but Fred beat me to it with three strides of his giant, swinging legs. He knelt and collected her into his arms gently, like a father preparing to take his little girl up to bed, and stood without any hint of exertion. She hung suspended well over the seat backs while Fred Moses's head nearly scraped the ceiling of the bus.

"I got you, Gibs," he said. "Let's go." He turned and carried her outside. Everyone else remained seated, looking back at me. Waiting. I took a breath and followed Fred down the steps out into the field.

He had laid her down gently in the field by the time I caught up to him. We stood together a moment under an endless, blue sky heavy with wide, low clouds. A flat horizon surrounded us for miles, and the peaks of mountains were just visible in the distance behind us. Fred held out his hand to me for the shovel.

"No," I said.

He nodded without comment and took two steps back. Taking the e-tool in both hands, I began to dig.

The earth was composed of good soil and was easy to displace once the grass layer was cut through. It didn't take me very long to cut out a hole that was respectfully deep enough for its intended purpose. I'd guess I was at it for a half hour or so. The others from the bus had filtered out to surround us as I worked; they all stood by solemnly. Waiting. Always waiting. George leaned on his cane, his other arm resting on Davidson's strong and youthful shoulder. Rebecca and Monica were both crying openly. I looked about the faces briefly, trying to spot Kyle, before remembering.

I nodded to Fred. Quietly, he lifted Jessica only to lay her back down in the hole. He crossed her arms over her chest and then retreated to his place in the crowd. Without waiting, I began to shovel dirt over her, starting first with her angry leg, following with her body and the tattoos she had displayed so proudly (those that had started as a fuck-you to a better-forgotten husband but ended as an advertisement of inner fire), finishing with a still lovely face. I smoothed the patch over and dropped the shovel. I could think of nothing else to do, so I only stood and stared at where she had been along with a spot right next to her; a place that should have held Kyle, who had briefly been my young friend.

A throat cleared from somewhere behind me. I gritted my teeth and tried not to scowl; I always detested the social requirement to speak at these kinds of things.

George said: "I didn't know Jessica…"

"Collins," Wang supplied.

"Collins. I didn't know Jessica Collins as well as I would have liked. From what I saw, she appeared to be a kind and free spirit. She had a beautiful laugh. I'm sorry that I won't learn more than that."

"She was a good person," Wang agreed. "When we needed food, she was always one of the first volunteers to go out and find it for all of us. She was always ready to help. She was strong. She, uh, she was a manager at some sort of delivery service. I'm ashamed to say that I don't know more than that."

There was a silence weighing down the air around us after Wang finished speaking. It was thick and made me feel as though it was hard to breathe. From the corner of my eye, I could see some folks start to fidget, some of them shifting their stance around. I looked over and saw many of them looking back at me; I realized in horror that they were waiting on me to speak.

I looked back at the little patch of ground concealing Jessica's remains, furious that any of this should be necessary. I said the first thing that came to mind. "Kyle was on his way to becoming a fairly good hunter. It was something he did with his father. Though he never said as much to me, I'm certain Kyle loved his father a great deal. I hope he was able to say goodbye to the man properly when the time came."

To my left, Rose, little fourteen-year-old Rose Dempsey with her too skinny arms and shoulders, encircled mocha arms within her mother's darker, stronger arms, buried her head, and began to sob. Monica held her daughter and rocked her quietly, resting her lips on the girl's forehead, and shushed her. I wondered at the girl's attachment to Kyle, wondered at how much was there and how great it may have been. He had been a good looking, kind young man.

"Jessica… erm—" I cleared my throat and tried again, almost steady the second time around. "Jessica had backbone."

I picked up the E-tool and whispered, "I hope you find Pinch, either way."

I coughed and growled out a "goddamnit" under my breath. I returned to the bus and sat down in the driver's seat.

We rolled into Jackson, Wyoming a couple of days later, owing to a whim. I'd been driving pretty much aimlessly for a time, not paying so much attention to where I was going as I was to looking for someplace (any place) to stop and kill that engine for the last time. I can't share a great deal of my thought process from that period, mostly because I don't think I had much of one at all. The loss of my two friends was eating away at me, and I wasn't devoting a great deal of brain power to giving too much of a fuck about anything, save keeping on the move. Save looking for someplace to get the rest of those people that was different from where they'd come. Food was down to nothing, and I wasn't sleeping so much anymore. When I came to a crossroads that was blocked by cars or debris, I just took the easier path without thinking about it or asking for opinions, and no one really offered me any either way.

I remember driving along, thinking about how I'd been hungry the day before but that I wasn't hungry the day after, and thinking that was probably a bad thing. At some point, I saw a sign that said "Jackson" on it. I recall smiling and singing to myself, feeling better about the whole situation. Don't know why, anymore, except to say that something that I figured had been dead inside of me woke back up and started kicking again.

We approached from the south along Highway 191, skirting the edge of a vast expanse of mountains on the east side. The road was just laid right down on the edge of them, like God had traced the whole range out with a galactic crayon.

I hunched down closer to the wheel as we came closer to the edge of the city with my eyes almost perpetually glued to the gas gauge; there weren't any lights flashing at me yet but the needle was right on "E," and it was looking like a toss-up between driving or walking into the city. Davidson and Wang stood behind me with eyes peeled either for obstructions or any kind of movement.

Before the city came into view, I was spending a lot of energy weaving around vehicles in the middle of the road, and I began planning for the inevitable point where the road became unnavigable. When it came to that point, I decided we were leaving the bus where it was and continuing on foot. None of us had consumed a full meal for the last two days, and the last of our rations were eaten that morning. We were all weak with hunger by this time and needed to be dealing with calorie management; specifically, we needed to not be burning critical calories by pushing cars off the road. Once a new food source was secure, we could always come back for the bus. Secretly, I hoped to leave the damned thing behind for good.

Just as I was getting ready to call it quits and throw the vehicle in park, Wang muttered, "What the…"

I perked up and glanced back at him to get an idea of the direction he was looking in, only to find that direction was dead ahead. I faced forward and rubbed my eyes. Just beyond the nastiest snarl of traffic, everything suddenly opened up, offering clear, unobstructed passage into the city. This sudden opening in the road began roughly one hundred yards before we would encounter the first visible buildings. This was disturbing because the cars that had once clogged up the street were all still there; they were just pushed off to the shoulders. At some point, between the final die-off of the plague and right now, the main road had been cleared.

"Someone's been through here," Davidson said.

Whispers came from behind us; I heard Rebecca hiss, "Did he say someone's here already?"

I saw Davidson wince in the long, overhead mirror. He said, "Sorry, man."

"It's okay," I said. I had the bus coasting along the open road; we weren't even getting five miles per hour. "They would've figured it out without you saying anything. Try to hide something that obvious and nobody will trust you."

The pathway into the city stretched before us unobstructed with a bumper-to-bumper wall of vehicles lined up on either side; curbs and soft shoulders alike were completely occupied. We continued on at a crawl, leaning forward as far as we could into the windshield, straining to see onto rooftops as we passed by storefronts. There was no movement to be seen anywhere, which basically meant that I began to see movement everywhere.

A few blocks into the city, the frequency of cars and trucks stacked up on the sides of the street began to lessen; large gaps of sidewalk and buildings became visible as the cars thinned out. Beyond this point, nearing a kilometer in, the vehicles weren't even pushed to the side anymore, they just created little island barriers at odd points along the way. I put the bus in park and separated the power lines to keep from burning fuel in idle. Rather than move from my position at the seat, I sat and stared, trying to piece together what I was looking at.

Davidson finally lost patience and asked, "What now, Gibs?"

"You guys see anything funny about all these cars?"

"What, you mean besides the fact that they've all been shoved over?"

"The antennas!" Wang said.

"Correctomundo," I said, climbing out of the seat. As far as I could tell, every antenna coming out of every car that was within viewing distance had a little duct tape flag wrapped around the top in plain sight, whether the car was out in the middle of the street or pushed over to the side. I had some suspicions about what that might mean but didn't care to comment until I knew for sure. I walked to the rear of the bus past questioning glances, dug out the MOLLE gear, and started to put it on. The grenade belt went on after, strapped around my hips. Finally, I grabbed the hand pump along with its hoses and held it out to Oscar as I approached him.

"Take this, the M9, and come give me a hand, please," I said.

He jumped up from his seat and said, "You got it, boss."

I walked back to the front of the bus where Davidson stood with Wang and paused while Oscar situated himself. I looked at Davidson and said, "You hold onto that rifle," while pointing at the HK pinned behind the driver's seat. To Wang, I said, "Grab the binos and spot for us. Look for movement." He nodded and pulled the binoculars from the dashboard. Oscar approached from behind and slapped me on the shoulder (my left one, thankfully) to let me know he was ready.

I looked back to everyone else, who were all wide-eyed and white-knuckled in their seats, and said, "Just sit tight a bit. We're going to step out a while. See what's what."

Without waiting for a response, I stepped off the platform into the street. Oscar waited in the doorway, giving me time to look the area over before following and I made a mental note to give him a gold star or something for his caution. I walked a few paces away from the bus while looking in all directions, hardly daring to breathe; just looking and listening for any possible thing out there. I think I must have spent two or three minutes doing that. Aside from the sound of wind and the occasional bird call, the silence was a physical barrier.

I decided that if anything was going to happen, it would have happened by now, so I nodded to Oscar and gestured over to the closest car.

"Do you want to grab a gas can?" he asked.

"Not yet. Let's just see if we can get anything out of it."

He spent the next few minutes snaking a tube down into the tank while I continued to scan the area. I saw Wang inside the bus nearly spinning in place as he scanned rooftops and alley entrances.

"Dry," said Oscar.

I grimaced and said, "Next one over, then."

He moved up the line, popped the gas cap on the next car, and began to feed in hose while I adjusted position to stay close by. I happened to see Wang staring at us instead of watching the area and waved at him with my left hand. Recognition flashed in his eyes as they locked onto mine; I stabbed two fingers towards my eyes and then swung my hand around over my head in a few exaggerated circles. Wang jumped in place as though he had been startled and resumed monitoring the area.

"This one's dry, too," Oscar said, coming to stand next to me.

I sighed, "Yeah, okay, shit. Let's try some across the street."

He nodded and trotted over to the closest truck to get busy.

He completed three more vehicles, all of which had flagged antennas, all of which were bone dry. He wasn't waiting for me to command him on to the next one now; he was gamely moving from vehicle to vehicle to see what could be had. I stepped out around the side of the bus and looked back down the street from the direction we had come, setting eyes on a sea of little, flagged antennas. I looked back up the road in the opposite direction and was met with the same situation. I thought there might be an antenna or two that was bare far off in the distance and pulled the M4 up to get a visual assist from the optic.

"Hey, we okay?" Davidson called from the doorway of the bus behind me.

"Yeah, it's good. I'm just going blind in my old age."

It was true; off in the distance, I could just make out some car antennas that had no sign of any duct tape along their length. I was just getting ready to call Oscar back to the bus when an unfamiliar, flat voice spoke off to my left.

"These have all been tapped. You'll need to head a little further up."

I swung hard in the direction of the voice, heart instantly jackhammering in my chest and finger hooking fast around the trigger of the rifle. I slammed into a cheek weld so hard that a bruise actually developed on my face later that day.

Without giving it a great deal of thought, I was already shouting, "Hands! Show me your goddamned hands, motherfucker!" It was only after I shouted this that I realized he already did have both of his hands held up in front of him, palms out in my direction.

He was leaning against the corner of a building as though he had just come from the alleyway behind it, and yet what he said to me suggested he had been watching us at least a little while. He was dressed lightly, probably owing to the warm season (we were either in July or August during this time, but I can't remember for sure anymore); he was wearing some jeans, a heavy set of hiking boots, and a plain, white T-shirt. He had a full beard that was just beginning to look wooly and a thick head of long, straight hair that was held out of his eyes by a red bandanna tied 1980s-style above his ears and eyebrows. He appeared to be in good physical shape, with noticeable muscular definition visible through his shirt at the shoulders and neck. He stood there, maybe thirty feet away from me, as calm as you please with his hands held out like he wanted to play Patty Cake.

"Here they are," he said. "Please don't shoot me." He was spooky-calm—Hannibal Lecter calm—which only served to ratchet my unease up through the roof.

I heard footsteps run up from behind me but resisted the urge to turn; if whoever was coming hadn't been friendly, Oscar would have called out to me. Davidson came into my field of view on my left with his rifle (*my rifle*, goddamnit!) aimed at the new guy. "Covered," he declared.

I glanced back over my shoulder at the bus. "Hey, where the fuck were *you*, Wang?"

"I'm sorry!" he called back. "I don't know what happened; guy just came out of nowhere!"

"I said 'keep your eyes open,' Wang! It's not that goddamned difficult! It's not as though I asked you to eat some apples and shit a fruit salad, is it?"

Not waiting for a response, I looked back at the stranger. He hadn't moved an inch. I took a few heavy breaths to get my heart back under control. "Okay, let's have you turn around, on your kne…" I was going to finish with telling him to go down to his knees and put his hands on his head, but it was unnecessary; he was already down in the desired position before I was halfway through the sentence, like he was perfectly happy to do so. His whole demeanor was that of a person in complete control of the situation; a guy who had all the cards in the deck, plus a few extras from a few other decks. Just looking at him made me uncomfortable as hell.

"Oscar," I said, "Get your pistol out and go stand to the rear of the bus. Keep an eye out."

"Got it," he said without hesitating and ran off in that direction.

"Davidson, swing closer to the building and keep a clear line of fire on this guy. I'm going to approach and restrain him."

Davidson vectored along my ten o'clock to stand against the building wall across the street, keeping his muzzle on New Guy as he went.

"You hear that?" I called out. "I'm coming over there to restrain you. Just be cool, and you won't be hurt, understand? Don't be stupid, guy."

"Yes, of course. I won't resist."

Mother*fucker* but this guy was freaking me out. A part of me (a part of *younger* me) kept looking him over trying to spot the bomb vest, but he didn't have a stitch of clothing on him that could conceal anything. His jeans fit him well; I would have seen the bulge of a weapon along the length of his legs, and there was nothing. His shirt was a little tight across his back and looked nearly see-through. He was either covered by a buddy at range, or he really was out here alone and unarmed.

I pulled some flex cuffs from a side pouch on my rig and approached. As I came closer, I noticed the motion of his breathing through his shirt; even and regular. It was looking more and more like this wasn't an act. He was truly relaxed.

"Lay down on your belly. Hands behind your back."

He did, lowering himself gently to the sidewalk and turning his head to the right to rest his cheek on the ground. Seeing him in profile, I noted that his nose had the mashed-in, reverse stair-step appearance of a fighter. Whatever else he'd been through in life, it looked like someone had gone to work on his schnoz with a pipe wrench.

"Davidson, choke up on him. I don't want you to miss if you have to shoot."

"Yep, roger," he called and hustled up to get close. He nearly got the barrel into physical contact with the guy's head.

"Not that close, man. A little room to breathe, please."

"Sorry…" he said, pulling back. I was going to have to talk to him about keeping his weapon out of other peoples' reach when the opportunity presented itself.

"Okay," I said. "Here it comes. Don't be stupid."

"I'll do my best."

Suppressing about ten different reflexive retorts, I knelt down to place my knee into the small of his back. I let go of my rifle just long enough to pull the loops over his wrists and yank both ends tight. I returned to my feet and got the rifle on him. I realized I was breathing heavy again; he was incredibly unsettling.

The man lay there a moment and then tugged his hands in opposite directions a couple of times, saying, "Feels about right. Can I get up, now?"

I couldn't think of any reason why not so I said, "I'll help you up, but then you gotta sit on the curb."

"Understood."

Frustration got the better of me, and I asked, "You do this often, buddy?"

He thought it over and said, "Not really, no. You?"

"I don't make it a habit," I responded through clenched teeth.

"Oh. Well, you're doing fine." He raised an elbow up into the air to give me something to grab while helping him up.

I sighed and lifted him off the pavement, walked him over to the curb, and stood back as he squatted down easily. He arranged his legs out in front of him crossed at the ankles Indian-style and sat easily (I'd almost say happily) with his eyes forward, held on nothing in particular. From my left, I saw Davidson shrug and shake his head, wearing an expression suggesting he was amazed more than anything. I looked back at New Guy, who again had not moved after he settled into place, like a toy robot that turned off between periods of activity.

"Well?" I prompted.

"Yes?"

"Well, what are you doing, damn it?"

"I'm… waiting for you to question me?"

Before I could answer, Davidson said, "Man, the more you pull that Jedi Mind Trick shit, the closer you're getting to just being shot."

I looked over at Davidson and shook my head while frowning. We had the guy restrained; there was no need to start making threats. I wanted information, not a pissing contest.

"I assure you, I'm not pulling any… Jedi shit. I'm answering all questions as truthfully as I can."

"Let's start with names, huh?" I suggested. "I'm Gibson but just call me Gibs. My friend, here, is Tom."

"I'm glad to meet you, Gibs and Tom. Call me Jake."

I had begun to calm down as we talked. There was no sign of anyone else out there (there had been no sign of Jake before he showed up either, of course, but never mind) and the man in front of us was tied up. I let my rifle hang at rest and said, "I got this, Davidson. Keep an eye out, would you? Wang seems to need all the help he can get."

"I'm sorry!" Wang shouted from the bus.

Davidson stepped back and rotated away to watch up the street.

"Okay," I said. "Let's start with what you're doing out here."

"Same thing as you, I think. I was out scavenging."

"Did you have anything to do with these cars?"

"If you mean marking and moving them, yes."

I stood for a minute looking at him, trying to determine if he was shitting me. "You mean you did all of these on your own?" There were well over a few hundred.

"No, I did have some help sometimes."

Here we go. "There's people out here with you?"

"No, not right now. I do live with two other people, but they're back at home. Scavenging is mostly a solo activity."

"Where's home?" I asked.

"Back down the road the way you came in. I can show you if you like."

I don't know if I felt confusion or discomfort at what he said; everything about the way he was behaving indicated that he was setting some kind of trap or that he held his own personal safety in complete disregard... or both. Either possibility made him dangerous as hell.

"You're just gonna lead the guy with the gun back to your house, huh?"

He looked down at my gun pointedly and then returned my gaze. "Do I have a choice?"

"Alright, goddamnit, you can just cut out all of that cute shit before I grow a hard-on with your name on it. What the hell's going on here? Straight answer."

Jake sighed and began to explain in the same tone you'd use to explain to a kid why the sky is blue: "Honestly, the only thing that's going on is that you people looked like you could use a hand. I'm here to offer my help if you want it."

"Yeah? What makes you think we need any help?"

"You're limping along in a bus that looks like it was salvaged from a monster truck show, for one thing. You're missing a rear tire, half the windows are busted out, and the whole left side has an I-just-rammed-someone-off-the-road appearance. For another, it looked like you were trying to find fuel. You'll need to go a little further up the road if that's true."

"Okay, but why would you just step out to talk to us?" I asked. "We're all armed. You don't even appear to have a Swiss Army knife."

"First, you're not *all* armed. You have two rifles and some sort of pistol between a large group of people. But aside from that, you folks are safe."

"Safe?" I asked, shocked, despite my position. "Just how the fuck can you tell we're safe?"

"You have women and children with you, and they're not under duress. You don't go armed all the time; when you guys are just riding along in the bus, no one is carrying a weapon. From what I could see, you even keep your weapons stacked in a pile in the back. You're driving around with a busload of free, unrestricted people."

"How… how long have you been watching us?"

"Oh, for quite a while. Another thing: you're taking great pains to protect them all. You were the first person off the bus. You made it a point to scan the area first before bringing anyone else off; putting yourself at risk first. The weak and infirm (children mostly but I thought I saw some elderly, too) are kept on the bus in relative safety. You're protecting weak people who don't appear to be capable of doing very much to contribute to your own survival. You're for your people, not for yourself. You folks are safe."

I was dumbstruck. The man had eyes on us at least since we approached Jackson, with enough visibility to determine age ranges and capabilities. He knew our armament. He could have easily picked us off from a distance if he possessed the skills and had been so inclined. I broke into a cold sweat as I realized how close we could have come to another Denver.

I brushed a hand across my forehead and asked, "And why are you going to help us, man?"

"Because I'm for my people, too, Gibs. Things are ugly, but

they can become a lot uglier if we allow it. Sometimes, chances are worthy."

I stood a while looking down at him. For his part, Jake's gaze had dropped down to center again, the computer going back into standby. I realized he didn't make me feel uneasy anymore. Now, he just made me feel tired.

"He kinda has a point, Top," said Davidson from behind me.

"Damn it, don't call me that," I said irritably. "I never went past Staff Sergeant."

Jake was looking back up at me. "Keep my hands tied, if you like."

I scratched my chin and considered him. Finally, I called out: "Oscar!"

"Yeah?" he responded, his voice made distant by his position behind the bus.

"Stand down. I don't think the dickhead's dangerous. He's just a regular dickhead." Jake smiled for the first time when I said that; it was slight, but it was there.

"Come on," I said to Jake while looping a hand into his arm to help him up. I removed my multi-tool from its pouch and used the cutters to sever the nylon straps at his wrists. His arms fell down to his sides as I walked around to his front to face him. His hands hung unmoving; overall, he was very still.

"Okay," I prompted. "Make with the helping."

"Sure," he said, turned left, and immediately started walking up the street in the direction our bus had been traveling.

"Hey!" I barked. "Where're you going?"

"To get my truck," he called back. "You need some gas, right? Come on, you'll see."

After a moment's hesitation, I followed after him while muttering, "Fucked up as a left-handed football bat..." Davidson honked in laughter.

8

AMWAY

Gibs

Jake led me a few blocks north and then a couple of blocks west. I stayed behind him the entire time with the M4 aimed at his back. He didn't seem to care; he just walked at an even pace, arms swinging lightly. I almost expected him to start whistling or try to make small talk or something. He did none of that; just walked happily along. As we rounded a final corner, we came upon a blue Ford pickup so high off the ground that the hood was level with my shoulder line. It was facing towards me and, as I moved further out to my right to pass around the front, I saw a long trailer behind it loaded down with a few plastic fifty-five-gallon drums.

"Holy shit," I whispered. "Are those all filled with fuel?"

"Not completely but I've had a good run today. It's pretty easy to get a line of cars going once they've been pushed out of the street."

I looked in his direction and saw him regarding me calmly. "Any diesel?"

He nodded. "Yes, a couple of those drums have a duct tape 'X' on the lid. They have diesel."

I stood for a moment while chewing my lip, trying to decide how to play this. After a few moments of indecision, I realized I didn't have the first clue. A lack of food and sleep had made me dumber than a box of rocks.

I finally gave up on trying to be clever and let the rifle hang. "Okay, Jake," I said. "What's the plan?"

"I propose we drive back to your bus, fuel it up, and you follow me back to my place. We'll get your people fed and figure out what comes next."

"Why?" I asked, exhausted. When he didn't answer, I shrugged and looked around. "What is this, a Jesus thing? You're gonna try to convert us? Cook us in a pot? Sell us Amway? What?"

Jake looked off in a random direction, apparently to collect his thoughts. He looked back at me and then began to walk towards me. He held his hands out where I could see them, but it didn't even occur to me to put the muzzle upon him at that point. I had just about surrendered to the stupid by that point. He stopped about a foot away, and I noticed he was a few inches shorter than me.

"I suppose you've been shot at? Shot a bunch of people as well?"

I nodded.

"Lost some people?"

I nodded again.

Jake breathed in deep; let it out. "Me too. I've met some good people out here as well, though. Just like you have. You wouldn't be running yourself ragged trying to protect them if that wasn't the case."

He fished the truck keys out of his pocket, unlocked the Ford's driver side door, and turned back to me.

"We're stronger together," he said. "We can do more together. How long are you going to stay out here looking? How long have you even been out here looking?"

I had no answer for him, so I only shook my head.

"You have to take a chance, Gibs," he called over his shoulder as he climbed into the truck. He shut the door and looked back out at me through the open driver's side window. "Whether it's with me or that road, you're going to have to take a chance."

He turned the key in the ignition; the deep, rattling growl of a diesel engine echoed down the street. He faced forward in the driver's seat and waited.

I scoffed at myself. *Fuck it*, I thought. I walked around the front of the truck to hop into the passenger seat.

It was a quick little drive to return to the bus; Jake pulled us up nose to nose with the grill while Oscar and Davidson stood aside. Both of them looked about as confused as a dog with a bone-shaped dildo. Jake shut off the engine, and I spoke up quickly before he could hop out of the truck.

"Let me go talk to them first, huh?"

"Of course," he replied without looking over at me. He was eyeballing the two men standing outside, perhaps wondering what they were planning to get up to with their weapons. His face was passive, with no hint of aggression at all, but I knew mean-mugging when I saw it. I prayed for everyone to just keep relaxed and happy.

I jumped out of the truck and walked over to them; fanned my hands gently towards the ground in a "remain calm" gesture as I approached.

"Go back to his trailer, find a drum with a taped 'X' on the lid, and muscle it over to the bus's tank. Get whatever tools you need to fill up, even if you need to transfer to a can first with the hand pump."

Oscar looked over at Jake and said, "He's cool, right?"

"Looks that way," I agreed. "Try not to empty the whole barrel, okay? Let's not start out by being shitheads."

They both made off for the trailer; Davidson actually waving and nodding at Jake as he passed. Jake nodded back. I took a deep breath and climbed up onto the bus to address the crowd, who must have been fit to come out of their skins by that point.

"Hey, everyone, how we doing? Holding out okay?"

"I have to go to the bathroom," Maria whispered to me from the front.

"Oh, yeah. Yeah, I guess you would, huh, sweetie? Okay, anyone need a head call? Let's get that out of the way. Same as before: grownups with kids." Our kids were really just limited to Maria and Rose, who were nine and fourteen. Greg and Alan both looked like they were in their mid to late teens. Even so, I didn't want to single the kids out by name. Monica offered to take them both, Rose being her daughter and all. The three of them stepped off the bus and went to go find an open storefront with a bathroom. It had become standard practice by this point; leaving little, unflushed care packages in our wake as we traveled. It probably wouldn't take that much effort for a skilled tracker to trace our journey—just follow the trail of abused toilets.

"Anyone else need a refresher?" I asked.

A few heads nodded, and George said, "I'd like to hear what we're doing first." Others voiced their agreement.

I nodded and rested my hands on the front seat backs. "Well, it turns out that this guy isn't as much of a-. Well, he's…" I struggled to redirect my train of thought, "he's not a threat, as I originally may have suspected."

"Is that gas they're moving over back here?" asked Jeff (a

skinny, little waif of a man) as he looked out the side window at Oscar and Davidson fighting the fuel barrel into submission.

"Diesel, yeah," I agreed. "This guy we ran into, Jake is his name, is helping us to fuel up and has invited us back to his place for…" I struggled to say the next part in a way that didn't sound idiotic and failed. Drawing a blank, I opted for blowing a raspberry: "ppfffttt, for dinner, I guess. He's invited us over for dinner." I put my head down, waiting for the questions and the arguing and all the other bullshit to commence.

When none of that happened, I looked back up at them and was met with row on row of curious, expectant faces.

Edgar (Mr. Asshole himself) said, "Well, I don't know about the rest of you, but I'm fairly hungry." Several others chimed in agreement. Barbara said, "It's very nice of him to offer. I wish we had something to bring with us…"

I couldn't have been any more surprised if they had all spontaneously started sucking their thumbs and farting the Benny Hill theme song. I had been certain I was going to have to swim through a wave of protests and arguments but, apparently, these people were all ready to go out to a dinner party. I turned and sat back down in the driver's seat, resting my hands on the wheel while slouching into the backrest. I looked out the windshield and saw Jake looking back at me. He smiled and waved.

I smiled and waved back, saying, "Well, why not? Must be 'Confuse a Jarhead Tuesday.'"

Davidson climbed up the stairs into the bus, I suspected to go get the refueling tools from the back. He stopped next to me and asked, "You want me to carry all that back with me?" He was pointing at my chest rig and rifle.

"Sure," I said. "Thanks." I shrugged out of everything and handed it all over, which he slung one item at a time over his shoulder. He wedged my MR556 back behind the driver's seat, took up the M4, and shuffle-stepped towards the rear of the bus.

In the meantime, various folks passed by the front and exited, on their way to go find some relief.

I felt rather than heard someone sit down behind me. Looking up in the rearview, I was surprised to see a shock of curly, red hair and a set of bright, green eyes looking back at me. I said nothing, waiting for her to talk first.

"You okay?" Rebecca asked.

I nodded and said, "I'm just tired. I really need a vacation, is all."

She laughed quietly and said, "Some of us are worried. People are talking."

"Oh?" I asked, perking up. "Saying what?"

"They're just worried about you. Afraid that you're going to get yourself hurt or killed trying to spread too thin, do too many things at once. I happen to agree."

I snorted. "We'll just ask the world for a time-out, then, huh?" It sounded shitty and petulant as soon as I said it. I was too tired to even try to take it back but, thankfully, she seemed not to mind.

"I'm just saying you could probably spread the load a little."

"I know, Rebecca. I know. I'm sorry. Last time I tried that, though, two of our own bought it."

A hand reached out and rested on my shoulder, then my neck. I felt a stirring in my shorts despite the topic and tamped it back down in disgusted anger.

"That wasn't you," she said, soft hand squeezing. "You can't let that break you."

I said nothing but shifted around to face her; mostly to get her distracting hand off my neck.

"You remember where you found me?" she asked.

"I remember. You weren't in the best shape."

"Well you don't know what happened before that," she said and rested her chin on the horizontal bar between us. "Like most people, I had ended up in a tent camp towards the end. You know how it went. There was a small group of us survivors who just weren't getting sick while everyone else died off."

I nodded. I remembered.

"There were three of us girls, all about the same age. The worse things got, the closer we became. Towards the end we started calling each other sisters. Wanda, that was one of us, even started calling our group The Survivor Sisters. She said we were all going to get a redneck tattoo of our gang name if we ever got to a point where we could settle back into homes again and hope-fully find someone who could do the tattoo." She laughed, face sad. "Rebecca, Wanda, and Emily…"

I jolted in my seat at the name "Emily," thinking of Pinch; thinking of the girl I was never going to meet but whose face I could still see in my thoughts regardless. I felt a wave of mental double vision (or perhaps split perception) in my mind as I strug-gled to track the two different Emily personalities, one established and older by a day, the other newly formed and taking shape as Rebecca spoke to me. I attributed the sensation to sheer exhaustion.

Rebecca continued on as though nothing had happened. "We left the camp for the road to find a new home. We weren't on the road for very long before we were found…"

Her chin remained propped on the bar, but her eyes no longer looked at me. They looked inward. Back.

"They chased us for hours that felt like days. I don't know where they came from, but we knew what they were after. We could hear it in their excited hollering and the jokes they shouted at each other. They were so excited. They wanted to make them-selves a… little club."

I grimaced. She was silent a short while longer, then, looking back at me, she said, "Wanda and Emily got pinned down, but I got away. I… I left them behind."

Neither her chin nor lip quivered but her eyes, those

dangerous goddamned green eyes, began to well up with water as they stared into my own eyes unblinking. I was held in place by her stare, hypnotized, unable to move, trapped; like I was pinned by the gaze of some half-goddess/half-viper hybrid. She blinked, and tears ran down both cheeks, breaking whatever the hell spell it was that held me. It felt like a physical cord had been cut. Heat bloomed in my face as I looked away.

She continued: "I don't know what happened to them. If I had stayed, it would have happened to me. I'm ashamed that I ran; I regret that I did and wish I could have stayed. At the same time, the part of me that I don't really like is grateful… *grateful*… that I was such a little fucking coward."

I looked back at her sharply, opening my mouth to argue but she talked over me.

"I couldn't have done anything," she repeated. "I know that. I'm basically a weak set of tits and a round ass out here. That's how it is now. I'm fucking sick of it, Gibs. I've done that since I grew a set of tits. I don't want it anymore."

She lifted her chin off the bar, and the sad, heartbroken little girl wasn't there anymore. There was fire there, and not just in her fancy hair. She started looking born again hard.

"None of that shit was my fault; that belongs to the animals that were chasing us." She leaned forward and stabbed a finger into my chest; it was light, she barely made contact, but it got my attention—I took a moment to determine if I wanted to be pissed or not and decided to let it go. "Kyle and Jessica weren't your fault. That belongs to those fucks that shot them. A lot of people on this bus feel like I do, Gibs. They don't like their chances in this world. Now, will you man the fuck up and help us or not?"

I snapped my mouth shut and took a minute to regain composure.

"Did I just get no-ballsed by the Instagram hottie?" I asked without thinking.

A guffaw was shocked out of her. She put her hand over her mouth and began to shake violently with mad laughter. She coughed, cleared her throat, and said, "Sure, if that's what you want to call it."

I nodded and put my fist out. She bumped it just like the young guys in the platoon used to do, like even the damned officers were doing, right around the time I left.

"Let's get some chow," I said. "My brain works better on a full stomach."

Davidson and Oscar finished fueling up the bus not long after my little "pep talk" with Rebecca. They reported filling a gas can four times and transferring the result into the bus's tank, twenty gallons in other words, which Jake agreed would probably be enough fuel to get us where he intended to go. I was pleased to see that what we had taken apparently hadn't put much of a dent in the fuel barrel's level, based on how hard Oscar, Davidson, and Jake were all struggling to get it loaded back on the trailer; I had no desire to be so deep in debt that I couldn't climb back out again if I had to—those things add up.

As everyone else was coming back onto the bus to settle in, I took my opportunity to run off for my own little evacuation drill. It seemed our group had found their way into some sort of vehicle rental agency offering everything from regular street transportation to quads and snowmobiles. I found the restroom sign in the low light and went to go have a look.

There were two *his* and *hers* heads, both with a single commode and one with the standard wall urinal. Between fifteen people (even fifteen underfed, dehydrated people), both restrooms looked like they just came out of the losing side of an abusive relationship. I looked down at a toilet already overfilled with the canned food of Christmas past and shuddered; the smell alone was enough to make a guy second guess his religion. Picturing the process of coming close to that mess was enough to elicit a shiver running through my body, and I shook my head in disgust. My gut churned, growling at me in aggravation, and I began looking around the room for alternatives.

The urinal was out of the question; it was just as bad as the commode, and I had no desire at all to take any splash damage. Squatting in a corner was more uncivilized than I was in the mood to be; I hadn't crapped into a hole in the floor since the Philippines and was in no hurry to resurrect the practice. My gut growled up at me again, a sharp stab driving all the way through to my pelvis.

I regret to report that I finally landed on the only option remaining to me; the sink. Major drunken tears aside, this was the first time I had ever attempted such a maneuver, and it was a learning experience, to say the least. If you think it difficult to get the job done from a handicap John that elevates you a few inches higher than desired off the ground, try doing it sometime from a perch that has your feet swinging out in space. Finding the appropriate… leverage… is a challenge.

If there's one thing they teach the Marines, though, it's how to improvise, adapt, and overcome (Semper Gumby, as the saying goes); in the great battle between the sink and my ass, the sink lost, and I thankfully didn't take any casualties. Having finished the shameful act (honestly, I don't know if I'd be relating this right now if I hadn't spiked my morning coffee with Jack), I hobble-stepped away to see to the aftermath with a trusty pack of wet wipes.

I returned to the bus with a lighter heart only to find everyone in their seats waiting for me, which was frankly a little unnerving given what I had just been up to. There was no way they could know what I had just done, but I felt a little heat in my cheeks, regardless.

As I sat down in the seat and leaned over to re-twist and tape the power lines together, Wang muttered, "Everything come out okay?"

"Can it." I touched the ignition lines long enough to fire up the engine and then taped the ends up as before.

"You know, you don't have to be the last one to go," he said. "We won't mind if you take your turn sooner."

"No, trust me; it's really better this way."

I could hear the start of laughter in his voice and prepared myself to exercise restraint. I would not let this little shit break me. I was not about to break character and start laughing—that would ruin the whole damned joke.

"If it's a question of safety, we could always send someone with a rifle to kind of watch over you; maybe offer a little moral support?"

I looked up to respond but made sure to keep my voice low. "Wang, just how the hell were you the fastest sperm? You bunch of ratbags don't have hands clean enough to hold my nose."

He cracked and began belly laughing. He sat back in his seat, shaking his head. I turned forward in my seat, allowing a smile only when I knew my face was hidden from view. I waved out the window to signal at Jake, who responded by throwing his truck into drive and passing by on our left. Once he cleared our length, he stopped and waited for me to get turned around. I pulled up behind him and shot a thumbs-up through the windshield.

He led us back down the highway towards the mountain range we had just passed, now on our left side, and continued on for five miles before turning off a crossroad and driving straight towards the range. In time, I saw that the road actually delved into the range itself; Jake passed through without slowing down.

I started out by trying to keep track of where we were and where we went, but there were so many twists, turns, and switchbacks as we continued on a gentle but increasing grade that I soon abandoned the practice. I heard a few people behind me comment on how beautiful the landscape was and, taking a minute to just glance out the window and see it all, I had to agree. It was subtle and crept up on you as you traveled. At first, the landscape all around us was brown; dotted by barren scrub brush and yet, as we got in deeper, we learned that this was really only the case for the largest mountain faces aiming south and taking the biggest brunt of the sun and wind. Once into the heart of the mountains, much of the landscape was shielded from the elements, and we began to see vast expanses of tall evergreen trees spreading out over and covering everything.

Our battered, janky bus was doing alright, for the most part, until we came to the point where the paved road ended, and we were forced to venture onto dirt. The vehicle swayed like an old drunk as it stepped down off the asphalt, making me and a lot of others sit up in our seats. The grade increased even more so I began to baby the hell out of the gas pedal, certain I could feel the tires trying to slip loose and stutter on several occasions. I was on the edge of blowing the horn at Jake and offloading everyone into his truck for the rest of the trip when the ground leveled off, we broke through a narrow, tree-lined cleft, and emptied out into the bowl.

That was a surreal experience for me. I'm not ancient, but I am old enough that they were still having the kids read Laura Ingalls Wilder books when I attended elementary school (God knows what they had them reading at the end, if they had them reading at all). Driving into the valley made me think of those stories, especially with the cabin socked back into the tree line. Jake led us directly toward it over the dirt road that ran along the center of the field. As we went, he began to honk the truck horn several times. The cabin appeared to be about a kilometer or so from where we emerged, positioned as it was on the extreme opposite edge of the valley entrance, yet I could tell it would take us a bit of time to get there based on the speed we traveled over the dirt trail. It became rough along the way, and I started to worry about the missing tire on the rear axle. It had held up pretty well so far, but I had to assume they stacked four wheels up on the rear of the bus for a good reason; I didn't have any clue how long we could drive like that before we ran into trouble.

Voices began to filter up to me from the rear of the bus; I heard Barbara's in particular as she described dreaming of just such a place for her retirement (a dream, I expect, she may have let go of when her husband died of a heart attack years ago; she flirted relentlessly with me, but I'm well aware that she never stopped loving him).

As we pulled up in front of the home, the larger garage came into view, although at the time we didn't realize it was a garage. Well, we knew it was garage-like, of course, but there could have been anything in there when we first clapped eyes on it. I *may* have begun to dream about floor to ceiling rows of long life food supplies. Such a hoard would keep us fed for an incredibly long time; maybe even a year or two. We could pull back from the daily grind. Day to day life wouldn't have to be about digging through heaps of trash trying to find something we could eat. There was no such hoard in there, unfortunately, or at least, not in the capacity I wanted. I didn't know this at the time, though. As I put the bus in park, set the brake, and killed the engine, that building hid unlimited possibilities. It was like a giant present under the Christmas tree.

As I was stepping off the bus, I heard Jake ahead of me (who had already exited his vehicle) call out, "It's okay! I brought them back on my own. Come out."

I looked to the entrance of the house expecting his buddies to come out, but no such thing occurred. One hundred yards off to the left of the home, a small figure emerged from the trees and began walking our way at a fast march. I could tell she was female right off from the long hair and the way she moved. She didn't waggle her hips around like a stripper or anything; maybe it was the way her body was shaped or, perhaps, maybe her long hair programmed me to see the movements of a female.

She wore clothing that would blend in well with the surroundings; not exactly woodland MARPAT but using the same color scheme, each article was a solid color rather than a camo pattern. It looked like the kind of outdoor gear you'd buy from REI if REI was still a thing that existed. A small, angry-looking little rifle was strapped to her chest. As she came closer to Jake, I was able to see that it was a bullpup of some sort, though I was unfamiliar with the manufacturer. I hated (and still do hate) bullpups. I tried shooting a buddy's once at the range; reloading the thing was just slow, uncomfortable, and awkward for me. I had years' and years' worth of muscle memory stored up in expecting the trigger group to be aft of the receiver. Reversing their positions was, for me, like trying to teach an old dog quantum physics. Having that one experience with my buddy's old Bushmaster, I had decided to happily disregard the design ever since.

Without looking at us, she walked directly up to Jake, positioned herself with her back to the rest of us, and leaned in close to talk to him. Sensing some trouble in paradise, I held out a hand to my group, who were just stepping into the open, to signal that they should stay back and give the two some space to chat. On a scale of Spring Break Florida to Mogadishu, I'd have to rate our welcome somewhere around Detroit. They stood like this for a few minutes, heads close together, probably arguing over our very presence. I began to think about loading everyone back on and leaving as I watched them.

In the end, before I could look back at the group and signal that they shouldn't get too attached to the area, I saw Jake nod towards us with his eyebrows while the woman was in the middle of saying something; which I could tell only because I could see the back of her head shaking from the motions of her jaw moving. She turned to look over her right shoulder, showing an attractive profile in rich, brown skin and features that might have been either Mexican or Native American. It's usually really hard for me to tell, actually; I grew up classifying people by color (black, white, brown, red) before all the various groups started marching every time an apparent dinosaur like me stuttered. I don't know what the hell happened. Towards the end, I started feeling like I wanted to carry around an application form that people would have to fill out before I could talk to them—one of the entries would have said, "Please list those labels that you're okay with and any others that are likely to trigger you into a frothing rage." I have mixed feelings about the world ending, honestly. On one hand, I don't miss the fact that one wrong word taken out of context on social media could potentially destroy your private and professional life. For a guy like me (your average jarhead, in other words), that could be every other word!

On the other hand, given enough alcohol I'd suck start a she-male for a donut, so badly do I miss those little sugared morsels of fried bread.

Where the hell was I?

Right: the woman was looking back in our direction, first with an expression that suggested that someone somewhere was getting an ass-chewing, followed by a complete softening of said expression. I didn't realize what had happened until I saw the angle of her gaze; she was looking low rather than high. I followed her gaze to see Maria standing very close to her father, Oscar, and looking all around the area with wide, intent eyes.

That's right, kid, I thought. *You just keep being disgustingly cute. Win me a dinner.*

I glanced back at the woman and had to work hard to keep a

grin from spreading on my face. She was crumpling. I could literally see her folding under the awesome power of Maria's cuteness. *Oh, Jesus, come on, lady. Just give in. Where's Sarah McLachlan when you need her?* I would have superglued a fly to the kid's face if I thought it would have helped. I would have settled for Sally Struthers.

The woman turned her head away from view again and said more to Jake, who nodded. She dipped her head, shook it slightly, and shrugged.

Oh, shit yeah, Maria! Oo-freaking-rah!

She turned and approached us along with Jake, now with a smile on her face, which continued to look fierce regardless of its softening. Jake said, "Everyone, this is Amanda. Amanda, this is everyone… many of whose names I have yet to learn."

She nodded and waved to us. Now that she was close, it struck me that she was tiny. The top of her head wouldn't have even brushed my chin. Even compared to Jake, who was a few inches shorter than me, she was still shy about a half a foot. I looked down at the rifle that hung comfortably across her chest and also noticed a sidearm strapped to her thigh. She looked like she was used to going around like that.

Amanda smiled and said, "Well, we can learn everyone's names over dinner, can't we? Why don't you put the truck away and I'll go dig out some tables?"

"You folks relax a bit," Jake advised. "We'll have you fed shortly."

Dinner turned out to be a certified feast, although it didn't follow any coherent theme. "Ghetto potluck" was how Oscar described it. Our hosts pulled out some folding picnic tables to lay out a spread but there weren't anywhere near enough chairs for everyone to have a seat, so we all stood with the exception of George and Barbara, who took chairs on the home's front porch.

The food itself filled a wide variety of canned tastes. White rice was used as a filling base for the whole meal; a large tray was put out in the center with spoons and paper plates. Around this were various smaller plates and trays filled with all manner of things like baked beans, whole potatoes, green beans, corn, and meats. There was even a small bowl of fruit off to the side for anyone who wanted it. All of this stuff came out of a can; I mean, when I say "meats," I'm talking about stuff like Spam and Potted Meat. Much of it was stuff I would have turned my nose up at back in the day. Today, I and the rest of the whole group annihilated every bite.

We learned that Amanda had a daughter, Elizabeth, who had come out to greet us after the tables had been set out but while the food was still being heated up on a few propane grills running in overtime (all told, it had taken around an hour to get the food out, mainly because that was how long it took to get all the rice cooked). Lizzy (as both her mother and Jake called her) fell in almost instantly with Maria and even Rose, who I would have thought was getting a little out of the younger girls' age range. Rose would have been fourteen during this time, as I think I mentioned already; she was at that in-between state where she wasn't a little girl anymore but also wasn't quite ready to be grown up as well. Greg and Alan looked on from the sidelines, most likely pondering both a lack of any males as well as any females in their age range. Like the rest of the men still possessing a pulse, they would have to content themselves for the time being by staring after Rebecca like lost pups.

"I'm sorry about the seating situation," Jake said, having finished a small plate of food. "We've never had so many people here before. Folding chairs were never a priority."

"Don't mention it, Jake," Fred called from a little down the line. "Most of us were sick of sitting, anyway, spending all day on that damned bus. It's good to stretch the legs out a bit."

Jake nodded and was silent for a time. I looked at him standing at the head of the table, there, next to Amanda, almost but not quite touching elbows; just on the edge of contact with each other. I wondered at their relationship.

"How long have you three been living out here?" I asked.

"Either three or four months, now, I guess," Jake said.

"Four," Amanda confirmed.

"Four, then."

"So then you guys found this place? That was lucky," I said as I looked around the valley. It was buried back deep into the mountains. I couldn't imagine anyone happening by on accident. It looked to be prime real estate, well protected on all sides by high mountain walls with a single, narrow point of access.

"Well, we had a friend who brought us here," Amanda said. "He owned the place. We lost him not too long ago. Shootout."

"I'm sorry for that," I said. "We lost some people too."

"I think everyone must have, by now," Rebecca added, looking pointedly in my direction.

I suppressed an eye roll and nodded at her. *Alright, already. I get it.*

I was deciding how to respond to her statement, or at least trying to decide if I should respond to it, when Edgar chose that moment to start speaking. I winced inwardly, trying like hell to keep it from showing on my face. I caught Wang's eye, who only shrugged; it seemed he and I were both taken by surprise.

"I was hoping you all might indulge me a moment," he said. "It's no secret that we were in poor shape when you found us. We had eaten our last morsel of food, which was admittedly not a full meal at that (you must understand that we were all feeling the pangs of hunger well before our encounter in Jackson) and consumed our last drop of water. We had been chased from the streets of Denver by a band of deplorable, bloodthirsty savages, losing some of our own, as already noted, but also gaining new friends in the process." He waved a hand expansively to Alish and the Page brothers. "What I'm trying to say is that we have learned to expect only famine and savagery out on this hard road. For this kindness you have shown to us, our people are in your debt."

Edgar raised his water bottle and looked around expectantly at all of us. I became concerned that he was about to start reciting poetry or something soon, so I hoisted mine as well and said, "Erm, yeah, hear, hear…"

There were a few belated chimes of agreement from around the table. For Jake's part, he looked as though he was put off balance by the whole display; he had his head down through the delivery, only looking up at the end when Edgar finished speaking. The expression on his face was unreadable. If he was confused or uncomfortable, I sure couldn't blame him. While blessedly short, Edgar's speech had killed any further conversation (any natural conversation, anyway) and drew everyone's attention to a major, nagging question: now that we had been fed, what came next? Honestly, the exchange made me feel like a bit of a moron. I was certain there was a list of subtexts that had gone right over my head, mostly because I was unsettled by the outcome and couldn't put my finger on why. My gut was telling me that something clumsy and ill-handled had transpired, only I couldn't tell who was fully to blame or if we all held a piece of it. I decided to classify the matter as above my paygrade and opted instead to spoon another wad of rice into my mouth.

Up at the head of the table, Amanda leaned in close to Jake and whispered something into his ear. His face betrayed no expression as she spoke to him; the expression on her face indicated that she was having trouble in choosing between speaking to him and biting a chunk out of his face. Without waiting for a response, she departed towards the house, mounted the short flight of steps to the porch, and disappeared behind the front door.

Jake looked up at the rest of us and said, "Would you all please excuse me for a moment? Please, there's plenty of food to go around; you must eat and enjoy the evening."

With a nod, he turned and followed after Amanda.

I sighed and spooned up another bite. Wang came over to my side and quietly asked, "What do you think all that was about?"

Through a mouthful, I asked, "You ever bring home a stray animal as a kid?"

"Kind of," he said. "I caught a bullfrog once and wanted to keep it in an aquarium. My mom was pissed."

"Well," I shrugged, digging around on my paper plate, "I think Jake's being told to take us back to the swamp and leave us there."

9

MOUTHS TO FEED

Amanda

"So, I'm wondering, Jake. Was this *our* place or just *your* place?"

"I beg your pardon?" he asked. For all of the things in him that I admired, his deadpan calm really used to drive me crazy. I could never tell if he was playing it safe, hiding his own emotions (in the last few months of living together, I had learned that emotions were certainly a thing that he possessed in his own strange, hidden way), or if he just really was as clueless as he sometimes seemed. It didn't help at all that he always became more relaxed in response to me getting more worked up. It's hard to explain but, sometimes, I would have been a lot happier with him shouting back.

"You heard what I said," I shot at him.

He took a moment before responding: "This is *our* home, of course."

"I see. Do you think you might have checked with me before you came home with an actual busload of strangers?"

"Ah. Well, it would have been hard to consult with you at the time; I was out there alone and had to make a snap decision."

"No," I scoffed. "No, you really didn't. It never occurred to you to just have them wait out there while you came back to talk to me?"

He was quiet for much longer this time as he considered. "Honestly, it didn't. I don't know why." He looked confused. Uncertain.

"I do," I responded. "Jake, Lizzy and I both owe you a lot. You've done things for us—well, we've all done things for each other—that go beyond friends. We're all family in a lot of ways. But you can be really, really inconsiderate sometimes, you know that?"

A pained expression settled onto his face, which sucked some of the fire out of me. It was hard for me to stay angry at him when he was like that. I had stopped being afraid of Jake some time ago, either because we just became familiar with each other's behaviors and moods or because I simply understood that he would never do anything to hurt us. It was probably some combination of those things. Dealing with him could still be exhausting sometimes, though. Most times, it's hard to know what you're dealing with when you interact with Jake. Is he hard as nails and feels things only a little, or does he feel everything but put all of his energy into hiding it? I still haven't decided what the answer to that question is for sure. When he got that expression on his face, though, I sometimes wondered if he was a little of what my mom used to call "touched…" what my generation would later describe as being "on the spectrum."

It was nearly impossible for me to stay angry at times like this; it became more like kicking a puppy than having an argument. Maybe I was still just too used to Eddie. He and I used to get into some terrific arguments. We never took them too far or anything, but he and I both grew up with thick skin, so we could always unload. We could just get things off our chest and out into the open without having to worry about hurt feelings. It was really great how we worked together... and I have to admit the make-up sex was pretty awesome too.

My relationship with Jake was a complete opposite; it was either smooth sailing or eggshells for me. I could just never be sure if I was hurting him and doing real damage to both him and our friendship or if it was all just rolling off him. It could be very tiring.

I took a deep breath, all anger expended and replaced by a kind of exhausted regret. "Jake, you can't make those kinds of decisions for us on your own. I understand that these things are important to you, but you have to remember that Lizzy and I are in this with you, too. Bringing people back here is a really big deal. I don't think I need to remind you..." I trailed off, not wanting to complete the thought; it felt petty and hurtful.

He was nodding. "You're... you're absolutely right. It won't happen again. I'm sorry."

I reached across the space between us (we sat in chairs facing each other in the library in front of the small fireplace; a place we usually went when we needed to discuss something serious and didn't want Lizzy to overhear) and squeezed his shoulder, which had become noticeably thicker in our short time at the cabin.

"Forgiven," I said. "Just keep it in mind, kay?"

He nodded again, staring into the cold ashes of the fire pit, falling deeper into his own private thoughts. Before he could go too far under, I asked, "So, what now?"

He looked back up to meet my gaze and asked, "Huh?"

"They're here now. What do we do with them?"

He breathed in and blew air out through his lips. "Well honestly, I thought they'd be helpful around here. We could spread a lot of work out among ourselves."

I started laughing despite myself. "Jake... there are *sixteen* of them! Who brings home sixteen people? Where are we going to put them all?"

"I'll admit I haven't solved that problem yet."

"Well, we can't stick them in the garage," I said. "It's getting down to the high 40's in the evenings."

"Not without space heaters, no," he agreed. He looked up at me. "We should probably get some space heaters the next time we're in town. Winter isn't far away."

"Okay," I said, "Maybe that works for later. We have a problem right now, Jake."

"Yeah, I know." He spent a few moments looking back into the ash pit and then said, "You and Lizzy take the master tonight. We can cram two people into your bed and another two into the guest room, which covers four. We can jam another six into the bunks in Lizzy's room."

"Right, that's ten people," I said. What will you do with the other seven, including yourself?"

"We have a few sleeping bags; we can spread the rest out over the couches and floor. I don't have any problem sleeping in the easy chair; I end up falling asleep there most nights, anyway."

"This is gonna be so crowded. Nineteen people and just three bathrooms. I'm not sure the septic tank can take it."

"It's just for the night… maybe tomorrow as well," he assured me. "We can get this figured out. Hey, look, we haven't even discussed this with them, yet. We might offer and have them tell us 'thanks but no thanks.'"

"We'll see." I was unconvinced. "So what about the food?"

"Food?"

I rolled my eyes. "Uh, yeah? What did we say we have right now? Eight months of food to pull us through the winter, right?"

"Yeah, eight months plus maybe a bit extra before we should start growing our own."

"That's eight months for three people. Or…" I did some math

in my head, "...twenty four months for one person. What's twenty-four divided by nineteen?"

"I... ah," he muttered.

"Exactly. We're suddenly down to less than a month and a half of food," I said. "What's the plan for that?"

"I don't know," he admitted. "There are a lot more of us, though, if they decide to stay. We can scavenge a lot more at a much faster rate."

"Enough to make up for that many mouths?"

"Well... I really have no idea. I suppose we'll have to see how it goes and make some sort of projection. Billy was the numbers guy, not me."

"Yeah, well, you better find a replacement if you're gonna be the new mayor," I said, leaning back in my chair and crossing my arms.

"Mayor?" He looked unhappy just saying the word.

"Oh, yeah. If we're going to do this, there can't be any question in these peoples' minds who's in charge, here. Didn't you read any of those books Billy left us? Someone has to be in charge. Usually, the turd floats to the top of the group naturally, but this started out as our home, and it needs to stay that way. We can't leave it up to natural group dynamics. Sorry, buddy: you brought them home. You get to be the turd."

He sighed: "I realize all that, certainly. But I'm not calling myself Mayor. Besides, a title like mayor implies the consent of the governed."

"Huh?" I said.

"I mean it suggests I was voted into position. As you say, we can't let a vote happen here. We'll have to play this more like they're house guests than some sort of village situation. I'd suspect it will become reflexive for everyone after too long and we won't have to keep tiptoeing around it."

"So how do you want to do this?" I asked.

"Let's go determine the leaders in their group and have a sit-down with them. Who was it, Edgar? That made that clumsy speech? I can't imagine it's him in charge; it felt like he was trying too hard to put himself out in front through that whole performance."

"I agree," I said. "I saw some people roll their eyes, too."

"Good, but let's make sure we invite him into the meeting anyway."

"Oh, why?" I asked.

"Because if there are issues within their group, I want to know about them. I need you there in a background position, watching everyone. You're going to catch things I miss; you're better at this than I am."

PROPOSALS AND OPPORTUNITIES

Amanda

Jake led us out of the front door, where he turned abruptly and went over to sit down next to the older woman and man on the porch (who I later learned were George and Barbara), striking up a quiet conversation with them both. People from the new group had spread out all over the immediate property. Elizabeth, who had helped to prepare the food and came out to eat with everyone soon after, was sitting down at the opposite end of the porch with two young girls. She had her deck of cards out (a gift from a friend met on the road) and was dealing between the three of them.

There were a handful of people still milling around the tables, a giant of a black man among them holding a paper plate and plastic fork that looked tiny in his hands. He had what Jake later described to me as 'the awkward posture of an overburdened frame'; basically, the man was so large that the weight of his body made him look like he was out of energy all the time. He didn't walk around; he lumbered. He didn't sit down; he eased into chairs with a groan. You could see it the most in his legs and also his feet if he went without shoes. He had long, skinny legs with knees that looked like they might fold in the wrong direction if he came down on them too hard. His feet looked spread out and mashed into the ground as though carrying the body above them had aged them prematurely. I felt physically uncomfortable whenever I looked at the man and, when he sat down, I always felt like I could breathe a little easier for him.

Next to him stood about the most attractive woman I think I've ever seen in person. She was one of those people who looked so effortlessly beautiful that you felt like a troll just standing next to her. She was tall, probably the same height as Jake (who was just a hair above average for a man); with long, perfect, white legs exposed by a pair of shorts I never would have been brave enough to wear. And when I say her skin was white, you have to understand: it glowed. A lot of people with pale skin typically get blotchy in different temperatures, hot or cold, and sometimes appear like they're breaking out in some sort of rash in extreme cases. This blotchiness, along with the usual tracing of visible blue veins just beneath the surface of the skin, is why the ability to tan is so desirable. For her, tanning was unnecessary. Her skin was smooth, even, and flawless. She had a mane of fiery red hair that fell just below her shoulders but most likely extended to the center of her back or lower if pulled straight. It was arranged in thick, wavy curls that most of my friends would have had to spend three hours with a curling iron to achieve; I had to imagine it happened on her naturally given that she had been living on a bus. I'm struggling for words to describe it; her hair was so thick that it stood out from her head in such a way that... headdress! That's it; her hair was like a giant, Indian headdress! I would have killed for hair like that. My hair was basically straight and dark brown, which my mother claimed I got from my Indian heritage. I don't know if that's true or not; I do know that it thinned out and became even more useless after I had Lizzy.

She stood chatting with a black woman who was more on my level: shorter, thicker, and darker. Her hair was pulled back into a stiff ponytail, and it looked like she had been living hard on the road for some time, as we all did, but the miles, lack of beauty products, and grime could not hide the strength and quiet dignity that she carried. I liked her on sight and admired her for all of the reasons my instincts told me to disregard the other, prettier woman.

I was startled by Jake appearing at my side, an annoying, unconscious habit that he still has and that others besides me have commented on. He called out into the open with a clear voice, "Gibs, Wang, and Edgar: could I beg a moment of your time, please?"

The three men approached all wearing different levels of curiosity on their faces. If I had to assign ratings for intensity, I'd have to say that the Asian man (Wang) had the most guarded expression; the taller, bearded man (Gibs) was somewhere in the middle; and the final person, a dead ringer for Ichabod Crane (Edgar), looked like he had just been called on to address the president.

Jake looked over at George, nodded, and asked, "Shall we?" The man called George pushed off from the low deck chair with the help of his cane and approached the front door, which Jake was holding open. Gibs, Wang, and Edgar followed into the house after George. Jake glanced over to the older woman left behind in the remaining chair and said, "Have him back in a minute," before indicating to me that I should follow into the house. I noticed that Barbara didn't smile at Jake or respond to his comment, which was odd. She seemed to smile at just about everything. Jake came into the cabin behind me and shut the door.

The entry hall (what a fancy-pants would call a "foyer") was nearly crowded with five people standing around in it. The three men looked about themselves in appreciation, obviously pleased with all of the masculine wood and furniture. I couldn't blame them; I always did think Billy's home was attractive, though I personally would have added a bit of color if I had been in charge of decorating. Jake and I had once considered changing a few things up but ultimately decided not to. The home was always going to be Billy's place; we didn't want to turn it into something he wouldn't have been happy with.

"Why don't we head into the front room? There's more than enough space in there for us," suggested Jake. He slipped by all of them as he said this and walked into the formal front room where Jake, Billy, Elizabeth, and I had spent so many quiet evenings. He sat down in Billy's old leather chair positioned just off to the right of the large fireplace and gestured to the rest of the seating surrounding the low coffee table. The rest of us filtered in and occupied various positions. Gibs, George, and Wang took the long sofa on the other side of the table while Edgar took a solitary chair off to the side of the room closest to the front door, a detail I was sure Jake caught. I sat down in the mate to Jake's chair, which was located on the opposite end of the fireplace, placing Jake and I shoulder to shoulder with a span of probably six feet between us. The positioning was well arranged, giving me the ability to see everyone's faces equally (Edgar's was almost in profile). The whole environment struck me as a little surreal; I'd never been in anything like a boardroom meeting before, but I imagined that this might have been pretty close.

Without waiting for anyone to start asking questions, Jake said, "I've asked you all to meet with me in this way because I think it's probably a good idea that we lay out everyone's intentions before too much time passes. Bringing in the leaders of your group seemed the best way to do that; large groups can devolve into a lot of chatter."

I noted that when Jake said "leaders," different people had different reactions. Gibs looked tired but resigned while Wang passively revealed very little. George looked surprised, as though he hadn't expected to be lumped into such a group, and Edgar straightened up in his chair.

"Well, that's fair," Gibs said as he leaned back into the couch. "What are your intentions?"

I was curious how Jake was going to play this. Saying, "Hey, come live with us," sounds a little nuts when you just blurt it out like that.

"If it's alright," Jake responded, "I was hoping I could ask you to share what your plans were before I ran into you all in Jackson."

"That seems reasonable," George said quietly. Gibs seemed to take a cue from this and nodded gently.

"Okay," Gibs said. "Our plans were fairly simple. Find a place that doesn't suck, dig in, and scavenge for food and supplies."

"How has that been working out?" Jake asked.

Gibs's left leg began to bounce rapidly on the ball of his foot, but he seemed not to notice; he met Jake dead in the eye. "Could be better."

"I'll say we started strong, but things got a bit harder as we went," George supplied. "Got a lot harder, really."

"And you all started out together?"

"No," said George. "I had started out with Gibs and Tom, that's Tom Davidson, in a sick camp down in Texas. This was when things had really started to go south, you understand; we just sorta nodded to each other one day, got up, and left. We ran into Oscar and his daughter Maria not long after that, Rebecca was out on the road."

"Rebecca is the redhead?" I asked.

"That's right," said George.

Jake said, "You just picked up the rest along the way?"

"More or less," Gibs said, wobbling his head back and forth. "We ran into Wang and his crew in Colorado Springs... that would be Jeff, Fred, Monica and Rose, Wang and Edgar here and… Kyle and Jessica."

"Jeff was the quiet one, wasn't he? He didn't say much while we were eating," said Jake.

"Yeah, but he's alright once you get to know him," said Gibs. "Doesn't complain, carries his weight. Helps out with the kids, also."

"You said 'Kyle' and 'Jessica,'" prompted Jake.

"Yes," Gibs nodded. "I lost them." 'I' not 'We.' His leg was drumming almost frantically. I was surprised no one pointed it out but I certainly wasn't going to. My job was mostly to watch them and compare notes later with Jake.

In the meantime, Jake nodded to himself and stood from his chair. He walked to a cabinet in the back of the room (up against the wall that was shared by the kitchen on the other side) and asked, "Can I offer any of you a drink?"

"I'd love a vodka," Edgar said hopefully.

After a brief pause in which he turned back to consider all of us, Jake returned with a tray carrying six tumblers and a fresh bottle of Crown Royal. Placing the tray down next to the Chess set on the table, he began to remove the wrapping from the bottle. He made no comment at all regarding the fact that he brought back Canadian whiskey rather than vodka, met no one's eyes as he poured. He didn't even attempt an apology over having no vodka on hand, which would have been a lie anyway. He poured a couple of fingers' worth into each glass, selected one from the bunch, and then settled back into his chair. He took the first sip and sighed, wearing his unreadable smile, and nodded to Edgar, who looked more than a little dazed as he reached out hesitantly to take his glass.

Jake nodded to him happily and said, "It's quite good."

Edgar looked at his glass as though he expected to find something floating in it. Apparently finding nothing, he looked up and smiled around at the rest of us before taking a sip. Personally, I've never been a fan of whiskey, which is why I felt sympathetic when one of Edgar's eyes squinted, and he just managed to suppress a shudder.

"It's very good," he agreed, and Jake nodded again happily.

I looked at the others and saw that Gibs wasn't paying attention to the interplay at all, choosing instead to warm his glass between his hands. His leg was still running a hundred miles an hour, and he appeared to be locked within his own black thoughts. George seemed amused by Jake; he sat with his hand covering his mouth, but I could see a smile in his eyes. Wang looked completely confused by the whole affair.

"That's whiskey," Wang said.

"Hmm?" Jake asked in a distracted tone.

"That's not vodka. It's whiskey."

Jake looked down at the bottle for a beat then back up at Edgar. "Oh, no! You did ask for vodka, didn't you? How stupid of me; here let me take that. I'll get you fixed up right now."

"Oh, well if you insist," said Edgar.

"I do," Jake said as he snatched the glass from his hand. He disappeared back into the kitchen where we heard him discard the glass into the sink.

He came back out and squatted down in front of the liquor cabinet. He called back to us over his shoulder, saying "Okay, you'll need to pick one. I don't really know anything about vodka." He stood and approached the group with two bottles in his hand, one of which said "Tovaritch" across the front. The other was a terribly gaudy pink bottle that looked like it had been bedazzled near to death. It said "Alizé" along the front of its face.

Edgar's eyebrows pulled up high on his forehead, and I briefly wondered if he was as put off by the bottle of disco vodka as I was. To my surprise, he pointed right at it and said, "That'll do fine," in a whisper that quavered.

Jake's expression didn't alter in any way that you could see but, having lived with him now for months, I noticed his demeanor shift. His side of the room chilled slightly, though he continued to smile as if nothing had happened (nothing did happen as far as I could see). "As you wish," he nodded and turned to fill a glass. He returned to his chair, reaching out to hand the glass to Edgar before settling in, who took it carefully with both of his. He took a sip and looked intensely satisfied.

I should mention here that this was the last time Jake actively addressed Edgar that evening, instead only choosing to respond to him politely when spoken to directly. George shook silently in suppressed amusement, which aggravated me; I hated being left out of a joke.

Jake now looked back to Blake Gibson, who always insisted on being "Just Gibs" and said, "You were saying, please?"

Gibs looked up from his glass and nodded. He raised it to his lips, threw the entire thing back in one gulp, and said, "We were heading for open country free of any nuclear power plants when we started out. That meant heading north from Texas for Colorado."

Jake and I both settled back into our chairs to listen to Gibs fill us in on the last few weeks of their lives together. His narrative was supplemented at times by the others when it seemed he might pass by a detail that was important to them. Gibs didn't mind being interrupted at all and yielded the floor happily to anyone who cared to add additional perspective.

I won't recount the details of his story here as I believe he's already relayed as much to you during his own interviews. I will say that both Jake and I were horrified by their encounter in Denver. In our entire time together, we had not once run into such a large and apparently organized group of aggressively hostile people. While we'd definitely had some run-ins with some incredibly unsavory people (and dealt with them accordingly), these were always limited to very small groups. In the total of my experiences, we had only come up against perhaps two of what I would consider to be evil people. Maybe only one. Everyone else seemed to be in the same boat we were; just stumbling around attempting to find a new place in the world while at the same time trying to avoid getting killed by everyone else.

A pack of people on motorcycles chasing down a group on foot, one of them badly wounded, didn't sound to me like an innocent mistake. That wasn't just the average struggle for limited resources. It sounded to me like a pack of hyenas. I felt a prickle along the sleeves of my shirt and looked down to see goosebumps along my arms.

I also noticed, during Gibs's story, when Edgar spoke up at the death of Kyle and Jessica. He said, "A needless loss." Wang, who was reserved and could be very hard to read, frowned in Edgar's direction. I was a little surprised myself; his tone was just shy of accusatory. Even more surprising, Gibs said nothing to defend himself. He only nodded his agreement.

The rest of the story was finished between all of them with focus jumping from person to person as one filled in any details that the other may have missed. The narrative ended with Jake being handcuffed on the pavement. I wanted to reach out and hit him when I heard that. As stupid as it sounded to me, it was just like something my Jake would do.

"Essentially," Jake concluded, "You've all just been looking for a place to settle." They all nodded, and a couple of them vocalized agreement. After letting the silence hang just a little longer than what was comfortable, he said, "What are your thoughts on this area?"

Gibs sat up straight on the couch and said, "What, you mean this valley? Are you asking us to move in?"

Rather than answer, Jake took a sip from his glass and waited.

Gibs looked among his other companions and then looked at

Jake again. "You don't even know us, man. Why the hell would you do that?"

"You're not murderers, I know that. I can sniff out a murderer… none of you fit. I've already explained what I've seen so far; I don't think I need to spend a lot of time repeating myself."

"Right, but 'not murderers' is a rather weak basis for such an offer, wouldn't you agree?" Gibs asked. I found myself agreeing with him.

Jake nodded and said, "Can I top that up for you?" while pointing at Gibs's glass. Gibs shrugged and held it out for a refill.

"Look," Jake said as he settled back into his chair, "You're right. Under normal circumstances, we'd be feeding you all and sending you on your way the next day. But I'm not making this offer because I'm such a nice guy. Or, at least, that's not the entire reason."

George was leaning forward now, resting both hands on the head of his cane. It was the most intent I'd seen him through the entire discussion.

"Amanda and I have been working on and adding to a list of things that need to be accomplished over the next several months. There are all kinds of lovely, thoughtful names we can apply to this list but the bottom line is that it defines our expiration date for survival."

I crossed my arms over my chest and suppressed a shudder. He was drifting into territory that I did my best not to think too much about; the dark things that kept me awake in the late hours of the night.

"The best way to describe this is that we're in a race right now to get to a point where we're not relying on any of the supplies of the old world when they run out. We're already well on our way to that point, actually. Fresh bread, meat, and dairy simply don't exist anymore unless we make it… which we can't; anything that was packaged and put on a shelf went bad a long time ago. It won't be long before gasoline stops working, either. We've been working to harvest as much of that as possible, as you've seen, and we've treated what we have so far with fuel stabilizers. Even so, within a couple of months, give or take, whatever we haven't pulled out of a tank will have gone inert."

He took another drink without looking away from them. There was an impression that he was holding eye contact with all four of them at the same time, though that was impossible. They sat motionless and silent.

"After that will be the canned and freeze-dried food, which is currently the majority of our food supply. The dates will vary, there, depending on the food type, but I don't think we can reasonably rely on more than a year in that case. After that, our only option will be MRES and what we can hunt, fish, or farm. The problem with that is there are only three of us here."

"I'm starting to see the problem," George said.

"Indeed," Jake agreed. "For a workable subsistence farm, we're probably looking at one acre per person if we're talking about vegetables alone. Add in grains and livestock, which we'll need to do for dietary diversity, and that number increases to five working acres per person. These are all round numbers, of course, but they work as a good baseline. This is further complicated by the fact that the area we're in has one of the shortest growing seasons in the whole state; there isn't really any growing season to speak of at all for tender vegetation. We're looking mostly at roots and the like."

"Have you thought of moving to a better climate?" asked Wang.

"Sometimes but not seriously," Jake said. "For one, it's hard to beat the area. It's secluded, hard to find if you don't know what you're looking for, and naturally defended on all sides. You'll excuse me if I mention the fact that you all had your asses kicked across Colorado looking for something similar."

This woke me up. It was always an event when Jake decided to curse; I wondered what had brought it out.

Gibs, who had settled back and seemed a little loose around his second glass of whiskey, said, "Kicked a little ass too, fella."

"Oh, that's understood," Jake said and lifted his glass to Gibs, who in turn gave a lazy salute. "And, for another thing, we killed quite a few people to protect this place. We lost a dear friend in doing so. This is Billy's place. He believed there was a way to make it work here and we have a lot of his initial planning to see it through. We're not prepared to walk away just yet."

Gibs nodded at this statement. He got it.

"Anyway, outside of the farming situation, there're plenty of other things to do. There is a lot of relearning of lost trades and arts that must be accomplished so that we can be ready for the day when all of these leftover products just aren't viable anymore. Things like metalworking, pottery, building permanent housing without milled lumber. We need to know how to find water; this place has a well, but wells go dry. Aqueducts, animal processing, skinning and tanning, food preservation. On top of that, I need to be looking to our defenses, stockpiling more weapons and ammunition, even preparing for the day when we eventually fire the last bullet. That day is out there on the timeline, and it'll be here a lot sooner than we'd like if we're not careful."

Jake drained the last of his glass and smiled.

"This is an awful lot of work for three people, one of them being a child. Like I said: this isn't about us playing the role of Charitable Savior. We need help. The three of us on our own can survive… maybe. A community of people can thrive."

"So… who's in charge?" asked Edgar. George and Wang looked in his direction; George nodded slightly. Gibs was looking down at his empty glass as though he found it offensive.

Jake looked in his direction as well, and here I have to say that things started to get a little uncomfortable in the room. Jake smiled and nodded; there was no indication that he was annoyed by the question, and I honestly don't believe that he was, but there was a tangible feeling of *measuring* in his regard. I'm convinced Edgar felt it too because he began to squirm a bit in his chair.

"That's a very good question," Jake said. "A *penetrating* question. I suspect we'll have to feel that out as we go. To some degree, the people who live here will determine who is in charge. A man... or woman," he nodded to me, "can stand up to proclaim themselves King all day long, yet it means nothing if they're ignored by the subjects. People must consent to follow. You can dominate their choice, of course, but then, you'll never truly be in charge. You certainly won't be pretending for very long, either."

Edgar was quiet as he considered this. The statement was delivered in a friendly, offhand manner. I couldn't help feeling as though there was a message buried underneath it, though I wasn't sure who it might be intended for. Maybe all of us.

"The intent is that this property be our property," Jake elaborated. "The Bowl, as Amanda calls it, will be the home of everyone. Our land, our responsibility, with each person holding an equal share. The only limitation I must set," he looked down at the brim of his glass and rubbed it with a thumbnail, "is that this cabin remains a private residence. This isn't a community center; this is the home Amanda and I fought for to protect. I don't think we're ready to turn it into a clubhouse. I feel as though it's only fair to be clear on that point up front."

A few of the men nodded, though Edgar remained thoughtfully silent.

Jake cleared his throat. "Everything else is open to carve up as seems best to you all, with the exception of a tree that I'll show you all later."

"A tree?" Gibs asked.

"Billy's Tree," I supplied.

"Oh… understood."

"Can I refill your glass for you, Edgar?" Jake asked. He was smiling again.

Edgar looked down at his glass, then back up at Jake sidelong from the corner of his eyes. "Thank you, but no. I should go slowly."

"What if we're not interested?" Wang asked.

"That's fine," Jake shrugged. "You'll all still be welcome to spend the night, although we'll have to insist that you make plans to leave in due course. We can't afford to feed such a large group for very long if you won't be staying, you see."

"How much food is on hand?" Gibs asked, looking up again.

"That would be one of the first problems we'll have to address if you do stay," Jake said. "For three people, we're good to get through the winter. Should you all decide to join us; there isn't enough food to get through two months."

Gibs scoffed. "That's a pretty big a—uh, a big problem, wouldn't you say?"

"It is, and yet it's still manageable. There was about six months' worth of provisions when we first came here. Since then, we've managed to sock away an additional two. That's with only one person scavenging on select days out of each week; we were also going out for other stuff like gas, tools, gear, and so on. On top of that, we've been eating from those stores while we've been adding to them. All that considered we've been here about four months with only one person ever gathering food for less than half that time, in a half-hearted fashion at that. With organized, motivated teams, I believe that those numbers could be drastically improved."

"He's making good points," George said. "Not all of us could go out," he held up his cane in illustration, "but many could. We could get a lot done together."

"I'm not sure we want to just jump in with both feet here, guys," Edgar interrupted.

Gibs held his hands out. "Stop. Just hang on a second. Before we go any further, we'd all better go over this with the rest of the group."

"Of course," Jake agreed. "An answer doesn't have to happen immediately. We'll make room for you all to sleep here tonight, obviously. If you decide to stay with us, we can see to more permanent solutions tomorrow."

Jake leaned forward, placed his glass on the low coffee table, and stood, signaling that the meeting or interview or whatever the hell it was that we just had was over. The rest of them placed their glasses on the table as well and began to shuffle from the room. Among them, Gibs stopped to turn and look at both of us. "Thanks. For the food and the drinks. I, uh… Just thanks."

Jake nodded, and I said, "You're welcome," feeling like an ass for making such a stink about them showing up earlier. Gibs shut the door behind them as they stepped out onto the porch.

***

"So what was all that business with the whiskey and the vodka?" I asked.

Jake, who had settled back down into his chair, grunted softly but did not look up to return my gaze. With all of the people having left the room, he had quit smiling like a goofball all the time, reverting instead to a Jake smile; a tightening around his eyes and a raised eyebrow. They say you can spot an evil man because he'll smile only with his mouth but not his eyes. Whether that's true or not, Jake smiles only with his eyes when he's being genuine.

Instead of answering me, he instead asked, "What did you see, please?"

I sat down on the couch across from Jake so I could look straight at him. "None of the right guys want to be in charge in that group, that's what."

"Mmm," Jake nodded. "That's a good point. I was having a hard time pinpointing who to focus on, but that makes things much clearer. Gibs is probably as close as it gets but did you see him when he recounted Denver? I believe he's taken the reins only because he refuses to trust anyone else."

"Oh, trust issues? Do you think that will be a problem?"

"Potentially, but not because he's malicious. He'll have a hard time living with himself after Kyle and Jessica; he's considering civilian deaths his own personal fault."

"Civilian?" I said.

"Yes, he's still very much a Marine in his mind."

I didn't know what to say to that, so I picked my glass up off the table to give my hands something to do. Finally, I held it up and asked, "So, are you going to explain your big performance to me, or what?"

He shrugged again. "Edgar gave me an opportunity, really. I took it."

"An opportunity for what?"

Jake finally looked in my direction. He seemed tired. "To get a sense of who he is. He was a bit of a question mark before then."

I couldn't even begin to figure out what Jake had discovered through his little act and lacked the energy to spend on it. "Fill me in."

"He's a coward who has convinced himself that he's brave. He'll see to his own needs first. Unfortunately, the group is a package deal. He'll need watching."

11

THE SLEEPOVER

Gibs

After the meeting with Jake and Amanda, the four of us gathered everyone else together out by the food tables, which by then had been completely cleaned of any food. Not a scrap was left; everyone had made it a point to eat everything they could carry. I saw more than a few food blisters with guts pushing out past their belts.

The kids were perfectly happy to hang out on the porch, so we left them alone, which was probably best anyway given our discussion. The exception here were the Page brothers (Greg and Alan). You could legitimately argue either that they were kids or adults based on any number of factors. They had both insisted on being included in our conversation, which cemented them as adults for me.

George, Wang, Edgar, and I laid out the whole discussion for everyone else to consider in short order. I think we all did a pretty good job. Editorializing was kept to a minimum in favor of relaying solid facts. When we had finished, George, who was leaning against one of the tables, asked everyone what they thought.

"It sounds pretty good to me, honestly," said Fred. "I mean, I don't know what the rest of y'all think, but I'm sick and tired of not having a place. First, it was a damned grocery store, and now we're living on a school bus? The hell of it is I don't even know which of those is worse."

"There isn't actually a place for us to stay, here," Monica said, looking around at everyone. "It's a big valley, a single house, and a giant garage. You can bet they're not putting all of us in the house. They gonna stick us in the garage or are we just on our own on the bus?"

"Hell, put my ass in a tent for now. We can always put a roof up," Fred replied. Oscar pointed in Fred's direction and shot him a thumbs-up, which the much larger man returned with a nod.

George laughed softly and said, "Well, they've already made it clear that we can stay here for the night. Whether we do or not, I think we all know we can survive another evening sleeping on the bus. We would have ended up doing that here or anywhere. As Fred suggests, though, this could be a place to build on."

A few people nodded to this and considered things silently. I kept my yap shut, feeling that it wasn't my place to try and sway people one way or the other. If they were going to stay, they needed to come around to that decision on their own.

"I feel I should point out that this isn't our only choice," said Wang. Everyone in the group turned their attention on him, and he continued, "This valley isn't the only place in the area we can stay. I know I saw at least a couple of neighborhoods in the surrounding area as we drove in. We could just drive into one of those, pick whatever houses we like, and set up there. It's not like we need to talk to a realtor or anything."

"That'd be a little awkward, wouldn't it?" asked Rebecca.

"Awkward how?"

"Well," she said, "we'd be setting ourselves up as competitors, wouldn't we? It's like Jake said; wherever we end up, we need to be collecting as much food as we can to buy enough time to figure something better out. If we do what you say, we're basically fighting over the same food in this area."

"That's a really good point," George said. "Things could come to a head."

"Not to mention our first night would probably be spent dragging bodies out of homes and fumigating…" Rebecca shuddered.

"I don't think going to any random set of homes should be an option," stated Jeff, surprising myself and others. Jeff Durand, who I'd always thought of as an ageless man-boy, was whisper-quiet most of the time. He was of average height with the build of a perpetually underweight teenager. His bearing and appearance made it damned hard to tell his actual age but, if I were forced to guess, I'd say he was a lot closer to his thirties than his teens. He was exactly the kind of person you'd expect to be playing a high school student in a bad 80's movie.

"How would we prevent someone from just coming by and forcing their way in?" Jeff asked. "We need a place that's protected. Somewhere we can keep the kids safe while we're out doing our thing."

Monica and Oscar both considered this, very carefully it seemed.

"This whole thing has me pretty concerned, frankly," Edgar blurted. When he didn't elaborate, I said, "Go on."

He looked at me and said, "Look, I know you, and I haven't always seen eye to eye but just hear me out on this one, okay?"

"I'm listening, man, we all are. Let's hear it."

"I'm worried about us all becoming a bunch of second class citizens around here," he said. "They seem pretty friendly, but Jake didn't make any effort to hide their chief interest. They need help accomplishing things here. Labor. What keeps them from setting themselves up pretty while we all bust around like a bunch of worker drones?"

"Well, there are sixteen of us," I offered.

"Meaning what, exactly? You're suggesting we kill them and take this place?" he asked. His expression was horrified, which went a long way to restore some of my faith in him.

"Oh, hell no, I'll break my foot off in anyone who suggests doing so seriously. You," I pointed at Fred, "I might just have to shoot. You might hurt me." He laughed and shook his head before shambling over to the other table and leaning his weight against it. He kept closer to the end where he would be over the table legs, and thus the strongest point, but it still sagged alarmingly under him.

I continued, "I just meant that two people can't really force sixteen people to do anything, can they? What are they going to do? Hold us at gunpoint? Two people can't keep sixteen people under control like that and still have them mobile enough to be doing work around here. They'd spend more time guarding us than doing anything else."

"It wouldn't necessarily happen like that," Edgar responded. "They could do it slowly."

His statement stopped me. I couldn't see how but something about the way he said it tickled something at the back of my mind. "I'm listening."

"How do you think dictators and fascists hold onto their power? They used to control whole nations where everyone lived under horrible, substandard conditions. What kept the citizens from rising up against the guy in charge?"

George was nodding, now, and said, "Primus inter pares."

I wasn't exactly a scholar of extinct languages, but I'd caught up with the concept by that point.

"I'm sorry, what does that mean?" Alish asked.

"What they mean," I said, "Is that, over a period of time, they establish a hierarchy around here; a small power structure. Within that hierarchy, some people will enjoy more privileges, get nicer things. We're talking about a long game, here. This isn't something where they come out tomorrow and say 'Okay, Alish, you're now the President of the well and it's your job to ration out water.' That wouldn't work. But over a long period of time, months probably, you could build up enough structures and relationships around here where certain people just have it nicer than others. It might be as simple as job assignments, you know? The idea is that those people with the nicer setups will want to hold onto that and will work for the ones in charge to maintain the status quo."

"Jesus Christ," Monica whispered. "You really think they'd try that?" She looked around at us, and a realization seemed to strike her. "Do you really think that would work on us?"

"Probably not," George said. "I don't think the group is large enough for something like that to take hold. We're too small and too tight. I used to cover this stuff when I taught high school history. I think you'd need at least fifty people to get something like that off the ground. Your population needs to reach some critical mass where folks can exist as acquaintances or even strangers. It's still a damned good point that Edgar makes. It's something to keep in the backs of our minds, anyway."

"Agreed," I said, and Edgar looked surprised.

Davidson chose that moment to speak up. "So, will someone tell me what the hell we're doing? I feel like we've been going in circles."

"I vote we stay," Oscar said. "My man Jeff is right. All this other stuff aside, you can't beat the area. We can leave the kids here with a small number of grownups while we go out and get the bacon. They'll be safe here. If that Jake dude wants to get stupid, I can just give him a little beat down to keep him in line, like."

"You think Jake is someone you can just give a little beat down?" asked Barbara, who had been uncharacteristically silent since we'd arrived.

"What's on your mind, Barbara? You seem worried," George asked.

"I don't know," she said. "Amanda seems okay. She's a hard woman, but she has a young daughter. I can understand and respect that. Jake is… something else. He makes me nervous."

"How?" I asked.

"I just said I don't know. Look, does anyone else get the impression that something is off with him?"

"Yes," Wang said. "I felt like he was playing a role."

"Could just be playing his cards close," Fred suggested. "He did just invite sixteen armed people to come live with him."

"Yeah, maybe," Barbara said.

"I could try to get close to him and see," suggested Rebecca.

"What?" I asked.

She rolled her eyes at me. "Come on. You know…"

"Holy shit," I said. "Sorry, excuse me. No, you're not doing that. Nobody has to do that."

Rebecca nodded, cheeks burning, looking relieved. I saw Davidson loosen up as well out of the corner of my eye.

We all had an awkward little silence after that, which I suspect we all needed after Rebecca's unsettling fucking offer. It made me feel really uncomfortable that we were in a situation where she felt like such a thing needed to be an option. The fact that I had considered it, even if only for a fraction of a second, was equally alarming. I remember feeling thrown way off balance at this point and lost myself for a few moments digging around in my own head; asking myself questions and finding no answers. When I came back to myself, I noticed a lot of faces staring back at me, all packing unanswered questions behind their eyes. This elevated my personal level of agitation even higher, obviously.

"What? What's everyone looking at?"

Davidson shot an exaggerated shrug at me, "Are we staying or not, man?"

"Oh, goddamnit, that ain't my call. You people have to agree on what seems right for you. I'm just in charge of keeping you all safe—"

"Can I suggest," George cut in over my tirade, "that we play it by ear? It's late enough now that we're probably not going anywhere tonight, anyway. It's just Jake and Amanda. They can't force us to stay if we don't wish to do so. It could be that this is just what we were looking for. Let's sleep on it."

Several nodded at this, to my great relief, and the tight little knot of people began to break up. Smaller subgroups wandered off to various areas; I noticed Fred and Barbara began to bustle about the tables, stacking up trays and cleaning up. Most of the cookware was ceramic or Tupperware, yet there was still a good deal of trash out there to be taken care of. I began to idly wonder about how they disposed of trash around here. It wasn't as though a city trash service came through to offload the refuse and take it to the dump. This thought led me naturally to the challenge of waste disposal.

Jake's cabin would have been built with a septic tank; there's no way a tie-in for city sewage was brought all the way out to this location. So, in a pinch, we could use the toilets in the cabin, assuming we had enough water on hand to charge the tank for a flush. The only problem there was that Jake and Amanda probably wouldn't be terribly happy about sixteen people stomping through the house all day and night to make a head call. This would be one of those problems we'd need to solve soon to avoid wearing out our welcome. I started looking around the area for a good spot to dig a deep hole.

"Give us a minute, please, guys," George said, bringing me back to the present.

Davidson, Wang, and Edgar were all muttering some form of the phrase "no problem" and moving off to positions of their choice a respectful distance away. I looked to George and asked, "What's this?"

"Gibs, I have a pretty good handle on where you're coming from with these folks, but, well, if you're going to be in charge, you need to be in charge. You can't suddenly abdicate if you get asked a hard question."

Maybe it was his choice of words or the way he delivered them, but I started to get a little pissed. "Hey, horse shit, alright? This wasn't some issue concerning the group's safety, the question under discussion was basically, 'Hey, Gibs, tell us where we'd like to live.' Exactly how much hand-holding do you consider to be appropriate, here? Shall I wipe noses and asses while I'm at it?"

George had his hands up with the palms extended at me in a 'calm down' gesture. "Okay, okay, easy. I'm sure I delivered that wrong. All I'm trying to say is that when you establish yourself as the leader under one set of circumstances, people are going to expect you to take charge under all circumstances. If you look indecisive under any of these, they're going to start second guessing you when it counts, or at least when it has to do with a subject about which you feel strongly. Can you see what I'm saying? You can't have it both ways with followers. You're either all the way in charge, or you're not in charge at all."

"Yeah," I agreed, "that sounds a lot better than talking some shit about 'abdicating responsibility.' Nice revise."

I was starting to cool off a bit and got a good look at George, who was staring off in the direction of Jake's huge garage. He had that kicked-dog expression that always drives me up the wall. I used to get it all the time from my Marines after lighting them up for some stupid thing they had done. It used to infuriate me. You walk in on some moron igniting his pubic hair with a fucking zippo, and suddenly you've gotta feel like the asshole for spoiling everyone's fun. I never understood how it was that I ended up being the dick after correcting someone else for their stupid shit, but there it was.

"Hey, never mind," I said to George. "I get what you're saying. But, man, I can't be the mother duck. I left that shit behind for a reason; poor sleep and premature hair loss are only a part of it. I'll snap asses back when it comes to safety, and I'll absolutely take a round to keep these people alive. I just can't do their thinking for them. I'm drawing the line there."

George nodded, glanced back at the cabin, and looked back at me. "Well, let's play it by ear, like I said. Maybe it's a problem that takes care of itself."

I wasn't sure what he was alluding to, but I frankly didn't have enough energy to give a shit; I just let the comment pass by like so much dust on the wind. My nerves had been ratcheted up to eleven for the last several days. I was only getting a couple of hours of sleep a night towards the end; a combination of trying to rack out on that goddamned bus, worrying about keeping everyone fed, and my stupid brain trying to turn every little sound heard in the middle of the night into creeping bandits. We were finally in a strong, isolated area where provisions were no longer an immediate problem to be solved, and I didn't feel like I had to be constantly looking over my shoulder for an ambush. As I felt my body starting to crash from running too long at full capacity on fumes, I was a little shocked to realize that I desperately hoped Jake was on the up and up. I wanted terribly for this place to work out for us. I couldn't lose any more people on some endless hunt for a home.

"Hey, where are you off to?" George asked from behind me; my feet had started moving (almost on their own) without me signaling my intent.

"I'm going to go tell them it's a deal and beg for a rack. If I have to sleep in a bus for one more night, I'm going to shoot myself."

The front door opened almost as soon as I knocked, revealing Jake on the other side. I could see Amanda standing not far behind him. He said nothing; only looked at me and waited to hear what I would say.

"We, uh, would like to take you up on your offer. I'm not sure where you're going to put us all, but we're willing if you are."

He smiled at me then, and I want to say it was the first time I saw him really smile, though he'd been doing it at everyone all day. There was something in the way it made you feel that let you know for sure. There wasn't a great deal of change in his face when he did it, but his eyes let me know it was for real; they made all the difference.

"I'm glad," he said and extended his hand to shake. I took it and was mildly shocked at how it felt. His hand was fat and meaty through the palm and, though it was only of average size, I had a hard time getting a good grip around it. The texture of the skin was all leathery, and the surface of the palm was sharp with callus. I could feel the bones moving around inside of it until he started to squeeze; when he did, the soft parts broadened and became hard, like his fist itself was expanding. The pressure exerted on my hand stopped just short of discomfort.

He let go of my hand and said, "I don't think we'll ask you to sleep on the bus or outdoors tonight; you've all had a rough road. I'm sure we can find room for you all here even if we have to break out the air mattresses."

"I assure you," I said, "air mattresses would be just fu—just freaking dandy."

From behind Jake, Amanda called out to me with a smile, "You've done that a few times today; correct yourself mid-sentence like that." She walked up to stand beside Jake in the entry.

I grimaced and nodded. "Yeah, sorry. That's my underdeveloped vocabulary coming through. I only have about half of it available when I'm in polite company."

Her smile widened, and I saw that she was genuinely, almost exotically attractive. Then again, I've always had a thing for the Hispanic girls.

"Gibs, I can't speak for everyone else but, as far as I'm concerned, strong language doesn't bother me a fucking bit. You should have seen the cousins I grew up with. They used "fuck" like a comma."

I snickered and said, "I think I may have served with your cousins."

"Well, that's unlikely," she said. "They tended to end up in jail every so often. I know the Corps frowns on that. Anyway, all I'm saying is you don't need to be like that around me. Just say what you're going to say."

"Okay, I'll keep that in mind," I said. "So, should I grab everyone, then? Oh, hell! I don't mean to be pushy but what are you guys doing for showers around here? We've all got at least a week or more of *road* caked onto us. You probably don't want us crawling into beds smelling like bags of smashed ass."

"Linens can be washed, but we can get a bath going for you guys," Jake said. "It'll probably take the rest of the evening for everyone to get a turn. We have a couple of rain barrels outside that we can draw from. This will take a while, though; we should heat it up over a fire, or it'll be like ice. I'm also sorry to say that there won't be enough for everyone to get a fresh bath… we'll have to reuse the water a bit."

My skin was already starting to crawl before he'd finished the sentence. The thought of sponging off with other peoples' ass grease set me to squirming on the spot. It didn't help that I knew, intellectually, that I'd been caked head to heel in some of the foulest material imaginable in my long, lovely career in the

Infantry or that I was every bit as nasty as everyone else. Sure I was disgusting, but that was all my filth. All that other filth was… foreign filth; tainted.

I suppressed a shiver and said, "We'll make it work. I'll head out and let everyone know."

"Excellent," said Jake. He turned to Amanda and started asking about air mattresses as I walked back out of the house to update everyone on the plans for the night.

It took the rest of the evening to get all sixteen of us washed and presentable, the whole thing turning into a group effort as we went. They had an old oil drum set up as a hobo fire pit outside between the cabin and garage where they burned most of their trash. There was a good cord of wood stacked up along the wall of the cabin outside just under the bedroom windows; some of the logs were thrown into the drum along with our trash from the evening and ignited. Very soon there was a strong blaze jutting up out of the top of the barrel and over this was positioned a grill and a massive, five-gallon kettle filled with water from the rain barrels. We placed it there long enough to just start boiling (which was a pretty decent amount of time given how much water it could hold), after which two of us would grab it by the handles and haul it inside to the bottom floor bathroom to dump in the tub.

One pot translated into depressingly very little water in the tub, so we had to boil two pots to get enough water to cover just up to a person's ankles. Once we had that (and once the water had cooled enough to just be on the safe side of scalding), we'd send someone in to sit in the puddle with a washrag and a bar of soap with the goal of taking up no more than five minutes; at ten I'd start hammering on the door.

Our original plan was to try and get three people to one fill, but the water was so horrifyingly grimy after just two that I vetoed the whole idea. There were some people who were willing to do it, but I don't think I could have slept that night if I'd allowed it. Despite the fact that we had to boil sixteen kettles of water that night and depleted one fifty-five-gallon rain barrel down to nearly empty, we got a pretty good rhythm going once we got the hang of it. The trick was to have a kettle on the fire at all times, whether we thought we needed it or not. In that way, we could have one up to a boil right around the time the second person was stepping out of the tub. We also learned that it wasn't necessary to bring both kettles up to a boil; just the first one. For the second, it was enough to get it lukewarm; once it was poured into the scalding water in the tub, the combined temperatures would normalize down to something a human being could handle, and the water would remain comfortable long enough to accommodate two people.

Each person had a new set of clothes waiting for them after the bath was over. In most cases, these were shirts and baggy sweat pants with the exception of Fred, who would have looked like he was wearing capris. He got a pair of athletic shorts just large enough to be comfortable, though they were still too snug to be decent (the poor guy was walking around hunched over at the hips with his face flushed; I considered calling him "Knuckles" as a gag but decided against it, not wanting to chance getting hammered flat into the ground).

Sleeping arrangements were handled efficiently. Amanda and Elizabeth took the master bedroom upstairs while Barbara and Rebecca shared the bed in the second room on the other side of the loft. George and Oscar took the king bed downstairs, and Monica, her daughter Rose, Maria, Alish, Greg, and Alan all took bunks in the last room, which typically belonged to Elizabeth. Jeff and Wang took couches in the rear entertainment room while Edgar took the easy chair. Fred and Davidson each got an air mattress; we stuck one in the center of the entertainment room between the couches and the other in the dining area; we pulled the table and chairs over tight up against the kitchen.

That left me with the couch in the front room where we had all conducted our meeting with Jake and Amanda earlier that day. I was surprised to see Jake easing back into his chair across from me at the end of the night when everyone else was settled into their various beds.

Quietly, so as not to disturb anyone else in the house, I asked, "You're sleeping there?"

He smiled. "Not many places left. It's this or pitch a tent outside."

"Huh. I would have thought you'd just take the bed up with Amanda."

"Why?"

I stumbled over the answer for this. I realized I had been making some assumptions about them without any real evidence. "Well, I guess I just thought that you two… you know."

Jake nodded slowly and said, "It's not like that. It's different."

I didn't know what the hell to make of that, so I just grunted. Jake killed the lantern and put his chin down on his chest. The house was already filling up with the soft sound of snoring from all the different corners that had been stuffed full of people.

I closed my eyes, went under almost instantly, and had an unrestful sleep.

1 2

INTERVIEWS, ONE

Wang

I remember that our earliest days on the commune were full of interviews. This is strange, now, for me to recall because it feels like a whole lifetime ago and I'm not sure if any of us knew what was going on while this was happening. We all kind of compared notes sometime after we'd settled in and figured out that both Jake and Amanda had worked through each of us early on, getting a handle on who we are; our strengths and probably our weaknesses too.

I can't even tell you who was approached first or what sequence this happened in. All I know for sure is when Jake came to find me.

I'm pretty sure I woke up before anyone else on the first morning. It was still dark, and I was disoriented enough that I reached out into empty space trying to find the back of a bus seat with my hand to orient myself; after several seconds of confusion, I remembered where I was. I heard the sounds of deep breathing and Fred's snoring soon after; realized everything was probably okay.

I felt a sharp cramp in my stomach, deep down between my hips, and realized that this is what must have woken me up. The pain felt like a knife digging around inside of me; I immediately understood that I had to go to the bathroom. It had been a few days since any of us had had a decent meal and last night I'd stuffed myself full, so I guess my body was just having a hard time getting used to being fed again. I think that canned fruit might have played a part as well.

I carefully stood from the couch and walked around Tom and Fred, who were both lined up on the floor on air mattresses. I was having a hard time seeing anything; for one thing, I was still fuzzy from sleep, but there's also the fact that not a lot of moonlight makes it into the back part of that house. The rear is pretty much covered with thick tree growth, plus the largest opening in the back had been covered over with a big sheet of wood. The rear of the house is dim even during the middle of the day because of this. Once I turned left around the corner into the main hall, it became easier to see as more light from the moon and stars was able to come in through the front windows.

I had a shock when I came through the front room and saw Jake sitting in his chair. At first, I thought he was just sitting there quietly next to Gibs, who was still asleep and waiting for the rest of us to wake up, which would have been intensely disturbing. I froze in place for a few seconds waiting for him to acknowledge me before I realized that his chin was down and he was asleep. My stomach cramped again, reminding me that I had problems to take care of, so I continued down the main hall towards the front door, rounded the corner back down the smaller side hall, and found the bathroom.

I'm not going to get all gross about what happened in there but what I'll offer here is that I had forgotten how nice it was to use a clean toilet that still flushed. We'd all been sharing dead commodes on the road for so long that using "pre-filled" facilities was something we were all familiar with. Being able to sit down and… take some time on an unspoiled toilet had become a luxury. When I found the full roll of toilet paper, I thought I'd died and gone to heaven.

I knew it was time to leave when I started feeling pins and needles in my legs. I finished up, put myself back together, and flushed; the sound of the toilet doing what toilets do was surreal. It was so… normal! I'd gone so long without hearing it that I experienced something like a wave of nostalgia or déjà vu… or something. This is harder to describe than I thought it would be; I was confused by that sound, as though there was a part of me that knew there was supposed to be a world in which light switches made light, toilets flushed, and ordinary people didn't try to shoot each other, and still another part of me that understood that all of this was now gone, perhaps forever.

There were two large jugs of water on the sink, both of which I poured into the toilet tank for the next person that would inevitably be in there. I collected the jugs to refill outside of the house at the rain barrel.

I exited through the front door of the house and probably would have crapped myself if I hadn't just taken care of business a moment ago. Jake was sitting out on the front porch, now awake, apparently. I never heard him move through the house or open the door; I suffered a childish urge to look back into the house and see if he was still sleeping in the front room. Ultimately I didn't… but I can't say that I wasn't at least a little nervous about what I would have seen if I did.

It was a shock to see him sitting there, like I said, and I blurted out something like, "What the hell?"

Jake raised a hand and whispered, "Easy. You'll wake the others."

"Sorry," I whispered back. "I wasn't expecting you there."

He nodded and gestured to a chair to his right on the other

side of a small wooden table that still had some of the tree bark on it. "Join me?"

"I should refill these," I said stupidly, holding up the jugs.

"You've refilled the tank already, right? You have time. We'll hear the next time the toilet flushes. You can refill them and take them back then."

I shrugged and moved around him to have a seat, placing the jugs on the table between us.

"I'll make coffee in a little while when the others start to wake up," he said. I was a tea drinker, personally, but I knew a lot of the others would appreciate this.

He fell silent for a while after that. I glanced over at him out of the corner of my eye while trying not to be obvious about it. He seemed to have forgotten that I was out there with him; his eyes were cast up to the sky with an expression hard to describe. His eyebrows were raised a little and beetled together at the center; the eyes themselves squinted and shined. His lips were cracked open just enough so that he could breathe; it was clear to anyone that whatever was left of his nose didn't do much more than take up area on his face. He sounded like an old boxer when he spoke; like a mouth breather. It gave you incorrect impressions about who he was. Thinking back on it, I'd have to use the word "wonder" to describe what I saw in his eyes.

"I don't know if I'm ever going to get used to this view," he said quietly, eyes still locked forward.

I looked out in the same direction and saw what he meant. The sun was just starting to peak up over the horizon but was still hidden behind the mountain wall, so the only hint of it we could see was the outline of the mountain ridge itself, a pure black contrast, lined by a deep red sky which immediately gave way to indigo before reverting to black. There wasn't a cloud up there; the entire sky was packed end to end with stars, just big, sweeping, bright waves of stars everywhere. The world all around us was impenetrable, solid black with that yawning sky stretched out above us. I felt as though I was looking down into a reflection on the surface of some great lake; like I might begin to fall up into the sky if I didn't look away.

I said the first thing that came to mind. "Holy shit. I've never seen anything like this."

"I feel sometimes as though I have no business seeing this."

"What?" I asked. "Why?"

Finally, he turned to look at me. I was certain he was going to answer; the shadow of his lips flexed like he was about to form words. He turned his head back to look out ahead of us again and sighed just loud enough for me to hear.

"It'll get better shortly as the sun moves higher," he said.

He was right. During the normal day time, you don't notice the sun so much. It's the last thing you want to look at because it will hurt you, so you're really only aware of it as something bright and hot above you somewhere. Mostly, what you see is the blue sky above. You don't realize how deceptively fast the sun moves across the sky unless you watch a sunrise or a sunset. As we sat there, not talking, the heavens above us shifted from black to red-pink to blue, and the valley out in front of us morphed from formless void to open, green fields ringed on all sides by tree covered mountains.

"You know," I said, "I think this is the first time I've ever sat out and watched a sunrise."

"Not an outdoor type?"

"Not really. Most of my life has been spent with my head in a book, like my parents. They spent their whole lives in books. My mom was a copy editor, see? My dad, well, he was something else."

Jake looked at me (and I mean *really* looked at me for probably the first time) and said, "Tell me." He rested his chin on his right fist.

I chewed a lip while mentally composing the most efficient way to explain. "My dad was an architect. Mostly, that means he spent all of his time buried in paperwork. He was either reviewing proposals, going over plans, meeting with clients, reviewing cost estimates, or off in a meeting somewhere. And, because he was an architect, it means I was studying to be one as well. Like I said: lots of books."

"Oh, really?" he said, perking up. "How far along in your studies were you?"

"I was about a year out from graduating. I was far enough along that I was interning at a firm."

"Did you enjoy it?"

His question pulled me up short. Before, when all was still normal, people always sounded impressed if I told them what I was studying in college. There was this initial reaction of "Oh, wow! That must be really cool!" and then they'd spend the next several minutes asking me what an architect actually does. No one had ever asked me if I enjoyed it before. I had to think about it.

"Well," I finally said, "my dad would have told you 'yes.' Then again, he also would have confidently listed my four favorite foods and gotten all of them wrong. He was a lot better at drinking and demanding silence than he was at knowing things about me."

"I see."

"Maybe you see, but I'm not sure." I sighed. "I don't know, man. It was okay, I guess. I seemed to be good at it, what little of it I actually got to do before being an architect became obsolete."

"Oh, I wouldn't say it's obsolete," Jake said, shifting in his seat. "I'm sure there're all kinds of ways to put a specialized skill like that to use these days."

"Doing what?" I laughed. "Designing a new shopping mall? Organizing client meetings and submitting plans to the city? Hey,

I know!" I pointed out in front of us at a spot on the ground some thirty feet away. "We'll put a giant exterior water feature right over there; it'll really class the place up."

I leaned back in my chair and sighed. "I'll get on the phone after lunch and start lining up subcontractors. Can I use your landline or is that, like, a thing?"

Jake took everything I said passively, which I suppose I was happy for. If he'd been annoyed at my outburst, it wouldn't have been the first time my mouth got me in trouble.

Finally, he said, "Everyone has to adapt, Wang. Even architects. There are new requirements, now, certainly, but there are things we can all do to be useful. You'll learn to handle a weapon soon, if you haven't already, and you'll contribute at the least with scavenging and protecting your people. But don't completely throw away your skills from the old world. One day, we'll need to build something bigger than a wooden box, and you'll be there to help us figure out how. More importantly, you'll be there to pass on what you know and what you learn to the children so that the knowledge we took for granted doesn't become a lost secret."

He stood up from his seat, stretched his arms out to either side, triceps bunching up and twitching as he did, and growled. "And now, speaking of adaptation," he said, "I have my own to see to."

He nodded to me and trotted off the front porch.

"Where you going?" I called after him.

"Garage. I have some heavy things to move around."

I stood up and moved to follow. "Do you need a hand?"

He stopped, turned back to me, looked me up and down, and smiled. "Sure," he said. "Come on. I'll teach you how to squat."

"What?"

13

INTERVIEWS, TWO

Fred

I don't rightly know how the rest of the folks I was traveling with felt about staying at Jake's place on that first night, but for me? I was sold on the whole thing. I had just woke up from the first good night's sleep that I could remember in I don't know how long and, for once, my knees and my hips weren't hurting me. Remember, now, that I had gone from sleeping on a hard, linoleum supermarket floor that I had tried (and failed) to soften up with scraps of clothing and other shit, to sleeping on the nasty ass floor of that school bus. I'd tried at first to stretch across the rows of seats, but it just didn't work out. I was too wide to lie on the seat properly, and the bench rows on those buses are staggered, so I couldn't get my legs across the aisle right. I always ended up on the floor.

I was on the floor again in Jake's house as well, only this time, they put me on a large air mattress. And even if my feet did hang off and my ass was starting to rest on the floor by the time I woke up, it was still a night of sleep with no pressure on my spine or any of my joints. I woke up happy.

I noticed everyone else was awake already when I sat up and started moving around. Tom and Jeff were talking quietly, and Gibs was over on my right poking around in the kitchen. Wang was gone already, I noticed, along with Edgar.

"Mornin'," I said. "How long's everyone been up?"

"Forever, Sunshine," Gibs said from the kitchen. "We couldn't sleep through all your snoring."

"Yeah, least I wasn't fartin' all night, asshole," I said. "What the hell, Tom? We need to get you to see a doctor, or what?"

"That wasn't me, man! That was Wang!"

"Wang?" I laughed. "Wang ain't big enough to bust ass as nasty as what I smelled."

"Whatever, man," Tom said. "Wasn't me."

I tried to sit up out of my bed, but it was so low on air that the damned thing just spooned me back into the ground every time I tried. I struggled around on my back like some kind of drunk turtle when Gibs approached from the side, laughing, the bastard.

"Hey, can I give you a hand, Fred?"

"You mean can you stop laughing long enough to help me up? Yes, please."

He took one of my hands in both of his and pulled me around to at least a kneeling position; I made it up the rest of the way after that. My back popped in all the right places as I got up, and I groaned happily. I hadn't been able to take deep, real chest-expanding breaths in weeks but I was beginning to feel like everything might be settling back into its right place that morning.

I pulled a deep stretch and held it just long enough for a muscle in my back to cramp up before shaking everything out and groaning happily. Tensing everything up like that woke my bladder up as well, so I said, "Just a minute, boys. Gotta see a man about a horse," and went down the hallway to find the bathroom.

Using the facilities was its own little treat as well, being as how the toilet was clean and all. I finished up my business, flushed, and enjoyed the sound of working, running water for a moment before walking back out to return to the kitchen.

The only complaint I can really come up with from that morning was how tight and uncomfortable those damned shorts were. I was grateful to have something clean to wear, but I couldn't do much more than shuffle around without danger of detaching something important or busting loose. I began to shift my balls around with my right hand while scratching my ass with my left as I came through the entryway to the dining area and said, "So what's a man have to do around here to get some breakfast?"

I was met with Amanda staring back at me while I just stood there like an idiot holding my boys and Gibs started laughing so hard from his spot by the sink that, if anyone in that house was still asleep, they had sure woken the fuck up by that point.

She very kindly kept from commenting on the situation or looking below my chest but she also didn't bother hiding a smile as she said, "Well, you need to help set the tables up outside and drag the burner out to start."

I let everything drop and looked for some better place to put my hands, placing them on my hips first and then deciding that crossing my arms in front of me was better.

"'Scuse me. Yeah, I can do that. I'll just get some shoes on and get at it."

"Wash your hands first, okay?" she giggled, and both Gibs and Tom started rolling again. "I'll go grab you guys a few things."

She walked out of the room and that asshole Tom called out after her, "Yeah, I think we've grabbed enough things of our own, thanks!" That one even made me laugh.

I shot Tom a "Dick…" and dug my shoes out from under the corner of my mattress after I pulled the plug to let all the air out. I folded the thing up as tight as I could get it (they never get as tight as they were when you first opened the box) and slid it under the table before sitting down in a chair to put my shoes on. Standing up and yawning, I stretched one last time, loving the ability to do it right, and started walking towards the door in that tired, early morning slide-step you do when you're still trying to get your day going.

"Oh, damn, are you going outside like that?" asked Gibs.

"Ain't got anything that'll fit me except my jeans from before, and I can't bring myself to put them on now that I'm clean."

"Huh. Good point. We'll look into getting you squared away. There has to be some sort of Big Ass Hombre clothing store around town."

"Appreciate it," I said and went through the front door.

Once outside, I stepped off the porch and walked around to the side of the house where I'd stacked the tables from the night before, grabbed one in each hand, and walked them back out to where I'd first seen them set up last night. I got them positioned and was just about to go looking for the propane camping grill when I heard the unmistakable sound of metal barbell plates clanging together coming from the direction of the garage. I noticed then that the roll-up door was open; I walked toward it to see what was up.

When the opening came into view, I saw for the first time just how big that garage really was. It'll fool you at first because it's hard to see how far back it goes from all the trees wrapped around it; when you see inside, you see all the way back. That building is deep and tall. All us folks could have probably lived in there if it hadn't been full of a bunch of shit already. There was a large Ford off to the side and what looked like a whole garage shop deep in the back. The floor around the center was stacked full of piles of what looked to me like all the food in the world, although we found out later that it wasn't nearly as much as we would have liked. Along the right wall, I saw Jake standing with his hands on his hips staring intently at Wang, who had a barbell up on his shoulders loaded with what looked like some decent warm-up weight for his size. He took a deep breath, squatted down low, and came up again, slowing down only a little at the midpoint. Jake helped him walk it back into the rack after that. I waited until Wang had the weight off his back before saying anything.

"Looking good, there, young man!" I called as I walked in to join them.

Wang looked at me and smiled but said nothing; he was breathing heavy and sweating.

"I was just teaching him how to squat. He's actually pretty good; it didn't take long at all for him to get the movement pattern down," said Jake.

"Yeah, I saw," I agreed. "Straight bar path and the plates didn't spin on the way up."

Jake's eyebrows rose. "Are you a lifter?"

"Not so much anymore. I played ball in high school—defensive tackle—so I know my way around a barbell."

"Oh, nice," Jake said. "Well, the rack is here, and you're welcome to it any time. I recommend everyone use it if they can."

"Thanks but I'd better get this clothing situation taken care of first. I'm indecent enough already without squatting down and sticking my ass out," I said.

Jake nodded. "Yes, there is that. I'm going to head out today and start looking for long term shelter solutions for you guys; I'll keep my eye out for some clothing for you. What's your size in pants?"

"Forty-inch waist, thirty-four-inch length."

He blinked for a minute and then said, "Well… we'll see what's out there."

"You think that's bad? Try keeping him fed. It's like trying to bury a Buick in sand with a teaspoon," said Wang.

I started laughing and slapped my gut, which was a lot smaller these days than I was used to it being. "On second thought, better make that a thirty-eight-inch waist. I'm not as thick as I once was."

"Very well," Jake agreed.

"Hey, listen," I said, "where did you guys stash the grill? Amanda asked me to set it up so we can get some breakfast going."

"It's in a closet in the house. Come on with me, and I'll show you."

"Hey, I'm going to stay here and do some more," said Wang.

"Nope," Jake said. "You got your three sets of five. Don't overdo it or you'll screw everything up."

"Screw what up? You mean I'll hurt myself?"

"No, no. I have a book that explains all of this. I'll show you. It covers everything."

Jake led us both back to the house and dug the grill out from the closet under the stairs for me and then took Wang back to the library. Amanda was back in the dining area, now, talking to Gibs. I could see that she had laid out a whole selection of plastic cups, toothbrushes, and toothpaste for everyone on the table. My mouth hung open at the sight of this, and I almost dropped the grill at my feet to go grab one of each and put it all to use. With our recent water shortage and lack of supplies, caring for our teeth had been reduced mainly to rubbing over them with a corner of our shirts, which were already nasty as hell. Clean toothbrushes and full tubes of toothpaste looked like a stack of gold to me.

Amanda came over to me with a big bag of Krusteaz pancake mix under one arm and a gallon jug of water in the other. "You get the tables out?" she asked.

I said I had and she nodded at me all businesslike. She called back behind herself as she stepped around me, "Bring the skillet and that other stuff when you can, Gibs, okay?"

"Roger," he said from the back.

She had the door propped open and was waiting for me. I sighed and made a note to come back for a toothbrush as soon as I could get away. We both went outside and started laying everything out at the table. As soon as she put her stuff down, she turned and ran back to the house.

Amanda's like that. She's always rushing everywhere, like Gibs, except Gibs refuses to run unless there's some sort of life or death situation. Gibs just walks twice as fast as everyone else. Amanda jogs or runs, though. It's funny for me to watch her when she works with Jake, who never rushes anything. The more time he takes, the more carefully he moves, the more agitated and twitchy she gets. She doesn't seem to get mad behind it; I think it might be unconscious. It sure is funny as hell to watch, though.

She had already returned with plates, forks, and syrup when I was just finishing with getting the mini-propane tank screwed on. Gibs came stomping out behind her carrying a big iron skillet along with a plastic bowl containing a bottle of oil, a big wooden spoon, and a spatula.

Other folks started to emerge from the house as she bustled around the table laying things out and called their good-mornings to us from the porch. Amanda thrust a bowl full of watered pancake mix into my hands, passed me the wooden spoon, and said, "If you get going on that I'll go grab us some new potatoes." That sounded fine to me, and I went to work.

"So who was the last person to use the toilet?" Oscar called down from the porch. He was holding the pitchers from the bathroom in his hands; the pitchers I hadn't filled, actually.

"Shit, that was me, man. Sorry 'bout that."

Oscar grinned and said, "It's cool, buddy. Just keep working on breakfast, and we'll call it even." As he came down the steps to go find the rain barrels, he asked, "Whatcha mixing up over there?"

"Pancakes, young man!"

"Awe, yeah, white boy tortillas," he laughed as he disappeared around the side.

Amanda came back with a large pot filled with several unopened cans of potatoes. "How's that going?"

"Getting there," I said, "but it's still lumpy as all hell. Gimme a bit, and we'll be good."

The next few minutes passed in silence as we worked together, Amanda hopping around underfoot like a hummingbird and me just shambling around, like I do, trying not to step on her. Gibs had one of those old-school metal coffee percolators going on the grill by this time; we didn't want to start the potatoes before the pancakes since they would be ready way too soon if we did. We began to smell the coffee right as the batter was finally starting to come into line; the aroma hit me so hard that I almost wanted to cry. I'm not exaggerating here, either. I actually teared up a little. When Gibs put a full cup in front of me, the best I could manage was to choke out a "Thanks" before handing the bowl over to Amanda.

Amanda set the bowl down and started spreading a touch of oil on the skillet. As she prepared to get the pancakes going, she said, "Guys, I'm sure there's a graceful way to bring this up and I'm sure Jake would have been able to do it if he had been out here instead of me, but I'm what you're stuck with, so you're going to get 'blunt' rather than 'finesse.'"

Gibs and I both looked at each other over the rims of our cups with the same wide-eyed expression. Gibs said, "Oh, Christ. This isn't where you tell us about the weekly blood sacrifice, is it?"

"No," she laughed. Amanda is one of those with an honest, hang-it-all-out laugh; it put me at ease. "What I was about to say is that we need to get an idea of everyone's skill set. There are a lot of jobs around here that need to be done; more now that so many people are here. Some of you will come with skills and knowledge that'll be useful to all of us. In some cases, those skills might define what you're expected to do around here."

"Job interviews?" I asked. "I haven't done one of those since I was a kid."

"No, not job interviews," she said. "You guys are all with us whether you're a bunch of geniuses or… not so much geniuses. But the point is, what if one of you were, like, a dentist or a doctor or something? That would be a good thing to know, right?"

"She's got a point," Gibs said quietly before taking a sip of coffee.

"On that subject," Amanda continued, "Gibs? Jake was hoping he could talk to you if you have a minute."

"Well, okay then," said Gibs. "I saw him head inside with Wang. I'll go catch up with him." He saluted both of us with his coffee cup and went off towards the cabin.

"So how about you, big guy?" Amanda asked.

"Been a welder now, oh, fifteen years."

"Really?" she said, sounding pleased. "What kind?"

"Mostly construction stuff, fabrication, all that kind of thing. Had my own truck rig and such; did quite a lot of business in the greater Wichita area."

"Kansas, huh?"

"Yes, ma'am, born and raised," I said.

"So I get what welding is," she said, "but describe fabrication to me."

"Oh, hell, that's just a fancy way to say that I made stuff that you couldn't easily buy already made. Say someone needs a wrought iron fence put up on their property, but they wanted a special gate on it that was a little bit fancier than what you can get from the big name manufacturers? Or even, say someone needed a custom built rolling rack to fit a specific dimension so they could load it with stuff and roll it around on a shop floor? It's basically using my skills as a welder to make some one-off thing to fulfill a specific purpose."

"Sounds like a creative job," Amanda said.

"Yeah, it was," I agreed. "I really enjoyed it; I was good at it too. Before that, I was a forklift operator, but that's pretty mindless work. I wasn't going anywhere with that and got tired of answering to some warehouse boss, so at twenty-nine I decided it was time for a change and went to school."

I finished my coffee and thought for a moment. "I don't really see how this helps us right now, though. We don't have a rig out here; don't have the power to run it…"

"Maybe, maybe not," said Amanda. "From what you're saying, it sounds like you know how to do more than just stick two pieces of metal together. Have you seen the shop?"

"What shop?" Oscar interrupted as he came over to join us. Amanda had gotten a good little stack of pancakes lined up on the side of the table under a towel and was starting to heat up a couple of cans of potatoes on the side. "You got some guero tortillas ready to go, yet?"

"Under the towel," Amanda pointed with her chin.

"You want a plate, Oscar?" I asked.

"Nah, bro, I'm good," he said as he lifted one of the pancakes out from under the cloth, rolled it up just like the tortilla he suggested it was, and bit the end of. His eyes crossed as he groaned. "Oh, holy shit, man. That's really tasty."

"Don't you want any syrup?" asked Amanda. She was laughing at Oscar's expression, which was pretty comical, honestly.

"Nah, it wouldn't be right without butter."

"Oh, hell yes," Amanda nodded. "I miss butter so much. If I could find any that was still good, I think I'd just eat a few spoonfuls of it without anything else."

I could see I was with *my kind of people* and began to laugh out loud. Pointing at them both, I said, "You two are talking my language now! Either of you ever had deep fried butter?"

Oscar hopped in place, pointed back at me, and nodded happily. He put his hand out and bumped fists with me.

"Holy crap, no. It's probably delicious, but I don't think my thighs could have taken it," said Amanda. "I'd just have to cut out the middle man and rub it directly on my legs."

We all stood around laughing at Amanda as she pantomimed the act of spreading butter over her thighs, twisting her face all around and sticking her tongue out.

After we got some control of ourselves, Oscar tried again: "So what was that about a shop?"

"It's in the back of the garage," she said. "There's a whole workshop back there with all kinds of tools and stuff. I don't know how half of them work, but it sounds like Fred might."

"Well, so would Oscar," I said, nodding at him. "He was in construction too, right."

"Yeah," he agreed, "I was a foreman at the end, there. Mostly did a lot of warehouses and stuff but I used to go and work for residential outfits building homes when the work slowed down."

He crammed the last of the pancake into his mouth and, still chewing, asked, "'s it cool if I go over and check it out?"

"Sure," Amanda said. "Don't try to run anything, though. I think we have to switch the batteries over before you do."

"Hey, that reminds me of something I was thinking about this morning," Oscar said after he swallowed. "You said your friend Billy had this place custom built, right?"

"That's right," she said.

"So maybe you know. I get that this place is sitting on a septic tank, right?"

"If you say so."

"Okay, cool, but, um, where's the water coming from?"

"Sorry?" Amanda asked.

"You're, like, a single house out in the middle of nowhere," said Oscar. "There's no way the city runs water all the way out here just for this one place, so where did the water come from that used to fill the toilets back up after they were flushed? I mean before we had to fill the tanks manually? This place is basically off the grid. I remember Jake even mentioned all the power comes from either solar or a propane generator, right?"

"Yes, that's right," Amanda said, almost to herself.

"What's up?" I asked.

"I was just thinking about something Billy told us once," she said. "Would they have run electricity out here?"

Oscar shrugged. "I doubt it, really. There ain't nothing out here. You see any power lines running to the house?"

"Huh," she said quietly.

"City isn't just gonna run electrical out to nowhere, even if there is a house. You'd have to get a bunch of people living out here for them to do that. I don't even know if this area's considered part of Jackson."

"You look like somethings bothering you, girl," I said.

"Yeah, it kind of is," she said. "Billy used to talk about this place like it ran off the power grid. I remember: he even said that a grid failure would knock his power out and he had wanted to install solar on the main cabin before the plague hit."

Oscar raised his eyebrows and took a deep breath. He blew it out through his lips like a horse and said, "I don't know about any of that, but that place there," he pointed at the cabin, "was never on no city grid."

14

INTERVIEWS, THREE

Gibs

"I'd like to talk about your time as a Marine if that's okay."

We'd ended up in the library/office at the back of the house; it was where I found Jake when I came in looking for him. He'd been back there talking with Wang, and he gave him a book which many of us on the compound would eventually become familiar with. Mark Rippetoe's *Starting Strength* became a kind of combination bible/manual/safety guide that everyone had to read if they wanted to utilize the weights in the garage. Wang had the big, blue book tucked under his arm as he left the room.

We were sitting by the small fireplace in a couple of well-worn Windsor chairs that were surprisingly comfortable despite their spindly, wooden construction. You could lean into them and have your back supported just the way you wanted to, without the chair trying to slump you over and spill you back out onto the floor. I held my coffee cup in one hand and concentrated on not jackhammering my leg around like a little kid. Jake never moved, or at least, he never moved more than he had to. He just sat in his chair with his hands rested in his lap as though he'd forgotten them. He always looked like he was sitting for a painting.

"What do you want to know?" I asked.

"Mostly what you did while you were in, when you got out, experiences, and so on. Oh, and tell me if we're going somewhere in the discussion that you don't like, please. I don't intend for this to be adversarial."

"I don't think it'll be a problem," I said. "There isn't anything I did that I'm ashamed of."

A strange expression seemed to pass over Jake's face but disappeared so fast that I assumed I'd only imagined it.

"So, let's see," I said. "I enlisted when I was eighteen years old (just out of high school) and went to boot camp at Parris Island. I was in Platoon 3120, 3rd Recruit Battalion, and graduated on January 7th, 1994…"

"Yes?" Jake asked.

"Oh, nothing. I was just thinking about my SDI… that's Senior Drill Instructor. Staff Sergeant MacBride."

I must have been quiet for a while because Jake asked, "Are you alright?"

His voice made me jump. "Yeah, fine. My mom died just before I enlisted so when I graduated, there wasn't really anyone there to see it except my uncle (her brother). It was good of him to show up since we'd never been that close. I think he came more for his sister than he did for me, though. He shook my hand, told me Mom would have been proud, and that was his obligation satisfied as far as he was concerned. He got in his truck and went home.

"Anyway, we could have ten days of leave, if we wanted them, before reporting for SOI, and I had just made up my mind that I didn't want any of it. I'm standing around in a crowd of newly minted Marines hugging their mothers and fathers, sticking out like a bleeding asshole, when SSgt MacBride puts his eyes on me from across the way. He started walking in my direction, and I internally groaned as I braced myself for one last parting shit sandwich.

"'Private Gibson, where are your family?' he says. 'Haven't any left, sir!' I said back."

I finished my coffee and put the cup down on a table. I hadn't thought about this in years.

"He instructed me to meet him down at the Brig & Brew later that day (that was a local bar and grill on the Island). When I did, the man sat down and had a beer with me."

"He sounds like a hell of a person," Jake said quietly.

"He was a motherfucker!" I said. "He was the absolute eye of the shit storm, I kid you not. The other hats just kind of swirled around this guy, sucked the evil out of him to recharge their own fucked up batteries and then fluttered out again to bury us all in shit. All it took was a sideways look from that son of a bitch, and the kill hat would enthusiastically smoke the whole fucking platoon. No shit. Satan wore a campaign cover."

"But… he took you out for a beer," Jake said.

"Yeah. He took me out for a beer," I agreed. "I just don't want you getting the wrong idea about the guy. It wasn't like some movie. The guy wasn't a secretly cuddly father figure who actually loved all the recruits and desperately wanted us to succeed. Every one of us found ourselves pinned to the deck under his boot heel."

Jake nodded, seemingly accepting what I said, so I continued. "Anyway, after that I went on to SOI, that's School of Infantry, and trained my primary MOS: 0311 Rifleman."

"I'm sorry," Jake interrupted, "MOS?"

"Sorry. 'Military Occupational Specialty.' Everyone gets a job in the service, see? We don't just spend all day oiling rifles, marching in formation, and doing a bunch of pushups. There's shit to do and all sorts of different specialties to pursue. You could be an admin guy, you could go work in intelligence, you could go work in comms… shit, you could even be a mechanic, okay?"

"I see."

"So for me, I wanted to go Infantry, and that's what I got. That ended up being a predictable run, if not routine. You deploy for a stretch, come home, keep current on training, head out again. After a while, you get used to shuffling around a bit. Then 9/11 happened, and things got special. I went to both Iraq and Afghanistan more times than I care to remember."

"I remember seeing it on TV," Jake said. "It must have been rough."

"You get used to it," I said. "I was good at what I did, kept my head down, and did my job. I promoted when I was supposed to promote, and ended at Staff Sergeant, MOS 0369 Infantry Unit Leader before I left."

Jake sat up and leaned forward. "Why *did* you leave, if you don't mind?"

I considered his question, trying to find the best way to condense my reasons down into a salient point. Finally, I said, "Mandatory Fun Day."

"What?"

"They were these fucking events that everyone had to show up for. Could have been anything; barbecue, bowling, family fun day, you name it. As a Staff Sergeant, it was even my job to organize a few, though I mostly kept them to barbecues where everyone understood they could leave in fifteen minutes if they wanted. The ones that finally did it for me were these balls that they'd hold. These were formal affairs that everyone had to show up to, married, dating, or single. The event was formal, so you showed up in your dress uniform. Regs require that you get all your medals mounted for this, by the way. Well, not only do you have to pay for that, you have to buy the medals, ribbons, and mounts as well."

Jake pulled a confused look and said, "You're talking about medals you're awarded?"

"That's right. You pay for everything, and some of those fuckers were pricy. I think the one that pissed me off the most was the Purple Heart. It was something like fifty bucks. Think about that for a second, okay? Say you pulled a Gump and took a round to the ass; you have to pay for the privilege of owning the medal that commemorates that proud event."

"Uh, I'm sorry if I'm missing the point," Jake said, "but that doesn't sound like such a big thing, really. You buy the medal once, and then you're good, no?"

"You know how much a PFC makes, Jake? Call it about thirty-nine grand a year, including drill and hazard pay, okay? That's an E2. I took every dollar those men and women had to spend on such shit as a personal insult. I can think of at least two occasions where I ended up helping one of my Marines pay for his getup because he'd fucked up his pay, albeit usually at a titty bar, if I'm being fair. Even so, they were humiliated to ask for my help both times, though I told them it was fine, and they always paid me back."

I could tell I was winding up for a rant at this point and didn't care. I restrained myself from standing up out of my chair and pacing around the room.

"It's never a single thing that makes that one final straw for you... until it is. It's a bunch of little things added up over time. Bureaucracy had totally taken over, and everyone was more worried about perception than they were reality. By the time I left, it was just fine to skate along at the bare minimum so long as the PowerPoint slides were up to snuff. So long as the platoon had a nice collective tick mark next to the sexual harassment training box. On those occasions that we screwed something up, we weren't supposed to acknowledge it for fear that it might look bad. Do you know how hard it is to learn from a fuck up if you can't even say that you fucked up?"

Jake shook his head and spread his hands out helplessly.

"Pretty fucking hard. They tell you at the Infantry Unit Leader's course that the most important role of a leader is to get your guys to suck it the fuck up when they want to give in. It's the leader that says, 'Bullshit, job's not done, so just grab the closest goat and keep on fucking.' And if you're good, if you're respected, your guys will absolutely take ahold of that goat and reach for the closest bottle of lube. They tell you that, and yet in the normal day to day life, you don't actually see enough leaders doing that. Everyone above a certain level is getting all political and shit. They're chasing a bunch of meaningless paperwork while the big-deal shit, the most important of all shit, slips right through the cracks."

"I think you're describing most organizations, really," Jake said.

I sighed and collected my thoughts. "Jake, when you have that kind of groupthink in other organizations, profits drop, stocks go to shit, and maybe workers take a pay cut. In the Corps, that shit results in dead Marines. Look, as a Staff Sergeant, one of my jobs, maybe my most important job, was to mentor my Marines. I worked with them every day, worked on their weaknesses, helped them line up their career tracks. I even helped them with their family shit when they needed me. A lot of these guys were working second jobs waiting tables to help make ends meet or pay for college, by the way. These people were my family. I've been married twice; both times it didn't last, either because of my charming personality or theirs. Wives walk out on you. My boys in the pit were always there. They looked to me to help guide them in an organization in which (it seemed clear to me) the priority was placed on appearances rather than the wellbeing of its people. And maybe it was always like this from the time that I enlisted, and I was just too young and stupid to see it; maybe we all are. But I had to get out in the end. I couldn't keep looking my family in the face and believe what I was telling them anymore. They deserved better than bullshit. Better than me."

I'd run out of things to say and stopped talking entirely. I was looking up at one of the bookshelves and reading off the titles, many of which I was mildly entertained to note had been on the Commandant's List not so long ago.

Jake said, "I don't think I believe that. I don't think your Marines would have either."

"Beg pardon?" I asked, mildly annoyed.

"I mean, I believe you felt as you say, certainly. But I also think you sell yourself short. If you were supremely confident in your abilities as a leader or mentor, I think I'd have an easier time believing that you were bullshit."

"Well, have it your way," I said, not interested in arguing the point.

"Given everything you've just shared with me," Jake continued, "I'm not entirely sure how to bring up my next point."

"The best way is usually to just spit it the hell out."

"So it is," Jake agreed. "What is your assessment of the people here?"

"What, here right now? They seem to be pretty decent to me… even Edgar has his good points if I'm being fair."

Jake smiled and asked, "What do you think of them in a fight?"

"Oh," I said. I raised my shoulders and let them drop. "Like trying to herd autistic kittens for the most part. I went shoulder to shoulder with Davidson, and he wasn't too bad, but that was close in and ugly; mostly a bunch of spray 'n' pray. Oscar's good too. Keeps his head on. I don't think we'd have made it out of Denver without him driving if you want to know the truth."

Jake adjusted his position in the chair; crossed a leg over his knee. "So, two people that you rate as 'kind of good' and the rest are newborn kittens with birth defects. What do you think it would take to make them competent riflemen?"

Looking back on our discussion, it's easy for me to see now that Jake was leading things in this direction. Without the benefit of hindsight, the question caught me flatfooted.

"You mean, like, turn them into Marines?"

"Well, perhaps not full Marines but approximating a Marine's competency? Someone who knows how to fight in a group and coordinate attacks. You'll have to excuse me; I don't know the appropriate terminology."

"I think I get what you're asking," I said. "You're talking about fire teams and infantry tactics."

"Okay, sure. How about it?"

I gave it some honest consideration before answering. "I really won't know until I get some time with them. I think everyone here should be able to handle a weapon; that's just basic. People like George and Barbara shouldn't go much further than that, though. They're not able-bodied. The younger people though… maybe."

"And is that a role you'd be willing to take on here with us?"

He was looking at me intently; either trying to gauge my reaction or I had a dick growing out of my ear. When I didn't answer, he said, "Do you think Denver would have gone differently if you'd had more competent people in the fight?"

"Fuck's sake," I said.

15

SHELTERS AND SHITTERS

Oscar

What you have to understand is that back in those early days, no one was actually pointing fingers at people and saying, "Okay, you're gonna be in charge of building… and You? You're gonna be in charge of farming," and the like. There was just a list of things that had to get done and, once everybody got an idea of what we all could do, people jumped in based on what they knew. After a while, the same people kept taking on the same kinds of jobs and everybody just kinda fell into their roles.

On our first day there, Jake and Amanda were already laying all the groundwork. They were talking to each of us, either on our own or in little groups, and figuring out backgrounds; strengths and weaknesses, you know? It was crazy because everyone had their own idea about what was going on. People who Jake had talked to were convinced that he was just being friendly and bull-shitting with them; dude was smooth, like. He could just rap with you a while and get whatever he needed out of you. Amanda came right at you, all direct and everything. The people she talked to knew what was up immediately because she told them. Different people had different ideas about this; some of them appreciated Amanda just coming out and saying, "Look, everyone has a job around here. There ain't no free rides, *sabes*?" On the other hand, Jake's method put a lot of people at ease. He creeped out a few of us when we first met him (it took Barbara a long time to get used to him) and being able to talk to him like that convinced a lot of people that the dude was just the quiet type.

For me, all I knew was that I was relieved that Maria had a place to sleep and a full belly. I would have put up with a lot of shit just for that and, honestly, Jake and Amanda are cool. Gibs is *the man,* and I think we would have probably found a place on our own eventually, but we won the fucking lottery when Jake found us, no lie.

Right off the bat, we had a little powwow out in the garage by the whiteboard, where Jake started listing off all these projects we had to get going on. I should probably make it clear here that they had a stack of three or four different whiteboards that they used to keep track of various projects. They had some pegs set up on the right inner wall of the building that they could just throw a board on and get to work. Jake was sitting down on a shop stool while Amanda wrote for him at the board, which was a good thing. Jake's writing looks like some kinda jacked up Chinese.

So Jake starts describing all the stuff we need to do, and by that time everyone's got it figured out if they hadn't before.

He goes, "We have a list of items we need to get going on immediately so that we can be in a good position when the snows come, which could be as early as October around here. When it does, the roads may become impassable unless we can find and operate a snowplow or some similar tool, so we'll need to have the ability to hunker down here in the bowl for long periods of time if we're forced to do so.

"We have four major areas to tackle: provisions, shelter, sanitation, and supplies. There's a lot more than that, of course, but these are the main items that we need to get moving on immediately, listed in order of importance."

He had our complete attention by that point; we all wanted to know how we were going to handle these things. Some of us had gone in a few circles arguing the issue. Why were we sticking in the valley when there were whole tracts of housing outside of the mountains in easy to reach areas? The valley only had the one house and a garage, so there were already a lot of areas that we had to play catch-up on. What we kept coming back to was the reliable water supply (both the well and the seasonal stream that ran through the area on the northeast side) and the seclusion. Denver was still fresh on everyone's minds.

Jake continued: "First, provisions. The food we have laid aside may look like a lot, and it is. It's enough to sustain three people for about eight months. Now, please don't get me wrong, we're happy to have you all with us, but that same amount of food will only carry nineteen people a little over a month. Before you arrived, the plan was to coast out the winter on our existing food stores and then work on a subsistence farming solution as soon as spring came. The winter would have essentially been used to lay out our plans and prepare for that first crop. At the same time, we were going to begin scavenging again as soon as the roads opened back up. The idea was to supplement our scavenging with our first crops (we were looking at beets and potatoes to start) and see what percentage of our meals came from which source. Based on that, we would have known how much more we had to ramp up farming for the following season. This is critical data that we have to collect because, as you surely all know, the food that's just lying around is going to run out, probably sooner than we'd all like. If we're not ready for when that time comes, things are going to get really hard; a lot harder than anyone realizes. Things have been really easy so far because everything we need is basically just out there for the taking. This cannot and will not last."

I felt a lot of people shift around during this speech and even heard one or two people mutter quietly towards the end. I guess they thought that Jake's definition of "easy" was a bit different from their own. I could see it from both sides. Yes, it was technically easy to go pick a bunch of stuff up and bring it all home. On the other hand, getting shot at by random strangers is bullshit. I grew up in a pretty rough area, but my past was a cakewalk compared to how things were now.

"Our plans don't necessarily change now that you've all come to stay with us," Jake said. "They just have to scale up. We'll need to do everything we can to get our food stores up to an acceptable level; enough so that we'll be sustained through winter. Scavenging is going to be everyone's responsibility, with the obvious exception of the children. We have enough vehicles to support everyone who can do it; we'll go out in teams and comb the area in grids. It's going to be tight, but I believe it's entirely possible if we keep organized."

That fucker Jeff said, "Someone will need to stay behind with the kids, won't they?"

"That's right," Jake agreed. "I suppose we could draw lots for work duty or something similar—"

"Or, some of us might be better at certain jobs," Jeff said. "I know that Alish and George were both teachers once. I wasn't, but I used to do a lot of community work with the YMCA and such."

"That's a good point," Jake said, "but I also want to avoid people getting pigeonholed as much as possible. The sad fact is that everyone needs to be competent with firearms and be able to fight as a team if the need arises. There's no way around it. But your point is noted. I'm sure we'll be able to work up a solution with little trouble."

Jake looked around us for a bit to see if there was anything else. Amanda stood behind him banging away at the whiteboard, collecting the important points. When nobody said anything, he continued, "So much for provisions; the next item is shelter. Now, please don't get me wrong. As I said, we're very happy to have you all here with us, but, well, we've got to get you all your own residences."

"Hell yes," Tom said. "Fred snores loud enough to wake up a dead man."

"Oh, hush now, fool. Ain't that bad," Fred shot back.

"I'll take Fred's snoring over your horrible, horrible singing," Wang said.

"Dude," said Tom, "my singing *rules*."

"Alright, goddamnit, secure your pie holes," growled Gibs. I mean, dude straight up growled; you could always tell when he was getting pissed. If you get him worked up enough, he'll go from growling to full blast in, like, zero-point-three seconds. I've seen him do it a few times. It's epic.

There were a few muttered sorries, which Jake waved away. "So as I was saying, we need to figure something out for your homes. I had considered putting you all up on cots here in the garage to start, but I'm against it for a few reasons. First, it's a temporary solution at best. The building isn't insulated, and you'll all freeze once the snows start in. On top of that, living in a garage on cots in a big group of people is just a miserable way to be. It's like living in a shelter; actually, no, it is precisely living in a shelter. People need a home, a place that's theirs. So we might as well skip the whole shelter concept and get busy working on something more permanent.

"Oscar, I'd like you to start working on some ideas for that; your background in the construction industry will give you some unique insight into the problem. That alright with you?"

"Uh, sure, man," I said, wondering how the hell I was going to house sixteen people without a work crew. "No sweat, I guess."

"Keep in mind," Gibs offered, "that you don't have to worry about inspectors, OSHA, or any of... of that. What we come up with needs to be safe to live in but it doesn't need to be a palace. One of the first things we could do is board up the windows on the bus, rip out all the seating, and build in a bed, some living area, maybe throw in a camping stove. See what I mean?"

"Yeah," I said, nodding. "Yeah, that's a good point, man." I looked back at Jake, a little excited, and said, "Okay, bro, lemme work on this a bit. I think I got a few ideas that'll do."

"Thank you, Oscar, that's much appreciated," said Jake. "Next item: sanitation. As some of you may realize, the cabin sits on a septic system. I'm not sure exactly how old the cabin is but let's guess and call it five years, for much of which it sat idle; our friend Billy used it as a summer getaway. The average septic system lasts about forty years, so given the lack of use this place saw, we'll assume a total of forty years of good, future use. Now, this average of forty years is based on your typical American family unit; call it four people. That's forty years for four people. Another way to look at it would be to say that the system would last for one hundred sixty years if used by only one person, right? One hundred sixty divided by four people puts you at forty years, basically."

People were nodding while Amanda was writing these numbers out on the board. I already knew where this was going.

"So, if we follow that math, we can extrapolate and say that the same septic system only lasts about eight and a half years when used consistently by nineteen people. One hundred sixty divided by nineteen is around eight and a half, see? There's a decent chance we're going to be here longer than that, so a single septic system divided among us all isn't going to cut it. On top of that, you need water to drive normal toilets, and we don't want to use as much water as it will take to flush for nearly twenty people."

Gibs was nodding while shifting around from foot to foot and waved at Jake. Jake raised his eyebrows and nodded back, letting him know he should speak.

"I can take this one on if you like. I have some experience in this area."

"What do you recommend?" Jake asked.

"Well, in the absence of chemical toilets, the obvious choice is a pit latrine. Basically, you dig a six-foot pit, put a cover on top of it with a little hole cut out, and then build up an outhouse around that. We could dig his and hers pits."

"Drawbacks?" Amanda asked from behind Jake.

"A few," said Gibs. "First, you wouldn't want to do this if you're sitting on a high water table… does anyone know if we are?"

"I think we're okay, there," Jake said. "Our well is sunk fairly deep."

"Alright, good to go. Other problems include the obvious smell and the fact that contaminants from the waste material will leach into the nearby soil, so we have to keep this well removed from the main living area and any farmland we plan on cultivating. Can I get at that whiteboard?"

"Absolutely," Jake said, and Amanda handed over the marker as Gibs approached. Gibs started by drawing out a wobbly circle with a break in the line at the bottom right corner. At the top left corner, he drew two rectangles.

"Okay, so this is the valley, and these two boxes up here are the cabin and garage, right? This break down here is the entrance into our valley," said Gibs while pointing at the board. "Off to the northeast of the garage is the well. What do you call it, Jake? Thirty yards?"

"Sure, close enough," Jake agreed.

"Good. Some distance up from there in the same direction is the river, right? I haven't seen it yet; does it always have water?"

"It's more of a stream, really. It runs out the cleft alongside the road," said Jake. "I'm pretty sure it's all fed by snowmelt. It's more or less a mud patch right now. I haven't seen how heavy it gets when the season is right."

"Okay, probably doesn't matter either way. I'm gonna say we put the pit latrines down here." He drew a couple of X's along the edge of the circle southwest of the house. "We'll say a hundred yards out from the house; that's a total minimum distance of a hundred and thirty yards out from any main water source. Additionally, let's say we maintain a minimum distance of one hundred yards between this location and any crops we eventually grow. That should keep our food and water supply safe. So that's another disadvantage; you'll have to go for a walk any time you want to deuce."

Gibs handed the marker back to Amanda and resumed his place among the group. He said, "Finally, these things will fill up. When the fill level of the pit comes to within a foot of the cover, we'll need to fill in the hole with dirt, tamp it down, and move the whole setup to another location; relatively close but not close enough that the new pit breaks into the old one."

"How long would it take to fill one of these things up?" asked Barbara with a sour expression.

"Can't say for sure," Gibs said. "I don't have a lot of experience with these. Mostly, we were either in small groups straddling trenches or in groups large enough that we needed burn out latrines."

"Burn... out?" Barbara asked.

"Yeah. In our case out here, you'd basically build up an outhouse-like enclosure around some metal drums. You cut the drums in half, so you get two units per drum. People squat into that and, once per day, you pull them out, add in some diesel or

MORGAS, and burn the contents. It's typically a no-no to do unless you're in some third world sh—uh—an underdeveloped nation. Environmental regulations, see? Not exactly a problem anymore."

"So, they'd need fuel," Jake said. "Good to note."

"Not in our case," Gibs said. "It's too valuable, but there are other options. There's a lot of water in crap, so letting it dry out enough to be combustible isn't the best option. We could get the fire going by burning our garbage over it, which would theoretically burn off the initial moisture—"

"I think this might be the most disgusting conversation I've ever heard," Rebecca said.

"—or we could look at making charcoal from the local wood supply, which wouldn't be difficult. I haven't tried this before personally, but I think it would be possible to build a, uh, a poop barbecue. It would take a lot longer to completely burn the material out but if you expose it to extreme heat for long enough, all the water cooks off, and then the waste itself eventually converts to ash. Charcoal burns really hot for a long time, so... you know. But all that's for when you have a lot of people; say a hundred or more. I think the pits are good enough for now."

"So that covers number two," said Monica. "What about number one? I'm assuming we're good to do *everything* in the pits, aren't we?"

"You know, we can make some pretty powerful fertilizer with the urine," Barbara said.

Everyone stopped and looked at her, this little, old lady with short, mom-hair. "Why, Barbara," Gibs said, smiling, "what *have* you been up to?"

"I loved to garden," she said, sounding defensive. "I liked reading about this stuff. Anyway, we can let it ripen up a bit and mix it into compost. It's like fertilizer steroids."

"That's an outstanding call," Gibs said. "We upcycle what we can; put the rest in the pits."

"That's agreed," Jake said. "Okay, final item: supplies. To put it bluntly, we need to find poor Fred a pair of pants that fit."

"God bless you, sir," Fred boomed, and the rest of us laughed our asses off.

The comment about pulling the seats out of the bus got me thinking about ways we could quickly get everyone into their own homes. After the meeting broke up, I ran over to Jake to talk to him about it.

"Hey, what's up, Oscar?" he asked.

"I got an idea about housing everyone, but I'm gonna need to borrow your truck."

"Oh, yeah?"

"Trailers, dude," I said. "Fifth wheels and stuff. That truck already has a ball hitch. I just gotta go out into the neighborhoods, find them, and bring them back."

"Okay," he nodded. "Not bad at all but do you think you can find enough?"

"I don't know," I admitted. "Maybe not. I'm pretty certain I can find at least two to start. They usually sleep at least six people, so that would be twelve taken care of on the first night, assuming I get lucky."

"Good… good, that covers the short term. What about long term? People will want their own place to live eventually."

"Two options," I said. "For one, there're a ton of trees around here. I'm pretty confident I could put up a simple cabin with a raised floor if I had some people to help me."

Jake raised his eyebrows and leaned back all surprised. "You think you can build a log cabin?"

"Oh, shit yeah, man. I could build a house by myself if I had enough material. I used to do it all; framing, plumbing, roofing, and drywall. The only stuff I never got into was electrical and tile, which aren't a big deal anymore. The interior finish work might be a little jacked 'cause I didn't do cabinetry and all that, but the place would be livable. I'd almost just recommend doing that but we can't 'cause there wouldn't be enough material. The local Home Depot or whatever they got around here probably wouldn't have enough framing lumber for more than a couple of small homes; not enough for everyone."

"That's true, but now that you mention it, we should probably head down there anyway and clean the place out," Jake said, almost like he was talking to himself.

"Yeah, sure, we can do that, but it won't solve the housing situation. Anyway, we can do cabins, but I'll need help for that because the logs'll be too fuckin' heavy to lift on my own. I'd need, like, a couple of dudes to help me. The main drawback, though, is that it'll take so long to build them."

"Yes, but it sounds like the most desirable thing, long term. People used to fantasize about such things not long ago. So, a couple of campers now, which we think covers twelve people, and then start to work on cabins?"

"Well, that's twelve if we find two campers. We might find three or only one. But I got another idea in case that doesn't work out at all."

"Yes? What's that?"

"I'll explain if it goes that far," I said. "For now, I just wanna get out there and start looking."

Jake thought it over; absently scratching at his beard while looking off toward the bus (we hadn't moved it since we arrived). "Take Amanda with you. She'll keep you safe," he said. "Go in the jeep first to scout. I want to minimize diesel use; that stuff is always hard to find."

"Aw, look, man. I'll be fine. What can she do? She's even shorter than I am!"

Jake looked at me, then, and the look on his face shut me up. He wasn't trying to mad dog me or anything; don't think of it like that. The dude can just go from chill to goofy without warning. We used to see dudes like that in the *barrio* back in the day. I grew up in a pretty tough area, so you had to be tough to get along. The thing is, a lot of us spent a lot of time just acting tough, putting up a front to try to keep from getting fucked with. A lot of times, that was enough because you can't actually tell if you're dealing with someone who's tough or someone who's faking. Then you had those loco motherfuckers. For the most part, you knew who they were, stayed away from them, and it was cool. I even had a few friends who were like that. You just didn't want to catch them on a bad day.

I never seen Jake lose his cool before. I've seen him go to work a few times and I know he's hard, but he ain't mean or cruel. Irregardless of all that, sometimes he gives me that look, and I'm pretty sure I'm looking at another loco motherfucker.

"She's little," he said, "but you haven't seen what she can do, either. Take her with you, please."

"Uh, yeah. Okay, bro."

I found Amanda not long after that; she was off to the side talking to her daughter Elizabeth while my girl Maria and Rose stood close by. Like an idiot, I happily walked up to them only to find out that Lizzy was getting told.

Amanda was saying, "I don't care that you're in a group now. You three need to stay close to the cabin. Period." She put out her index finger and started stabbing it at each of the girls in turn: "Every… one… of you. Got it?"

The kids all had that pissed off look that they get when they decide to disagree silently. I decided to weigh in and said,

"*Mija, ya.* You remember what it was like getting shot at? Either of you remember Kyle and Jessica? This ain't a world anymore where you get to disobey and just get grounded. If you screw up now, people die. Ain't no grounding for that. You get somebody killed because you're feeling like rebels; you just won't ever be able to forgive yourself... and neither will anyone else around you."

The looks on their faces fell, and I wondered if I hit them too hard. They were all remembering their own friends that were gone; all of the fight had escaped them. Amanda was looking at me funny, and I couldn't tell if she was upset or what.

"Sorry to butt in," I said.

"No, it's fine," she said. "It's been a while since I've heard someone else speak Spanish. It was nice to hear."

"Oh, man," I smiled. "There's more where that came from."

She shook her head and asked, "What's up?"

"Jake asked me to get you. I want to head into the city, and he told me to take you with me."

She looked back at the girls and chewed her lip, almost certainly wondering what to do with her kid. I didn't realize it at the time, but Jeff must have been in earshot because he spoke out from behind us.

"I can keep an eye on them if that's what you're worried about. Jake is taking some of the others out in the Dodge to go looking for food, and stuff and I think Gibs and Fred are going to start digging those pits. I don't have much to do right now."

"Okay, that works," Amanda said. "Thanks." She looked back at the girls, "You all pay attention to what Jeff says, okay?"

They nodded, and Lizzy mumbled a "yes, ma'am."

"Lizzy, come over here," Amanda said. She took the girl over to the other side of the porch and whispered to her a while. I couldn't tell what she was saying, but she looked serious as a heart attack, so I looked away to give them their privacy.

As I waited, I looked over at my little girl and said, "Like Amanda says, okay *Mijita*? Do as you're told."

You know how you have those situations in your life where you wish more than anything in the world that you could go back and just change one decision? Even having nightmares where you're screaming at yourself to do something different?

Yeah.

16

PISSING MATCH

Gibs

That first week was a flurry of activity. Everyone had taken Jake's little speech about food to heart, and it was clear they were all moving at full blast to make up the difference. If the snow was likely to come in October, we only had a little over a month to get ready.

Every day, people divided into two basic groups: scavengers and builders. The scavengers would head out into the city in one or more of the gas vehicles, taking along an armed guard; either Jake, Amanda, or myself. In the case of the Jeep, it was almost always a two-man team so that the rear seats could be folded down for more storage space. With the Dodge, there was a whole truck bed available, so four or five people usually made the trip there. Because of this, we found that the truck was always going out for bulk supplies (mostly food and such) while the Jeep went out for harder to find specialty items.

Poor Oscar often found himself torn between duties. He and Fred knew more about building things (or at least, building things the right way rather than just slapping any old shit together) than the rest of us combined but they were both also very strong and could lug heavy things around all day long. Additionally, Oscar usually had to go out to find stuff that he needed to build with. Sometimes he could just tell the rest of us what was required, but he was often afraid he either wouldn't explain the needed items well enough or that we'd misunderstand and end up wasting gas getting the wrong items. You could tell it frustrated the hell out of him because it ended up taking him twice as long to finish a lot of projects.

Fred and I had the shit holes dug and ready on day one but, not surprisingly, no one was really in a rush to start using them because they were just a couple of holes out in the middle of nowhere. Most everyone else was out in the city, except for George and Barbara, looking for food and other stuff so I couldn't tell Oscar the work was done and that it was time to get going on the outhouses. He was out working on the shelter problem, anyway, so I figured it would be a while before the pits were put to active use, which was actually a little galling. Why the hell had I jumped in so quick to dig a couple of shit pits, making myself all sweaty and dirty, if they weren't going into service for a few days?

Walking up to the edge of one of them, I unzipped and relieved myself.

"Oh, you're just gonna whip your stuff out and get busy, ain'tcha?" Fred said, mildly disgusted.

"I'm testing my handiwork, man."

"That's just nasty. Can't just be pulling out your dick like that. At least turn away or something."

"Hell, it's not like I give a damn," I said, shaking off. "I lost all those barriers a long time ago." I packed it away, pulled out some wet wipes from a bag we'd kept by our water bottles, and wiped off my hands. "You know what it's like doing a piss test in the Marines?"

Fred shook his head.

I walked over to him and stood shoulder to shoulder, then leaned my head close to his and looked down his front. I whispered, "An observer is there, standing close by just like I am now, to watch you fill the bottle. He could almost put his arm around your shoulders..." I said as I started to creep my left arm around him and rest my palm against his back.

"Hey, get the fuck off me, man!" he erupted through nervous laughter.

I laughed as well and said, "Sorry, man. You just get used to it. I got out of the habit for a long time, what with all the civilized behavior I was exposed to when I left the Marines, but it's one of those skills you can always fall back to, like riding a bike."

I went over to grab the shovel, waters, and other stuff to walk back to the house. "We'll need to put some plywood over these to keep them from filling in and keep people from falling in. Would you grab the pick?" I turned and was mildly surprised to see Fred, with his back to me, pissing into the hole next to the one I'd just used.

"No, man. That's the lady's room," I said.

His shoulders started to shake as he laughed and he said, "Hey, kiss my ass, Gibs."

"This ain't one of those gender identity things, is it? Do I need to dig a third hole or something?"

He laughed hard at that but then turned and said, "Alright, man, that'll do." He said it amiably enough, and his smile was genuine, but I could detect just a hint of an edge underneath his voice like he was getting ready to start taking offense if I didn't lay off.

"Hey, no problem, man. No offense, okay?"

He flapped his arms at me as he walked back in my direction, as though I was being silly, and said, "Hey, it's cool, man. We all are just fucking around here."

He slapped me on the shoulder, hard enough to jerk the top of my body to the side, and squeezed my arm. He then deliberately pulled the pack of wipes out of my hand, removed a few of them, and began to wash his hands, all while smiling at me in good-natured fashion.

"The fuck was that?" I said, voice low.

He pulled a confused expression and said, "What, man?"

"Don't pull that innocent cunt look with me like a what-the-fuck grenade just went off in your face. You know good and goddamned fucking well what's going on here. How far do you want to escalate this, Fred?"

I didn't realize it at the time, but I had taken a few steps towards him. He backed up a couple of paces, putting his heels on the edge of one of the pits. I'd dropped the bottles of water but was still holding the shovel. Belatedly, I dropped that too.

"Hey, Gibs, look—" he said.

"It's too late to pretend you didn't mean anything, Daisy. We both know perfectly well how I feel about proper sanitation. You're counting on me not calling out that you just purposefully rubbed your fucking mitt all over me before washing your hands… some fucking moronic dominance horse shit. Only now here I am in your face, and you look about as vicious to me as a bowl of Ovaltine."

He stayed quiet a moment while he considered me and I began to wonder what would happen next. I'd gotten the worst of my annoyance off my chest and was just remembering the fact that I was only really up to Fred's chin and he probably outweighed me by eighty pounds. I was beginning to wonder if I wouldn't just be better off shoving him into the hole and running off for a bazooka.

Finally, Fred sighed and slowly picked a water bottle up off the ground. Uncapping it, he dumped the entire thing over his hands and washed them thoroughly. He held one hand out to me and said, "Look, sometimes things piss me off, and I take it the wrong way. We're both assholes. Do over?"

I considered for a moment just how much of an asshole I wanted to be but decided ultimately that he was sincere. I took his hand and nodded. "I'll tone the ribbing down."

Right about the time Fred and I were wrapping up our little pissing match, Oscar and Amanda were returning to the valley from the day's first excursion. They rolled up in the jeep just as we were dragging a plywood sheet out of the garage.

"Hey, any luck, you guys?" called Fred as they climbed out of the Jeep. In answer, Amanda walked around to the back to open the rear door, exposing row on row of clothing stacked up as high as the seat backs.

"We found a few things for you guys while we were out scouting for campers," Amanda said. "I'm pretty sure we found some clothes that will fit you, big guy."

"Oh, thank you, Jesus," Fred said. "You have no idea how much more uncomfortable these shorts are after digging in the dirt for the last few hours." He looked at me and asked, "Okay with you if I change right quick?"

"Nah, get after it," I said. "I can get someone else to drag this with me."

Fred's voice thundered out through the field as he advised the others to get their butts over to help unload the jeep. Those people who weren't out with Jake looking for food, such as Alish, Barbara, Jeff, and all of the kids, spilled out from various nearby areas to help unload. Meanwhile, Oscar had run up to grab the other end of the plywood sheet and nodded to me to get moving.

"Thanks," I said as I started walking. "These things are heavier than they look."

"Oh, yeah," said Oscar. "Especially this three-quarter stuff. A full sheet of this is both heavy and awkward."

We humped the sheet of plywood across the field for a while, maybe thirty or forty seconds, before the silence started making me feel all twitchy, so I said, "How's the search for trailers going?"

"Good and bad. Good in that we already found two today. Bad because one of them is just a teardrop camper. It'll only sleep three people... cramped."

"Oh, well, it's a start anyway," I said. "The main thing is beds and shelter."

"That's a part of it," Oscar agreed, "but I gotta get people spread out into their own space, too. We can't keep being crammed on top of each other like we are. People will start tearing each other's heads off otherwise."

I thought of Fred and muttered, "No shit."

We approached the holes and laid the sheet over them, taking care to ensure that both were sufficiently covered. I said, "We'll have to build little houses over these. The critical factor is that the floor have a good seal all away around the hole and also that the box we end up sitting on has a lid that seals uptight as well. If any part of the pit is left open, this whole area'll get completely overrun with flies."

"No problem, man," he said. "I know how it can be done. It'll take maybe a couple of days to do the whole thing once I have all the material up here."

I said, "You're going to be a busy guy for the next forever, I think. You just let the rest of us know how we can help. You and Fred don't have to remain as the only guys who know how to build shit. We can get you set up with, well, apprentices, I guess. Greg and Alan both have a couple of strong backs on them... trust me, I know."

"Hey, let me ask you something," Oscar said. The tone of his voice told me something was bugging him, so I gave him my full attention. "What's your take on Amanda and Jake?"

"Oh, well, they seem okay, so far. Jake can be kind of a weirdo, but then, I think anyone who survives what we all have comes out a little touched if you know what I'm saying."

"Naw, man. I mean Jake and Amanda… *together*."

"Oh," I said. "Uh… hadn't given it much thought, really."

Oscar looked back in the direction of the cabin, silently getting into his own head.

"What?" I asked.

"I just kind of assumed they were together, you know? Like, every so often she'll put a hand on his shoulder or his arm and leave it there just a little longer than normal, right?"

"I guess," I said. "I don't know if that means anything. Some people are just more touchy-feely than others."

"Yeah, come on, you know what I mean. Plus, does Amanda seem like the touchy-feely type to you?"

"Huh. You do have a point there," I said. Piss her off enough and Amanda seemed a lot more like she could be the shooty-stabby type, honestly.

"She asked me to help her build a house for her and Lizzy while we were out alone today," Oscar said, still looking at the cabin. "She was… um… really serious. 'Serious' isn't the right word, actually, but I'm having trouble thinking of one that fits."

"Insistent?"

He snapped his fingers and pointed at me. "There you go. She was insistent."

"You don't think Jake's putting hands on her, do you?"

"Nah," Oscar said. "I don't get that feeling from her. We knew women back in the *barrio* that used to get smacked around by their husbands. Amanda doesn't act like them at all."

"Well, shit. Maybe she just wants her own place, man. Did you ask her?"

"Not about that, no."

"But you did ask her something? What was it?"

"Never mind," Oscar said.

Amanda asked me to head back out with her and Oscar to retrieve the two campers; to provide another set of hands, eyes, and cover. I told her I was happy to do so, and she spent the next few minutes waiting by the truck while I retrieved my rifle and scavenged rig. She and Oscar both were already wearing some sort of sleek, black, lightweight body armor that appeared to have taken a beating in its service life. They had been wearing this stuff when they made their first excursion that morning.

They had stumbled upon an RV park located in the rough center of Jackson south of the 191. The thing was right in the middle of the city, right next to a bar and library; surrounded by parking lots and businesses. I wondered about the kind of people who would come to camp at such a location given the fact that Jackson itself was sitting ass-to-shoulders with both Yellowstone and the Grand Teton national parks. I suppose they must have charged more affordable rates, but honestly, why come to this area with an RV just to park it by the fucking drug store?

The park itself had been mostly emptied out by the time we got to it; nearly all of the stalls were vacant, and many of the trailers that were still there had been trashed, gutted, or rendered otherwise unusable. There were two exceptions; one little teardrop trailer and a much larger RV truck. Jake was still out with Wang and the others in the Dodge collecting food, so the three of us (Oscar, Amanda, and me) decided to throw a couple of filled gas cans into the Ford and head out to retrieve Oscar's first score.

We took a detour on the way, driving further north to an Ace

Hardware store, where Oscar lost his goddamned mind and ran around grabbing everything in sight. He wanted to start by loading the truck bed up with a shit ton of lumber, which I only talked him out of by explaining it would be better for us to come back with the trailer because it could hold a lot more. He agreed and instead spent the next hour and a half hauling armloads of whatever tools had been spared from looting outside to throw in the bed. He also lined up several five-gallon buckets and proceeded to fill them with box after box of nails and screws of all sizes; not putting the whole box in, of course, but opening the boxes and dumping their contents into the buckets. By the time we were done, the truck looked like it was loaded with enough shit to build a housing tract. I was just rubbing a knot in my back when Oscar scurried back to the passenger side of the truck cab, jumped in, and slapped his hand on the outside door panel.

"*Andale!*"

"Jesus Christ, alright, Speedy," I said as I eased up into the back seat. "Keep your sombrero on."

"Racist…" said Oscar.

"Oh, hell, there he goes again," I said.

"I don't know if I'd call that racist," Amanda said to Oscar as she got the truck moving. "You are moving pretty fast."

"C'mon, I know the dude's not racist," Oscar laughed.

"You missed it, Amanda," I said. "He got me with that early on when we first met. I made some stupid comment or other—"

"It wasn't that stupid, man," said Oscar.

"—and he ribbed me a bit."

Amanda smiled. "What did you say?"

"He asked me if I spoke 'Mexican,'" Oscar said.

"Oh, shit," laughed Amanda.

"So right away, the little jerk launches into a whole routine," I said. "Why I gotta be a Mexican? Why is it all the brown people south of the border only come from Mexico with you people? So I start trying to smooth things over and tell him, 'oh, man, I'm sorry, I didn't mean to assume, where did your family originate from,' and all that."

"I told him we came from Mexico," Oscar hooted. "He got all pissed off. Fuckin' priceless."

"Hey," I said to Oscar. "Language, man."

Amanda scoffed from behind the wheel. "Gibs, we talked about this already. I absolve you of any need to watch your language around me. It's fine. I don't care."

"Huh," I grunted. "Well, fair enough, I guess."

We circled back down the 191 to return to the RV park. As we drove onto the premises, I had a nasty thought and asked, "Hey, did you guys check out these campers you found? We're not gonna have to clear out bodies, are we?"

"Both abandoned," Oscar assured me. "We're good."

The RV and camper were located at different ends of the park, so they dropped me off at the RV along with my rifle and the gas cans. I decided to pour only one five gallon can into the tank, reasoning that I could always add in more along the way if I needed to. I doubted that I'd burn five gallons' worth of gas on the way back, but I wasn't entirely sure. No matter; I didn't want to put in all ten gallons only to have to siphon out what I didn't use when we got the RV parked back at home. Wherever we parked it back in the valley was likely to be permanent.

The RV itself was of decent size. It wasn't palatial like a lot of the luxury buses you'd see on the road or on TV promos; it looked like a solid, affordable family RV that had been loved and well taken care of. It was the variety of vehicle that had started life as a large utility truck only to be surrounded by a metal frame and plywood living enclosure. There was a full sized bed in the back as well as another large bed up over the cab that was accessed by a little ladder behind the front passenger's seat. There was also a small dinette area that would obviously convert into a bed. It looked like it could house five people reasonably; six if we put Maria and Rose in the dinette bed together. It wasn't the answer to everything, but it was certainly a nice little start.

I set the gas cans down in the cramped excuse for a head at the rear of the living area and closed them in behind the door. Pulling out my multi-tool, I advanced on the driver's seat, only to find the keys sitting in a pile on the center console. I had mixed feelings about this. On one hand, I was happy that I wouldn't have to fuck around with the ignition to get the engine started. On the other, I had been interested to see if I could hotwire the thing on my own and was bizarrely disappointed to miss an opportunity to try out my new skill.

The engine started up after a few moments of the starter bitching; it finally caught and turned over after I pumped the gas pedal a bit. I let it run for a while and listened for any sounds that might indicate a problem, hearing none. I shrugged, threw it into drive, and rolled over to the camper, which Oscar had just finished connecting to the Ford's trailer hitch. I noted Amanda stood close by, scanning the area while hugging her ever-present bullpup.

"We gotta take it really slow on the way back," Oscar was saying. "I think this'll be okay, but once we get onto dirt, one good dip in the road could pop this right off the hitch."

Amanda nodded up at me. "How's that thing look?"

"Seems to run okay once you get it going," I said. "Battery seems iffy, but it's nothing we couldn't jump if we had to."

"Good," she said. "Do you want to lead the way back?"

"Let me follow you," I said. "None of those roads are marked very well once you get into the mountains. I'm not sure I can find the way without a little more practice."

17

HOME IMPROVEMENT

Amanda

Things got moving fast, a lot faster than I'd imagined they could, that first week after Gibs and his people arrived. There was a constant flurry of activity and, if you took a moment to just stand back and watch everyone running from place to place, the valley looked a little like a kicked anthill. I didn't notice it too much, for the most part, because I was usually out there running alongside of them. Every so often, though, I would stand back to watch it all from the porch of the cabin and just... see.

I remember being nervous a lot back then. There were all these new faces to get used to, different personalities to deal with and so on. And throughout the whole time, there was the constant worry over not having enough of anything. Sometimes Jake would be on the porch next to me, planning his plans, making adjustments as needed.

I asked him once, "What the hell are we doing? The first snows are probably a month away. What chance do we have of collecting enough food to pull nineteen people through a winter season?"

He smiled out of the corner of his mouth while continuing to look out over the field and said, "We have exactly as much chance as we choose to create." He rested his hand on my shoulder for the slightest moment and then stepped off the deck to meet Oscar, Gibs, Fred, and Wang, who were all just returning with the second phase of Oscar's shelter project.

When it became clear that we wouldn't be able to set everyone up in their own private camper, Oscar immediately started working on Plan B with Jake. Watching the two of them discuss it was kind of fun; Oscar was enthusiastic from the start when he explained what he wanted to do while Jake went from reserved to animated (well, animated for Jake) during the discussion. For lack of a better word, it was "cute" to see the two of them feed each other's excitement as they planned out how the whole thing would work.

To me, housing people in shipping containers seemed crazy but Oscar was absolutely certain he could make it work, and Jake apparently had more imagination than I did because he got all the way on board after asking a few questions regarding how they were going to do it.

The boys returned to the valley driving the Dodge, blasting the horn in triumph as they came. Behind the Dodge lumbered a giant Mac truck, growling (and sometimes grinding) angrily as it plowed through the dirt on the way up to the cabin. I noticed as they came that the driver (who appeared to be Fred, though it was hard to tell from so far away) made it a point to keep within the compacted ruts of the existing track that had been carved into the valley's center, having evolved after months of near constant excursions out into Jackson. As he came closer to the cabin, I could see why; he swung out wide to the north of the road and turned in a lazy arc back towards the cabin, such that the two, forty-foot containers he was hauling lined up perpendicular to the track when he came to a stop—as he entered into the softer soil, his progress slowed noticeably and the truck's tires began to spin alarmingly in places, causing me to wonder if he would get stuck and never be able to move from that position again.

Some more grinding came from the giant, idling truck followed by an outraged, mechanical fart accompanied by a cloud of black smoke rising up into the air. The engine itself finally died just before the driver's side door opened and a shaky, grey Fred Moses climbed carefully down to the ground. Once both of his feet were set in the dirt, he took a deep breath and shook out his hands.

Oscar was on him before he was fully collected. "You… are… a… badass, Fred! That was some touch and go shit, but I never doubted you for a second, man!"

Fred grinned and nodded back, resting his right hand on one of the steps leading up to the cab to steady himself. "I didn't think I was going to make it. That grade coming up the hill is a queen bitch."

"Uh, damn, are you okay, dude?" asked Wang. "You look like you might want to sit down."

"Think I will, thanks," said Fred, and started walking slowly towards the house.

Jake called to his back as he walked away, "Fred, there's a cooler up there with a few beers in it. I put a little well water in there with them to cool them down a bit. It's not ice cold but it's the best I could do, and at least a couple of those beers have your name on them."

Fred nodded without looking back and offered a thumbs-up as he began to mount the steps of the deck.

Oscar whispered, "Fuck, man, I didn't think he was gonna make it!"

"Give the man some credit," Gibs said. "Mac trucks aren't designed for off-roading."

"I know, dude, that's what I mean! You think we'll be able to talk him into doing it again?"

"That sounds like an Oscar problem to me," Gibs said.

"That's very white of you," Oscar laughed.

"*Semper I*, motherfucker," Gibs responded happily. He had loosened up around me quite a bit over the last week and appeared to view me as one of the guys. He still wouldn't talk like that around the other women. I took it as a compliment.

"This is a great start," said Jake while looking over the big rig. He turned his gaze to Oscar and said, "What's next?"

"That's easy," he said. "We can reconfigure these pretty easily but, for now, I'll bet we can bunk four people in each one, which more than takes care of the immediate situation. I saw a few more of these on the road outside, and around Jackson, so we could haul even more up here and eventually have a situation where each person has their own private home if they want it."

"So we just leave them up there on the trailer?" asked Jake.

"No, probably don't want to do that. It'll make it too hard for me to work on them. Plus, I don't think people want to have to climb a ladder or a ramp every time they go to the bathroom. Too dangerous at night, right?"

"Good call," said Gibs.

"So… how do we get them off," asked Wang.

The sudden, stunned silence of the group was all of the answer any of us needed.

"You don't actually have a plan to get these unloaded, do you?" Wang asked.

"Um… well," Oscar said, scratching his forearm absently, "I, uh, I hadn't thought about that part, honestly…"

Gibs burst into hysterical laughter, doubling over on himself and bracing his hands against his knees. Despite himself, Oscar began to laugh as well, although not as hard.

"Hey, dick," he said, looking down at Gibs, "I can't think of everything. Let someone else problem solve for a bit, eh?"

"Well, maybe the trailer tilts or something," Wang said. "Do you see any controls or hydraulics or anything?"

"I don't think so," I said as I walked along the length of the two containers, looking under them. "This just looks like a couple of trailers joined together. I don't see anything obvious that would help unload them."

"I think they must have just used cranes," Gibs said, who had recovered and was looking the whole thing over as well.

"Do you think we could pull them off with the Ford?" I asked.

"Hell, no," said Oscar. "Maybe if it was on rollers or something but not like that. Those things have to be a couple of tons each. That truck would just spin its tires and dig a hole in the ground."

"Ugh, goddamnit, I can't believe we can't think of a way to get this thing unloaded," Gibs growled. "We're the most advanced lifeforms in the known universe; you'd think we could unload a fucking truck. Could we build a shallow ramp? We're not actually looking at finding some forklifts and bringing them back up here, are we? God knows we have enough propane…"

"No, no, just take it easy a moment," said Jake, who had been quietly assessing the truck, just rattling along in his own little world. He looked like he would say more but then fell silent again. He continued to walk along the two trailers while observing them closely, arms crossed over his chest and tapping his lips with an index finger.

Finally, Jake looked at Oscar and asked, "What's the largest dimension of beam lumber we have on hand right now?"

Gibs scoffed and said, "Hey, I was just joking about building a ramp, Jake."

"I don't want to build a ramp. It will take too long. Oscar?"

"We got some four-by-six," Oscar said hopefully.

"That's probably not big enough," he said quietly while looking back again at one of the containers. He clapped his hands once, surprising all of us. "Okay, let's hop in the truck and do some shopping, then."

"Shopping" turned out to be a trip to the local lumber yard (which excited Oscar, predictably). Out of all the places to have survived the apocalypse, it seemed that this had faired the best out of anything I'd yet seen. Apparently, a store specializing in all manner and dimension of board lumber is the last destination on anyone's list of places to go looting. We weren't there for very long at all; just the amount of time it took to load two eighteen foot long six-by-twelve beams into the back of the truck. As soon as they were positioned in the bed, Jake was already hustling us back out of the yard with Oscar resisting him every step of the way.

"Man, let's grab some more of this!" he kept saying. "Leaving all of this wood here is criminal. Do you have any idea what I could be doing with all this?"

"Focus, Oscar," Jake responded happily. "This will all be here later. We have a different problem to solve at the moment."

Oscar was finally nudged back into the truck, looking like a child who was being forced to leave Disneyland early. He kept glancing back at the store as we ushered him away as though someone was going to run up and snatch it any moment. I struggled not to laugh at him; the look on his face was a little adorable.

The next stop was a hardware store that was already becoming a regular destination for our whole group. This place hadn't gotten through the fall as well as the lumber yard; there were a lot of empty spaces on the shelves and some overturned displays belying obvious signs of desperation here. The evidence of struggle was as much in those things that were missing as what had been left behind; all lighting had been removed from the place long ago. One row of shelves in the power tools section was completely bare. Closer inspection revealed that it had once showcased gasoline generators of all shape and size.

Luckily for us (according to Jake), everything we cared about was still available: several hundred pounds worth of cinder blocks and bricks along with several yards of heavy duty chain. The final items he grabbed, while we were all offloading the heavy masonry to the bed of the truck, were four chunky, fist-sized, steel padlocks. With those taken care of, Jake rushed back to help us transfer bricks to the truck, carrying three times the weight of anyone else and almost running from point to point. We spent about an hour loading that truck up, cramming every available vacant inch of the bed with a block of some shape or size. It got so that we began to anticipate being done on each individual trip, but whenever one of us showed signs of slowing down, Jake would fan at us with his hands and say, "We're not done yet. Keep going. This is going to take a lot, and I don't want to make a return trip because we stopped early."

So we kept loading. We loaded the truck until the bed sat dangerously low on the rear axle with the insides of the wheel wells only a couple of inches away from the tops of the tires. We sat back a moment, looking uncertainly at the newly lopsided vehicle.

Gibs said, "I think we overdid it, man. This is apt to fuck the truck up permanently."

Jake nodded, hands on his hips, and said, "Yep. Don't care. There're plenty of other trucks out here. It just needs to get back to the valley."

Jake could be like that sometimes. I usually got sentimental over things like that. If someone had suggested to me that I run my jeep to destruction and then leave it behind on the road some-where, I would have pitched an almighty bitch. That jeep was my baby. Jake wasn't like that at all. When he focused in on some-thing, he went after it, and he would ride any machine into the ground or wear any tool down to nothing to achieve it. He would use anything until it died and then just leave it on the side of the road without a second thought.

The return trip was… interesting. The truck bottomed out at the slightest bounce, and it ended up taking much longer than we'd planned to get home because we had to drive so slow to get there. Jake drove, but I could still tell even from the passenger seat that the truck was handling sluggishly as we began to climb the dirt grade up into the Bowl. The engine sounded… wrong, like it was about to give out, and I kept glancing over at the driver's console looking for warning lights. I heard Gibs mutter, "He's gonna blow the tranny…" from the back seat.

Maybe I'm superstitious, but maybe, just maybe, we made it back only because Gibs said that the transmission was going to fail. If he hadn't actually said that, I'll bet it would have gone out. Anyway, we made it.

What we did with everything when we got back was so incredibly simple that Oscar, Wang, and I felt like a bunch of morons for not seeing it sooner.

Jake started by placing a beam at each end of the rear shipping container, front and back. The width of a container was just under eight feet, so with an eighteen-foot beam at each end, the whole arrangement would have looked like a capital "I" if you could somehow hover high up in the air and look down at the top of it all. With the beams in place, Jake took the lengths of chain (which he had cut into four segments with a hacksaw back at the store) and wrapped them around each beam on the outside of the container, threaded the ends of the chain through holes at the bottoms of each of the four corners of the container, and secured it all in place with the heavy padlocks. With all of that done, he started offloading bricks and cinder blocks from the truck, stacking them up under the four ends of each beam.

He started with the cinder blocks first, stacking them up in a two-by-two column, until they came within a foot or so of contacting the beam. He then filled in the rest of the space with bricks, stacking them up until he could wedge them tightly under the wood. We stood by watching him without comment, trying to figure out how this was going to help anything.

He stood back to look over his work, nodded, and then looked back at the rest of us.

"Make three more of these at each end, please, and get them as close to the trailer as you can."

Without waiting for a response, he made off towards the garage, waving at some of the others who were moving about outside as he passed.

"The fuck is he doing?" Gibs asked.

"I've found it's best to just go along when he gets like this," I said and started transferring blocks.

Jake returned only a few minutes later carrying something that looked like a red fire extinguisher without the top nozzle. It had a handle coming out of the side and a square base at the bottom. Gibs said, "Okay, you have a bottle jack. You could have just told us all this at the outset instead of being all Secret Squirrel about it."

"What?" I asked. "I don't get how this helps."

"He's going to jack it off the trailer," Wang said.

I still didn't understand how it was going to work but didn't say anything. The rest of the guys seemed to get it right off, and it made me feel a little stupid that I wasn't seeing it. I just stayed quiet and played along.

At three corners of the container, bricks were stacked up all the way to the bottom surface of the wooden beam, such that they were wedged in as tight as we could get them. At the final corner, we stacked blocks up only high enough so that the bottle jack could be wedged under the beam. With all of this in place, Jake rubbed his hands together and began to pump the handle.

After a minute or so of this, he began to slow down more and more until he finally came to a stop. He looked the whole thing over with a curious expression and asked, "Has that thing moved at all?"

"Negative," said Gibs.

"Huh," said Jake. He began to walk the perimeter of the container, looking it over at each point of contact.

"I see the problem," Wang said, crouching next to the brick pillar with the jack. We all walked over to join him. "It's actually working okay; it's just that the soil's soft enough that the blocks are compacting down into it."

"Well… shit," said Gibs. "Now what? Stack them higher? Do we have enough?"

"No, we don't need to do that," Wang said, shaking his head. He was still crouched down by the brick stack and gestured with both hands, palms down, towards the ground as he explained: "We just need to find a way to spread the load out over a wider area. You said we had some four-by-six boards, right Oscar?"

"Yeah, that's right."

"Okay, then let's cut those into five-foot lengths and put a few under each pile."

"Under each pile?" asked Gibs. "As in, we have to unstack and restack each pile?"

"Afraid so."

Gibs sighed, "Like a bunch of monkeys trying to fuck a bucket."

"Stand back, you guys," advised Jake. "I don't want you close when I'm operating the jack."

He turned a little silver knob on the side of the jack's base, which caused the central piston to lower back down into the bottle, and removed the jack from the pile. We all began to take each stack down while Oscar trotted back to the garage to select and cut the additional wooden beams. After all of the block stacks were moved aside (I had been shocked to find that the bottom cinder blocks couldn't actually be pulled out of their depressions in the soil without first wiggling them around hard), we all went around and did our best to smooth the dirt over and stamp it down level. Oscar returned around this time carrying three of the five-foot beams in an armload. Jake and Gibs ran back to the garage to retrieve the rest.

As suggested, we placed the beams side by side at each corner and began the painful process of stacking all of the cinder blocks and bricks back up to the bottoms of the beams that were chained to the container. We had a few bricks left over at each point this time due to the distance being shortened by the addition of the wood beams in the dirt.

With everything back in place, Jake replaced the bottle jack and began to pump the handle again. This time, a loud, echoing, metal groan issued from the trailer almost immediately, making us all jump a foot off the ground, and causing us to laugh in varying degrees as Jake continued to pump away at the handle. When the corner of the container was about three inches off the trailer, he stopped.

"Right, so now what?" I asked. "You don't have three more of those jacks, do you?"

"No," Jake said. "What we need to do is make another stack of bricks next to this jack going all the way up to the beam. Then I can lower the jack. This corner will stay raised up off the trailer because of the second stack. Then, we can move the first stack from this location over to another corner and jack that end up. Once we have the other end up, we'll increase the height of the initial stack at that end. We'll just do this at each corner, one at a time until each corner of the container is lifted three or four inches off the trailer. Once we do that, we can just drive the truck out from under it. Lowering it back down to the ground is just the reverse of that process."

"But if we try to do a second stack of bricks, won't that just bury into the dirt too?" I asked.

"Aw, shit," said Oscar. "Hang on; I'll go cut a couple more beams."

"Monkeys and buckets, people," grumbled Gibs. "Monkeys and goddamned buckets."

Within one week's time, we had the outhouses fully constructed along with four shipping containers all lined up next to each other and well on their way to being converted into livable homes. Oscar worked on these like a lunatic, driving himself from sunup to sundown each day, barely ever stopping to eat or rest. He pulled in the rest of us to help along the way, often times just grabbing whoever happened to be close by, yet some of us became regular helpers when we weren't out trying to get more food, that persistent, nagging worry that drove everyone (that still drives everyone today, honestly). Some of us kept coming back to help because we enjoyed learning how to do new things—some in our group had never even driven a nail before—and others pitched in out of simple curiosity; they wanted to see how a row of ugly, boxed containers would turn into anything that a sane person would want to live in.

Each container was spaced about fifty feet apart to help ensure that they would all catch a decent amount of crosswind for ventilation. I wasn't really sure how that mattered since they were just windowless boxes until Oscar explained that each unit would be getting a series of windows on each side for relief in the summer months.

He burned up a good amount of diesel traveling to and from Jackson in that first week alone just getting everything he would need. I usually ended up going along just to fill in guard duty, though we rarely saw anyone out there, and he almost always had one of the larger men along on the trip as well to help him carry items. With all the stuff we brought back to the Bowl, we almost could have built a regular house.

He started by having Fred cut windows out of each unit with the torch that had been left behind by Howard's group a few months earlier. These weren't any small windows either; each "home" got two large sash windows on each side, directly across from each other, which Oscar said would produce a good cross breeze in the warmer months. These windows were cut to a specific size to match—you guessed it—all of the frame windows Oscar had managed to lift from stores in the surrounding city. These were all the high quality double paned affairs, as well. It was fun to watch him go shopping for this stuff. You could see that he was taking extreme pleasure in grabbing the best and most expensive versions of every item he could find since price was no longer a barrier. It didn't help (or perhaps Oscar considered it a great help) that, with the exception of items like sandbags and certain tools like axes, sledgehammers, crowbars, and the like, most home improvement stores were generally untouched by rioting or destruction.

So, as I said, each unit got the two sash windows, not to mention an assortment of smaller windows at various points. Fred also cut holes for doors, in all cases along the longer side walls rather than on the ends, and three holes in each roof to install skylights. None of these units were getting electricity of any kind so Oscar was doing everything he could think of to cool and light them naturally.

The holes looked really ragged to start out, which caused some of us to share disturbed glances, but Oscar's obvious faith and self-confidence sustained us through our doubts. He never showed a moment's hesitation throughout the entire process of converting these units. No matter what part he was working on, he was always mentally further along. I came to realize just how gifted the guy is. It was like he would plan out whatever the current task was that he had to work on and then just stop thinking about it entirely; he would just tell his body to go do it, and it would. And while his body was busy working on that little project, his brain would be busy working out the planning for whatever phase came next. Jake, who is probably the smartest person I'll ever meet, used to just stand back and watch Oscar in either amazement or admiration… it's always hard to tell with Jake because his expressions are so damned subdued, but it was definitely one of those.

When all of the various holes had been cut into the containers, Oscar shifted gears and began to frame the insides with steel studs, screwing each piece directly into the walls of the container with a battery-powered drill. Once the internal framing of the unit was completed, he started up the generator and went around the outer perimeter with an angle grinder (which happened not to be cordless), smoothing out the sharp ends of all the screws that had punched through the surface. Later, he made a second pass around each building and smeared some kind of dark goop over each puncture, which he told us would harden up and seal the hole off from any outside moisture.

He installed all of the windows, skylights, and doors after that. What followed soon after was a bit of inspiration that I was certain came from insanity, yet I was soon proven wrong. Oscar insisted that the scavenging teams go out and get four new fifty-five-gallon drums, preferably plastic, or at least rain barrels if the drums couldn't be found. While the teams were out doing that, he climbed on top of each unit and poured some water over the roof to see which way it would run off (the ground was nearly level, and we hadn't bothered to flatten it out perfectly before setting the containers down, so there was a bit of a tilt to each container; Oscar had insisted this was a good thing as it would keep water from pooling on the tops of them when it rained). He then built a rain gutter running around the entire outside perimeter of each unit and positioned the spouts at their respective runoff points. This stage in the process took long enough that many of the barrels he would need had already shown up by the time he was finishing.

Each container home received a rain barrel (at or around fifty-five gallons) on a raised platform just underneath the spout of the rain gutter, with the gutter itself tied into the feed hose of the barrel through something Oscar referred to as a diverter. He ran the drain hose of the barrel through a hole in the wall into the inside of the home, which he connected to copper plumbing that ran down the wall frame and eventually terminated in a faucet.

When he had finished one of these, he stood back with his hands on his hips and smiled. He looked over at me and said, "So these places'll have running water… ish."

I was impressed, but there were parts of it that I still couldn't figure out. "Where does the water go, though?"

Oscar pointed below the faucet and said, "I'm going to build a sink right there with an open bottom, and we can put like a wash basin or a bucket under it. You'll still have to dump out the water when it fills up, but it's better than running down to the creek every time you need to wash something."

I shook my head, laughed, and said, "This is freaking brilliant! This would have never occurred to me in a million years." Oscar actually blushed when I said that.

I thought for a minute, then, and asked, "Wouldn't it just be easier to run the sink back outside, so we don't have to dump a bucket of water all the time?"

"I thought about that," he said, "but decided not to for a

couple of reasons. For one, we don't want to just dump water back into the dirt. Even if it's dirty, it's still water we could use for, like, crops or whatever, right? I also thought about just running it outside into another barrel, but I didn't like how out of sight that idea was. I was afraid that if we could just make water come and go when we wanted, we might fall back into old habits and waste the stuff carelessly. If we're forced to carry it out and do something with it each time the sink fills up, I think we'll be a lot more careful with it."

"I can't argue with any of that," I said. "So what's next?"

"Oh, all kinds of shit," he said as he walked towards the door. "I gotta pack insulation in all these walls, hang drywall, get it all taped off and sanded, figure out how I'm gonna do flooring… I'll probably give all the kids a bunch of painting equipment and have them paint the outsides of these things just to make sure they're fully protected from rust and whatnot."

"Oscar," I said. He stopped talking abruptly and looked back at me.

"This… this is really impressive. I had no idea you were this talented. I guess I was kind of pissed at Jake when he brought you all back here. I'm pretty sure I didn't hide it very well. Anyway, I just wanted to tell you I'm glad he did. Jake was right… again."

He laughed and said, "Don't worry about it, Amanda. You were feeling the same thing as the rest of us. And, yeah, from what I've seen, Jake seems to make a habit of being right a lot."

"The dick…" I said.

He laughed hard that time, nodded, and agreed, "Yep. The *Dick.*"

18

RANGE MASTER

Gibs

I f Jake didn't want me to turn our people into full Marines, it was at least strongly implied that he was looking for Marine-like objects. I didn't have the first clue how close I was going to be able to get to that goal, and never would until I had a good assessment of where everyone was at. I wasn't holding out a lot of hope for badass levels of competency, but I figured I could at least get them all moving in a similar direction without flagging each other. I didn't really know what to expect at the time and decided to just take things easy and see what might happen.

Getting people trained on weaponry means sending a lot of rounds downrange, so the first thing I had to do was get together with Jake and inventory the tools I had to work with. This was well back in the days before everyone kept a weapon either on their person or locked up in their home, so everything was centrally located up on the second floor of the garage by all of the reloading equipment. It was this whole wooden deck construction that appeared to be custom made after the garage building itself was put up; wrapping around the back of the building in a giant U-shape. There were safes up there at the time but the firearms he and Amanda owned by that point were so numerous that only a portion of them were locked in the garage; the rest were kept under lock and key in the cabin. He and I had both hauled them all over and laid them out on the floor.

I'm not going to belabor this document with a laundry list of manufacturers and features. I will say that, besides Jake's AK and Amanda's bullpup, there were a fair number of rifles in both 5.56x45 and 7.62x39, not to mention a shotgun and some hand-guns. Between that and what my group brought to the party, there was enough hardware there to keep half of our people armed all of the time, which wasn't such a bad start.

The real problem was the ammunition. There wasn't nearly enough of it.

"How many rounds do you have here?" I asked. "Of each?"

"I haven't done an exact count, but I'd estimate on the order of twenty thousand of the 5.56, another eight thousand or so of 7.62, five thousand of assorted shotgun rounds, and probably fifteen hundred of assorted handgun ammunition. Is… is that a problem?" he asked when I began to shake my head.

"That's not enough. We're going to shoot all that up before we even get started," I said.

He sat quietly and blinked at me for a few moments before saying, "You must be joking, of course."

"I'm absolutely not," I said. "I'm fairly certain most of these people have never even fired a weapon before. Look at this," I held up my hands to start ticking off names, "Davidson, Rebecca, Oscar, Wang… uh… Edgar, Jeff, Monica, Greg, Alan, and Alish. That's ten people, not counting yourself and Amanda, the chil-dren, or the infirm."

"Now, do you have any idea how many rounds I'll typically

go through on an average day at the range? I mean just taking it easy and keeping my skills current?"

"I don't."

"Maybe five hundred," I said. "Times ten people. Five thousand rounds, or thereabouts, on day one. And that'll just be enough to start getting them familiar with the various weapons. We've gotta do this for days. Fuck, we gotta do this for weeks to get that muscle memory built up. I need to get them shooting at distance, I need to get them drilling close in, I have to work with them moving in teams. Reloading drills, speed drills, run 'n' guns. What you have here will be about enough to get them to a point where they stop blinking every time a rifle fires. This is going to take an assload of bullets, Jake."

He sat back and boggled at this. "I… well, I never realized… we don't have nearly enough, do we?"

"No, man, we don't. We'll need to find a lot more."

"Shit," Jake whispered, looking down at the rifles and hand-guns all laid out on a blanket along the wooden planks. "Well, what can we do with what we have?"

I sighed and looked at the pile as well. "I suppose I could have them shooting halfway decent groups at a hundred yards. I'm telling you, you're looking at a shitzillion bullets to get them competent. This is what it takes: frequency. It makes all the difference between capable people and hobbyists."

He nodded, drew in a deep breath, and let it out.

"Start them on ARs," he said. "Use fifteen thousand rounds of 5.56 to get them going but don't exceed that. Find a way to stretch that out as much as you can. I'll work on discovering more ammunition. Save that brass; I'll start learning how to reload ammo. Billy had a ton of that material socked away here. It should help us to limp along for a little while, at least."

"Aye-aye," I said, and began pulling out the relevant rifles.

Amanda

I had some idea about what Jake and Gibs had discussed early on specifically because Jake had mentioned it to me beforehand to get my thoughts on the matter and plan out our approach. I did not realize, however, just how seriously Gibs would take his assignment.

By the time he really began making an effort to work with all of us, a general routine had already been established—this was after something like a week and a half or two weeks after his crew had been living with us on the property. Oscar was just finishing off the drywall in the first container home by this point and had built up such a rhythm that he always had the Page brothers (Alan and Greg) working alongside him. He was so impressed by how hard they were willing to work despite their young age and obviously thin frames that he flat out declared the second finished container would be their home without even consulting with Jake or anyone else. We all saw how hard they were driving themselves to get the shelters finished as fast as possible, though, so not a one of us complained over it. I think it also helped that the brothers both turned out to be a couple of jokers as well, once they loosened up around us and began to come out of their shells. Oscar himself was an epic knucklehead, so they fit right in with him.

Besides this activity, there was ongoing scavenging that had to be kept up every single day. The food situation was a constant anchor on everyone's psyche and, after a week of seeing just how much food nineteen people could actually put away, getting more became this constant race we never felt we could actually win.

The problem was that you could never just collect food and stash it away; you had to eat some of it while you were in the process of getting it. So if you found, say, thirty pounds of good, long-life food on a Monday, you'd have to eat some portion of that after you brought it home because people are basically just eating machines… you've got to keep fed every day. So you don't actually get to keep thirty pounds of food. Between nineteen people, you probably only get to keep fifty percent of thirty pounds of food. If you're not as fortunate on the following day and you find no food at all, you end up eating the remaining fifty percent of yesterday's find, and you're back to square one, see?

It was like this, day in and day out, always taking three steps forward and another two back. It really started to wear a lot of us down.

We kept the jeep and dodge truck operating pretty much every day, trying to make the best use of our stored gas before it all went stale. We were still collecting fuel back then, too, because you could still pull usable gas out of vehicle tanks. We knew, though, that whatever we had after winter hit was going to be all we would ever have from that point on, so a lot of our scavenging runs were still being divided up between getting food and keeping the gas barrels filled. Like I said, it was a constant, never-ending race against our own need to consume resources. It was horrible. I can remember looking at some people with resentment for even daring to complain about being hungry. I'd think about all that food Jake and I had managed to store and how long it would have carried us (how long it would have carried Elizabeth) before all these other mouths had shown up. It makes me cringe to remember how I looked at a lot of them back then. The only thing that kept it from coming to a head with me was how hard they were all obviously working. Not a single one of them was lazy. Everyone was looking for things to do; ways to be useful… even George, who could only get around with his cane. I think all of the lazy people must have died off naturally by that point, honestly.

The routine we had fallen into was that half of the people who were physically capable of going out into the city for food (based on age and fitness of body) would head out for the day while the other half stayed behind and covered housekeeping duties. This concept of housekeeping was really just a catch-all phrase that covered any activity we could carry out in the Bowl that benefitted the group. If you were cooking the return meal for the scavenging party, it was housekeeping. If you were washing clothes (we'd constructed a kind of water processing and reclamation station with wash basins out on the north side of the garage), it was housekeeping. Even if you were reading one of the books from Billy's library because you were trying to pick up some new, critical skill: housekeeping.

Small arms training with Gibs became just another aspect of housekeeping. It's probably not surprising, then, that we use the phrases "fire team" and "cleaning crew" interchangeably.

He'd apparently been preparing this for some time because when he invited the first group of us out for the initial session, he already had a little shooting range set up along the north edge of the valley. Two of our folding tables were laid out with a small collection of rifles, magazines, ammo boxes, and what I assumed were cleaning kits on top of them. Twenty yards away, there were six wooden targets with human-shaped, hand painted silhouettes positioned just in front of the tree line.

This first training session included me, Wang, Rebecca, the Page brothers, and Oscar. The others were out scavenging with Jake while George and Barbara stayed back to watch the kids. Gibs had rounded us all up and led us out to the range like a group of ducklings while delivering a speech that felt as though he'd either rehearsed or delivered it a few times already before presenting it to us.

He said, "As some of you may or may not know, Jake has asked me to spend some time with everyone to get you all up to speed on small arms and tactics. Specifically, he asked me to get you all functioning as close to Marines as I could manage."

He paused for a moment to let that sink in as we walked. A few of the others glanced back and forth, some of them looking at me. I kept my face passive and pointedly ignored them.

"The problem with that," he continued obliviously, "is that I'm not really sure if that's a reasonable request, or if it's even realistic. By the way, this isn't because learning to be a Marine is some mystical ability that only a small segment of the population is capable of achieving. Being a Marine really just consists of discipline, training, and repetition. It's a lot more about desire than it is about aptitude. No, what I'm getting at here is that I'm not certain whether I'm equal to the task and, moreover, I'm not sure that turning you all into a bunch of Marine knockoffs is what we should be going for."

As we approached the little impromptu firing range, Gibs turned to face the rest of us with his hands on his hips. "There's a whole list of things that Marines learn that just aren't relevant anymore. You guys don't need to march in formation all damned day. We don't need to spend a bunch of time on uniform regulations, inspections, or making your goddamned beds, obviously. As much as I hate to admit it, as much as it pains my old heart, the Corps is extinct. There's no more United States military, and we're simply not making any more Marines. I'd like to share some of the traditions that made me who I am with the rest of you but, for the most part, I need to be instructing you on those skills that will make you more competent fighters. I'm not treating you people like Marine recruits. You've all made it this far; you're obviously survivors. I'm going to drill you like survivors. Recruits are treated like unformed maggots. I'll assume you all have graduated from maggot status by this point; else you wouldn't be standing. Consequently, let's all just agree up front that I won't be screaming at you like this is boot camp, fair?"

We all nodded to this, to which Gibs responded with a thumbs up and continued, "All that being said, I tend to let my mouth get away from me when I'm talking shop. I'm going to apologize up front for any blue language, okay ladies? We're not men or women out here, now, we're just survivors. I'm not wasting any time tiptoeing around feelings and sensibilities; I have more important concerns right now. Is everyone good with that?"

I didn't bother to indicate one way or the other as Gibs had thrown all that out the window with me a while ago. Rebecca said, "Absolutely," and bounced in place a little, which caused me to suppress an eye roll.

I'm sure this is going to sound petty, but she really rubbed me the wrong way when they first showed up. At the time, I attributed my reaction to all sorts of unflattering aspects of her behavior. She was always flipping her hair around or shaking parts of herself, or she was winking at the guys and puckering her lips out; always putting out her hand to touch the guys on their shoulder or arm. Everything she did was a flirt. On their first evening here, she immediately zeroed in on Jake like a man-seeking-missile. It was tiring… or maybe just boring.

I pulled my eyes off her and put my attention back on Gibs, who was already continuing his speech.

"…will find a selection of AR variant weapons. Now, these are all outstanding, standardized firearms that are easy to operate and maintain, with a few notable exceptions that are just garbage; mainly due to poor manufacturing. Those examples aside, an AR produced by a reputable manufacturer and properly maint… *hey!* Nobody told you to pick anything up, goddamnit!"

The word "hey" had come blasting out of Gibs mouth like cannon fire, causing all of us to jolt in place as though we had been electrocuted. I turned to follow the direction of his gaze and saw Greg and Alan standing by the table, both of them holding rifles. They stood frozen, staring back at Gibs like two preschoolers caught with their hands in the cookie jar. They were holding the rifles such that each muzzle was pointed directly at the other. I cringed inwardly, knowing what came next. Though I had never seen Gibs fully unload by that point, I had spent enough time with him out in Jackson to know how seriously he took this stuff.

"Now, you two knuckleheads have demonstrated amply why it's so important that we're all out here today," Gibs said. "Put the damned rifles back down on the table; you've already flagged each other and everyone out here a dozen times already."

"These aren't even loaded, man," laughed Alan.

Shocked by his answer, I opened my mouth to tell him to just drop the thing, that he was about to be eaten alive, but Gibs was already moving through the group before I could draw breath.

"You ignorant fucking children, drop those fucking rifles on the deck right fucking now! Get your filthy fucking smug little fucking hands off of my fucking weaponry!"

The sheer volume of his voice was stunning. It bellowed across the valley like thunder. Birds dislodged from the trees overhead and flew away, calling back angrily in response to Gibs's unholy tirade. Alan and Greg both dropped the rifles onto the ground, faces pale, and took two full steps away from Gibs as he advanced on them. The backs of their legs bumped into the folding tables and nearly knocked the rest of the assembled weapons into the dirt.

He was in their faces almost instantly, snarling, as he thrust out a hand to point to a spot several feet away from the table, growling that they'd best displace to that point before they were annihilated. They stumbled over each other to move where they were ordered. In the meantime, Gibs reached up to the dead branch of a nearby tree and, yanking for all he was worth, pulled it down with a dry, grinding crack. He laid the length of it up against the trunk of the tree and kicked into the center of the branch, snapping it in half, such that he had two three-foot segments. He picked both of them up and walked over to the teenagers. He thrust a stick into the arms of each boy, both of whom flinched as though they would be struck.

"Here are the only weapons fit for such as you two," he barked. "You will both carry these around with you every fucking place you go, do you read me? You will sleep with them. You will shit with them. You will eat with them. On those occasions when you feel compelled to rub one out, your off-hand will be so occupied. Every time I see you two dumbasses, you'd better goddamn well be carrying those with you. And I swear to every deity that ever existed or will ever exist: if I see either of you *assholes* point the end of those sticks at anything breathing, I'll jam a foot up each of your asses and wear you around the valley like a pair of autistic fucking flip flops! Is all of that perfectly fucking clear?"

Greg shook his head vigorously while Alan nodded with his mouth hanging open.

"Say it, shit-for-brains," Gibs growled. "Say it's clear. I want to hear your childish, mewling voices."

"It's clear! We got it!"

"Out-fucking-standing! Now get the fuck out of here and do whatever it is little children do. When I think you're ready to try again, I'll come and find you."

The two of them literally ran out of the area back towards the safety of the teardrop camper, which they were both sharing. Gibs stood and watched them as they went, not turning back to the rest of us until they were completely out of sight. When they were no longer visible, he nodded and turned to address us.

"The main thing," he said in a calmer speaking voice, "is that a weapon is always loaded until you've cleared it. Let's all try not to forget that."

"What the fuck, man?" Oscar said, clearly disturbed at what he had just seen. "They're… they're just kids."

"Define 'kids,' Oscar," Gibs said. "Do you think they're too young to take a bullet?"

"Come on, Gibs, you know what I mean—"

"No, I don't really think I do, Oscar," said an annoyed Gibs. He didn't quite sound angry, but he was still relentless. "I've seen blue-on-blue casualties before. I'm pretty sure none of you have. I've seen what it does to the guy who pulled the trigger. He spends the rest of his life wishing he had that second back. I don't care if feelings get hurt around here, understand? My mission is to get you all competent and safeguard the group; not to make everyone feel good."

Oscar shook his head and looked down at the ground, unconvinced.

"Just trust me on this, Oscar. Let them sting for a couple of days, and I'll bring them back in. This'll be something they never forget, and I can almost guarantee they'll have their minds on safety forever after. Now, can we please continue?"

Gibs started everyone out on the basics, consisting mostly of the rules of safety, how the weapons were to be held, how they were fired, reloaded, and so on. His discussion on safety was to the point and about as crude as you'd expect. Concepts like muzzle awareness and the assumption that a weapon is always loaded were covered when he unleashed his tirade on Greg and Alan. The subject of trigger discipline was even more succinct; he said, "Keep your booger hook off the bang switch until you're ready to bring the heat." My face screwed up in distaste when he said this, but Rebecca absolutely gagged and coughed at his use of the word "booger." I'm convinced that it wasn't an act, either —she actually gagged violently. I may have had to suppress a bit of a smirk.

There weren't enough slings to go around, so we traded rifles between ourselves throughout the session so everyone could get some familiarity with the device. The only exception to any of this was my own rifle; I was free to fire it, but Gibs didn't want anyone else to use it. He said that he wanted all the newbies to build up muscle memory with a standard carbine and rotating in a bullpup would just complicate the process. Additionally, he had me work with one of the AR-15's to "expand my horizons." I did okay with the rifle even if I wasn't that big a fan. With the exception of the magazine, all of the controls were in familiar locations, and I already knew how to run it due to the brief period I carried an M16. I still didn't like it as much as my Tavor, though. It just felt really uncomfortable holding my left hand way far out in front of me, and Gibs insisted on all of us grabbing the front of the rifle in this hyper-aggressive fashion that had our thumbs wrapped over the top of the barrel, almost as though we were trying to corkscrew the whole weapon. He said doing it that way would help with barrel control and improve our target acquisition, but all it did for me was make my shoulder tired.

We shot a ridiculous amount of bullets. I'll bet we fired twenty times more rounds on that day than I had fired in my whole life up to that point. It was incredible; the whole process morphed over time from being a nerve-wracking rush to a sort of rhythmic routine. We were held to a rate of about one discharge per three seconds, or how long it took to reposition the sights on the target, take a breath, and squeeze the trigger without rushing. If we went any faster than that, Gibs would lightly rest a hand on our shoulders from behind us as a reminder to slow down. He divided his time between doing that and reloading magazines. None of us had to reload a magazine during the entire session. I'm not sure how he was able to divide his attention between this activity and correcting our mistakes (and there were plenty for him to correct, even by me) but he always had a full magazine ready to go when one of our rifles were empty. He just held out a full one and traded for the empty that we'd dropped. He kept us going nonstop for I don't know how long; fire until empty, reload, repeat. He had us shoot from standing, seated, and prone positions. Sometimes he would command us to shoot at other targets instead of our own. The only thing we weren't allowed to do was move around with the rifle; if we had to step back from the firing line, we were instructed to drop the mag, empty the chamber, and surrender the weapon over to Gibs.

Over time, I became numb to firing my rifle. It didn't even feel like firing a rifle towards the end of that session; it was more like I was reaching out with an invisible finger and just tapping the target. If I wanted to touch the head, I'd tap the head. If I wanted to touch the body, I'd tap there too. I didn't even have to think about what I was doing. I could almost feel the fibers of the plywood splintering under the pads of my fingertips. I mentioned this to Oscar after we were done that day and he said he had a similar experience; only he hadn't thought of tapping targets with his fingers.

When we were done shooting, Gibs took us back over to the tables to show us how to strip and clean the rifles, which was something I had never learned how to do with Billy even after we'd settled into the Bowl. He spent a little time monkeying around with my rifle after he had everyone else busy scrubbing out their barrels with wire brushes, trying to figure out how to take it apart. After a few moment's worth of cursing and turning the weapon around in his hands, he found the take-down pin at the butt that, when extracted, allowed the shoulder pad to swing open. From there, he was able to remove the bolt carrier group. Lifting the trigger pack out from the underside of the rifle took even less time. He and I both spent a little more time looking the rifle over to see if there were any other parts that looked like they required removal for proper cleaning. Failing to find anything obvious, I ran some CLP down the barrel while Gibs figured out how to remove the firing pin and extractor from the bolt.

We all must have spent an hour or so out there cleaning our rifles, doing god knows what to our lungs while breathing in all those harsh smelling chemicals. Wang and Oscar started cracking jokes back and forth at each other, causing themselves as well as the rest of us to giggle frequently. I didn't realize that Rebecca had edged up alongside me until I felt her tap on my shoulder.

"Hey, uh, d'you mind if I ask you something?"

I wasn't sure what to make of this, so I just shrugged. She bit her lip, seeming unsure of herself, and then pressed on. "I don't know if this sounds weird, or whatever, but the next time you head out into the city, do you think I could come along with you?"

Thoughtlessly, I said, "Oh, okay. Running low on eyeliner?" I regretted it as soon as I said it and laughed it off to show that I wasn't trying to be a bitch, which probably made it worse. She didn't respond but maintained her position off to my left; a presence I could only just make out from my peripheral vision and yet found impossible to ignore. I looked at her and was shocked by the expression on her face. She was flushed bright red, making the minimal spattering of freckles across her nose and cheeks stand out in contrast; her electric-green eyes shimmered.

"Never mind," she said and moved back toward the other side of the table.

"Hey… wait—" I began.

Whatever emotion had been painted across her face a moment before was now completely hidden, covered up by a perfect smile that failed to hide the tightness in her eyes. "I said it's fine," she emphasized. "Just never mind."

She bent over her rifle and proceeded to scrub at it with an old toothbrush, the plastic head clanging aggressively against the metal edges of the receiver. I caught Gibs looking at me uncomfortably from the corner of my eye and shrugged at him in a

"What?" gesture. He shook his head, clearly not wanting any part of the exchange, and sighed quietly as he began to organize the sundry parts lying along the table top. Thus arranging everything, he returned to the firing line and began to gather up all the spent shell casings into a bucket.

Nice one, I thought. *Queen Bitch of the Year Award goes to yours truly, I guess.*

19

RADIOS

Gibs

Like most men of greatness, my best ideas tend to come to me when I'm sitting on the shitter. The inspiration to go looking for team radios was no exception.

I'd been thinking about the firefight in Denver again, playing it over in my head, wondering about things I could have done better or at least differently. Thinking about Jessica and Kyle. I remembered a specific point when I was running back to the bus with the others, hauling Jessica's unresponsive body, with I don't know how many motorcycles riding up our asses when I thought how nice it would be to radio in for air support. Never mind air support; just being able to radio back to Davidson would have been a major advantage. We could have dug in at a building and call in some help, at least.

I thought back to how things were when the world made sense; when everything proceeded in a confident fog and all things critical to our survival were safely taken for granted. I used to see walkie-talkies everywhere. Security guards all had them; hell, even the cleaning staff for most moderate to large sized facilities carried the things on their hips all day long. Jackson wasn't a large city by any stretch of the imagination, but it still stood to reason that at least a few of these radios could be out there somewhere. All I had to do was go out and find them.

Feeling invigorated (and also a couple of pounds lighter), I finished up my business and tumbled from the outhouse in a rush to get back to the cabin and find Jake. Everyone else was out and about doing their own thing; no one waved at or called out to me as I advanced on the home. Jake never kept his door locked, so I just walked in.

"Jake? Hey, Jake!" I called from the entryway. I stood there for several moments and listened for a response, with only the sound of an empty, dead quiet homecoming back at me. I hesitated, trying to think of anywhere else he might be.

"Hello? Ja-ake? Sound off if you don't want me to take the high-dollar scotch."

I waited a little while longer before giving up, assuming that he was out somewhere working on any one of the dozens of ongoing projects that had to be completed before winter hit. I shrugged and exited back out the front door.

Out on the porch, I leaned against the railing and took in the view of the valley in a slow, sweeping arc. Progress on the Conex homes was just coming around to the finishing touches, with Oscar putting in the final internals including modified wash basins and some premade cabinetry that the group had managed to score out in the city; really, the stuff was intended to serve as simple garage wall cabinets, but Oscar figured out how to install them side by side along the floor and cap them with a little countertop. For a guy who claimed to know jack shit about cabinet making or finish carpentry, he really stepped up to turn those containers into some really nice homes. He'd even added a dividing wall in the center of each unit, with a private bedroom in the rear and a common living area on the opposite end where the front door had been installed. It was a little jarring; outside, they still looked like shipping containers with water barrels stacked on the side, although they were all covered in a solid coat of fresh brown paint and had an assortment of windows along both sides. When you stepped inside, you got the disorienting experience of walking into a nice little bachelor pad in the city... well, you had that experience as long as you didn't look too close at anything. Eventually, you noticed that there were no electrical outlets or switches, the plumbing looked a little off, and the walls had only been taped off but not painted (Oscar said the occupants could handle that themselves). Despite all that, Oscar and the boys had made some lovely homes for our people. With a little furniture, decoration, and TLC they'd end up a damned sight finer than the trailer and RV we'd managed to pick up, anyway.

Off to the right of the house and just outside of the tree line, Oscar had worked with Amanda to stake off a rough area for her future cabin. They'd done some preliminary work; setting up batter boards, running mason's string (what Oscar called dry line) around the perimeter, and so forth. Greg and Alan had been out there to set it up with him along with Amanda. Oscar had appreciated their help on the containers so much that he kind of adopted them both as apprentices and was looking for every opportunity to teach them something new. Each time he could show them a thing, especially something that required a bit of math, he'd tell them, "You pay attention to this, you guys. There weren't a lot of people who knew how to do a layout like this. This is what separates the journeymen from the laborers." He was adamant that his boys would learn to be carpenters and not just ditch diggers.

I'm not exaggerating, either. I overheard him say at one point to them both, "There ain't enough parents to go around anymore, so you boys are gonna be my sons now. I'm looking out for you two now like my little girl. You remember that."

He reminded me how much growing Greg and Alan both

had left to do. I kind of made it a point to get right with those two when I saw how Oscar interacted with them; made it a point to let them know they were still cool with me and invested some one on one time with both of them at the range. I don't know if I ever told Oscar how I learned from watching him with the boys. I guess I'd better before too much time goes by.

Jake's voice came from behind me, unexpected: "Were you looking for me, Gibs?"

I about jumped out of my skin; turned on my heel to see him standing in the open doorway of the house. "Where the hell did you come from? Jesus Christ!"

"From the house."

"Yeah?" I asked. "Why didn't you answer me when I called? I must have been standing in your doorway for a minute."

He nodded as he held up a paperback book that looked like it'd been beaten halfway to death and said, "Sorry. I was trying to learn how to build a smokehouse… meat preservation and all. I have to concentrate pretty hard when I read. I tend to tune everything out." He rolled the book up and mashed it into his back pocket. "What's up?" he asked.

"I want to organize a trip into town. I'll take a small team and go looking for radios."

Jake scratched his chin and looked out into the field. "I suppose you're not looking for new music…"

"No, two-way radios," I said. "FM or something like. There are all kinds of places out there where we should be able to find them. I want everyone to be able to stay in communication with each other when we're out scavenging. It's essential for coordinating activities or calling in help if we get into some shit. I can think of a few times already where they would have made a pretty big difference for me."

Jake lowered himself into one of the chairs on the deck and

asked, "What's the effective range on these things? Do you think they'd reach from Jackson back here?"

"I doubt it," I said. "With an unobstructed line of sight, I suppose we might get four miles or so over UHF. Twice that with VHF. But again, that's best case with a clear line of sight. There are a lot of mountains around here. I don't think the signal would make it. I wouldn't count on anything better than a two-mile range. Good enough for a couple of teams working through an area, though."

"Yes, I agree. You know, I never thought I'd say this, but I really miss cell phones."

I laughed and said, "No shit."

"When will you go?" asked Jake.

"As soon as I can get a team together. I'd like Amanda to come along if that's alright."

"Sure, as long as she's good with it," Jake said. "Out of curiosity, why her specifically? I would have suggested her anyway, certainly, but I'm interested in what you're seeing as well."

"Because she's a hell of a shot with that ass-backwards rifle of hers. She can hold a group as tight as I can at a hundred yards from a standing position, and I've been doing this for decades. And, from what I understand, she keeps her head in a fight. So I want to take her and a less experienced person out when I go. I'll feel better if there are two people who know their shit."

"Yes, well, she does seem to have a natural aptitude. You know, her husband wanted to be a Marine, yes?"

"That's what I hear," I said.

"Maybe the wrong person wanted to sign up."

I shrugged and glanced back over my shoulder into the valley. Davidson was hauling water in a couple of buckets over to the four new homes, probably charging the gravity tanks. He stopped long enough to wave at me. I nodded back. "You never can tell," I said. "I met plenty of people who dreamed about being Marines who made fantastic Marines. Then there were ones who should have excelled but didn't do so well. There's just no telling who'll keep their head when you hand them a rifle and order them to go fight. Trying to guess is typically just a waste of time."

Ultimately, I took Wang out with Amanda and me. I had a feeling about him. I'd never actually seen him in a serious fight; the ugliest one we'd had so far had him hunkered down in a bus along with everyone else while Davidson and I shot rifles out a back window. There were little things he did, though, that suggested he could be one of the good ones. He was smart and cagey, for one thing, which is always a bonus when combined with other abilities. Additionally, he'd expressed a desire to fight against numerically superior forces in defense of his group's territory out in Colorado Springs, rather than just bugging out to hide until they went away. I was well aware of the possibility that all of this could have just been Wang talking big, of course, but I had no indication yet that Wang was all talk. One never knew who might end up being a secret hard ass. If I had been pressed to make a bet, I would have put my money down on Wang, despite what I told Jake about the futility of guessing.

We went out in Amanda's jeep because it was the most agile and capable small vehicle we had. She drove since she knew the area better than either of us; I sat in the front passenger seat trying to clock everything at once, suppressing the urge to call out every little bit of trash in the road, and Wang was in the back. I was feeling pretty good about our loadout. With a small three-man team, there were enough weapons to go around such that we each had a rifle and sidearm. I was carrying my MR556 (the M4/M203 having become Davidson's weapon after I had the necessary time to get him up to speed on it) along with my Beretta M9.

I equipped Wang with a rifle from Jake's cabinet o' goodies; yet another AR variant of some sort. There were so many different manufacturers of these after Colt's patents expired in '77 that it became damned near impossible to keep up with all the different brands. There were a few manufacturer names where you just knew you'd be able to trust the weapon with your life, of course, and then there were the ones out in circulation that you learned to run from. The rifle I settled on for Wang was made by PWS (or Primary Weapons Systems). I'd never fired one of these personally, but I had read good things about the company in general so I took Wang out to the range and we both ran a few hundred rounds through it. I liked the way it operated, but the manufacturer name wasn't what drew me to the weapon; it was the barrel length. My rifle, as well as Davidson's M4, were both outstanding weapons, but they had shorter barrels, having both been designed to function well in CQB scenarios. The issue with a short barrel is that you're sacrificing a lot of muzzle energy, which becomes a problem when you're shooting 5.56 rounds.

The 5.56x45mm is a flat-out devastating round… provided it has enough ass behind it when it hits you. If the bullet strikes you with enough energy, it tends to yaw inside of you, fragments into shards, and dumps every bit of its energy into your soft tissues. As it passes through you, it creates a temporary cavity inside of your body that expands rapidly out from the center; there is basically a little kinetic bomb going off inside of you when it impacts. This temporary cavity can and will expand to the size of a bowling ball; even larger than a bowling ball, in some cases, if the bullet strikes bone, which seems to sharpen impact and transfer energy more violently. Anything in the path of this expanding bubble (your muscle, organs, and any other soft tissue) is ripped to shreds in the violent displacement and will bleed out rapidly after the temporary cavity collapses in on itself and everything slams back into place.

The catch is that the bullet has to really be moving for this to happen reliably; about 2,500 feet per second or better. Bullets lose speed over time. They start losing speed, in fact, as soon as they exit the muzzle of the rifle. When you have a longer rifle barrel, muzzle velocity is maximized, and the bullet will travel for farther distances at a faster rate.

When you're dealing with an M4 style carbine having a barrel length of fourteen and a half inches, you're giving up a tremendous amount of muzzle velocity over distance. You're basically creating a situation where the bullet isn't getting the energy it needs to do its job, cutting the effective range from around five hundred meters down to maybe three hundred or so. This was the primary criticism of the 5.56 round by the way, which I always felt was foolish. If a bullet requires a certain barrel length to perform properly (twenty inches, in this case, for best results), you don't cut five and a half inches off the barrel and then claim the round is a piece of shit when it doesn't behave the way you'd like. That's just moronic.

Wang's new rifle, incidentally, had an eighteen-inch barrel. I'd personally seen Wang perform better than everyone else in our group at distances in excess of three hundred yards on open iron sights; he was the right man to carry the long gun.

Amanda had her ever-present Israeli salad shooter with her as well as her Glock 17 in a leg holster. Along with these items, I was wearing my plate carrier and rig while the others had some sort of concealable ballistic vests which I had been informed would stand up to at least a .38 round at close range. I hadn't seen this myself nor was I aware of them being tested for any higher caliber, but I still felt better with my buddies wearing them. They were bound to be more effective than just t-shirts and good intentions.

Before we left, Oscar offered the tip that any large scale construction site would most likely have a collection of two-way radios. They had apparently used them all the time when he was in the business. Some of those buildings he worked on got up into the tens of thousands of square feet with the work crew spread out over the whole area, so it made more sense for the guys to communicate over radios than it did for them to hoof it from group to group to have a chit chat. We all thanked him and later cursed his name when we drove all over Jackson and the surrounding area looking for anything that resembled a moderate to large scale construction site.

In the grand scheme of things, Jackson is goddamned small. A Kmart is about as big as it gets in this town.

Now, I don't know how it happened, but at some point (a point that transpired some two hours after rolling all over the place) we realized that we'd completely forgotten why we were out there. We were looking for radios. We'd ended up searching exclusively for anything that looked like a large construction site.

"Look around for heavy equipment," I said after Amanda commented that it didn't appear as though we would find something anytime soon. "Earthmovers, cranes… a backhoe."

"I think it's time we give up on the construction angle, guys," Wang said from the back.

"What?" I said, turning in my seat to look at him.

"Oscar was being helpful by giving us options, but construction sites aren't the only place we'll find radios. Where's the closest bank? Banks had security guards, remember? They probably have a whole stack of radios wherever it is those guys had their break room."

I faced forward and sat for a moment with my mouth open, crafting a sufficiently toxic insult to apply to myself while Amanda began to laugh. "Well, I'm glad we brought him!" she said.

"What is it? What'd I do?" asked Wang.

"Nothing, man," I said. "She's just laughing at how stupid we seem to be. Amanda, do you know where the closest bank is from here?"

"Yeah, there's a Wells Fargo just off Buffalo Way. I'll have us there in ten."

"Good deal. Hey, Wang?" I said.

"Yeah, Gibs."

"Thanks for setting us straight. Not to be an ass or anything, but do you think you could do that before two hours go by next time?"

"Sorry, man. It had only just occurred to me, really. I had tunnel vision, too."

"I suppose that makes me feel better," Amanda said, still laughing.

"God, I sure don't," I said. "Remind me to slap Oscar the next time I see him."

"It's not his fault," Wang said. "He was just being helpful."

"Stop being reasonable, damn it. I really want this to be Oscar's fault."

Wang laughed at this and didn't bother to answer with anything further. We all felt like idiots by then. There wasn't much more to do but laugh it off.

What followed was one of the most bizarre, circuitous routes I had yet experienced since settling in the valley. Wells Fargo was probably the biggest personal banking location in the area, but it happened to be buried deep in the center of the city, far removed from any block we'd managed to clear out so far. We were lucky that Amanda was with us; she seemed to have a GPS map of Jackson programmed into her head. We drove through all manner of side roads, switching back and forth block by block, often giving up one block of progress to make up two blocks later.

I used to keep my eyes open on these little excursions hoping to spot military outposts or checkpoints along the way but had long since given up all hope along those lines. Apparently, there had been little to no government presence in Wyoming at all during the fall, owing to the state's low population and vast expanses of nothingness. The guys in planning and logistics evidently decided that it made more sense to ship people from Wyoming into nearby states that were more populous (and thus had emergency infrastructure already in place). Aside from the obvious drawback of having no gear to pillage, the city's never having any military presence meant that the streets had never been cleared off at any point outside of what the local government had managed to accomplish before the total breakdown. To my knowledge, any road clearing around here had been accomplished by our people.

This was evident as we made our way further north. I became convinced that Amanda had finally been defeated by the ubiquitous snarl when she rounded a corner onto a street so tightly packed with cars, trucks, and other vehicles that we couldn't have made it to the next intersection without jumping from roof to roof. Just as I opened my mouth to tell her that it was no big deal and bound to happen at some point, she pulled a hard right up onto the sidewalk and drove through the front yard of a single-family home, veering off to the left to miss the house itself and plow through an opening in the backyard fence. As we passed through a surreal landscape populated by yard toys, a couple of pitched tents, and a swing set, I noticed a line of tire tracks already imprinted into the ground in front of us, indicating that someone had driven through here already.

As we neared the end of the yard, I saw that the fence in front of us had another section knocked out, the leftover material of which was strewn across the ground close by. We drove through the opening into an adjoining yard, which we continued through, passed between another two houses, and emptied out onto a street one block over from where we'd started. This area was much more open in the direction we wanted to travel and made for comparatively smooth sailing.

"I didn't realize you'd been this way before," I said. "When did you open up those fences? Was that before we arrived?"

"That wasn't me," Amanda said. "I only found them that way. Someone else was responsible for that little side passage."

"Nice," said Wang. "Lucky you found it."

"The kicker," Amanda said, "is that I'd been up this way once before when we first arrived with Billy, and that path wasn't there. It was done sometime after we came to live here. There're still people out and about. We run into them from time to time."

"Bad?" I asked.

"Once," she said. "Most times they run away before you realize you've seen anything. We try to call out to them and get them to talk, but it doesn't work out."

"Imagine it has to do with the hardware you're carrying," I said, nodding to her rifle. "Jake left his rifle behind when he approached us, which was good. I might have dropped him otherwise."

"Yes, well, Jake has bigger balls than brains sometimes," Amanda grimaced. "I personally don't see how carrying a rifle makes a person any more dangerous these days. It's just another piece of gear. I'm not about to set mine aside so I can make a stranger feel comfortable."

Her tone didn't leave a lot of room for discussion on the matter, so I let it drop. I could see her point, though. The presence of a rifle didn't automatically indicate an evildoer. It sure as hell upped the ante if you happened to guess the wrong way as to a person's intentions, however.

We pulled into a bank parking lot eerily devoid of cars in a part of the city that was crippled by traffic congestion on the streets. The shape of the bank building was irregular, with jutting sections and recessed alcoves, which all served to capture garbage as it blew past, causing it to pile up waist-high in some areas. Dormant parking lot lights towered high overhead, never to function again; a few of them had fallen to lie at odd angles across the asphalt for tens of meters. The base of each one had a mangled appearance, and I guessed (because all I could do was guess) that they must have been struck by vehicles at some point.

The front door was an all-glass affair that had been thoroughly busted out, leaving the entrance and main lobby of the branch covered in a layer of the same filth that had stacked up against the outside walls. Amanda parked such that we were pointed directly into the structure and lit the inside with the jeep's headlights. The inside of the building looked angry. Hungry. It looked like some half-sleeping thing waiting patiently for three assholes to make the mistake of setting foot inside.

"I really hate how dark everything is on the inside, now," Amanda said as she regarded the entrance. "It doesn't matter if the place is a preschool; it always feels like something's just waiting to jump out and get you. It gets old."

"As long as it doesn't get routine," I said.

"What's that mean?" Wang asked.

I sighed. "You always want to feel that unease when you go in to clear a building. It means you're going to be alert. You want to be switched on like that. If you're bored, you're liable to do something stupid. More than likely you're liable to get a buddy killed." I got out of the jeep, patted down my rig to confirm all was in its place and adjusted my rifle. "Come on. It'll be less spooky once we've been through the place and know the layout."

I approached the bank entrance but stopped just short of walking in, waiting for the others to catch me up. When I sensed they stood close by, I said, "If nothing else, this'll be a good opportunity to practice moving as a team. I'll take point; Amanda, you get the rear. Ready?"

They said they were so I switched on my weapon light, gave what I could see of the lobby from the outside a quick sweep and, seeing no movement, advanced.

There were a series of offices encircling the lobby and entryway of the building, most of which were walled in glass. Regardless of my ability to see inside, I decided to clear each room individually; both to get the practice in for Wang and Amanda and also because each office had a wraparound desk that would easily conceal one or more people if they were crouched.

They moved pretty well and, to my satisfaction, successfully implemented many of the concepts I had covered with them back in the valley, which impressed me considering that I'd only just begun drilling them using the container homes as well as the cabin when Jake would allow it. I did note from time to time, however, that Wang had a habit of covering my sector; essentially, he was pointing his rifle in the same place I was. When you're moving in a team as we were, you want each person to be covering their own sector. You hug a wall whenever you can, and your point guy covers forward. The next guy in line should be covering out in the direction opposite the wall, and so on down the line until you get to the rear position, which needs to cover (surprise, surprise) the rear. The pattern and positions shift around depending on the area, whether you're moving down a hallway, up a staircase, where a door might be positioned within a room, and the like, but the overall concept is the same. Every person covers his own sector and you position in such a way that you can achieve overlapping sectors whenever possible.

Wang had a habit of just following wherever I put my weapon light. I didn't really blame the guy; each physical room layout has a predetermined set of positions that fire team members need to assume automatically. These positions are chosen for the purposes of maximum dominance (or coverage) as well as to ensure that team members aren't flagging each other. There's a lot of shit to remember, all of which changes based on your position in the team, and this all has to be muscle memory so that you can move fluidly through an area, focusing on the task at hand rather than worrying about where your position of dominance was supposed to be, whether you should take a knee or not, and so on. They all just needed a lot more drilling, which would only come with time. Given the circumstances, I was still pretty happy with his performance. All I had to do was whisper, "Wang: your sector," and his muzzle would snap to position (as evidenced by his shifting light).

I soon realized that Amanda seemed to have it all down, either because she'd managed to commit everything I'd covered thus far to memory or because she had a natural instinct for this kind of thing. It was good to know, yet not particularly amazing. You encountered people like her every so often; naturals who always seemed to be in the right place at the right time; folks who always put their feet right and only had to be told a thing once. In my own anecdotal (and also correct) experience, these were the same people who made outstanding dancers; people who seemed forever comfortable in their own bodies and could always move them exactly as they intended... natural athletes, in other words. I didn't know if this was the case with Amanda at the time, though I would later learn that she is, in fact, an outstanding dancer, but she did seem to be a natural. This did not excite me, however. Everyone has a weakness that needs to be worked, without exception. I was just still waiting to discover hers.

We went through the first few offices in quick order, stacking up at the door, moving in to find our points, pronouncing the room cleared, and moving on. By the fourth office, we made what I'll call an unfortunate discovery.

"Jesus Christ!" gasped Amanda. "What the hell?"

"Shit," said Wang.

And he was right. In the back of the office, hidden behind the desk, was a prodigious pile of the stuff. Arranged in various shapes, colors, and consistencies, as though an artist of the obscene had been laboring away for weeks (or maybe even months) at some kind of fucked up, Howard Hughes-level magnum opus of turd sculpture. Judging by the smell, much of it was fresh.

"Goddamn," said Wang, "why the hell wouldn't they just do this in the bathroom?"

"Perhaps the bathroom's already full?" I pointed out.

A gagging sound came from behind us. I turned to see Amanda bent over outside of the office, leaning her right shoulder against the glass partition separating the little room from the lobby. She hadn't actually emptied her stomach as far as I could see, but she looked close to it.

"Okay, come on. Let's move along," I said, and backed Wang out of the room. Shutting the door behind me, I placed a light hand on Amanda's left shoulder and asked, "Okay?"

She nodded without straightening up, panting, and shot a thumbs up over her shoulder. After a few moments her breathing returned to normal and she advanced a few steps forward before standing up, probably so she could put the room outside of her range of vision. Wiping sweat from her forehead, she said, "You forget how disgusting people can be sometimes, you know?"

I agreed with her, though I actually did not ever forget. A pile of shit in a corner is the least of what I've seen, even if it did look like an original Jackson Pollock.

"Hey, can we call this area covered, or what?" asked Wang.

"Have we cleared every office?" I asked.

"Well, no, but come on, man. They're all glass. We can see inside. There's no one here."

"They're not cleared until they're cleared, Wang," I said. "If it was a good idea to clear the first few, it's still a good idea to go through the rest."

"Fu-uck…" he groaned, tilting his head back. "Fine. You're right. Let's get it over with."

It turned out that they were all empty, as I knew they would be, but I didn't care. Empty rooms or not, it was still good practice, and Wang needed all he could get, whether he was willing to admit it or not. It was good for Amanda as well. She was still a little grey after nearly vomiting and moving around a bit helped her to re-center.

We completed the area and thus began to move down a hallway connecting the main lobby to what appeared to be a smaller back area containing additional offices, a cafeteria/rec room area, and, all the way at the end of the hall, what I hoped would be an employee locker room of sorts. I noted this last area, assuming that any kind of security shack or locker would likely be located there. Amanda had the same idea as well, judging by her reaction, but I held them to the plan of clearing area by area, which was probably not a bad idea, in hindsight.

We made our way down the hallway such that we had decent cross cover for a three-man team; I was along the right wall covering the left side of the hallway, Wang was along the left wall covering the right side, and Amanda was to the rear and in the center of us, covering dead ahead. As we advanced, I caught a hint of movement around the cafeteria door jamb on the left side of the hall and extended my hand to stop the others. They immediately tensed up.

My mind began racing furiously, running through options and discarding them as fast as they were considered. If this had been a normal situation, I would have pulled a flashbang off my vest, tossed it into the room, and rolled in hot. This was anything but a normal situation. I didn't know a damned thing about who or what was on the other side of that doorway. In fact, I didn't even know if it was human or not; it could just be a scared dog or nothing at all. It may have been that I just saw a shadow cast by my weapon light. If the room were empty, it would be a waste of a priceless bit of gear; it didn't look like we'd be stocking up on additional grenades any time soon. Even if the room wasn't empty, what if it was just a kid?

I really, really missed having decent intel at my disposal. We usually had a good idea who we'd find in a building when I used to do this stuff for a living; all the recon had already happened by the time we were sent in, for the most part, so we felt more confident about mixing it up. This situation, by contrast, was horse shit. I couldn't decide if I wanted to go in hot or easy.

I finally sighed, coughed out a *"fuck"* beneath my breath, and raised my voice to address no one in particular.

"Alright, goddamnit. Whoever's in there, I hear you… *existing.* I'm coming in right now. I'm armed to the teeth and prepared to ruin your whole fucking experience. I'm only interested in talking, okay? Bullets are expensive, and I hate wasting them, so you be cool and so will I. I guarantee, though, that if you play stupid games, you're going to win stupid prizes."

I glanced back at my buddies. Amanda was good to go. Wang, with his bugged-out eyes and hanging jaw, looked like a spilled can of fuck.

Well, fine. Two out of three ain't bad.

I moved to the left wall and choked up on the door, waiting for the others to stack behind me. When Wang tapped me on my shoulder, I hunkered and pushed in.

There were five of them within easy view as we positioned ourselves in the room, some of them behind an older wooden laminate folding table that had been turned on its side as a useless barrier, given that it would be ripped to splinters and dust by our rifles. Two men were standing out in the open; they were both armed (one with a pistol while the other had a rifle) but had their weapons pointed at the ground. They were all filthy and underfed, giving me flashbacks of the King Soopers in Colorado Springs.

When I saw that their weapons were lowered, I did the same with my rifle and said, "Muzzles down, guys," to the others. They complied, but all of us kept the rifle butts pulled into our shoulders, ready to raise them back up on a moment's notice.

There were two women and three men; two of these men stood armed, as I said. I gave up trying to determine their age. The grime caked onto their faces emphasized every crack and wrinkle, adding on years if not decades to their appearances. Their combined odor was at least as offensive as their appearance; they smelled like sweaty Funyuns and hot, buttery garbage. As I looked closer, I realized the two armed men were frozen solid with white-knuckled grips on their firearms. A loud fart could have knocked them over.

"Hey, ease up," I said. "We're not here to start anything, and we're definitely not here to take… whatever it is you might have. Just… just take it easy."

From my peripheral vision, I saw Amanda disengage the swivel stud on her sling and slowly lean her rifle up against the wall behind her. She resumed her position and let her hands hang at her sides.

Well, now who has more balls than brains? I thought, and refocused on the two men in front of me.

"Why are you here?" asked one of the women from behind the table.

"Just looking for radios," I said.

"Radios?" said one of the men, confusion clear in his voice. "What d'you mean?"

"Radios," I repeated. "Two-way radios, like what you'd see security guards carry. We come from a larger group of people, and we'd find them useful. I don't need to explain why, do I? We suck at smoke signals, is the main thing."

The other armed man snorted. "Yeah, makes sense. What are

you, military or something? You got the look, sorta, but your two friends look like they're wearing daddy's uniform."

I didn't like this one's tone. Of the two armed men, he stood to our right with a guarded (I'd almost say aggressive) posture. I rotated slightly to my right so that all it would take to put a bead on him would be to raise my muzzle. I heard Amanda shift to my rear left as well, but I couldn't see her anymore and so couldn't tell how she had positioned herself.

"Something," I said in answer to his question.

He snorted again and glanced at the others in his group. Turning his attention back to us, he said, "Well, I guess we're all in luck, anyways. There are, indeed, some radios here. We'll let you have them, too, in exchange for food and water."

"Crap," Wang said from behind me. "We don't have any."

"Oh, now I have to call bullshit on that," said the snorting man. "You all look well fed and strong, just look at how strong they all look," he glanced back to the others in his group as he gestured at us with a free hand, still holding his pistol in the other; I could see that it was a large framed revolver of some sort, chrome-finished and angry.

"He just means we didn't bring any with us," I said calmly. "Let's just take it easy, here. We can work something out. I'll trade you food and water for radios, no problem. We just have to go back and get it. Are you folks willing to wait here while we go?"

"He said he had a lot more people where he come from, right?" said the other armed man on the left; the one holding the rifle. "Suppose they all come back lookin' to fuck us up?"

"Teddy..." one of the women whimpered from behind the table.

"Hush, now," said the snorting man. I couldn't tell if he was Teddy or not; she may have been talking to the guy with the rifle, or just to the third guy hunkered behind the table with the women.

"Look," said Amanda before I could respond. "If we wanted to light you up, we would have done that by now. Do you see the hardware hanging off my friend's chest? He has at least a couple of grenades. He could have happily tossed one in here instead of talking to you guys. I just put my rifle down. What more do you need?"

"Hard to say," said the man with the revolver. "Could be y'all's just friendly. Could be, you just don't like the odds, one-sided or not. Could be you got six or twelve more like your-self… turns lopsided odds into a sure goddamned thing, don't it?"

"What does that mean, exactly?" I asked, moving my index finger down over the trigger of my rifle. "You don't intend to let us leave? Spell it out for me."

"Whoa, whoa," said the man with the rifle. "Nobody said that! Let's just work through this."

"Yes, let's do," I growled. "We're offering to get you all some food and water in exchange for the radios you say you have. Note: I'm not demanding to see them. I'll go get your munchies without demanding proof, see? What the fuck?"

"One of you stays here," said the snorting man. "Insurance, like…"

"Teddy!" barked the third man behind the table.

"I said to be quiet, goddamnit! I got this!"

"If you're dumb enough to think I'm leaving one of my people here with you, I have to question how it's even possible that you know how to breathe," I said.

Things got very quiet. There was a good five-count where nobody said anything, and then finally Teddy whispered, "I guess we have a real problem, then, don't we?"

Without raising the revolver, he cocked the hammer back. Three shots erupted from behind me, fast enough to sound like a full-auto machine gun except for the fact that the report was clearly from a pistol. Teddy dropped his revolver, grabbed at the center of his chest, and fell over.

I was on my knees and swinging my muzzle out to the left towards the guy with the rifle, only to see that he had thrown it to the ground, put his hands in the air, and was screaming, "*No, no, no*!" repeatedly. The women and third man had dived out of sight behind the table and were crying audibly.

I looked back to the left and saw Amanda with her Glock out; sweeping the barrel calmly from person to person (I supposed she was able to see the other three behind the table since she was still standing). Wang, to his credit, had his rifle up and trained on Teddy, who lay on the floor, still clutching his chest with one hand, and moaning, "Ah, fuckin' shot me. Fuckin' assholes… what the hell?" Wang's face had gone white as a sheet, and the barrel of his AR trembled visibly.

I engaged the safety on my rifle, stood up, and sidled over to Wang. Placing my hand gently on his weapon's rail, I pushed down steadily and said, "We're good, Wang. Secure that rifle and get a breather. It's okay."

He took a deep, trembling breath, and nodded shakily. There were tears standing out in his eyes, ready to spill over. It was the adrenaline, of course; there must have been about a pint of the stuff chugging through his veins, just like mine.

I walked around behind Amanda and picked up the castaway rifle without looking too closely at it; I felt a synthetic stock, but that was about all I gathered at the time. It turned out to be a Ruger 10/22 Takedown—not exactly an infantry weapon but probably great for small game. I stacked it up against the wall next to Amanda's Tavor and then retrieved Teddy's handgun: a Smith and Wesson .44 magnum.

I dropped out the cylinder and saw that the revolver was empty.

I snapped my attention up to look at Teddy. "You… stupid…

fucking, inbred, extra-chromosomed, sheep-raping, shit-eating, ass clown! Did you really just get yourself killed with an empty fucking gun? Goddamned moron, you should have been a blowjob!"

Teddy didn't answer me, as he had expired.

I stood there, staring at him, wanting to kick his stupid corpse a few times, before I felt something strike the back of my heel. It had been Amanda standing behind me, advising me wordlessly to pull my head out of my ass with a kick to my boot. I realized I'd been grinding my teeth and the muscles in both of my forearms had cramped up due to how hard I was clenching my fists.

"Gibs?" asked Wang.

"Yeah, just... just gimme a minute, will ya?" I took a few deep breaths and turned to have a look at the others in the room. I thought about telling the women to stop their crying and just calm down or about telling the remaining two men to relax that no one else was going to be hurt if everyone just stayed calm. I couldn't bring myself to say any of those things. Teddy had been a dipshit, but he was their dipshit; they were obviously hurting from his loss. I didn't know who he was to them, but they obviously cared. Trying to apologize now or insinuating that everything was going to be okay from here on out would have only been an insult. Instead, I looked at the man crouched behind the table, who could have been my age or twenty years older than me for all I could tell, and said, "You can... see to Teddy, there. I'm not gonna get in your way."

He looked back at me with reddened, enraged eyes but did not move. I shook my head and looked at the other man, who remained standing but was backed against the wall.

"Any more of you here?"

He muttered, "Naw."

Amanda was just slipping her pistol back into the holster on her thigh. She retrieved her rifle, popped her sling swivel back into the stock, and looked around the room impassively. The only thing about her demeanor that betrayed any feeling about what just happened was the jugular vein in her throat hammering rapidly in time with her pulse. She met my gaze, and then glanced away quickly.

"You two stay here," I said to my friends. "I'll go see if there even is a radio."

Disgusted with the whole situation, I moved through the remaining rooms adjoining the hallway rapidly and aggressively, first finding a warren-like sty of a sleeping area packed in among some cubicles with a paltry little pile of food and no water that I could see anywhere. The final room, the room I had assumed to contain the security lockers, was located at the end of the hall. My assumptions about security lockers and so forth were apparently off, though; there were a couple of file cabinets and an empty bookshelf that stood about elbow high. One of the file cabinets had been knocked over, its paper guts spilled all over the floor.

Perhaps even more surprising (or less, depending on how you chose to view the world around you); there were a couple of no-shit two-way radios with matching earpieces all plugged into a dormant charging station on the shelf. I picked up one of the earpieces and saw a small microphone mounted on a clip; the kind of thing you'd affix to your collar or vest.

"Well, thank fuck for that," I said and left the room.

As I walked in the opposite direction along the hall back towards the lobby, Wang called out through the doorway: "Any luck?"

"Yeah, wait one," I said. I moved back behind the teller counter into an area that had an array of desks and tables arranged at odd intervals. Not seeing what I was looking for, I began to knock tables over, yank drawers out of desks, and generally ransacked the hell out of everything. I was more interested in being fast than careful, so there was quite a bit of noise; enough that Wang came out into the main lobby to see what I was up to.

"Are… you okay out here, Gibs?"

"Fine," I said. "I'm just looking for a sack or something. Maybe a duffel bag. I recall seeing that kind of thing in banks. I'm hoping there's something out here because if I don't find it, I suppose the only other option is the vault."

I rummaged around a bit more, my energy beginning to flag as nothing turned up. "I guess it's not a big deal," I muttered. "It's a couple of radios and an AC adaptor. I'm not carrying it all home; it's just a walk out to the jeep." I kept tossing the room, regardless.

"Hey, Gibs?"

"Yeah, what's up?"

"You've been through that set of drawers three times now."

I stopped and looked around at what I'd done. Numerous tables lay on their sides with papers and little shitty ink pens scattered across the floor. Office chairs with broken wheels remained where they'd fallen, resembling either passed out drunks or prisoners too beaten to move anymore.

"What the fuck am I doing?" I asked myself. "A fucking duffel bag?"

Wang stood close by clutching his rifle, saying nothing. I met his gaze. The expression of worry or remorse or whatever the fuck it was made me angry and I struggled to hide it.

"Amanda's okay?"

"Those guys aren't doing anything," Wang responded. "I think they just want us to get the hell out of here."

"I can't blame them," I said as I returned to the hallway. "Let's give 'em what they want."

2 0

SQUARED AWAY

Gibs

We worried about leaving the firearms with Teddy's group for all of twenty seconds before we just decided to bring them out into the lobby. The survivors weren't exactly being responsive after Amanda killed one of their own; they mostly spent the rest of our time together alternating between huddling in a corner of the old cafeteria and glaring in our direction with righteous anger. You can't even apologize to people in such a state or talk your way off the hook. You just have to accept that you're the asshole and be about your business.

"Hey, listen, I'm not gonna leave these here," I said, gesturing at the rifle and pistol that Wang had repositioned on the sink's countertop, "but we're not taking them either. I'm going to stack these out in the center of the lobby where I can keep my eye on them. Then, we'll get in our car and get the hell out of your lives."

I grabbed the weapons while Amanda stood in the doorway, her rifle again held across her chest, and made to exit. Before stepping out of the room, I hesitated, looking down at the threshold where cracked linoleum gave way to shredded, low-pile carpet. Damn it.

"Look, I'm… uh… I'm sorry as hell about what happened—"

"Please just go," one of the women sobbed behind me.

"Right. Fuck me, anyway," I whispered to myself. I passed by Amanda without looking her in the eye, feeling like an ass, walked through the lobby (dropping the rifle and revolver on the floor as I went), and out to the parking lot where Wang waited by the Jeep. They both climbed into the vehicle after me, occupying the same positions we had on the way out. Amanda sighed, fired the engine up, and drove us out of there.

We traveled in silence like that for several minutes with Amanda picking her way back through the confused maze of streets and side roads. Wang was so silent in the back seat I forgot he was there; at one point he coughed loud enough to startle me.

"I'm really sorry," Amanda said.

"What? Why?" I asked.

"I shouldn't have killed him. He didn't even—"

"Hey, knock that shit off right now," I said. "You did the right thing. He cocked the freaking hammer back. How were you supposed to interpret that?"

"He didn't even lift it. It was still pointed at the ground."

"Horse shit," I said. "A person can lift a muzzle and drop someone at that range faster than it takes to respond if you're not ready to go."

"I noticed you didn't bother to put your rifle on him…"

"I should have," I said. "This whole thing was completely screwed up, Amanda, but Teddy died because he was a fucking dipshit, okay? Did he deserve to die? Hell no, but it was his own goddamned fault." I turned in my seat and faced her even though she had to keep her eyes on the road. "You keep your shit squared away, Rah?"

"*Rah*, what the hell does that—"

"*Oorah*, for Christ's sake, Amanda. Say 'Oorah.'"

She looked off into the distance, confused. "I'm not a Marine, Gibs."

"Hey, neither am I. Marines are extinct. I may be a dinosaur, but the thing that stuck with me from the Corps the most is the concept of brotherhood. Family. My family's all dead, both blood relations and the ones I signed up for. You people are the family I got now. And I'm giving you permission. *Oorah*."

"Gibs... I—"

"*Oorah*, you stubborn little shit."

She sighed. "Oorah?"

"Bullshit. Like you mean it."

"Oorah."

"OO-RAH!" I barked.

"Oorah!"

"Goddamned right. Hey, Wang! Oorah!"

"Oorah!" Wang called from the back seat.

"Fuckin' A," I growled and looked back out my window. Once-normal houses passed by, now made surreal in a world where housing tracts full of single-family homes were a relic of a past era.

I carried the radios into the garage when we returned, all cradled into an arm like a football. There was a little table close to an outlet by the battery pack array up on the second level that had reliable power since we rarely ever used the electricity provided by the solar panels. Amanda and Wang had gone off to lick their wounds; we were all dealing with the Teddy incident in our own way.

I set up the charging dock on the table, fished the little AC adaptor out of a pocket in my cargo pants, held my breath, and hooked the whole thing up. To my relief, a little red LED lit up on the dock. I wasn't ready to deal with the possibility that the gear wouldn't work.

Grabbing one of the little radios (they were the size of a small cellphone rather than the big, black brick of a team radio I used to lug on deployments) and turned it over in my hands to inspect it. It had round edges and a decent sized LCD screen which appeared as though it might be backlit, which meant they'd need to be concealed in some way. It was just as well, really. It was clear that they weren't anything close to being ruggedized; putting them inside of something might help to keep them protected in a fire-fight. About the only thing the little radios had going for them was that they were made by Motorola, which at least suggested that they wouldn't stop functioning after a couple of weeks. I seated the radio into the first slot of the charging dock, noting that the LCD screen did, in fact, illuminate in muted orange. By this point, I was just relieved to see that the thing was taking a charge and quickly seated the other unit.

They both lit up and began to report percentage complete statuses on their screens. I leaned back in the little rolling chair I occupied and wondered about their service life and who might have carried them. I wondered if there was some sort of logging procedure that might have been in place for the bank's security staff to first check the units out at the start of their day and then check them back in before they could leave. Or was it perhaps possible that said radios had been the property of the security guys rather than being provided by the bank? I didn't know how any of that stuff used to work when the world made sense, but I was pretty sure that banks just outsourced their security to other outfits; I guessed gear responsibilities might have been handled by the security contractor instead. I wondered what action, if any, these little radios might have seen. That bank branch had been a pretty good size; maybe had to cover the interests of the surrounding farms and ranches as well. Even so, Jackson was pretty small and remote. I had to imagine they hadn't been used a great deal.

"Well, you guys are gonna see some action now, anyway," I said to the little, yellow devices and got up to leave.

When I reached the bottom of the stairs, I stopped and took a breath. To my left was the palletized food supply that we all managed to build up in the few weeks we'd been scavenging thus far. I don't remember how long we had been living in the valley by that time; three or four weeks maybe, but I could be off.

As an individual, that pallet looked like a near-infinite supply of food. Living in a group of nineteen people, I knew how long it was all likely to last. We might make it halfway into the worst part of winter before it was all gone if we started rationing immediately, which we weren't. Everyone was working their asses off every day, just burning up calories like they were cheap and easily replaceable. This whole plan involving scavenging food from the nearby area simply wasn't getting it done. Food was only trickling in with this approach, and we needed to start hitting on some serious caches really soon.

At some point, maybe within the next month, we were going to have to arrive at a go-no-go decision. If we couldn't get enough food to carry us through the winter, we were going to have to pick up and leave for a warmer climate before we got snowed in, nuclear power plants or not. The nebulous threat of possibly being irradiated kind of took a back seat to the guaranteed outcome of starving to death.

I stood motionless, looking at the group's food, our food, and thought about the people back at Wells Fargo. Before I even knew what I was doing, I was going through the stack pulling out cans, whether it was fruit, beef stew, hash, or whatever. I figured at least two cans per person, or about seventeen hundred calories assuming the can contained some sort of meat. There were four people left, so eight cans. That oughta do it. Seventeen hundred calories per person was enough to make a difference. It could get those people back on their feet. It wouldn't save them; they were starving to death—you could see it in their sunken eyes and too tight faces. But this could put some strength back in them. It could get them back in the fight.

"You okay, Gibs?"

Jake stood in the entryway of the garage, silhouetted by the light outside, made unmistakable by his stillness, his long, shaggy hair, and the meat around his shoulders, which seemed larger since the time we first met, if that was even possible.

"We ran into some people," I said in answer.

"I know. I spoke with Amanda."

"How's she doing?" I asked.

"She's coping. She's with her daughter right now, either reminding herself what she fights for or that she's still human. She's been through some horrible things, but I believe this is the first time she's killed someone that may not have had it coming."

I scoffed. "Her reaction was the right one."

"Well. You and I know that, anyway," he said.

We stood quietly a while, not moving. I waited to be called out on what I was doing, a can of food in each hand, but Jake said nothing further. His silhouette remained planted in the center of the half-opened roll-up door, ape arms just hanging there. Not wanting to burn up a bunch of daylight waffling around, I said, "I'm gonna take some food back to those people… the ones at the bank." My voice sounded defensive even to me, and I hated the momentary weakness. I knew I was doing the right thing.

I also knew what the food situation was. I squared it personally by understanding that I was just going to have to collect more than anyone else the next time I was out; more than I had ever collected before. I'd stay out well past dark if I had to, if that's what it took to make up the debt. I prepared to explain this to

Jake; squared my own shoulders (higher off the ground than Jake's but nowhere near as wide or dense) to argue it out.

"I'll get a bag to carry those," said Jake. "Grab a couple of gallons of water and a first-aid kit as well. We can take the Dodge."

Edgar, George, and Barbara came along to intercept us on the way out to the truck. Well, they came to intercept Jake; I just happened to be out there with him at the time. We'd packed the food into a canvas bag, and I suppose I may have hoped that it would be concealed enough that none of them noticed, but things rarely work out just the way you'd like. I guess the outline of the cans in the bag was pretty obvious.

"Fellas," George said. "Where you off to?"

"What's with the cans?" Edgar asked.

Before I could say anything, Jake said, "Care package. Some new friends out in Jackson could use a little help, I think."

"New friends?" asked George. "They coming around our way?"

"I don't think so," Jake said. "They're more of the independent type."

"You're... taking them some of our food?" asked Edgar.

I answered before Jake could this time. "Yeah, I'm taking them some of our food. They're in bad shape and could use a hand. Is that a problem?"

"I, uh... well..." Edgar sputtered, running a hand through his hair and looking at the ground.

"It just seems a little off, hon," Barbara said helpfully. "Everyone's been busting their humps for weeks building that supply up, including you as well, of course. How are we going to make any headway if we give it all away?"

"I know Barbara, I get it," I said, taking an easier tone with her. "But it's not enough to make or break us. And you didn't see these people. You weren't there."

"It makes a person wonder why he should go out and get any more," mumbled Edgar.

"Easy," George said. "Gibs is a Marine Veteran. He tends to look out for people. We know this about him. We've all benefited from this attitude many times over, lest any of us forget. It's a little disingenuous to start complaining when the very attitude that makes him such an asset in our group gets directed at some strangers in need."

"Yes, George, that's all well and good, but the fact remains," Edgar interrupted. He turned his attention back to me and said, "First off, thank you for your service—"

"Don't… you… even… try to start in with that line," I said.

"I beg your pardon?" he asked, genuinely confused.

"That 'thank you for your service' bullshit. It's what a Vet usually hears right before he's told that he's basically wrong and irrelevant. If someone's gonna tell me I'm full of shit, I want to hear it outright. I don't want to be buttered up. You know how many times I heard that line right before someone told me in the same breath that I was full of shit and didn't know what the hell I was talking about? I'll give you a hint: it's like a big, old, sloppy blowjob in your basic, garden variety porn. It's foreplay, Edgar, and you've just told me that you like it rough."

Everyone stopped trying to say things for a bit after that, not that I could blame them. Being fair, it's probably hard to continue making your point when someone tells you to spit their dick out. Jake decided to step in, once again, to save everyone.

"Was there something I could help you folks with? I can't imagine you ran out to grab me over a couple of cans of food."

Appearing relieved, Barbara almost jumped to provide an answer. She had warmed to Jake considerably during our time there, having decided, apparently, that he was not, in fact, the Boogey Man. "It's about the kids, Jake. We're not doing enough for them here."

"Oh?" asked Jake, showing genuine concern.

"They're kept safe and fed but what about their education? They're more or less left to their own devices all day while everyone bustles around doing their thing, and all. If we don't take an active role in their development, well…"

"They're going to grow up to be a bunch of morons," I concluded for her.

"Okay, um… well, I wasn't going to use the word 'morons' but essentially, yes Gibs. Pretty much."

"We're not suggesting they be taught Shakespeare or Calculus," George said, "but there are basic skills from the old world that we need to hold onto and reinforce for everyone's survival, as you know."

Jake was nodding, looking off into the distance rather than anyone in particular. "This is a good point. I can't believe how much math I've had to employ just in figuring out how much farmland we'll need to support everyone going forward…"

"We have some preliminary plans for this," said George. "I was a high school history teacher, once upon a time, and it turns out our friend Alish taught sixth grade."

"Really?" I said, impressed. "I didn't know that about her."

"We don't know much about her at all," Edgar said. "She keeps to herself for the most part. I don't even know her last name."

"It's 'Rouhani,'" said Barbara.

Edgar stared at her, surprise painted across his face.

"All you have to do is ask, Edgar," Barbara chided.

I started shifting from foot to foot, anxious to be on my way. "Okay, okay, we have a history teacher and a sixth-grade teacher, which basically means a person who can teach everything at an introductory level. You guys have anyone else?"

"Well, I was an accountant," Edgar said, "so I can cover most math as long as it doesn't get too advanced. I haven't touched trigonometry in years, though, and anything higher than that, like calculus or physics, is a deal breaker."

"We were thinking Jeff, too," Barbara supplied.

"Jeff worked at one of those self-serve ceramics joints, didn't he?" I asked confused. "What does that have to do with teaching kids, outside of showing them how to clean a paintbrush?"

"I was thinking he could sort of apprentice with the others, like Greg and Alan have been doing with Oscar," said Barbara. "I think he's struggling to find a place here. Monica and Fred have both mentioned that he looks just all kinds of shaky and uncomfortable when they go out into Jackson."

"I'll second that," I said. "He holds a rifle like it's a snake. I'm not sure he's cut out for that kind of activity. He's not coming up to speed, and there's the real possibility that he's more of a danger than a help out there."

Barbara nodded, "I think it's why he spends so much time with the kids; watching them while the rest of us are out working and suchlike. He's looking for some way to be useful, and I don't believe he has many real-world skills that we need. I think that bugs him quite a bit. Plus, he seems to be good with them."

"Well, I can appreciate that," Jake said. "At least he's actively trying." He glanced at me and twitched an eyebrow in just such a way that I knew he was about to end the conversation; he was letting me know that he knew I was impatient to get going and he was about to handle it.

Sometimes people describe knowing each other so well after years of working or living together that they complete each other's sentences, express a complex idea with a wink and a smile, and so forth, which is a roundabout way to describe what

Jake had just done. Back in the day, I could hold entire conversations with my sergeants with nothing more than simple hand gestures and a few facial twitches. Low bandwidth, high resolution.

The catch is that you typically don't get up to this level of communication until you know someone for a significant amount of time because it's all based on knowing that specific person; all their little idio-whatevers, expressions, and moods. That is, unless you're Jake, apparently. Then you can just start doing that shit after a few weeks of hanging out. I don't know how the hell he managed it, honestly, but he always had a way of reading people.

"We need to be on our way," said Jake "but this dovetails pretty nicely with some things I've been wanting to bring up with the group. Let's get together, either tonight or tomorrow night. Does that work for everyone?"

They all glanced around at each other and nodded.

"Great. We can probably have this knocked out pretty fast, along with some other things. Ready, Gibs?"

I had thrown the food and water into the backseat of the truck and was elevated halfway into the driver's seat. "Yeah, man. Let's hit it."

He waved at the others and hopped into the passenger seat beside me. "Why don't you drive," he advised sarcastically as he checked the safety on his AK and then laid it into the foot-well next to his leg.

It took me a little longer to find my way back out to the bank than it would have taken Amanda, mostly because our first trip out there hadn't been a direct route; we'd spent most of the morning meandering around like idiots looking for a construction site. Jake eventually directed me along the right series of roads, pointing out various landmarks as we went, that got us further north towards the center of Jackson. Once we got into that general vicinity, and once I found Amanda's little backyard passage, I was golden and made directly for Wells Fargo.

The only thing that had changed about the place since I'd been there earlier that day was the position of the sun in the sky and the direction of the shadows along the ground. I asked Jake to grab the food and water, which he did without comment and approached the building lobby.

Sighing, I called into the blackness, "Uh, hey, everyone. I know I said I'd just leave you alone and all but I've brought you guys some food and water. I've got a first-aid kit here, too. I'm gonna bring it all in right now. Please… just, please don't try anything, okay? I'm just bringing some food. Okay?"

I stood there outside the main door, waiting. I must have waited thirty seconds with Jake standing patiently behind me, hoping for some kind of response.

I jerked my head forward to let Jake know I was proceeding into the building. I clicked on my weapon light, throwing the interior into sharp relief, and made a straight line for the cafeteria. It was empty. There was no sign at all that anything had happened there outside of a bloodstain on the floor.

I exited and went another door down the hallway into the tiny cubicle area, only to find it cleared out as well. There had been some blankets, sleeping bags, and a small pile of supplies on the floor the last time I'd been there. Now, there was nothing.

Being unable to think of anything useful to say, I instead landed on the obvious. "They're gone."

"It was a possibility," Jake said from behind me. "I'm sorry, Gibs."

"Fuck," I said. "*Fuck.*"

Jake nudged past me and set the water and bag of supplies down in the middle of the room. "We'll leave this here," he said. "There's always the chance that they come back. If we see them again—"

"Yeah, right," I scoffed.

"If we see them again," he pressed on, "we can do more. That's about the best we have right now."

I shook my head, looking at the meager offering in the center of the floor; things that would go to waste just sitting there. Also, things that I couldn't bring myself to collect and take back to the truck. Not wanting to be an ungrateful asshole, I said, "Hey, Jake. Thanks. Thanks for coming out here with me. You could have done different. Just… thanks for not arguing with me."

He nodded. "Don't worry about it. There are things we all have to do to get to sleep at night. Things we have to do in order to live with ourselves. I understand."

He made to pass by me but stopped just before he did. Standing next to me but facing the opposite direction, he raised a fist and bumped it lightly against my shoulder without looking at me. He exited the building, and I followed him.

21

THE SMOKE PIT

Amanda

I moved a bishop across the board, not paying a lot of attention to where it ended up. Sitting in a low-slung wooden chair on the cabin porch, I cupped my chin and looked out across the field in the valley. From somewhere off to my right, Lizzy said, "Are you okay, Mom?"

"Hmm?" I asked.

"I asked if you're okay."

"Why?"

She gestured to the side of the chess board on the little wooden table between us where a small army of my captured pieces stood huddled together. In comparison, only one of her pawns stood in my own little prison camp. "You're making some pretty bad moves."

"Oh, you always beat me at Chess, Mija."

"But not this bad," Lizzy said and captured the bishop.

"Crap," I muttered and moved a knight to try and fill in the hole.

"You can't do that, Mom."

"What? Why not?"

"Because knights don't move that way. They move two-by-one or one-by-two. They can't move two-by-two."

I sighed and examined the board. Based on her instruction, it turned out that I couldn't legally move my knight anywhere near the vicinity of where I intended due to my other pieces getting in the way. I reached out to move it back to where I originally had it only to realize that I no longer remembered where it was.

"Mija, I'm sorry, can we do this another time? My head's just not in it."

"Okay," she said, clearly disappointed. "I can ask if Jake wants to play when he gets back."

"You could ask one of the other kids to play," I suggested. "You could teach them if they don't know."

"I tried. None of them like it."

I *tsked* and nodded. "That is a problem."

"Did something bad happen when you went out with Gibs and Wang?" asked Lizzy.

I looked at her, small in her chair with her dark brown hair pulled back in a ponytail. Her face had thinned out; lost some of its baby fat. She was too young to be losing baby fat. She had always been a smart child, but she had matured quickly in the previous months. Her perception had become more adult, more penetrating. I decided it was best to be upfront with her. If I fibbed, she would know.

"I got in a fight," I hedged.

"Did you kill them?"

I sighed. "I'm afraid so."

"Good."

I jerked and looked at her, shocked. "What?"

"Good," she repeated. "You wouldn't have done it unless you had to. They must have deserved it."

I didn't know what to say to that or even how to approach it, so I stayed silent.

"I wish I could kill someone," she said quietly.

"What?" I sat up and turned in my chair, so I could look straight at her. "What did you say?"

She hesitated, clearly trying to decide if she wanted to admit to what she said when something inside of her seemed to harden. Defiantly, she said, "I wish I could kill someone."

"Baby," I whispered. "Why… why would you want that?"

"Because it's what we do now. It's what we have to do. It makes us stro—"

She was interrupted by my hand shooting out toward her face. I honestly don't know what I intended; if I was going to slap her or not. The action was almost out of instinct. My hand was definitely on a path to slap her but what she had begun to say had made my arm weak and shaky. I only knew I had to stop her from saying it; that she wasn't going to be able to take any of it back. Rather than hitting her, my fingertips only fluttered across her lips, interrupting her long enough for me to say, "Mija, no. Don't say that. You don't know what you're saying. Killing someone is horrible. You don't ever want to do it. It isn't a good thing."

A wall went up and locked into place between us. I could see it in her eyes as the passion that had been there just before muted, then died. No, that's not right. It hadn't died. It was masked but not hidden. There were many things she had learned from Jake, but the ability to hide all emotion wasn't one of them. Her look was sly and calculating.

"Okay, mom. I understand," she said. Her eyes said: *This is a thing I need to keep to myself, something I need to hide from the world.*

I grabbed her arm and pulled her out of her chair into my lap; wrapped my arms around her and buried her head under my chin. I rocked her like I did when she was a baby while I frantically tried to decide what I should do. I had never anticipated having a problem anything like this as a mother. Elizabeth was eight years old at the time.

"Yo, Amanda!" Fred's voice hollered out from the line of container homes.

"Goddamnit," I whispered over the top of Lizzy's head. I shouted, "What?"

"Look!" he called back.

I craned my head around to see him waving back at me with one hand; his other was pointed across the valley towards the cleft entrance where a dark, unfamiliar SUV lumbered slowly into the open.

"Shit," I hissed. "Get everyone who can fight out here with firearms and everyone else locked down!" I stood and threw open the door of the cabin. Shoving Elizabeth over the threshold, I said, "You know what to do. Get low."

She nodded and thrust my vest out to me, which had been hanging on a hook by the door. I yanked it over my head and pulled the Velcro straps down as tight as they would go. It fit me better than it used to as I'd thickened up a bit (I'd taken up weightlifting with Jake early on), but I still had to cinch it way down around my waist to keep it from swinging. I grabbed my Tavor, which had been placed up against the outside wall of the house, checked the magazine, and peaked into the chamber to confirm there was a round in the pipe.

Several people came scurrying out into the field as I situated myself, some people running flat out for the garage, while others, like Rebecca, Greg, and Alan, helped those who didn't get around so well. I saw Monica yanking her daughter Rose by the hand so powerfully that I half expected her to just pick the reedy girl up and carry her. Everyone made a straight shot for the garage without fail.

Tom and Oscar came running up by then, Tom with his

M4/M203 combo and Oscar lugging Billy's old Remington shot-gun. They looked keyed up, wide-eyed and breathing heavy.

"What the hell is this?" I barked. "I said, everyone!"

"All the other guns are locked up in the safes!" panted Tom.

"Oh, *chinga tu... Fred*!" I hollered at the big man as he ran across the field to the campers. He came to a skidding halt and looked back at me. I waved frantically at him to get back over to the porch. As he approached, I pulled the Glock from its holster on my thigh and thrust it into his hands' grip first.

"What's up?" asked Fred in a state of shock.

"We're out of time, that's what's up," I said back, looking over his shoulder at the advancing SUV. It was hard to make out at a distance, but I thought it might be a Chevy; I was almost certain that what I saw on the grill was the classic bowtie and not just a trick of the light.

"Tom, get upstairs and positioned at the front window. Oscar, hide yourself around the side of the house. Fred: other side. Wait for my signal before you do anything."

"What's your signal?" asked Tom.

"I'll start shooting," I responded, and pulled the rifle sling over my head. They all ran off to get situated, Tom diving through the front door and Oscar clomping off down the planks of the deck. Rather than going down the front steps and running the long way around, he just vaulted over the rail at the end of the deck and hit the ground running. Fred took a smoother approach, swinging first one leg and then the other over the railing on the opposite side; I assumed he took such care owing to his weight and the danger of landing awkwardly. I turned to regard the SUV as it advanced across the field and waited, thinking about the last time something like this had happened. I readied myself; I wasn't going to let it go any further than it needed to this time. Even funny looks would be met with gunfire.

I moved to one of the beams holding the roof up over the front porch and placed the palm of my left hand against it, arm fully extended. I stretched my left thumb out to the side, creating a little rest, and settled the foregrip of my rifle on top of it. I did my best to put the red dot of my optic at a point on the windshield where I thought the driver's head might be and wished (not for the last time) that it had some sort of magnification.

"Hey, Tom?" I called out.

"Yeah!" his voice was muted from his overhead position.

"Can you see what the driver or passenger looks like?"

"Um… negative. The sun's at a funny angle. I can see the driver's hands; he's either a black guy or wearing gloves. That's about it."

I thought back to the bank and tried to remember if any of the people there had been wearing gloves but couldn't recall for sure. Certainly, none of them had been African American. The SUV was unfamiliar as well. We hadn't seen anything like it in the parking lot when we had our mix up.

The vehicle lumbered closer as I tried to suppress my feelings of déjà vu. The SUV was halfway across the valley to our home; my home. I thumbed down the safety selector on my rifle's grip and prepared to blow out the windshield.

Suddenly, the vehicle (which turned out to be a Suburban) came to a halt in the middle of the field. I had just enough time to catch my breath and whisper, "What the fu—" when the high beams flashed three times. Following this, there was fluttering movement on either side of the truck, though with no magnification on my optic I couldn't see for sure what it was.

"Tom," I called to the man positioned overhead, "can you make out what that movement is?"

"Hands," he responded. "There are two sets of empty hands coming out of the passenger side and another set coming out of the driver's side window. They're just kind of waving around and stuff… wait. There's only one hand on the driver's side now…"

The Suburban began to roll forward again as Tom finished speaking, moving much slower than before but still at a good twenty or thirty mile per hour clip. My mind raced as I tried to decide if we were being screwed somehow. Uselessly, I wished that Jake and Gibs were with me. Either one of them would be able to come up with something better than just sitting around waiting for whoever this was to drive up to the front door. They weren't there, though. Almost as soon as we'd returned with our radios from the bank, Jake and Gibs had bundled up a bag of supplies, jumped in the Dodge, and headed off for a destination about which I could only guess. I was on my own; had to make do with the tools I had rather than the tools I wanted. My finger tightened down on the trigger, squeezing through the few millimeters of slop before the mechanism actually engaged and threatened to discharge the first round.

The truck was close enough to read the license plate now. I breathed and waited.

They were a hundred yards out from the common ground when it stopped for the last time. The driver, who I could just barely make out through the double distortion of dirty windshield and low sun glare, again hung his hands out the side window and waved them around, making a big show for everyone watching. The door popped, swung out, and a black man stepped into the open, hands extended high over his head.

"Muzzles up!" I shouted immediately, the urgency in my voice startling even to myself. "Holster weapons! These are friends!"

I popped the swivel stud on my sling and tossed my rifle into the chair I had occupied a few minutes earlier. I vaulted down the steps of the porch to the dirt ground, almost rolling my ankle like an idiot, and started to run at the SUV. I heard wild laughing as I ran; realized a moment later that the laughter was my own.

"Otis!" I shouted. "Otis, you made it, oh my God! I never thought we'd see you again!"

"Eh-hah, hey, hey, girl, I-OOF!" his voice was immediately cut off when I threw my arms around him and began to squeeze.

"I can't believe you're here! Did you guys make it to Oregon? What did you find? Oh, shit! Where's Ben?"

"Easy, easy, Amanda," he laughed. He disentangled himself from me, held me back at arm's length to look me up and down. "You lookin' good, sweetie. Strong."

A voice from off to my left tentatively said, "Dad?" I looked in the direction of the voice and saw Ben and Samantha coming around the front of the Chevy. "Ha-hah! Oh my God, look at you!" I laughed and threw an arm around the boy's neck to pull him in.

"Hey, Amanda," he said, voice muffled by my shoulder. Samantha gave a shy smile from behind him and waved. I looked around and saw that there were only three of them. I felt a flash of alarm, tried to stifle it from my voice and failed as I asked, "Robert?" I looked from face to face trying to find some hopeful sign; finding none.

"No," said Samantha.

"He's, uh, the reason we got out of Oregon," Otis said. "We wouldn't have made it if it wasn't for him. He saved us."

"Oh... oh," I said. I felt as though the wind had been knocked out of me. I thought back to when we last saw them and realized only a few months had passed; maybe four or five at the most.

"Seems like you've picked up some more people," Otis said, looking past me to the cabin. I followed his gaze and saw some of them coming out from cover; Oscar and Fred, Tom stepping off the front porch, Monica leading Rebecca, Jeff, and Edgar out of the garage. "Where's Jake? Billy?"

The sound of Billy's name was a second shot to my ribs. I

took a few moments to regain my composure and said, "Come on, Otis. We all have some things to talk about."

––––––

Jake and Gibs returned an hour later, well after I'd gotten our old friends settled in and somewhat fed. The grownups were sharing a bottle of wine while the kids all had some Kool-aid that was actually cool (as in, it had been left out overnight and then placed in the shade to keep it as cool as possible; we always tried to have a pitcher on hand for the kids if the mix was available). We had this sort-of community bonfire that we ran, not every night but close enough, which was really just an old oil drum stood up on its side about two hundred feet away from the cabin, smack in the middle of everything. We'd throw some scrap wood into it at dusk (there was a lot of scrap lumber left over from Oscar's various projects most times) as well as the day's trash, and light it all up just as the last light of the day was failing. We had all kinds of camping chairs and the like circling the drum, close in enough to feel the heat but not so close that we were breathing down a lungful of smoke; and this was how we typically closed out our days after the evening meal. We would chat, tell stories, make plans, sometimes tell jokes or sometimes cry. It was a good place to meet and end your day. Everyone spent most of their days scurrying around chasing after their individual or group projects—there was always another project to work on, always another problem that wanted to be solved—but the fire brought us all together to reconnect, always.

There was no fire running yet as there was still some daylight left. We all sat around it in our chairs in anticipation of the first spark, everyone agreeing silently that the drum would be set alight after Jake and Gibs returned. Otis wanted to know what had happened to Billy right away, so I told him about the night

Howard had come calling with his people, how incredibly screwed up it had all gotten, and I made it a point to emphasize how hard Howard had tried to bring the situation to a peaceful resolution before he'd been killed by one of his own group. That part seemed intensely important to me. I described how Billy had gone down shooting and what Jake and I had to do in order to finish the job.

I hesitate to mention something here because I'd spent so much of my life being told that such things don't matter, especially in the world as it is now, and yet if I ignore it I'm probably being dishonest; with myself and anyone who reads this. Otis, Fred, and Monica all hit it off immediately as though they'd been friends for years. They were different with each other; their voices became more energetic, and they were quicker to laugh than I had been used to. No matter how you might struggle to ignore or disregard such a thing, their shared heritage and experiences growing up in America created a kind of common footing between them; they seemed to fold themselves up in it like it was armor, and they appeared stronger and more vibrant because of it. I recalled that same experience in my own lifetime; dancing at a quinceañera for any one of my seemingly hundreds of cousins; sitting around a table piled high with masa making tamales with my father and uncles; walking to school with my sister, who I can still barely bring myself to recall or name. Otis, Fred, and Monica laughed together, squeezed each other's arms, and commiserated; allowed the rest of us to be included within their family, pulled us in with their soft smiles and loud voices. And I felt a homesickness that nearly doubled me over from shock of heartbreak. It seemed to me that the stance our society had tried to adopt for the last generation, that skin color doesn't matter, was all wrong. Strip away society, burn it to the ground, and you'll absolutely see how much it does matter. There was a lot of hate being pushed by a lot of different groups towards the end of the world, all of whom were pushing for their own selfish reasons, and underneath it all as a backdrop were row on row of militant youth shouting that race doesn't matter, sexuality doesn't matter, religion doesn't matter, and so on. It all seemed so clear to me sitting around that oil drum, listening to people talk; it mattered so much. What those young, angry kids all missed was that it matters in the right way. All those things that make us different from each other; those are the best things. And all you had to do to get it was to sit down with some friends and tell stories.

"So, let me meet all these new folks you have here with you," Otis said before I could ask him about his own doings over the past few months (I felt he was holding off on telling that story until Jake returned so he wouldn't have to tell it twice). "How did everyone here get together?"

"Actually," Edgar said, "the relationship came about rather organically. I believe we all realized that we could benefit each other and so fell in together naturally."

"That's one way to say it," Wang nodded. "Another way to say it would be that Jake appeared out of nowhere when we were on the verge of starving, took us in, and fed us."

Otis' laughter erupted from deep within his chest. "Yeah, that sounds like Jake, alright." He looked at Edgar, apparently noticed a sour look on his face, and reached a hand out to him, even though they were separated by a distance of some twenty feet on opposite ends of the circle, and said, "Don't take it so hard. He did the same for us once upon a time." He reached back with his left hand and lightly patted the Bushmaster hanging from the back of his chair by its sling; a present from a hundred years ago.

"Well, let's see," George said, "You've gotten a few of our names, but maybe it makes sense if we share our professions as well—"

"Professions?" Otis said, sounding a little surprised.

"That's right," agreed George. "Everyone has a skill set."

"It's basically our plan to not die," Wang said. "There're too many things we have to accomplish in order to get self-sufficient here in the valley for everyone to just be doing whatever they feel like. We have to specialize in certain trades if we're going to have any chance of surviving."

"Hey, bro, you think maybe you could say certain things a little differently?" Oscar said, jerking his head slightly in the direction of his daughter.

"Crap. Sorry, Oscar."

"Wang is blunt, but he's basically got it right," George continued. "There's a lot to do, a lot of us have certain skillsets that transfer well into this environment, so we use them to advance the group's aims, even if that skill is only tangentially useful. For example, I was a history teacher until I retired. Outside of some odd handyman experience I picked up maintaining my own home and the stunning ability to balance a checkbook and pay bills, that's about what I have. I know about stuff that happened a long time ago, and I'm good at telling other people about it."

"I don't want to be rude, sir, but how is that useful?" asked Ben. "It seems like a mechanic or someone like that would be really good to have around right now if you see what I mean."

George smiled and nodded. "That's absolutely correct!" He looked at Otis and raised his glass. "Nice job, Dad. That's a perceptive young man." Turning to address Ben, he said, "So what happens is a certain set of skills and abilities come along with being a teacher, if you're any good at it, at least. Basically: you know how to teach people, which is a lot harder than you might guess. And there are a lot of things that we all need to learn here, especially forgotten things that you can only find in books. As you can see, there are more than a few children here now, all of whom need to continue their education in reading, writing, and math at the very least. These basic abilities are critical because many of the skills we need to survive can now only be learned from reading books. For example, could you make a vessel to carry water over a long distance right now, knowing what you know?"

Ben looked a little surprised. "Well, I suppose I'd just find a water bottle and fill it up."

"Okay, that's fair," interrupted George. "But we're not always going to be able to rely on finding things. What happens when all of the food lying around runs out? How are we going to get more?"

"Grow it or kill it, I guess."

"Correct. Do you know how to do that?"

Ben began to nod his head but then stopped and thought about the question. After a moment, he said, "Yeah, I guess I don't. It's easy to say you should just go kill a deer or plant some food, but there must be more to it than that."

"That's right," agreed George. "And most of us here don't know how to do a lot of what we need to know how to do. So we'll have to learn from reading books and experimenting. You kids will need to learn how to teach yourselves in this way as well, and that's where people like me, Alish, Edgar, and Jeff can help." He pointed at himself and the others in turn as he said their names. "We were all teachers in one way or another at one time; it's the thing we're good at that we can give to the group. We can teach you kids how to teach yourselves."

"I wasn't a teacher," Edgar said. Everyone looked at him, and he held his hands up to the group. "I just don't want you guys to get the wrong idea. We were going to talk with Jake about this when he got back, remember? I didn't think that meant I instantly got my teaching credential. I was just an accountant, guys. It's not that I don't want to do my part. I'm just worried about not doing a good enough job."

A few people around the circle looked surprised to hear him say this; I know I certainly was. Edgar was typically the kind of guy that saw to his own comfort before worrying about others, or at least, that was the aura he usually projected. Listening to him express concern over his ability to help adequately made me second guess my initial impressions of him.

"Besides," he continued, "I'm not exactly great with kids. I didn't have any of my own for a reason. I liked my Porsche a lot more."

On second thought…

"Man," groaned Ben. "I was really happy without math."

"Sorry, bro, but you need math. You can't build anything better than a shack without it," Oscar said.

"That's Oscar," said George. "He and Fred take on all of the building projects."

"And even if you don't have a really useful skill you can always pick one up," Barbara offered. "I never really did anything but putt around in my garden; my husband Lyle worked while I stayed home to… to run the house." She seemed to have stumbled at the end of her statement. She shook her head, coughed nervously, and pressed on. "Well, now Jake has me working with him to put together a crop schedule for next year when spring hits. I guess I'll be the resident farmer."

"A lot of us are kind of in a wait-and-see place right now, too," Monica said. "I was a prison guard myself, back in the day, which you may or may not be surprised to learn has jack to do with surviving in the wilderness." There was some laughter at this; Monica had a no-nonsense attitude that a lot of us enjoyed. "So right now, I help out by going out with the scavenging teams and finding as much food for the group as I can. We think, or at least hope that we'll be living off the land by this time next year and my thoughts are that I have that much time to fall into a new role by then."

"There hasn't been a lot of time to really plan any of this out,"

Edgar admitted. "Mostly it's just been a lot of scrambling to put away enough food to last us through the winter."

"Well, I can definitely help with that," Otis said. "Scavenging, I mean. I have several months' worth of practice built up by now."

"What did you do for a living before the fall?" asked George. His question surprised me; I realized I didn't know the answer and yet felt as though I should have. Otis seemed to me like this old friend that I'd had for years, and I knew virtually nothing about the guy.

He seemed to swell up a bit as he said, "I owned a barbecue joint. Best damned Southern barbecue in New Mexico; I was even featured on some TV shows in my time. Called it *The Smoke Pit.*"

"*Only* Southern barbecue in New Mexico, you mean," Ben muttered.

"Now, that ain't true, boy, we had competition," Otis laughed. "Maybe the only authentic Southern barbecue; I'll let you get away with that."

"I had no idea, Otis," I said smiling.

"It's a long story," he said. "We had a joint back in Atlanta that was family-owned; I kinda broke away to go do my own thing. I used to butt heads with my dad a lot." Ben snorted, nodding to himself as he drew in the dirt with a stick. Otis smiled at his son and struck him lightly on the shoulder.

"Could you butcher an animal, Otis?" asked George thoughtfully.

Otis's expression was mildly surprised. "Well, I s'pose I could try. I've never done the job before, though. The meat always came to the restaurant all carved up and ready to go. I mean, I know where the cuts come from and all; that was my whole business, but my guess is I'd probably be an embarrassment to a real butcher. Probably take me three times as long and screw it up a bit, besides."

"Okay, that's fair," said George. "What about preserving the meat? Long term storage, and such. Do you know about that?"

"Oh, sure. Shoot, I learned a lot of that just from my mamma. Main thing is: we'll need a lot of salt and a smokehouse for that. Vinegar, too, if we want to pickle anything."

"You don't know how to hunt, do you?" asked Wang, mild excitement showing in his eyes.

"'Fraid I can't help you there. Bought my meat, like I said."

"Crap," said Wang, deflating. "Well, it's a start, at least."

"I can't imagine it'll be that hard to hunt down some game," Tom began but was interrupted by Rebecca when she pointed out to the valley entrance and said, "Hey, they're back, you guys."

I turned to see the Dodge coming toward us at a comfortable pace, either Jake or Gibs extending a hand out the driver's side window to wave and let us know all was well. From the corner of my eye, I saw Wang light a match and drop it into the oil drum. The contents began to smolder not long after.

22

THE OREGON TRAIL

Gibs

I knew things were gonna be different when Jake and I returned. A new and unfamiliar suv parked out in the middle of your front yard in the exact spot you'd expect to see nothing at all tends to clue you in on shit like that.

I didn't come out of the truck switched on and ready to snarl, of course. Everyone was sitting all Kumbaya-style around the camp barrel getting ready to roast marshmallows and whatnot, so I was able to utilize my considerable powers of deduction and reason out that the situation was probably not dire. A quick head-count also told me we were having some guests for dinner. I began to say as much to Jake, but before I could even open my mouth, he was already stepping out of the passenger side of the truck while the damned thing was still rolling.

Startled, I called out, "Hey, shit, Jake, come on…" but he'd already slammed the door and was running back around the bed of the truck. I took it out of gear, set the brake, killed the engine, and hopped out while grumbling to myself the whole time. I was met with enthusiastic laughter from one of the newcomers; a black man about my age or a little older, hair grown out a little bushy and graying at the temples with a beard and mustache that was threatening to graduate to Hobo Status any time. He had Jake's hand grasped between both of his and was pumping the damned thing like he was trying to get water to spray out of the other man's ass. They were both yammering at each other, but I missed most of what was said; I had my eyes on who I assumed to be his son, who stood close by, as well as a young girl either in her late teens or early twenties. I started calculating for mouths and calories, thinking glumly about the food I'd just left in the middle of nowhere; it would have easily kept these new people fed for a day. Things were feeling a lot like one step forward and two back these days, and we were running out of time. It was starting to piss me off.

Jake was calling over to me, startling me out of my black thoughts. I walked over to meet the new mouths.

"Gibs, I want to introduce you to Otis, his son Ben, and Samantha. These are good friends of ours met on the road earlier in the year, before Amanda and I had ever set foot in Wyoming."

I nodded and shook first Otis's and then Ben's hand; Samantha kept hers jammed in her pockets, so I passed her a relaxed salute and a smile. She blushed and waved, which served to remind me of my intense powers of animal magnetism, of course. Actually, she made me feel like a dick. I'd just been grousing about the need to feed three new people only seconds ago; her shyness and uncertainty reminded me that I was dealing with more than just mouths. These were people, and they had seen real shit just like the rest of us. I owed them all better. Taking this on board, I straightened up and said, "It's a pleasure to meet all of you. Welcome."

"I guess they've all had some time to chat while we were out," Jake said. "We ought to have a sit-down and get up to speed." He gestured to a collection of chairs at one side of the fire. Some of the others had already coalesced around this point; folks like George, Barbara, Wang, Oscar, and so on. Around the other side of the fire, I saw Jeff surrounded by the kids—Maria, Lizzy, Rose, the new kid Ben walked over to join them, even Greg and Alan, though they tried to hold themselves apart to look cool. Jeff appeared to be telling the children a ghost story that wasn't much for thrills and chills; the kids were all laughing their asses off at him, which he seemed to encourage and went to lengths to amplify. Rebecca and Monica sat by to watch, laughing along with the kids and clapping, while the new girl Samantha was drawn in like a meteor falling into a planet. I realized that he'd succeeded in segregating the adults off into a private bubble and was impressed.

"He's so good with those kids," Barbara said quietly from beside me. "I think we may have found what he was meant to do."

"Maybe so," I agreed and looked over to the adult section. Jake sat in the center next to Otis, who was on his left. Amanda was to his right, and the others fanned out from there. There was an empty chair next to Otis, between him and George. Amanda nodded at me and pointed at the seat.

"Christ," I grumbled under my breath and moved to sit down. I noticed that I was almost directly across from Jeff, who fingered constantly at his wrist whenever he wasn't gesturing around with his hands.

He wore one of those old ID bracelets; it flashed and shimmered in the firelight, looking more like a darting fish under water than a silver chain. He constantly rotated it with his free hand, creating that fishy illusion.

"What happened to Robert?" asked Jake, drawing my attention back.

"I guess I'd better start with Oregon," Otis began.

Otis

We made the side trips that you folks suggested when we parted ways, skippin' down to Barnes first and then up to the tent city Amanda told us about. We had fairly good luck in both places, and from what I could tell, it didn't look like many people had been through to ransack either of them. You could argue that Barnes is kind of isolated—out in the middle of nowhere as it is, even though it has some big, red letters painted along the front— and maybe you could say that the tent city out by Cedar Fort is a bit off the main drag, but I don't think these explanations tell the whole story. For the most part, I think Utah is just empty land now. Weren't that many folks living there to begin with and what was there was mostly killed off when e'rything went to hell. I suspect whoever was left just picked up what they had and lit out. Can't prove any of that, uh'course. I do know that we didn't see a soul in the whole state after partin' ways with Jake's people.

We made our way up toward Oregon through Idaho, taking things easy; never pushin' too hard. We kept our eyes open for other survivors but never saw any. Maybe they wasn't any. Or maybe they was, and they just kept they heads down as we passed. You wouldn't blame them, uh'course. We seen all the good and the bad, out there, and you never could tell which it was gonna be. After a time, it got to feeling like we was the only people left in the world. I recall Ben mentionin' that he felt like you folks, Jake and Billy and Amanda, even little Lizzy, had all been some kind of dream. He said the only evidence he had that any of that happened was his missin' deck of cards. We all thought a lot about you folks during this time. We wondered if it hadn't just been better if we'd followed along with you instead.

The minivan died in Glenns Ferry; a little splat of a town

along the 84 in Idaho, surrounded by a bunch of farmland and such. I couldn't tell you what it was that killed it. I ain't no mechanic; I can change oil or change a belt, but anything worse than that meant a trip to the shop for me, so we lost 'bout a day and a half finding somethin' new, getting' all our things moved over to it, and getting' it all gassed up. It was that old Suburban we found, and it actually ended up working out for us in the end; we had a hell of a time getting' that minivan through certain areas. Felt mighty top-heavy and unstable when you took it off the pavement. That Suburban did just fine any time we had to roll off-road. I wanted to kick myself for not getting' one sooner, once I saw how well it handled that kinda thing.

We took our time gettin' from A to B, like I said. A drive that woulda taken a day once upon a time took us 'bout a week, I'd guess. We made frequent stops for gas like you guys advised, which always ate up a good portion of the day. We got where we was going in the end, slow but sure.

My in-laws (Ben's grandparents) lived in a neighborhood in Portland called Woodstock. I don't know what I expected or hoped to find when we got there. Mainly, I think I wanted to find someone from my wife's side of the family for Ben because he'd lost his mom at such an early age. I wanted him to have someone besides me that he could ask questions about her; about who she was as a little girl and such. I think... I think I may have wanted them for myself as well. Miss my wife. I was lookin' forward to being with her for a long time, and even when she got the cancer, I thought we still had some decent years ahead. It just... ripped her away from us so fast; like to take your breath away.

There was no one there when we arrived. Someone had left a note tacked to the front door (I think it was my mother-in-law, Beatrice—looked like her writing, at least) that said, "Left for camps. May God bless and keep us all." I didn't really know what to do at that point, so the four of us moved into the little house, and I decided to spend some time searching the area. Didn't have what you'd call a long term plan; we just figured one place was as good as another. Portland was pretty big, had lots of dense populated area; plenty of things to scavenge and such. So that's what we did for a while.

During the days, Robert and I would head out into the area to go looking for things; water mostly but anything that was useful, like. At night, we did what we could to keep entertained. We played board games, told stories, and read books. It turned out that Robert had a good speakin' voice and would read out loud for the rest of us often enough if we asked him to. I spent a lot of nights lookin' through old photo albums with Ben, showin' him pictures of his mother as she grew up. I think it's easier for him since he was so young when we lost her. I had a harder time with it; seein' my Gerty again brought a lot of things back, made my chest feel so constricted with grief I could hardly breathe. Did my best to hide it, though, 'cause it seemed to make Ben so happy.

We saw the first people after livin' there... oh... I'd guess it was three weeks or so. We saw them at a distance, Robert and I, and they was skittish, runnin' off and disappearing, like, when they noticed we was there. Couldn't get much of a read on them except to say that there was three of them and they weren't interested in making friends.

Wasn't long after that when a couple of people broke into our house. All four of us was home, thank God; I don't know what would have happened if it'd just been Ben and Samantha that was home when they came through the window. I tried to talk to them, thinking they might just be goin' house to house lookin' for food and just tryin' to let them know this one was occupied. They wasn't interested in talkin', so Robert and I did for them and then gave 'em a look-over when it was done. They did happen to have a duffel bag between them loaded with some supplies, a couple of pistols, and one rifle between them. We took all of that and threw it onto our pile. There wasn't anything else about them that was very special, except that they had red bandanas tied around their arms, just at the elbow. I wasn't sure what that meant at the time, though I was familiar with gang culture and all that foolishness, and what I saw made me uneasy, knowin' what all that might mean.

That encounter shook us up a bit, and we spent the next few days locked up inside, waitin' to see if any more would come callin'. No more came, and yet it took us a while longer to get over it. *We were in an ugly spot surrounded by bad options*, as my mamma would say sometimes. Going out into the city was necessary because that was the only way to get more food, but it was also dangerous because there was obviously people out there waitin' to be found; some friendly and others not so much. So, we didn't want to go out into that alone. It just felt better having someone you trusted to watch your back. Robert had done a lot of growin' up between Utah and Oregon, and he'd become someone I depended on daily. I knew I could rely on him to protect all of us and havin' him at my back with a rifle put my mind to ease. To th'other hand, Ben was too young for any of that kind of activity and Samantha was either too fidgety or too scared to fight. The few times I actually got her to pick up a gun, she'd pinch it in her fingers and pull back into herself like she was waitin' for the whole world to end.

So if we went out lookin' for food and water, it felt really risky without two people to do it but, when we did that, we was leavin' our people undefended at home, and we already knew for a fact that people would find the place and try to come in because it had happened before.

It broke my heart, but we eventually decided it would be best to leave. The house, as it was in the middle of Woodstock, was too out in the open, too hard to defend, and too hard to fortify. We agreed between the three of us (Ben wouldn't agree and didn't want to leave) that we'd pick up and move to a more remote location outside of the city; probably somewhere's high, where visitors would have to work they way uphill to get to it, and hopefully under cover so it wouldn't just draw strangers from miles off by simply existin'.

Leaving that home had been harder than I expected. We'd fought so damned hard to get there, and the place had become a kind of King's X for me; I'd traveled towards it for weeks telling myself that all will be better when we get there, everything just gonna be fine and click into place. And now we was leavin', and it weren't fine. I wanted to take everything in that house with us. There was things all throughout that I recognized from my life with my Gerty, my gal, that her folks had held onto. Her mamma kept a little curio shelf in the front room, and I saw keepsakes that my wife had kept in her room when we was dating, some of 'em given to her by me. I left 'em all there, thinkin' they was more likely to get broke on the road with me.

I took a single photo album with us; one of the ones that had the most pictures of Ben's mamma from the time she was a girl to when she was a woman, even some of our wedding pictures. There was a framed portrait of her and her family hanging in the hallway. I think she was fifteen or so in that picture. I stopped there and kissed the glass over my dead wife's lips and then kissed the glass over her mother's forehead as well, a thank you for givin' birth to the love of this tired, ol' man's life. We lit out.

We spent some daylight movin' 'round the city, trying to get out of it. The streets was all a mess, as you can well imagine, and it took careful plannin' to plot a way through all the chaos that wouldn't see us wedged into a corner someplace. After a while, I got the impression we was bein' herded along; always when I thought we'd gone far as we could, we'd find a way that was open through the worst part of the snarl and it was always feeding us in the same, damn direction. I mean, it may have switched back every so often for a block or two but our direction would always correct back to the same path: northwest—almost the opposite direction we wanted to travel, which was southwest across the Willamette for less populated areas like Shadowood and such.

We eventually came to a place so piled up with cars and garbage that there was simply no way to get through by drivin'. We could either turn around or try to clear away some of the wreckage to get by. I was just getting ready to turn us 'round when Robert said, "Hey, let's get out and try to clear a path. I think we're in luck, here."

I asked him what he meant and, in answer, he pushed a city map into my hands and pointed at it.

"Look, we're right about here, I think, just coming up on Clinton, right? Well, if we can just find a way to push through a couple of blocks west from here, it'll dump us onto these train tracks. They run all the way down until... here, where they split off and go east. We can get off at that point and try to pick up the 99, see? That'll definitely get us going in the direction we want."

It looked really good from the perspective of the map. The main thing was just breakin' through the snarl ahead to get on the other side. There was so much crap piled up at the intersection that you couldn't see over the top of it and, at the center of it all, two trucks had been left spanning the gap, overlappin' and facin' each other in the street.

I nodded to the tangle and said, "Any of that look planned to anyone else?"

"I was just thinking the same thing," Samantha said.

"We don't even have to move both of them," Robert pressed. "I think if we just push one of those trucks back, we can squeak by."

I sighed and nodded. We'd spent all mornin' and the better part of the afternoon getting to this spot. I didn't want to turn back now; we'd have lost the whole day travelin' basically nowhere's.

"Get your rifle, Robert. Let's see what we can do." I looked at the others in the back seat. "You two sit tight."

Robert and I climbed out of the SUV and made it about halfway to the trucks when an ear-piercin' whistle echoed out along the street corridor. We froze in place, both of us liftin' our rifles up, as row on row of heads popped up from behind all the garbage, shop windows, alleyways, and busted-out cars. I never got a complete count of how many was out there, but I'd guess they was at least twenty of 'em. All of them was armed with some sort of gun, and all of them had red bandanas tied 'round they arms.

"Okay, easy, folks! Easy! Let's put those rifles down," a voice called out.

As you might imagine, the sight of several people poppin' up out of nowhere with guns caused me 'n' Robert to do the exact opposite.

A voice, muted more than the first, sang out from behind me, "There they go, he's drawing down, Mike. He's going for it!"

"Whoa, WHOA!" the first one yelled. "Nobody shoots, you hear! Everyone just settle the fuck down!" He popped up from his cover behind the truck that was blockin' the street and skittered out into the open in front of us, wavin' over his head wildly as he came. "Just... Jesus Fuckbunnies, just everyone chill a minute, will yah? Just everyone be cool! I need everyone to not be a bunch of stupids, right on? Disco-titties!"

The answer that floated down from the barricades was patches of silence interlaced with muffled snickers, I'm assumin' because the man who jumped out had such an odd way of cursin'. The good news was that it seemed no one was actually getting ready to shoot us, though there were plenty of barrels pointed straight at us from all angles. I saw a lot of the people behind those barrels ease up and settle back. I took a relieved breath and felt Robert loosen up a bit beside me.

"Hey, guys," the man said, dragging out the word "guys" as though he had some genuinely depressin' news to deliver and he wanted to soften the blow, "my name's Mike. Or, Mikey, if you like; that's what my friends always used to call me." He smiled, half extended his hand to shake, and then drew it back at the last second and wiped it down the front of his jean jacket. He had what looked like sports-gear strapped down over his left shoulder, as though he'd cut a set of football pads in half, cinched one side down over the joint, and strapped it in place with nylon tie straps. I looked around at some of the others and saw that they was all decked out the same, with knee pads, shin guards, and such, and wondered what the hell they thought they was on about. That stuff would work fine in a fist fight, I guess, but most people was carryin' firearms; pistols at least. That hard plastic nonsense wouldn't even slow a bullet down.

Off to my left, Robert snorted and said, "Hey, what the hell is all this, guys? You supposed to be a Comicon cosplay group or something?"

"Easy," I hissed at him. "Those guns're real enough."

"We make it kind of a point to look uniform," Mike said, still soundin' like a used car salesman. "Kind of dress the same? Wear these little armbands and all. Helps us to know who's on our team, you see? It's important to know whose team you're on around here."

"Okay," Robert said, "unless someone just gets a red bandanna and ties it around their arm, right? What's stopping someone from doing that?"

Mike smiled, not unkindly, and said, "Don't think that would work... yet, anyway. Maybe there're enough of us that we don't all know everyone's name, but there's few enough that an unfamiliar face gets noticed."

Nobody said anything after that for at least a good fifteen seconds. It was like some sort of conversation stopper that pulled the life out of everyone. When I got sick of standing around, I finally said, "Say, what is this, Mike? Why're you stopping us? We ain't starting nothin'; we just passing through."

Mike raised his hands in a "hang-on" gesture while bowing his head slightly. "I know, I know, and I'm sorry, you guys. I keep telling folks we need to put some decent signage up, so travelers know what the hell to expect around here, but one thing at a time, you know? The deal is this: you're kind of in a group territory. People don't get to come through this way without they check in, get cataloged, pay a little tax. You know. Mainly, you gotta meet with Raul."

"Raul?" asked Robert. "Who's this, now? Gang leader?"

Mike winced thoughtfully as he wobbled his head back and forth, making a more-or-less gesture with his hand. "Eh, you could say we all kind of fell in behind him, I suppose. I don't know if I'd use the word *gang*, though. Organization, maybe."

"Oh, hell," I said, disgusted. "So you tellin' me you folks are charging tolls for people to pass by? What sort of foolishness is this? Y'all just robbin' people passing by, right?"

Mike was waving his hands over his head again, agitated. "Okay, okay, okay, dude, I hear what you're saying, but I hate to say that this is really how it has to be. There are something like a good hundred and fifty—"

"Two hundred, Mikey," called the man behind him.

"Two hundred! Fine, that's even worse. There're a good two hundred folks in our crew. That's a ton of mouths to feed, man. Can you imagine trying to keep two hundred bellies full on a day to day basis? It's a fucking chore, dude. Believe you me."

He completely dropped the barrel of his weapon, lettin' it hang off his shoulder as he began to build up a momentum.

"We do our best to get by on scavenging, and that's mostly enough to keep us fed, but we run into a real problem when travelers just come... *flitting* through the area. As far as us in our crew are concerned, this is our area that we staked out, you know? We defend it, keep it clean, keep the streets safe at night and all. And now here comes some random people, drawn to the spoils of the fat, dense city, trying to get all set up to compete with us for food and shit. What would you suggest we do? Kick a can and go, 'awe, shucks, guess we'll have to just search that much harder, now'? We have mouths to feed, man. A lot of them are kids."

I dropped my rifle and motioned for Robert to do the same. "I see your point," I said. "Fact remains: you're aimin' to steal from me, whether you call it a toll or not. We just passing through, like I said. We ain't takin' any food out this'ere area. We just wanna leave."

"Cool, cool, cool," said Mike. "But you might also want to stay, you know? Two hundred people could easily turn into Two hundred and… uh, four? Looks like you got two people in your… yeah. Two hundred and four, hey?"

"We join your group just like that, right?" Robert said with sarcasm.

"Well… yeah," said a perplexed Mike. "More eyes, more arms, more strength, right? Why the hell not? How did you think we got so many people? We sure as hell aren't holding entrance exams."

"Okay, look," I interrupted. "We ain't interested in joining up, no offense. Like I said, we're just passing through."

"Yeah, right, I know," Mike laughed while waving me off like I was some obstinate child. "They always want to be stubborn. Either way, come on. We'll go see Raul, figure out what's what, and decide what happens next."

"We'll pass, Mike. Don't feel like goin' to see anyone and we sure 'nough don't feel like joinin'."

Mike's face took on an aggrieved expression, and he said, "Aw, shit. Look, man, this isn't a discussion, okay? You're coming along with us. We're not gonna hurt you or anything like that, but this is how it is. It isn't perfect, but this is what we got."

All around me I saw rifle barrels raise back up and, from some locations, I heard the ratcheting sound of weapon actions as they were cycled.

They loaded Robert and me into the bed of one of the trucks blockin' the street while Ben and Samantha was left in the Suburban. Mike and the fella that kept correctin' him jumped into the bed along with us, keeping they rifles leveled at all times, though they didn't trouble to tie our hands up. Mike said doing so would've been rude. Two other men from Mike's crew climbed into the front seat of our suv. So, all in all, it was a lead truck, followed by the truck me and Robert were ridin' in, and finally our Suburban in the rear.

"We're gonna head back across the Willamette River and travel up into the hills for a bit, okay?" said Mike. "Your suv's gonna stay behind us so's you can look back from time to time and see that no one's dicking around with your friends, see? Everything is totally above board, here."

"Yeah, above board. All except for the whole kidnapping thing, right?" said Robert.

Mike grimaced and said, "It's temporary, kid. Trust me, I'd much rather be drinking a beer and reading a girlie mag."

"Maybe watch that attitude," said Mike's friend. "Someone might end up having to fuck yer face up a bit—"

Mike jerked in his spot over the rear truck wheel and groaned loudly. "Oh, son of a dildo-swinging… can we just not, Pete? Huh? For once, can we just please not have you start off by assuming god-tier levels of douchebaggery? What the hell is it with you, anyway? You watch too many eighties action flicks as a kid? It's like you're trying on every cliché you can think of. You were probably a Verhoeven fan, right?"

Pete looked confused, between his slackened jaw and loosened grip on the rifle. He stared at Mike for a few beats before he said, "Ver… wha? What the fuck're you talking about?"

Mike rolled his eyes and looked back at me. "Right, probably more of a Cameron guy. You're a shoo-in as Henchman Number Three for that Burke dickhead."

"I… what?" Pete reiterated.

Mike ignored him and continued to address me and Robert. "Look, I'm sorry about him and sorry about all the rest of this. Nobody's fucking up anyone's faces," he shot a pointed look at Pete, "unless you guys do something really stupid. We just got this way of doing things. It ain't the best way by a long shot, no sir. But goddamnit, we need *some sorta way*, or everything just runs to shit. Seen it a hundred times. Raul's seen it, too."

I didn't want to get into a big philosophical debate and tried to steer the conversation towards somethin' approaching useful. "Okay, Mike, okay. So we're goin' 'cross the river. Fine. Whereabouts? You got a town hall over there or something like?"

He straightened up and smiled. "Oh, naw, dude. We'll take you up to The Man's house. He's got himself set up in some really nice digs; a place they used to call Pittock Mansion. Some kind of museum or something. You know, that's been, by far, the absolute best thing about this whole little reset? We used to live in a world of complete and total inequity, right? There was, like, this vanishingly small percentage of assholes that owned everything everywhere, a slightly larger group of shlubs who could barely grind out a comfortable living, and then a massive horde of people who had to go without, right?"

He reached over to a cooler, opened it, and pulled out a bottle of water. He grabbed an extra one and held it up questioningly to me and Robert, but we both turned him down, not wantin' to owe anything. He shrugged and handed it over to Pete.

Taking a sip from his own bottle, he continued, "Now, I'm not saying that everyone who was rich was a cock donkey or that everyone who was poor was an unwashed, noble saint, but you have to admit: a violently leveled playing field is kind of fun, ain't it? Take me. Before this all happened, I drove a forklift in a warehouse. I barely scraped enough money together to pay for my shitty-ass apartment from month to month. And now? I'm living The Life in an eight hundred thousand dollar home up in the hills, man. Sure it sucks for all those people who had to die and all, but I'll tell you, this is really working out for those of us that're left and have the brains to organize appropriately."

"This Raul fella," I said, "he knows how to organize appropriately? He raised you all into an army, or what?"

"Naw, we ain't big enough to be called an army," he scoffed, taking another drink. "We're only a hundred and fifty, like I said—"

"Two hundred, Mike," interrupted Pete.

Mike snorted and rolled his eyes again. "Fuck. Yes, two hundred. Thanks again, Pete. But, no, we ain't no army. We're just set up in work crews, plus we have outposts just like the one you ran into all along the river. We have positive control all through the South Waterfront, Downtown, the Pearl District, and the Northwest District. We hold just about everything west of the Willamette, man. Nothing really happens around here without we know about it first. It's really not bad at all."

I looked over at Robert to try and get a sense of whether he was buyin' into any of this. Mike did a good job of sellin' the concept, but I knew Old Boy shit when I heard it. For every nice little perk he was describin', I'm sure there were at least five gotchas just waitin' to rear they heads, every one of them poppin' up right after you signed on the dotted line. I was gettin' a vibe off

Mike, alright. I figured he was lyin' like a no-legged dog. Only question in my mind was: could Robert see it?

Robert didn't give me much to work with; no expression, wink, or nod. Probably best, too. Them other fellas was right up in our business. They'd have caught on if me or Robert tried to get cute. Still, made it hard for me to know how to move forward. I figured I'd need to find a good point where they guard was down and make a grab for one of their rifles. They'd thrown ours in the back of the Suburban, obviously with the intention to keep everything we had whether we decided to hang around or not. I don't know how things would have ended up, either way. If we'd all gone before this Raul, listened to his pitch, and told him 'thanks but no thanks,' would they have killed us or turned us loose?

I honestly can't say. Could be, they'd have just taken everything we owned and dumped us on the road outside the city limit. I s'pose that would have been as good as killin' us. Sure wouldn't have gotten far that way. Won't never know, though, 'cause we never met the son of a bitch.

I don't recall what street we was on when it all went down. All I can honestly remember from right when the you-know-what hit the fan was that gunfire erupted from all around us to start, I saw the silhouettes of helmeted heads and shoulders popping up from rooftops, and Pete hollered out, "Army!" before divin' off the back of the truck with his rifle.

Mike followed over the side soon after, shoutin' over his shoulder as he went, "You'll want to seek some shelter!" He hit the ground, ran across the street, and dove around the side of a building. His head peeked out from around the corner so he could keep an eye on the goings-on.

The doors on both our truck and the one in front of us had opened in the meantime, people fallin' out of both vehicles with weapons firin' at the rooftops. I noticed the driver of our truck wasn't movin', and then realized the whole back window and windshield was webbed out with cracks, and there was blood all up in the cab. Robert grabbed onto my shoulder and hauled me off the back of the truck, causin' me to land awkwardly and wrench my knee a bit. He didn't slow down and kept pullin' on me as he drug us both over to the alley where Mike had holed up. As we closed the distance, the two men sittin' in the front seat of our suv spilled out and ran up to the head of our column to join the fight.

"Wise choice, you guys," Mike panted when we rounded the corner. "I don't think they're doing a lot of discriminating between red armbands and random-ass people."

"What the hell is this?" I yelled, tryin' to be heard over the gunfire.

"Army leftovers," Mike yelled back. "They have a base of some sort set up at the Portland International Airport. I don't think they have much of a command structure left, though; they seem to be pretty disorganized. They've been trying to take our section of the city back for weeks."

"You assholes are at war with the Army?" shouted a disbelieving Robert.

"Eh, I don't know if I'd call it a war. We just sort of disagree on a few key points, you know?"

A bullet whined and snapped as it flew by a few inches overhead, and we all ducked in reflex. I said, "Look, Mike, this is all beyond us. Just let us go. You guys got your hands full. We don't want a damned thing to do with any of this!"

Mike was already shaking his head before I'd finished speakin'. "No can do, my man. The rules are absolute; you gotta see Raul. Just chill here a bit; we'll get this all figured out soon enough."

"Hell with this!" growled Robert. He reached out, wrapped both his hands around the stock of Mike's rifle and yanked hard enough to pull the man off the wall and across the whole damned alley. They rolled all around with the weapon locked between them, lookin' like a couple of 'coons fighting over a hotdog.

"Jee-zus… the fuck're you doin'!" snarled Mike while arching his back and writhin' all around in the trash of the alley. Robert didn't bother to answer, instead lettin' go of the rifle with one of his hands to start hammerin' Mike repeatedly in the face. He got in 'bout five or six solid shots, splittin' Mike's lips, breakin' his nose, and causin' all kinds of mayhem in general.

It was a mistake, though. With only one of Robert's hands holdin' the rifle, Mike had the leverage to angle it back into the boy's chest and fire.

The shot surprised me; sounded somehow louder than all of the other gunfire goin' on around the corner, which was beginnin' to taper off a bit, even though the shot had been muffled due to the muzzle bein' jammed into Robert's body. Robert didn't seem to react at all, outside of shiftin' his body slightly, adjustin' the grip of his left hand closer to the muzzle so he could push it away, and continuin' to hammer punches down on Mike's head. I stood there, horrified; watchin' a patch of red bloom over the boy's left shoulder.

Mike eventually lost all sense and his grip loosened to the point that Robert could yank the rifle from his hand. Robert stood up, leveled the weapon, and fired three rounds into Mike's chest, point blank. He turned to look at me and panted, "We gotta get the fuck outta here." You ever hear someone say, "Such and such a thing turned my bowels to water"? I never really understood the phrase until that moment when Robert spoke to me. I'd been scared and excited in my life before that, but the physical experience of it was always more like a flush of heat runnin' through me or my heart a-jackhammerin' in my chest. This time, the sound of Robert's voice honest to God made my insides churn like they was all liquid an' gettin' stirred up by a paddle.

The boy's voice was all wrong; had gone all croupy and

wheezy. There was this clickin' deep in his throat when he breathed, almost like what you'd hear when you put a playin' card in some bicycle spokes, only slow, like. And he was breathin' hard, breathin' like he was trying to suck down e'ry last bit of oxygen in the area and still couldn't get enough.

I looked down at his body and saw the matchin' red bloom in his shirt over his right chest. I said, "You hit, son," and was shocked at how hard my voice shook.

It only seemed to make him angry. He said, "Damn it, Otis, did you hear me? Come on!" He grabbed me by the collar and pulled me along after him. I did my best to keep up with the one gimp leg but had to hobble pretty fast, takin' a couple of steps for each one of his.

He poked his head out to see what was happening up the street only to yank it back out of sight when a bullet exploded a brick on the wall close by. He fanned dust out of his hair, and I heard Pete's voice call out from across the street, "Mike, what the hell's going on over there? Get your ass out here and fight! Frank's dead! Albert's dead! We gotta get the fuck out of here!"

"He doesn't know what happened. He still thinks he has a buddy back here," Robert wheezed just before launchin' into a coughing fit. He coughed a long time, body doubling over, while the gunfire kept rolling up the street and Pete kept yellin' for his friend Mike to help stir the pot. When he got control of himself, he said, "I'm going to step out and give you some cover. You get your ass over to the suv. Get it started up and ready to roll."

"You're gonna get hit," I said. "There's another way. We can circle back around this building, come out 'round the other side and work our way up from behind—"

He was shakin' his head impatiently. "I can't walk that far." He was leanin' hard into the wall like he was tryin' to keep the building from fallin' over.

"There's not a lot of time," he wheezed. His face got really serious before he said, "Don't you fucking waste this, Otis!"

He swung out around the corner and commenced to light up the entire street. I didn't see what all he was firin' at; I was already hobble-skipping at full speed over to the driver's side of the suv. I just saw Pete go down out of the corner of my eye as I slammed the door behind me. Samantha and Ben was both screaming from their huddled position in the back seat, but I either didn't understand or don't remember what they was shouting.

I had the engine runnin' and the transmission thrown into reverse. I almost stomped on the gas but looked up to Robert instead. He was on his knees by that point. He was still shootin', but the red patch over his shoulder was a lot bigger, and there were new patches of red all over the rest of him as well. He fanned out behind himself with his left hand, shooin' me away like I was some kind of annoyance he was just too tired to deal with. He keeled over onto his side, lifted the rifle up, and kept firing.

I hit the gas.

Gibs

Otis had gone quiet, not bothering to indicate that he was done speaking. He just stared into the flames licking up out of the barrel, lost in his own head, playing back what had happened and no doubt seeing all the things he could have done differently to save his friend. Children laughed from across the way, and I realized Jeff was still over there doing his thing; keeping them all entertained and out of our conversation. I saw that the girl

Samantha sat silently, looking troubled, and I wondered if she had heard anything, or how much she'd heard.

I waited about a minute to give someone else the chance to say something. When no one took it, I asked, "How certain are you that those men on the rooftops were soldiers?"

Otis looked at me, surprised, and shrugged. "I ain't, I guess. Sure dressed the part, from what I could see. They had the helmets, anyway."

"Why do you ask, Gibs?" Jake asked.

"Well, it sounds like they had an ambush set up, only it was poorly executed. When you lay an ambush like that, you typically want an element to close in from the rear and block off any kind of escape, only you folks drove right out of there. I'm just a little surprised."

"I don't think they was interested in prisoners," Otis said slowly. "They never called out at us to surrender or anything. They just up and started firin'."

"Well, as to that," I said, "that all depends on their past history with your group of red-armed bandits. If they'd mixed it up enough with that group, they certainly wouldn't greet them with a handshake."

"Maybe they didn't expect the third vehicle?" Amanda suggested. "Maybe the train was too long, and they couldn't close in from behind?"

"That shouldn't have mattered," I said. "There's typically enough flexibility built into the kill zone that you can correct for things like that."

"Maybe they were just undermanned," said Jake as he rose from his chair. "There could be any number of explanations. Fruitless to speculate, though, with the information we have."

"Where're you going, Jake?" asked Amanda. He was moving across the circle of people towards the cabin.

"I'm going to go grab something. Why don't you take Otis over to Billy's Tree? I'll meet you there."

A few minutes later, Amanda and Otis stood in front of a massive fir tree, though I couldn't tell you the exact kind of tree it was, with Barbara, Wang, George, myself, and the rest of the grownups all standing back from them by a few feet to give them some space. I couldn't see much in the black of night as we were pretty removed from the fire; there were just two people-shaped voids standing out in front of me, about ten feet away. I heard soft footsteps approaching on the right, and Jake's apparition appeared next to them.

"That's Billy, then?" Otis asked.

"It is," said Jake.

There was the sound of a sniffle, followed by Otis again. "You folks saved us all, back then. Didn't have to." His voice shook.

"We're glad you came to find us," said Amanda. I thought I saw an arm go around a set of shoulders, but it was so damned dark I couldn't be sure.

There was the sound of liquid swirling in a bottle, followed by a gasp. Jake said, "Here," and then that same swirling sound and another gasp, this time with a cough.

"Hah!" Otis growled. "This the same stuff we had last time?"

"The same bottle," Jake confirmed. Another round of swirling; this time Amanda gasping.

They were quiet a while. Finally, Otis said, "Always wondered, Jake. What did you say to Robert that day? That boy grew into a different person after we parted ways. He grew into a man. What'd you tell him?"

Jake didn't answer for a good, long time and I thought no answer would be forthcoming, which we'd all grown used to. He surprised us all, though, and said, "Just told him a bit about me. Where I'd been. Where he was heading if he didn't watch it." Another swirl and a cough.

"Yeah," agreed Otis.

I must have been bouncing on the balls of my feet. I'd never heard Jake give up that much before and was holding my breath just waiting for him to say something else. Within my head, my inside voice—that part of me that does the yelling when I become aggravated—was screaming, "What? Fuck, man, don't stop there! More, goddamnit!"

Instead, I said in a calm and controlled tone: "Where is it you've been, Jake?"

I could feel the people standing around me tense up. We were all waiting to hear what he'd say. In the dark, a hand reached out and squeezed mine, though I have no clue who it was. The flesh was soft and loose; I suspected Barbara.

In the darkness, Jake's voice floated back to us, hollow and remote. "Here and there."

A sound of swirling liquid, splattering in the dirt, and Jake was gone.

23

POWDER KEG

Gibs

Though Oscar had busted his ass both day and night to produce housing adequate to meet the demand of our group, it remained that there were still pockets of people packed in tighter than could reasonably be considered comfortable. With three additional people moving into the neighborhood, Oscar, Greg, and Alan redoubled their efforts with urgency to find ways to get everyone housed. This was especially critical, as the housing distribution had not ended up being equitable in some situations; mostly due to the composition of our little subgroups. For example, people with familial relationships naturally wanted to be housed together, and yet these relationships all consisted of no more than two people; Greg and Alan, Monica and Rose, Oscar, and Maria, and Amanda and Lizzy. We simply had to fit more than two people to a residence in order to make the best use of our space, which essentially meant that we were asking families to take on adoptees.

The challenge is that family members paired with acquaintances creates an us-and-them dynamic, which boiled down to the very real problem that most individuals didn't feel comfortable being paired up to live with a family, whether that family was fine with having that person in the home or not. There were cases where it worked out, of course. Rebecca ended up living with Monica and Rose in a container home, as they all did a pretty good job getting along. Alish, who was at the time still struggling to fit in and find her place in the community, ended up staying with the Page brothers, again in another container home; an arrangement I suppose came about naturally just because all three of them had spent the most time together and were all at ease in each other's company.

On the other hand, you had Oscar and his little girl Maria, who had a whole container home to themselves, due in large part to the fact that most people had no desire to encroach on that father-daughter relationship, especially with her at such a young age. It was naturally agreed without the need for discussion that those two just required their own place to be their own way.

A lot of these little live-in relationships came about naturally like I said, but the problem was that the leftovers created some rough dynamics that needed some pretty rapid resolution before shit came to a head. You had Fred Moses, for one, who nobody in their right mind wanted to room with; not because he was a slob or anything—he just snores like a motherfucker. Sleeping anywhere within twenty feet of the man is basically pronouncing a death sentence on quality sleep (unless you're a veteran; guys like me can sleep through anything). Not only that, he had a quirky personality, as I've taken the trouble to illustrate in past entries. I'm still trying to find a good way to describe Fred's temperament and, so far, I've failed to find anything that fits without running my mouth for fifteen minutes to describe him into the ground. Most of the time, the guy is totally personable, right? Quick to laugh, quick to joke, always the first guy to pitch in to help when help is needed, and he'll absolutely break his damned back in the process of helping you out. And yet every so often, you find patches of his hide that are paper thin. It's bizarre. With most people, you just know; you can either talk shit with them or you can't. With Fred, you can talk shit with him *most of the time*, until you find whatever random hot button that manages to piss him off for that day. Then it's all hurt feelings and dick measuring contests until he gets over it. It's tough for me to put my finger on—I hesitate to label the guy a bully; I've seen how they operate, and Fred doesn't fit the profile. But there is definitely a kind of you-got-me-so-now-I'm-gonna-get-you-harder thing going on with him.

So, yeah, people are cool with Fred, for the most part, but nobody wants to live with his Baby Huey ass.

Same deal with Wang and Edgar, for obvious reasons, I should think. Wang has a sharp fucking tongue; a point I've discussed with him on more than one occasion. He's been good about taking the criticism, and I've noted him making an effort to dial it back, but all it takes is a little stress to bring out the personality that I've begun to think of as Belligerent Wang. That guy can do some outright damage with his mouth, and he knows just how to hit those little-exposed nerves that you work so hard to keep covered. He just... lifts the flap off 'em and braises 'em with a torch.

So, a little stress and Wang starts throwing darts. As bad luck would have it, we were all feeling stress in those days because the food situation was a constant concern that just wasn't getting any better and Old Man Winter (the inconsiderate prick) just kept getting closer.

Then there was Edgar. I'm starting to think he doesn't realize how he comes off; the reality is that he's an effortless douche canoe. He doesn't even have to try. It's like he's a virtuoso of condescension and backhanded compliments. He's just always convinced that he knows better than everyone around him, which is only made more insufferable by the fact that the guy is actually pretty smart and does have good ideas.

So, taking all that into consideration, we knew right off that bunking Wang up with Fred was just weapons-grade levels of stupid, so we stuck Edgar and Wang together instead. Yeah, maybe it was kind of a dick move, given that Wang wasn't Edgar's biggest fan either, but Jake and I figured that Fred would have murdered either one of them eventually, so it was what it had to be.

If you're keeping score, this left me, Barbara, George, Davidson, Jeff, and Fred dividing up the available space in the camper and RV we'd found so far. Now, we added Otis, his son Ben, and Samantha into the mix. We had just been treading water in the sleeping situation up to this point, and now we were back to scrambling in order to find a life preserver. As a stopgap measure, we had them assigned to bunks in Lizzy's room in those earliest days when they came to stay with us.

Even with the on again, off again help of Greg and Alan, Oscar found himself hard-pressed to meet demand, so I took time off from slinging a rifle to fill in as unskilled labor. The container homes had been a good idea and had worked out pretty well, but they had just taken too damned long to get into a livable state, and we had folks that needed a roof right now, so we put the scavenging crews back on the hunt for more camping trailers of any shape or size. When time was a factor, you simply could not argue with the ability to tow a ready-made and furnished home back to the valley. All you had to do was get lucky and find one; then it was just a day's worth of effort before folks were moving in.

The morning after Otis's group arrived, I was out on the site of Amanda's future cabin, having been assigned to mixing duty at a wheelbarrow. And by mixing, what I really mean is hour after backbreaking hour of hauling water buckets, upending bags of sand and masonry cement, and mixing up said components into mortar. With a goddamned shovel. I don't know if you realize just how heavy mortar is but in its mixed, liquid form, it's worse. Mixing and slinging that shit for an hour will drain all of the life out of you, never mind doing it all damned day.

We needed the mortar because you can't just build a wood structure right onto the dirt, apparently, because it'll pick up moisture and rot. To counteract this, Oscar's plan was to lay a foundation using cinder blocks, which would be all glued together by the mortar I was mixing up. Thankfully, the stuff we needed to make this happen had all been gathered up from local home improvement stores on earlier excursions; Oscar did the layout on Amanda's cabin, realized what it was actually going to take to get the job done (no, you can't just chop down trees and stack them like Lincoln Logs), and had to put the whole thing on hold while a team went out and stocked up on masonry materials.

It turned out people were happy to help with this project, mostly because they knew that Amanda's cabin was going to end up being a prototype of sorts. Once we figured out the process to build these things, we'd have the main kinks worked out and know how to do the job better and faster, just as we'd seen with the container homes. With this understanding, a lot of folks wanted Amanda's cabin to succeed so that we could learn what mistakes there were to be made (because we would damned-well make them). Basically, a lot of people wanted their own cabins down the line, and they knew that in order for that reality to happen, we had to learn how to build them in the first place.

So, Oscar and Amanda were lining up a block foundation while my tortured ass mixed up batch after batch of mortar. A few hours in and I gave up any hope of actually finishing on that day; resigned instead to just mix the shit either until my arms fell off or some strange evildoer came along and granted me the sweet release of death. At one point, I asked Oscar how much of the stuff he thought we'd actually need to get the foundation laid just so I could gauge how much there was left to do. The son of a bitch said, "Just keep mixing 'till I'm tired, homes," and then issued his little Speedy Gonzales giggle while picking up a cinder block with each hand in an effortless pinch grip that made them look like they weighed no more than a couple of pounds. He carried them over to the line he was constructing and laid them into a shallow trench, leaving me to reminisce sadly on a time when my hands could still work that deftly; they had become so cramped and blistered by that point that I doubted my ability to wipe my own ass.

Oscar called a lunch break towards the middle of the day, right as the morning's scavenging crew was returning from their excursion. These scavenging activities were broken into shifts between a morning and afternoon crew, which helped to ensure that Housekeeping kept moving forward as well as spread out the limited number of firearms. The Page brothers had gone out that morning with Fred and Monica; they would be followed that day by Wang, Rebecca, Davidson, and Alish.

There was a bit of a handoff meeting between the two shift teams that happened during this period; the morning crew would eat lunch with the noon crew and discuss what ground had been covered, what they found or who they may have run into, areas that could use some more careful searching, and so on. As they all settled into chairs at a long table outside the garage, Amanda was setting up our own little picnic spot next to her future home, pulling the lid off a cooler loaded with food and drink while Oscar and I made a low table and stools out of cinder blocks and a few sandbags. The fare was decent; crackers just shy of going stale and some canned meat that she'd cooked up early that morning before wrapping it up in tinfoil.

"I never thought I'd say this," I said, slapping a slice of meat between two crackers and stuffing the wad into my mouth, "but I'd kill for a fresh salad."

"You didn't like salad?" Amanda asked.

"No, not before," I said. "It was pretty much steak, potatoes, and cheese for me. Pasta too, I guess, but all that green stuff wasn't food. It was the shit *my food* ate. I never thought I'd miss it." I turned another cracker-meat sandwich over in my hands, regarding it dubiously, and said, "Damned if I wouldn't do unspeakable things for a fresh wedge of cold iceberg lettuce smothered in ranch. God forgive me…"

"I miss tacos," Oscar said through a mouthful, which surprised a snort out of me.

"Hah, way to perpetuate the stereotype, fella," I said while trying to keep from coughing on my cracker.

Oscar smiled but said, "Hey, bite me, alright? I love it; the white guy who lived off steak and potatoes wants to tell me I'm a stereotype. You doing that on purpose or are you just, like, clueless?"

I shrugged and nodded. "Fair point."

"What I was talking about," Oscar continued, "were the tacos my wife used to make. She'd bust 'em out once a month at least. She made everything up fresh that day; the salsa, guacamole, beans, rice, steak… all that. Man, no one made guacamole like my old lady. And then, right before she put it all out on the table, she'd fry the tortillas in oil on the stove. Her tacos were unbeatable. Every time was the best time, man, no lie."

"What was your wife like?" Amanda asked. "I think this is the first time I've heard you talk about her."

Oscar was quiet for a time, not looking at either of us, before he said, "It's still hard to talk about her, you know? Like, I can talk about things she did, but it's hard to describe her. Who she was. Do you get what I mean? Maybe I'm full of shit…" he trailed off.

"No," I shot out, surprising them both. "You're not full of shit. I think I can speak for Amanda and say we both understand."

Amanda nodded, shifting her gaze from me back to Oscar.

Oscar went quiet again, flipping a cracker between his fingers like it was an edible poker chip. Finally, he heaved a deep sigh and said, "She stayed with me when she had every right—every reason—to ditch my stupid ass and find something better. And she gave me Maria. Everything good about my little girl is because of her mother; I'm too hard and fuckin' stupid to be responsible for any of that. She… I…" He cleared his throat hard, the sound halfway between a scream and a growl. "…can't even say her name without…"

Just like that, Oscar was hunched over and shaking silently, trying to hold in the sobs that I'm sure he was ashamed of, a long life of growing up hard having conditioned him to believe he was embarrassing himself; *behaving womanly*. He had the heel of his right hand jammed over his mouth, with the fingers of his left hand wrapped around the wrist in a vice grip, and his arm muscles bulged as he fought to stop up his mouth with the palm.

Amanda positioned herself closer to him, wrapped her arms around him while resting her chin on his shoulder, and began to rock him slowly while he struggled to master himself. As I shifted to get up from my seat, she and I both nodded at each other wordlessly, and I walked a respectful distance away to stand guard, ready to tell anyone who might approach to fuck off.

I stood that way a few minutes with my back to them, looking out over the valley. The two scavenging crews were still up at the table enjoying their lunch, it seemed, and I wondered idly how much time I had left before I had to wrap my hands around that hateful shovel. Presently, I could hear Amanda and Oscar talking to each other, though their voices were low and guarded. I didn't move; they'd call me when they were ready. I looked down at the patch of ground I was standing on and toed a clump of grass with my boot.

A shout erupted from across the field, yanking my attention

back up towards the cabin to see a snarl of flailing limbs and a bunch of people skipping around in circles by the picnic table. The sight was so unexpected that it took me several seconds to process what was actually happening. At first, I thought Wang was choking on some food or something, that the surrounding people were freaking out over it, and that Fred was trying to help clear his airway. Pulling a mental double-take, I soon realized what was really going on: Fred had Wang in a bully choke while in the process of fending off Monica and Davidson, who were trying to pull him away, and he looked as though he was about to knock Wang's whole fucking head off.

A fraction of a second before this all clicked into place, Davidson's panicked voice tore through the valley: "GIIIBS!"

Fred must have outweighed Wang by a good hundred to a hundred and thirty pounds; if he got a hand free enough to take a swing and connect, it would probably be a world-ender. Without waiting to see what Amanda or Oscar were up to, I dug into the ground with both feet like a track runner and launched myself in Fred's direction, not knowing if I could get there in time but pushing with everything I had despite the uncertainty.

I was about three-quarters of the way there when Fred jerked hard to the side. I don't know if he swung with his fist or elbow, or even if he swung at all, but the result was that Davidson fell off of him and ran into Alan. Both of them went sprawling into the dirt from the impact, and I understood that neither of them would be getting back into the fight in time to provide any further hindrance.

As I closed the distance, I realized that Fred was shouting into Wang's face, who only struggled in the larger man's grip with his teeth bared in a grimace and the whites of his eyes exposed, resembling a terrified horse rearing back from a snake. I'm unable to recall the details of what Fred said exactly but the gist of what I caught during the few remaining steps it took to close the gap told me everything I needed to know about what was happening. In essence, what Fred yelled was, "What you got to say now?"

So, Wang had been running his mouth again, apparently. Briefly, I contemplated just letting Fred clock the dumb bastard. No sane man wants to step in front of an enraged bull, after all.

I couldn't do that, of course, and instead reached out to wrap both of my arms around Fred's elbow, which was already drawn back to full cock and ready to fire out. I'm sure I yelled a few choice phrases and suggestions into Fred's ear as well, but I'll be damned if I can remember what I said anymore. I was so jacked on adrenaline at the time that the details of that exact moment all run together. I can recall that I half expected Fred to drop Wang and redirect at me, which is a big part of what I was trying to do by unloading every insult I could think of at him. Instead of giving me what I hoped for, Fred drew the arm I was trying to hold back across his chest, which pulled me up off my feet, and then drove his elbow back into my chest, which rocketed me through the air square onto my back several feet away. The wind was driven from my lungs completely, leaving me to groan and writhe around on the deck while trying to will every muscle in my torso to unclench. All I could think of was trying to get back onto my feet—or at least to my knees so I could wrap my arms around Fred's legs for a takedown. I kept telling myself, "Get moving! Breathe later!" and my whole damned nervous system responded with, "Hey, fuck you, guy!"

The best I had managed was to roll onto my right side so I resigned myself to the reality that Wang was about to get bulldozed and that I'd better start refreshing myself on the battlefield medicine for a caved-in face. Fred's blow never landed, though. Jake appeared from out of nowhere (I'm sure he heard all the screaming from inside the house and must have come clomping down the stairs of the front porch right around when I was getting my ass handed to me), positioned himself between Fred and

Wang, and swung his arm up between them in a vicious arc, his forearm slamming into Fred's outstretched wrist. Fred's grip on Wang's collar was broken utterly, and Jake used the opportunity to shove Wang back behind him, who collided into the food table and nearly knocked the whole thing over.

Now Fred was distracted, alright, and redirected his anger on Jake almost without missing a beat. For his part, Jake was backing away, both hands out in a let's-be-friends gesture, and saying all the calming things you're supposed to say in such a situation (assuming you keep company with angry drunks and have experience in dealing with this kind of bullshit).

Fred wasn't having any of it, instead opting to throw a haymaker left that was aimed right at Jake's temple. Jake leaned back away from the swing to let it pass in front of his face, appearing almost bored, and I realized in that moment what kind of experience he must have carried with him. No one *just leans* away from a punch like that without all kinds of prior practice. Whatever else he'd been through, Jake was used to having people try to get physical with him, and he had the means to deal with it. Seeing Fred's wild movements—his planted stance and utter lack of footwork—compared to Jake's calm and competent evasion, it occurred to me that Fred was in fairly deep trouble.

"Fred!" I yelled out. "You'd better cut that shit out before you piss him off!" Other people surrounding the whole goat fuck shouted their agreement, though none of them attempted to jump in between the two men, having seen what happened to me for my troubles. Jake still had his hands up, was still backing up, and was still trying to placate the man.

Fred either didn't hear or chose to ignore all of us, instead following up his left hook with another wild overhand right. Jake, who had apparently decided he had enough of the whole experience, slipped low and to the left just under Fred's fist, close enough that his unruly length of hair was ruffled by its passage.

At his lowered position, I was just able to catch a violent twist in Jake's shoulders, his body appearing to blur as he drove up from his heels with everything he had, sinking a balled up left hand deep into the lower right side of Fred's gut, at the bottom of his ribcage and directly into his liver.

Now, I have seen body knockouts on TV in boxing matches and whatnot, but this was the first time I'd ever seen it happen up close. Fred seized over as though someone had swung a sledgehammer into his midsection, ratcheting so quickly that his feet actually left contact with the ground. Let me make this clear, now: he wasn't lifted off the ground from Jake's punch—the contraction of his doubling over was so violent that it *pulled his feet up off the ground* before gravity had a chance to bring him back to Earth. He seemed to hover there in place for the briefest of periods just before we all saw him crash into the dirt hip-first and roll over into a big, tortured ball. I can't ever recall seeing such a rapid reaction to pain before or since that encounter, not even from a guy taking a kick full-force to the beanbag. Just seeing it happen made me feel queasy. Well… it was either that, or I was still recovering from being winded.

Jake was already crouched by Fred before the rest of us knew what was happening, cradling his head, looking into his eyes, and calling out to see if the man could answer. Fred could only grunt and moan, so Jake let him stay rolled over on his side and began to rub his back aggressively like he was trying to help the guy get some air back in his lungs. It occurred to me to bitch about the fact that I'd received no such aid but was so disoriented from a lack of air, not to mention having witnessed Jake go from Whoop-ass to Assistance mode so rapidly, that all I could really do was breathe in and out and be thankful for the fact that I had that ability again.

"Anyone want to tell me what the hell happened out here," asked Jake, actually sounding annoyed.

"It was me," Wang said quickly. "I was talking smack and got him going."

"That's a bunch of bull!" Monica interrupted.

The rest of us looked at her and Jake asked, "Wang wasn't talking smack?"

"No, he was doing that, alright," she responded. "But you can't fault him for what Fred did. Runnin' your mouth isn't any cause to get manhandled like that."

Jake sighed and looked down at Fred, who had stopped moaning but still lay on the ground clutching at his side. Looking up at Wang, Jake asked, "What did you say?"

Glancing briefly at Fred, Wang said, "They didn't have a good run this morning. They almost didn't find any food at all." He looked away, clearly embarrassed. "I guess they covered a lot of ground and came back hungry. He, uh, he was eating a lot of food. I said, 'If you found food half as well as you shoveled it in, some of us might have a chance to survive the winter.' Among some other things…"

"Oh, shit. Bad choice, bro," whispered Oscar.

Jake had returned to a standing position, with his hands on his hips, staring at the ground, and shaking his head in little jerking motions like there was something inside his skull that he couldn't quite understand and hoped he could make go away just by rattling it to death.

"That is a pretty lousy thing to say," Jake agreed, "but that didn't give him the right to attack you, as Monica said." She nodded angrily in agreement.

Jake sighed heavily again and said, "Come on, Oscar. Help me get him to his bed. He'll want to rest a while until his side stops hurting." As he hunkered down next to Fred to take him by an arm, Jake leaned close and said, "You and I are going to discuss this later, yes?"

Fred nodded his head as he attempted to roll into a sitting position and grunted, "Yeah, I know."

Oscar got Fred's other side, and the two men helped the near-crippled giant hobble off to his bed in the larger RV.

I resisted following them at first, instead looking around to see if anyone else had been hurt. Davidson's collision looked pretty dramatic, and Wang had spent more time getting rag-dolled around than you'd like if you're interested in leading a productive, healthy life. As I gave them a quick going-over, I heard the hissed and angry conversations of the people left milling around the scene; a small amount of which were directing snark at Wang while the vast majority talked a foul, blue streak about Fred in glorious 5.1 surround sound. I cringed inwardly while I listened, foreseeing an ever-increasing gap expanding through the center of the group, with people taking opposing sides and ending in eventual fragmentation.

Fred had significantly damaged his standing in the community with his little outburst, and I saw no easy way back to harmony. People were going to be watching him askance, now, and no amount of apologies or attempts at reconciliation on his part would be able to rectify the whole mess. Worse, if it happened again... or hell, even if it didn't happen, but he got agitated and showed his temper, the other people in the group were apt to call bullshit and demand his removal. I wondered how something like that would shake out. Fred represented a unique combination of skills and abilities. His total dismantling at the hands of Jake notwithstanding, he was a large, powerfully built man who had thus far demonstrated an aptitude with firearms and a willingness to work hard. Additionally, if he was turned out of the group his metalworking and fabrication knowledge would be sorely missed in the challenges ahead.

It was a nasty problem that needed patching fast. Unfortunately, community trust isn't a thing that you get back with a "sorry" and a gift fruitcake. Like all worthwhile aspects of a relationship, trust required time and consistency. We needed time and consistency out of a guy with a volatile temper. Fuck me with a stick.

I excused myself from the group with a whispered comment to Amanda to come get me if any of them looked like grabbing torches and pitchforks. Dusting off my hands, I made the long walk to the camper trailer that Jake had led the other men to and stood outside the door wondering if I should enter. Not wanting to barge in, I decided to take a seat in one of the camp chairs that were set up outside just under a green, fold-down awning that extended from the side of the RV. I didn't have to wait for very long before the door swung open and Oscar hopped out.

Noticing my presence, he shut the door and said, "Hey, Gibs." His voice was solemn, as though he was still shaken by the events of the afternoon.

I hooked a thumb at the camper behind me and said, "Everything okay in there?"

"Yeah. Well, kind of. Fred's getting told *right now*."

"Oh?" I asked with raised eyebrows. "Getting told what, exactly?"

Oscar scratched his forearm, no doubt a nervous tick, and said, "I don't wanna go into details. Seemed kind of private, you know?"

I scoffed. "Be general, then."

Sighing, Oscar said, "Basically, Jake said this was Fred's one free major fuck up. Next time he does something like this, he'll be driven out to the edge of town and left there."

"Huh," I nodded and directed my view forward. I looked down at my fingernails, which were dirty underneath with grime from that morning's work, and noticed a blister had risen along the pad of my thumb. I bit it so that it would dry out faster, spit out a hunk of skin, and asked, "You alright, Oscar?"

"I think so. Yeah. I'm gonna go get back to work on that foundation." He seemed fidgety, which made me worried. I was worried for all of us.

"Go ahead, man. I'll be back out there with you shortly. I need to speak with Jake."

"Right on," he said and headed off to meet up with Amanda. They appeared to chat between themselves as well as with some of the others before separating off from the pack to stack more cinder blocks. I knew they had enough mortar to work with for now, but I'd need to get back over there soon to mix up a new batch. I crossed an ankle over my knee and watched the noon crew load up into the Dodge, rifle team shrugging into borrowed vests and adjusting themselves as they stepped up into the back seat. I focused on ignoring the stinging throb growing in my thumb, which worked about as well as you'd expect.

The RV door opened again, after which I heard Jake's voice from my left. "Gibs…"

"Jake…" I greeted him back.

He came around and sat down to my right in another chair but said nothing further. I quickly realized that he knew I had things to get off my chest and was waiting for me to begin. I was still organizing my thoughts, and so delayed by saying, "Fred okay? You can kill a guy by gut-shotting him like that, you know. Rupture his liver."

I detected nodding from the corner of my eye and looked over in his direction. Jake sat straight in his chair, feet flat on the ground, with each hand rested lightly on an armrest. He looked as though he'd been arranged. "I'm aware, but he's too big for me to catch him a good shot on the chin. Too much reach. Besides, I dislike headshots. You have to shake someone's brain for a knockout. There's too much danger of doing serious damage with that if all you're trying to do is control a person. Then, too, you can break a hand if you're not careful."

"So he is, or he isn't okay?"

"Oh, he'll be fine. He stated that the pain was getting better a moment ago. He'll be up and around not long from now. He'll have a hell of a bruise for the next few days."

"We have to deal with this, you know," I said. "This won't be the last time it happens if we don't."

Jake sighed; a deep, heavy thing that made me exhausted just to hear it. "I know. If we could just get out ahead of this… this fucking food situation, I suspect a lot of this would work itself out."

I was semi-shocked to hear him say "fucking." It wasn't a term he dropped liberally. Recovering quickly, I said, "We've got to do something about the morale in general around here. We've all been going balls-out for weeks now, with no end in sight, and the most critical factor (food) isn't improving the way we need it to. People are run down and starting to feel like their efforts are futile. It's important… no, fuck that. It's *imperative* that we do something to pick 'em back up."

"It's *imperative* that we get more food," Jake countered. "These people aren't fools, Gibs. No matter what… team building…" he said the term with pronounced disgust "exercise we concoct to distract them, the situation doesn't change. Starvation is an inescapable danger."

"I understand what you're saying… and you're wrong," I said. I met his quizzical gaze head-on. "I'm not suggesting we fall into each other's arms or hold a fucking group enema. There just needs to be some sort of effort taken to lighten things up. It could be as simple as handing out pieces of chocolate for tasks well accomplished."

He leaned away from me and pulled a disturbed expression. "You mean like doggy treats? That's a little insulting, isn't it?"

"Oh, Christ, you don't pat them on the head and ask, 'who's a good boy,' Jake. Do you know what some people would do for a fucking Snickers at this point? Do you have any idea? I could tell you what I'd do, but I don't want to lower your opinion of me. Trust me: it would work."

"Huh," said Jake.

"The main thing is," I continued, "whatever we do needs to come along with a recovery plan. Like you said, we're not dumb-asses around here. They need to know that we have some new ideas to get through the winter. What we're doing *right now* clearly isn't getting the job done."

"Agree," he said simply.

We sat quietly for a while, watching as Amanda and Oscar slapped more blocks into place in the dirt. A giggle flitted our way over the field signaling that George was about to begin an afternoon lesson with the kids; they were beginning to arrange themselves on the front porch of Jake's cabin in a loose circle around the older man, who lowered himself into a wooden chair.

"Let me chew on it a while," Jake said as he rose to his feet.

"Don't chew on it too long," I said to his retreating back. "This is only going to get worse if we don't square it away."

He turned back to me, pushed his hair behind an ear, and said, "No. I've heard you loud and clear. I may have some ideas, and I'll definitely run them by you soon, but just give me a bit to work out a few details."

24

BARN DANCE

Gibs

It took Jake about two days to get those few details worked out. I don't know if that's because some of that time included reading or he had a little preparation to do in order to get things set up; maybe he was just waiting for things to cool off a bit after Fred's big blowup. The logistics were finalized a day after the fight, definitely, because he and I met that evening to hammer out particulars. He gave me a week to plan—get my shit together—which was more than I felt like I needed or wanted, but which was probably a good idea in the long run. Once I had a target, I wanted to go execute. Jake insisted on the extra time for planning. I'll admit he was right.

Two days after Fred had been buffaloed, I was finishing off an afternoon training session with a handful of folks including Amanda, Rebecca, Wang, Edgar, and Alan. Experience demonstrated I'd be better off keeping the Page brothers separated as it cut out any impulses for buffoonery. I had Edgar along because, like Jeff, he didn't seem to be developing any aptitude at all so I was banking on the hope that keeping him around some of the better performers like Amanda and Wang would benefit his progress to some degree. I had yet to see if there'd be any payoff in that regard.

I'd had them working targets at three hundred yards that afternoon, followed by cleaning their weapons, and then some room clearing drills in Oscar's place. Despite the fact that the container had a fairly simple two-room layout, I was happy with everyone's progress overall and was looking forward to getting multiple teams going at once, coordinating their movement between different structures over the radios. Seemed like every time I had them out they were getting better; taking on new skills or improving existing ones. I'll admit to some degree of satisfaction in the process.

We'd wrapped up for the day and were just filing out of Oscar's house, discussing what we'd done, how it had gone, and who needed to tighten up, when Jake's answer to improving morale began to make itself apparent. It had been timed perfectly, just when my group was finishing up as well as when the final scavenging team had returned for the day and were busy washing up (but before they'd had a chance to begin unloading the truck).

As we stood around in a loose circle chatting, the sound of talking and laughter came from behind us, back in the direction of the garage. It sounded *off* somehow, as though it was filtered, and the voices came from people I didn't recognize. The sound was jarring, and there was only enough time for Amanda to say, "Hey, what is that?" before the funky, laidback sound of a bass guitar line accompanied by clapping and what I suspect must have been a cowbell rolled out across the field.

We turned in unison to regard the garage, which had its roll-up door opened all the way, and saw the muted glow of the overhead LEDs shining from within as well as the edge of a picnic table just poking out through the door, bisecting the opening. From our left, folks from the scavenging team were slowly walking up the path as though they were sleepwalking while others still came foggily from the campers on the opposite side of the field, southwest of the cabin.

From some thirty yards away, I heard Otis say, "Hey, is that—?"

Before he could finish, a falsetto, ghostly voice echoed out from the garage. I didn't understand what that voice said at the time because the quality of the music as it issued from the garage was too distant and distorted, but I learned later from Fred that the song's opening lines were, "*I used to go out to parties, and stand around…*"

It turned out that Jake's solution to a group morale problem was to rub some Marvin Gaye on it… which, I suppose, is not such a bad idea at all.

"That's right!" Otis shouted, unable to contain his laughter. "*Got to Give It Up!*"

People were moving faster towards the garage, now, and I had to remind my group that they were still carrying rifles and that they needed to continue practicing some kind of muzzle awareness, despite the fact that none of them had seated mags. They all listened with one ear, moving towards the garage as though called by hypnosis. It was like trying to get a group of kids to wash their hands before diving into a birthday cake.

Whether planned or not, everyone arrived at the garage door at about the same moment, so we all saw the same thing at once. A folding table loaded with a variety of food had been set up close to the open roll-up door. The Super Duty was absent, having been parked around the side of the garage earlier that day, and it appeared as though the palletized provisions had been moved upstairs to clear out floor space. The trailer that was usually connected to the Ford by virtue of a ball hitch was centered to the rear of the garage. Another of our folding tables had been set up on the trailer—on the table was one of those large boombox CD players; it appeared as though the unit's speakers had been detached or otherwise removed and there were two larger cabinet speakers (standing about as high as a man's knee) set on the floor to either side of the trailer with red and black speaker wire leading back to the player. An orange extension cord ran from the back of the folding table to the solar battery array in the back of the shop. Jake was up on the trailer, too, sitting in a folding chair behind the table. As soon as we came in, he waved at us and shouted something, though we couldn't understand what he was saying due to the volume of the music. I looked back over my shoulder and saw a line of adult faces all reduced to a state of childhood wonder. A few of those faces had wet eyes and glistening cheeks.

Jake had stepped down from the trailer and was approaching us still talking, his voice barely understandable with the music blasting in the background. I shook my head at him vigorously and closed the distance. Wrapping my hand around the back of his neck, I put my mouth close to his ear and shouted, "Okay, try again!"

Rather than leaning in for just me to hear, he ratcheted his voice up as loud as it would go and hollered, "This is going to be a pretty pathetic dance party if none of you guys actually dance!"

The sound of screaming laughter erupted from behind me, made small by the overpowering thump-thump of the music, and I stood rooted in place, bemused, as several people including Monica, her daughter Rose, Rebecca, Otis, Maria, and Amanda all filed out to the center of the floor. They began moving at a walk, like normal people, but something happened to them as they came closer to the center of the floor. Their spines went loose while their hips wobbled around under them. Their knees bent, lowering their centers of gravity, and never quite straightened up again, while arms extended out, fingers snapped, and eyes closed. I had just been working with some of these people only a few minutes ago, helping to refine their skills in small arms and fire team tactics (in other words, we were all practicing getting better at shooting people we didn't like) and now here they were, shaking their asses like a bunch of teenagers.

More people followed these brave trailblazers out onto the floor before I knew what was happening. Otis's son Ben had Lizzy by the hands, and they both bounced around happily. George kept a death-grip on his cane with one hand while holding onto Barbara's fingertips with his other; both of them executing a subdued and refined adaptation of what looked to me like an old-fashioned Two Step made only slightly ungainly by George's bad knee. Only a few people hung back on the sidelines, including Jeff and Davidson. Fred was nowhere in sight, probably still keeping to himself in embarrassment for his earlier display.

Looking at Jake, who smiled mildly at the group of dancing, laughing people, I shouted, "You sneaky, cagey fuck!"

He snorted, but the sound was lost to the music; a visceral beat that you could feel through the souls of your boots. He leaned closer to me so he wouldn't have to yell as much and said, "They look happy, don't they?"

I jerked my head at the table and said, "How much of the food did you lay out for this?"

He shrugged and said, "More than we could spare but not so much that it'll hurt immediately. We should still be okay by the time you get back."

I grimaced and said, "You know, we're fucked if I don't find anything, right?"

In answer, he pinned me with one of his trademark Jake stares and said, "Sure, but this isn't going to make it any worse. We need to get their minds off of food right now. The best way to get peoples' minds off food is to fill their bellies."

I shrugged, not disagreeing with him but not fully subscribing to the idea, either. To me, the whole thing felt like a hell of a gamble. I'd had a day to think about the plan (well, less than a day, I suppose) since we'd finished working out the details the previous night and, no matter how many times I rolled it over in my head, the whole thing felt like one hell of a Hail Mary pass.

Jake heaved his shoulders in an exaggerated sigh and waved me over to a position towards the rear of the shop just removed from the impromptu DJ table he'd built for himself. Around the side of the trailer was a tarp draped over some sort of box. He pulled the tarp off to reveal an electric box cooler, which he opened and leaned into while I stood behind him, dumbfounded. He straightened up holding a beer bottle, which he slipped under an opener screwed into the side of a nearby workbench and popped the cap off onto the concrete floor. He held it out to me and said, "Have a drink," though I couldn't hear a damned thing because we were right next to a speaker; I had to read his lips.

Hesitantly, I reached out to take the bottle. It was ice cold to the touch. My expression must have been pretty comical because it caused Jake to smile and I shouted, "How the fuck?"

He shook his head, exasperated, and pointed at the bottle insistently. I put it to my lips and tilted it back, my perception of the world narrowing down to a pinpoint as I felt shockingly cold lager carrying the smallest of ice crystals roll over my tongue and swirl in the back of my mouth, beginning at once to foam. I swallowed hard, gulping it all down and burping almost immediately after, causing my eyes to water. Before I realized what was happening, I was chugging again, and Jake had his hand out to try and slow me down. I looked down at the bottle and saw it only had one swallow left swishing around in the bottom. Breathing heavily, I pulled the bottle back to my lips fast enough that the rim clacked painfully against my teeth, but I didn't care. I had that ice cold, sweet-yet-bitter liquid rolling over my tongue again; all other concerns could just fucking wait.

I pulled the emptied bottle away from my lips, making a

hollow popping sound from the suction, and growled out a satisfied, "Ahhh!"

"You alright?" Jake shouted into my ear.

I held the empty bottle out to him and yelled, "Again!"

He rolled his eyes and retrieved another from the cooler. The initial song seemed to be ending by the time he put the second bottle in my hand, so he jumped up onto the trailer and killed playback just as the final notes were dying in the air. The noise in the garage suddenly took on a hyperreal quality, as that otherworldly music was replaced by the much more familiar chattering and laughter of voices I recognized. Many people retained their position on the dance floor (which was really just a cleared out space on the concrete) and clapped loudly, shouting for more.

Jake put his hands up and waved them all quiet. When the commotion died down enough, he said, "Well, I guess I'd like to thank everyone for coming to my little party…"

Everyone in the room instantly broke into cheering laughter, and Oscar split the air with one of his ear-shattering whistles. Jake patiently waited for everyone to calm down again before continuing.

"That's much appreciated, everyone, but you don't have me to thank for this. It was all Gibs's idea."

"Alright Gibs!" shouted Otis, which fired everyone up again. I took a sip off my second beer, resolving to take it easy this time around, and resigned myself to the possibility that we'd all be here for a while.

"I want to apologize to you all," Jake continued. Many people stopped cheering at that, and several shushing hisses filtered out from the group as everyone took the hint that the topic was about to become serious. "We've all been working so hard to get ready for this winter; it's been such a concern on my mind, as I'm sure it has been on yours, that I think I forgot one of the most important components of human existence: being connected. Everyone has been working together so well, and we just haven't taken the time to sit back and enjoy that success; that so many people from such diverse walks of life could all be dumped together in the midst of unimaginable tragedy and commit themselves to each other's survival. I forgot that people sometimes need time to unwind and for that, I'm sorry. I'll do better."

For a moment, Jake stopped speaking and looked around. He seemed to be taking a head count as his eyes passed over each person. After a bit, he apparently found what he was looking for, as he called Wang up to the trailer and leaned down to whisper in his ear. When he finished, he stood back up again but kept his attention fixed on Wang, eyebrows raised and hopeful.

Wang rubbed his chin while his other hand rested on his hip, looking as though he was trying to settle on an important decision for which he liked neither option. Finally, he nodded to himself, looked back up at Jake, and said, "Yeah. You're right. I'll go."

"Thank you, Wang," Jake said as the other trotted out of the garage exit. As Wang left, Jake addressed himself to the rest of the group. "Diverse walks of life, indeed. We have teachers among us, and blue-collar folk who made things of beauty and utility with their own hands. Folks from academia, who bent their minds to complex, important social issues and concerns relevant to our times. Men and women of both thinking and action. Men and women who defended our society with their lives," he looked at Monica and me as he said this, "along with men and women who enjoyed the security such sacrifice afforded and contributed back to the machine, thus paying back into the system in their own ways.

"The way I see it, the chief difference between then and now is that before, most of us never would have known each other because we lived in a world where people could easily wall themselves off if that was their desire. They could... well, they could live behind a screen." He seemed to falter for a moment. He looked down at his hands, picking at his nails a moment uncertainly. Just before it became uncomfortable, there was movement over by the door, which caused Jake to look up and nod. He said, "Ah, here we are. Thanks for joining us."

At the front of the garage, Fred entered uneasily, partially led by Wang, who stayed at his side. The rest of the people (men, women, and children) all went deathly silent and regarded the two as they moved across the floor, hardly daring to breathe. I realized I was breathing shallowly myself, wondering what the hell would come next.

Before anyone could speak, Fred said, "Need to apologize to you people. I, uh… well, there just ain't no excuse for what I did. Guess I've had a way for a long time now. Got me in trouble some…" he trailed off, looking down at his feet. Without looking up again, he said, "I'm just sorry, is all. Don't know what else to say."

The room remained silent; silent enough that I could hear the low hum of no-sound leaking out from the speakers. I looked from face to face, seeing uncertainty and maybe a little anger in some places.

Wang was the first to speak up. "I'm good with it. Fred and I have talked, and I'm over it. And, I apologized to him as well, because I was being an insensitive prick." He rested his hand on Fred's shoulder, having to reach high up to do so. Fred seemed to straighten up a little from that simple point of contact. "I probably could have used a few more beatings growing up," Wang continued. "But all that aside, I forgive Fred. And, seeing how I had the worst of it, it seems it won't kill the rest of you to do the same." He said the last part defiantly, almost daring anyone to tell him he was wrong.

They were silent a bit longer, a silence eventually broken by a grunt. We looked towards the source, which turned out to be Davidson. "Come on, guys, he looks miserable. I'm good with it."

"Yeah, let's call it squashed," Oscar agreed, clearly wanting to put the uncomfortable moment behind us all and get back to the partying.

Fred looked up across the crowd to me, almost ignoring everyone else. "Gibs, I gave you a hell of a shot. You alright with this, too?"

I laughed. "I've had worse, big boy. Come over here and get yourself a cold one."

"Whoa, *cold one*?" called George. "Since when do we have cold beer?"

"Had the jenny running," Jake said. "Let's everyone get a drink, huh? Think we should have a toast or something."

Everyone lined up temporarily by the cold box and grabbed a drink of their choice (the choices being beer, wine coolers, waters, or soda) and returned to their general positions in front of the makeshift stage. I noticed that Fred was now mingled in among them, absent the uncomfortable gap in space that would have been there only a moment before. Certain of the people continued to eye him suspiciously, though, and held themselves out on the edges; people like Edgar, Monica, and Alish. The kids stayed well away from him too, I noticed.

As I had suspected; everyone may have agreed to let him back in, but it was on a probationary basis at best. Fred had some hard work ahead of him before he came close to enjoying anything like unconditional trust.

Holding his own beer, Jake continued his speech. "This proves my point. We're different, but we pull together. We have disagreements, and yet we put them aside. This is the reason we're going to survive. It won't be the guns or the food we find or the shelters we build or even the new things we learn. It all starts with a basic ability to see the kind of world we want to have and then create it. This world of ours has been reset back to zero…" he trailed off and looked down at his own beer, which he spun idly in his hands. He cleared his throat, "Erm, back to zero. Whatever happened before now… it just doesn't matter anymore. However things used to be done, whatever responsibilities we used to have. Whomever you may have… have wronged once upon a time. It's over now. Gone. All that matters now is what this world could be. It can and will be whatever we decide to make it."

He held his beer out to the crowd. We all responded by hoisting our drinks up into the air, aimed back in Jake's direction. "It's whatever we decide it is," he said and drank.

There were disjointed calls of agreement from the group, ranging from "hear, hear" to "hell yes," and everyone took a drink; even the children, who had their own sodas or waters.

"There's plenty of food and drink," Jake said, gesturing out to both the table and the cooler. "Some of you may have concerns about the extravagance of the food I've put out, but I'm here to tell you we have a plan we're working on; have been working on for the last couple of days."

People looked at Jake inquisitively, their attention fully paid to the shaggy, hulking caveman as he stood up on the trailer. "You see, this get together doubles as a going away party of sorts. Gibs and I have been doing some planning—there are places out there, places some of us have been to, that I believe have the things we need. I'm talking about food, medical supplies, ammunition… all of the things we're short on. It's a long drive, stretching from here down to Vegas, but we can make it quickly. Gibs and I did some math, and we figure the trip can be done in the Ford without any stops to refuel. It has the hundred-gallon reserve tank in the bed, for one thing. That plus another fifty-five-gallon drum of diesel will cover way more than is needed to do the whole trip. I've asked Gibs to select a team to go with him; the purpose being both to watch each other's backs but also so that they can drive around the clock all the way through. With a little luck, they can be back to us within a few short days."

People in the crowd started to mutter, and I saw uncertain glances being traded back and forth. Heads came close together as people whispered among each other.

"You folks are doing a lot of chattering out there," I said. "If anyone has a problem, now is the time to sound off."

Edgar stepped forward from the group to answer. "It's just that some of us are a little confused, Jake. Or, maybe concerned is the right word. Yes: concerned. We've been scrambling to get enough food laid by for the winter. Despite the slow progress, we are actually making progress. I just don't see how diverting four people for a long distance trip improves our situation. Those are people we could have out looking for food."

"They will be out looking for food," Jake insisted. "Just a little further away than we'd all like."

"Oh, you know what I mean," Edgar said. "You're targeting… what? Three or four days for this trip?"

"I'd like to see no more than three."

"Okay, three," said Edgar. "For the distance you're suggesting, that's three days consisting mostly of driving. They won't be out gathering anything for most of their time away. They'll be playing Travel Bingo."

I moved forward to speak up but was stopped at a subtle gesture from Jake; a slight straightening of his left index finger in my direction from a handheld immobile at his side. It was expertly done; the signal to me was loud and clear though I don't think anyone else noticed it.

"There is a difference, here," said Jake. "All of the local searching we've been doing has run according to chance. While we've done our best to proceed methodically, our ability to be successful is still governed by whether we stumble onto useful resources. Gibs is traveling to places which have demonstrated high yield in the past."

"And what was our last known status of any of those locations?" Edgar asked.

Jake was silent a moment before answering. It was only a momentary beat, but it was noticed. "I'd guess three to four months ago, is that right Otis? Was that when you went through?"

"I couldn't call it for certain," said Otis. "Tend to lose track of dates these days. But… oh, sure, call it that."

"How'd the tent city look when you passed through?"

"Relatively good shape," Otis said. "Some things was fallin' apart, as you'd expect, but there was still plenty to be had. Least, they was, anyway. Packed up as much as we could carry and didn't even scratch the top."

Jake looked expectantly at Edgar, who only shrugged and said, "A lot can happen in four months, Jake."

"Indeed. A lot can happen in only three days, as well."

"Yes, but you can't say what *will* happen," Edgar shot back. I winced, wondering how Jake would respond. Looking around at the faces in the room, I saw a lot of people on the fence. I contemplated what might happen if people just outright said "No" to the plan. Would Jake override them? What would happen if he did? Would that signal the beginning of the first cracks leading to the eventual breakdown?

In response, Jake slumped, took a deep breath, and let it out. He walked to the edge of the trailer, where he hopped off the side, and then returned to the front of it to sit on the wheel fender. He looked smaller in that position. Deflated.

He took a swig from his bottle and said, "No, I can't. But bear with me a moment, please, while I share some thoughts. When you all came here, we determined there was enough food to last us all for about a month and a half, remember? Well, we're now breaking onto the edge of winter; we can expect the snows to start any time this month. We've all been out every day, gathering as much food and supplies as we possibly can. Would any of you say you haven't been pushing to the fullest extent possible to get us prepared for what's coming?"

Several heads shook emphatically, with a few spoken negatives to go along.

"Right. We've all been busting our tails. And how far has it gotten us? We've made progress, certainly, but we only have enough right now to get us halfway into December." He lifted up the hand holding his beer bottle, index and middle fingers extended and pointed at Edgar. "And no one is more aware of that than you, Edgar. You've been keeping a tally of the total stockpiled calories every day, so you should know exactly where we're at. Am I wrong?"

Heaving a sigh, Edgar said, "No. That's correct."

"Thank you. And may I assume that you've also projected how much more we're likely to get before the snows hit and we're stuck up here for the season, given our performance thus far?"

To his credit, Edgar met Jake's gaze solidly as he nodded. "I have. It isn't good."

"Not good," Jake agreed and took a drink. Everyone in the room was deathly quiet. The happy atmosphere from only a few moments ago was completely extinguished by this point.

He let the silence hang a while, not looking at anybody or anything, just sitting on the fender regarding the floor. Some of us began to shift around. I caught Barbara's eye; thought I saw a tear. I wondered just what in the blue fuck Jake thought he was doing.

Finally, he looked up and said, "You guys are asking me for a guarantee that this works out and I simply can't give you one. The best I have for you is that what we're doing right now isn't getting the job done. We have some pretty good data that suggests it won't get the job done no matter how hard we push. We need a big payout. This is the best way I can think of to make that happen. If they don't find anything, we're just back to where we started anyway. If they do find something, though…"

"You're suggesting the only risk is lost time," Edgar said. "You forget we were all chased from Colorado under fire. That two of us didn't make it out of Colorado at all. There's an additional risk right there. Gibs and his team may not come back at all."

Jake's demeanor went all cold, then, as he stapled Edgar to the deck with those shark's eyes of his. His body language died completely, as though someone had cut the puppet strings, and he said, "I'm not forgetting anything, Mr. Muller." Edgar took a step back at the sound of his surname, and the people surrounding him moved away reflexively. I hate to say that the temperature in the room dropped because it's a goddamned cliché but, if I'm being faithful to what happened, the temperature did seem to take a hit. Rebecca folded her arms, for one thing, and the fact that I wasn't distracted by the movement of her chest is a testament to just how tense the exchange had made everyone.

Then Jake took another pull of his beer and just like that, it was over. People could breathe again; could hear and produce sound again. Jake held out a hand and said, "We understand the risks. Gibs certainly does. That's why he's taking time to prepare. We're going to mitigate the risks as best we can. I'm sorry, I simply don't have the power to eliminate the danger from your lives. But I'd like you to consider the following…"

He stood and walked out into the crowd, standing among us. He looked from face to face as he said, "When it comes to risk, your whole life is a gamble. A coin toss. Every day, you're faced with decisions you have to make, and if you choose wrong, you could die. You can't know what the outcome will be, but you toss the coin anyway. You gamble. And, as we all know, when you gamble long enough you'll eventually lose."

He rotated slowly in place until his gaze settled on Edgar. "The problem is we were all thrown into the game against our will. We play simply by existing. You don't get to opt out; you're flipping the coin just by being here. Failing to make a decision is still a decision. Failure to take a risk is still, essentially, a risk. The only way to get out of the game is to die. Paradoxically, the penalty for gambling poorly is also death."

Edgar had shrunken somehow. He'd pulled back into himself and, though he still met Jake's gaze, his head was pulled to the side, as though he couldn't stand to meet his look full on.

Jake's hand rose from his side and rested on Edgar's shoulder. Softly, he said, "Under such circumstances, the only sane, reasonable choice is to flip the coin and bet for a win. You bet on hope, Edgar. You choose to take the risk. You do so because either choice is a risk in the end, be it heads or tails. If it's true that there really is no way to back out of playing, you make the hopeful bet that has some chance of paying out, remote though it may be."

Jake withdrew his hand from Edgar's shoulder and stuffed it into his front pocket. When he pulled it out, there was a dull, silver flash reflected from the overhead light as he popped his thumb. A quarter tumbled through the air, rang as it hit the concrete, and rolled only a few inches before landing on its side. During this time, Jake's eyes remained locked on Edgar's, who didn't move a muscle.

"What do you say, Edgar? Do you need to look at that coin for an empty promise? Or do you bet on hope? What will you take: risk or death?"

Without looking down at the coin, Edgar raised his drink to his mouth with a steady hand, took a deep pull, and said in a clear voice, "Risk."

I took that as my own personal cue to vault up to the CD player on the table and start thumbing through the CD's that had been spread out over the surface. "I thought we were supposed to be having a party here," I bawled. "Somebody needs to fire the damned DJ!"

This was met with explosive laughter from the crowd. I soon gave up trying to find the perfect artist or song, settling instead on a random dance mix that appeared to cover the whole gamut from pop to R&B and Motown. I dropped it into the tray, hit the play button, and twirled a hand at everybody on the floor in a get-your-asses-moving gesture. As the beat started to float out over the crowd (some kind of thumpy hip-hop song I'd never heard of and couldn't name if my life depended on it), they all began to move again, slowly getting back into their groove while deciding that everything was probably okay, or at least that it would all be okay for this night. They were safe right now, and they looked like cutting loose.

"Thanks," Jake said, having climbed back onto the platform to stand next to me. He leaned closer to me to ensure that I would hear and said, "I didn't know if they were going to buy that or not."

I leaned over to him and said, "Fuck you, Jake. You believed what you said every bit as much as the rest of us."

He pulled back and regarded me momentarily, perhaps wondering if he wanted to be offended. He apparently decided he was okay with it, as he nodded and returned his gaze to the small crowd of people whooping and hollering on the floor.

Overall, I think it ended up being a successful night, if not a little odd. Between the three of us (Jake, Amanda, and me) we had wondered how much resistance we were going to catch when we shared our plans for a road trip with everyone else… and what it would take to cut through it all. I was thankful that we wouldn't have to discover the results of Jake giving up and just saying, "Fuck you all, we're doing it." You never want to pull heavy rank like that if you can help it.

Everyone got out there on the floor at one point or another

that night, and some of them stayed out there the whole damned evening. One of the biggest shocks for me was Amanda, or more specifically, how she moved. It was such a different aspect to her personality from what I was used to, having known her in my time there only as a serious, competent person. Well, let's face it: if you spend any amount of time with these people, you eventually figure out that Amanda is essentially Jake's Hammer. In all my time living here in the commune, I've learned that Jake trusts and relies on her completely. He certainly trusts the rest of us as well, I'm sure, and there have been plenty of things for which he's leaned on me to handle, but… well, let's see. I'll put it like this; if Jake thought it was a good idea to kill someone in their sleep, he wouldn't ask me to do it. The only person he'd trust for a job like that would be Amanda.

Tonight, though, Amanda wasn't Jake's Hammer. She was just a woman who loved to dance, who dominated the floor and made everyone else appear shabby by comparison, even Rebecca, who could only manage a rough approximation of what the smaller woman achieved through instinct. Amanda had a way of moving, of getting low and growling with her body, that I'd simply never seen before. There were no choreographed steps that I could recognize, no easily identifiable patterns. She just closed her eyes and let go, like a creature responding to hereditary knowledge, and her entire body positively throbbed along the floor. Everyone in that room was thunderstruck by her movements; most of the men had to pick their jaws up off the floor. No one came close to her nor did they even look like trying. She was in a whole class by herself, and the rest of us were rendered lacking in her presence.

I realized as I watched her gyrate everyone else to shame that there was a little pocket of immobility to the right of the crowd; George, Barbara, and Davidson sat out along the sidelines. The older folks were either giving their joints a bit of a break, or they were just busy awaiting a better song, as the one that was currently playing was on the faster side. Davidson didn't look right, though. He was young; practically a kid. He should have been out on the floor.

Looking at Jake, I said, "Back in a bit. Wallflower."

He looked in the direction I indicated, seemed to understand, and gave me a thumbs-up. I jumped from the trailer and crossed the short distance to sit down next to Davidson along the wall.

"What gives?" I asked. "Why aren't you partying?"

He shrugged and said, "I've never been much of a dancer. Not too good at it."

I looked back into the crowd. Edgar was either doing some adaptation of the Chicken Dance or he was suffering a seizure and others, such as Wang and both of the Page brothers, appeared to rely on a minimalist strategy, basically standing rooted in place with their arms out and rocking slightly side to side like they were doing their best Snoop Dog impression.

Looking back at Davidson, I said, "You're joking, right? You couldn't possibly be any worse than the people out there right now... unless the only dance you know is some variant of the Russian Dick Stomping Cha-Cha."

He honked in laughter, shaking his head but saying no more. The animation slowly died from his face, and he looked back down at his hands while fidgeting with his fingers.

"Jesus H. Christ," I said in dismay. I looked back at the crowd. Some people had paired off to dance together (I noticed Lizzy wouldn't leave Ben's side and seemed to be eyeing Rose suspiciously) but there were plenty out there dancing alone quite happily. I decided I'd have to take some drastic action.

"Here, look at this," I said. "This shit ain't that difficult. Watch me."

Confirming I had his attention, I stood up and walked directly into the crowd, aiming straight for Rebecca without faltering.

Rather than looking surprised as I approached, she favored me with that blinding, heart-stopping smile of hers and shot me a mock salute.

"Hey, there, Sailor!" she said happily.

"Marine," I barked. "I worked for a living."

She laughed at that, which made me feel a little lightheaded and stupid, and said, "Fair enough: Marine. What can I do for you?"

"Need your help," I shouted over the music, my voice barely audible to either of us. "Davidson's smitten like a lost puppy. Said he's been thinking about asking you to dance only he's certain you'd turn him down on account of you're waiting to be asked to dance by the sexiest man in the room."

She almost doubled over laughing before she asked, "Yeah, and who would that be?"

"Come on, don't make me say it. It's embarrassing," I shouted back. "It's not my fault I'm such a specimen." She continued to laugh, so I pressed on. "Anyway, I think you must know that I've promised my heart to Barbara, only she seems to have chained herself to George for some unknown reason; maybe they're trading home remedies for arthritis or something. The point is I need your help to make my girl a little jealous and maybe show Davidson that you're probably a human like the rest of us. What do you say? We just waltz over there, and I'll dump you off before you have the chance to become addicted to my raw animal magnetism?"

She laughed harder than I'd thought she would, causing me to wonder if I should feel a little offended. When she finally came back under control, she said, "Well, only since you asked so nicely. Also, I don't think I can stand the idea of George coming between you and your true love."

"Right? What a jerk, huh?"

She looked back over her shoulder at Davidson, and a satisfied, mischievous grin spread slowly across her mouth. I'd seen looks like that before. They usually preceded wild, head-first dives followed by sudden stops right at the end, with no parachute or crash helmet to be had.

"Hey," I warned. "The kid's my friend. Don't break him, okay?"

She looked back at me with a hurt expression; a genuinely hurt expression, she wasn't putting on an act this time, and shouted, "He's my friend too, Gibs."

Feeling a little guilty, I backpedaled. "Okay, I know. You're right. Sorry."

She seemed to accept the olive branch, nodding once with a hard jerk, and said, "Well, get me over there, big guy."

I put my arms around her and got moving; holding her like a brother holds his sister to ensure that the wrong signals weren't sent out to anyone who happened to be watching. As we came closer to Davidson, who watched us openly with a lost, forlorn expression, I shouted a "Sorry!" into Rebecca's ear right before reversing my grip on her arm, pivoting on my heel, and snapping her out into open air like she was a wet towel that I was using to whip a buddy's ass. She got about one and a half revolutions before she tilted too far in one direction but my aim was good, and she tumbled right into Davidson's lap, laughing harder than at any other point that evening. The kid's face went beet red as he sat there stuttering like an asshole and I began to fear that the putz was about to blow my epic setup. Fortunately, Rebecca decided to take mercy on him; she just grabbed him by the hand and bodily yanked him up out of his chair and dragged his ass onto the floor like he was a cave bitch. It was about as good as I could hope for, all things considered.

I sat down in his place next to Barbara, who was laughing uncontrollably and clapping her hands. She shouted, "Oh my

God, I never thought he was going to get out there with her! Thank heavens you came along!"

"Yeah, well, sometimes nature needs a kick in the pants, you know?"

She nodded happily and gave me a playful elbow to the ribs.

"How about you," I asked. "Think I can pull you away from this chair long enough to make a circuit around the garage?"

She screwed up her face and shook her head. "Let's give it a while. This stuff is too fast for me."

"Yeah, I know what you mean," I said, looking back at Davidson as he struggled to keep up with Rebecca, who was still smiling and seemed to be having a grand old time, thank Christ.

I got Jake's attention up on the stage by waving at him. He shot me a "what?" head nod, so I pointed at my ear and then made a slow-down gesture with my hand. He returned an exaggerated nod and began shuffling through CD cases.

I looked back at Barbara and said, "Okay, I think we're covered." She smiled and tapped her foot.

Eventually, the song that was playing faded out and the music stopped entirely as Jake swapped CDs out of the player. He pressed a few buttons, waited a few seconds, and then pressed one more before straightening up and looking back at me. Almost instantly, a slow and simple guitar riff faded in while being backed by a lap steel guitar, instantly recognizable. I was unable to stop the world's biggest shit eating grin from breaking over my face as I nodded back to Jake, grabbed Barbara by the hand, and said, "This'll do," as I helped her up from the seat. We got out onto the floor along with everyone else, all of our friends pairing off and calming down to a warm, happy, mellow. Over the speakers, the voice of Don Williams issued forth as he sang *I Believe In You.*

"Oh, my God, I haven't heard this song in ages," Barbara laughed.

"Me either," I said. "It was my mom's favorite."

"She had good taste."

"Maybe," I said. "My dad was a bit of a… well, he left a lot to be desired."

She frowned and said, "I'm sorry to hear that. Still, she raised you up. She got some things right."

Let's hope so, I thought. The discussion died down for a bit, and we just concentrated on moving around, me taking it easy owing to Barbara's older age and weaker bones. Don't get me wrong; she moved well at her age, but you could tell the old girl had a bit of a hitch in her get-along. One person on a cane was enough as far as I was concerned. I didn't need to do something stupid and make that two people.

I looked out over the crowd as the song played out, saying the words to myself in my head and discovering with some small amount of joyful surprise that I still remembered them all. Amanda appeared to be taking a break by the food table, getting a bite to eat. Oscar came over to say something to her, and she looked back toward the stage, mild concern showing in her eyes. She looked back at Oscar, smiled, and shook her head politely. He held a hand up to her, palm out, and nodded before backing away.

"Huh," I said. "Some people can only move fast, I guess."

"What's that?" asked Barbara.

I smiled at her and said, "Nothing."

WEAPONIZED SUPER DUTY

Gibs

Per Jake's suggestion, I selected my team based on factors such as ability, group need, and group dynamics. As far as ability was concerned, I needed to use people who had demonstrated solid aptitude with regard to small arms training and fire team tactics. This didn't mean I just got to grab the best of everyone, though. As I said, the needs of the mission had to be weighed against overall group need, or rather the needs of the entire commune. I couldn't take Amanda, for example; she had proven to be the best gunfighter after me, mostly due to my years of experience... she certainly wasn't lacking in killer instinct. At any rate, I wanted her to stay back and keep an eye on things. Oscar and Fred couldn't go either; they had way too much work to do back at the valley.

After careful consideration, I selected Davidson, Wang, and, after a great deal or argument with some of the others, Greg to accompany me. They had all come along nicely with a rifle, the community wouldn't take too bad of a hit for their absence, and the four of us worked pretty well together. Every one of them agreed to come along without the slightest hesitation.

Greg was a hard choice for me to accept; I originally argued with Jake that I'd do just fine with only two other people, which he vetoed outright. Greg wasn't even eighteen yet at the time; younger than Kyle was when I'd lost him. He reminded me too much of Kyle… reminded me too much that I couldn't keep people protected.

The decision was finally settled when Jake made it clear that, one way or another, there were four people going on that trip, and I'd better get busy selecting the last person for the team before I completely pissed away our time. I was in the process of talking myself into taking Monica, who I also didn't like for the fact that she had a daughter depending on her, when Greg apparently got wind of the discussion and informed me in no uncertain terms that I was gonna have to break his legs to keep him from coming along. I had a hard time saying no to that kind of resolve. I finally agreed and shook with him on the matter, though it twisted my stomach into knots to do so.

It was thus that the day after our little barn dance, the four of us stood in the dining area of the cabin accompanied by Jake, Amanda, Otis, and George with several fold-out maps spread across the dinner table. These showed the states of Utah and Nevada at various levels of detail, some of them focusing just on the interstate highways while others dived into specific detail along areas such as Salt Lake City and Las Vegas, with additional street maps covering some of the cities in between. We had attempted to arrange a number of these in such a way that the interstates matched up, succeeding only some of the time but getting close enough that we could at least get a general idea of spatial relationships. We had a red Sharpie marker that kept getting passed between Jake, Amanda, and Otis as they recalled important landmarks, particularly bad traffic snarls, and other points of interest to avoid.

Jake was bent over the table while gesturing excitedly with his index card reading aid; a basic three-by-five card with a small hole punched out of its center. He always had this with him when there was reading to be done, either keeping it in his back pocket or folded in a book as a place marker. He used the thing like some sort of cheat code. The first time I saw him use it I was completely confused at what was going on; he laid the card over the page and started moving it slowly from left to right, lips silently moving as the card progressed. After a moment, I realized he was looking through the little hole like it was a window, so I asked him what it was all about.

To use his words, he'd explained that, "Text has always been a problem for me. Letters alone on a page don't bother me, and I can read my alphabet just fine, but when they get all jammed together into words, my mind starts to do funny things to them. It all falls into so much noise, and the meaning becomes lost."

He said that he noticed at a young age that using his finger to point out one letter at a time helped but not so much that it eliminated the problem entirely. He could still see those other letters, and if he got distracted (in other words, he wasn't able to keep one hundred percent of his attention locked on that single letter) all of the surrounding letters would collapse together, and he'd have to start over at the beginning of the word. Sometime later in his life, he figured out that he could cut a hole in a small piece of paper and move it over a page, such that he could limit his view to a single letter at a time, which had alleviated much of his troubles. After that, all he had to do was learn which letters went with which words.

Apparently, that's not as easy as it sounds. According to Jake, the average person is a visual reader; we see a word on a page, and we don't actually notice the individual characters. Our brains recognize the complete pattern of the word, and we automatically understand the meaning. Its instantaneous recognition and translation is automatic. In Jake's case, that pattern recognition is completely broken, so he had to memorize the series of letters that goes along with each idea or concept. The really fucked up thing is that, the way he explains it, he has to concentrate on the sound of the letters and map that information to the sound of the word; again his visual understanding of a word is just broken. So what that all really means is that while we map word patterns to concepts, Jake is busy mapping letter sounds to word sounds to concepts manually by taking in a single letter at a time.

If it sounds exhausting, that's because it is; you can probably appreciate why it takes him so damned long to read anything. It becomes even more shocking when you realize just how much reading he does. I don't know where the man finds the time, personally.

So, all that is to say that Jake was basically pointing at the maps with his combination Rosetta Stone and decoder ring.

"Your trip is just the reverse of what we did when we first came to the Valley," Jake explained. "You'll eventually pick up the 80, here, but don't try to take it into Salt Lake City; the whole area is a nightmare. Take the 189 at this point here, which will eventually run you into the 15… here. You'll then have to head north to get to the 73, which will take you out to the tent city out at Cedar Fort. That's the path you went, Otis, correct?"

"Yeah, that's right," he agreed. "You'll catch some knots here and there, but ain't nothin' you can't get around with that Ford."

"What was the status of the camp when you were last out there? I mean *exactly*?" I asked.

He considered my question for a moment and shrugged slightly before saying, "I could tell it'd been picked over a bit, if that's what you mean. They was some areas all torn up, and such… others not so bad."

"Did you see any field kitchens?"

"Not sure," Otis said. "Saw a lot of tents and trucks."

"It would have looked like a basic mess kitchen; stainless steel boxes, rolling racks with food... possibly inside a really large tent. It would be big enough to house several rows of tables and chairs."

He perked up at the mention of the large tent. "We did see something like that. We just never went in it."

"Amanda, did you ever eat in anything like that while you were there? Did you see such a tent?" asked Jake. Otis and I both looked at him confused; those tents would have been used by the military staff, but the people under quarantine wouldn't have been allowed anywhere near that area. They would have been kept in the sealed medical tents with their meals brought to them, as I had been during my own time in quarantine.

Amanda saw the confusion on our faces and explained, "Jake never stayed in a tent city."

"How the hell did you avoid that?" I asked.

"Things fell apart pretty fast in my area," he said without looking up from the map.

"The point is: there's probably something like that out there, so keep an eye out," said Amanda. "I kept to the outskirts with Lizzy. I was terrified that we'd be stopped and locked down if we got too deep toward the center. I wasn't really myself then, either. I don't remember a lot from then..."

"That's fair enough," I said, not wanting to work her up. She looked uncomfortable just thinking about it.

"Okay," Jake said while pointing further south on the map, "your next stop is here. It's just off the side of the 15 in the middle of nowhere with big, red letters on the front that say: Barnes. They were an ammo supplier of some note from before. We loaded a vehicle full the last time we were there a few months ago and didn't even scratch the surface. There's so much in there,

I don't think you could get it all out, even with the truck and trailer together. Or, at least, there was."

"Sounds good to me," said Davidson. "Are there specific calibers that you want more of?"

"Everything," Jake emphasized. "Grab everything. As much as you can. I suggest you use the entire truck bed for food and use the entire area of that trailer for ammo and weaponry."

"Jesus, Jake," whispered Otis. "You fixin' to go to war with… who? Russia?"

"I'd like to avoid future trips like this for as long as possible," Jake said. "Every time we send someone out, it's a risk… a risk that seems to increase with the amount of distance traveled. You guys need to get out there, grab what you can as fast as you can, and get home."

"What's the total distance?" George asked.

"Well, that brings me to my next point," Jake said. "If you guys cut the trip off here, that hundred-gallon reserve tank will be enough to get the job done."

"*If* we cut it off there," I said. "You said you had designs on Vegas, though."

Jake nodded and moved along to the more detailed Vegas city map. "I do. At this location… here, is a warehouse that was owned by a company called Botach. They had just about everything you could imagine there. Every kind of rifle, pistol, self-defense gear, you name it. It's where we got those body armor vests you guys use. They even served law enforcement, so you'll find riot gear there as well."

"Won't the place have been emptied out? That doesn't sound like the kind of stuff that just gets left lying around," Wang said.

"It's off the beaten path in a nondescript warehouse," Jake said. "It was the reason Billy made such a point of stopping by when we passed through that area. All the obvious places like outdoors outlets and such had been cleaned out, but he theorized that a place like this," he pointed at the map with his index card, "would have been relatively unknown. He was right too; we had to break the lock to get in."

He leaned back from the table and crossed two thick arms across his chest. "It's a risk versus reward thing. It's quite a drive, and there's a real possibility that the place is empty when you arrive. On the other hand, it's safe to assume that not many people knew about it before the world fell. Now, given the percentage of people who are gone, that number of people in the know becomes exceptionally small. There's a good chance that place bears fruit."

"Right. So we go to Vegas," I said.

"Not necessarily," Amanda interjected. Jake looked to be on the verge of saying something but held his silence. "You guys get to Barnes and then evaluate the situation at that time. If you've had a good run and you're feeling okay about things, maybe you decide to head south. But if things have gotten bad out there…" She hesitated, looking down at an undetermined spot on the map. A hard-line formed between her eyebrows and I was shocked to realize that she had become enraged. "Just come home if it looks bad."

Jake let out a breath and said, "Absolutely. That'll be your call."

"So the Vegas trip is why we'll load up the fifty-five-gallon drum, I take it?" George asked.

"That's right," nodded Jake. Directing his attention to me, he said, "I want you guys to refuel from the drum first before tapping the reserve tank. When the drum is empty, leave it on the side of the road. That will get you more cargo space for the return trip."

"Drive in shifts," said Amanda. "You guys are never idle at any point. You're either driving, refueling, or scavenging, understood?"

"Crap," Wang said, sounding annoyed. "I'd hoped that was an exaggeration. We can't stop to rest at any point? Like, at all?"

Jake and Amanda only stared at him, Jake's expression flat while hers said, "*You're shitting me, right?*"

"We don't want to spare the space for a tent, anyway," I said. "Don't worry about it. You can rest all you want when we get home."

Wang twirled his finger in the air and offered an unenthusiastic, "Hooray."

"Gibs, I understand you've been looking into some things with Fred, is that right?" asked Jake.

"That's affirmed. I was looking into armoring the truck."

"Oh, shit. Nice!" Davidson laughed.

I continued on without slowing down, "We took some heavy fire getting out of Colorado. I'd say we got out lucky except for the fact that two of us were killed in the process. If we were lucky, it was only in the fact that our bus was shot full of holes and yet the only casualty taken was a minor crease to my arm. It happened once so it can obviously happen again. I'd like to hang some armor off that truck."

"What would something like that take," asked Jake.

"Some high-grade steel plate, mostly," I said. "Unfortunately, you can't find a lot of that just laying around. The metal sheets that you can find up at Ace and some of those other hardware stores are no good. Even if you sandwich them together, a high powered round will punch right through."

"There may be some other areas around here that we could check," George said thoughtfully.

"No time," I said. "Like we've all been saying; snows are just around the corner. We have a week to get ready."

"Well, you wouldn't bring this up if you didn't have some idea, so…?" prompted Jake.

"That school bus has leaf springs," I said, gesturing in the general direction where we left it out in the field. "We'll jack it up, disassemble the axle, and pull them right off. Each leaf looks to be about a half inch thick or so. We can drill holes in the ends and mount them along the rear window of the truck on a frame that Fred will fabricate and bolt into the body."

"Is there enough to cover the whole window?"

I thought for a minute and said, "Eh, probably not, but that's okay. We can leave gaps between each band. A bullet might find its way through, but it's unlikely."

"And those bands will stop a bullet, huh?" Davidson asked.

"I think so," I said. "Your basic rifle and pistol rounds, sure. It might dent or crack, I guess, but I don't think they'd shatter. Fred was explaining about the kind of steel they'd have to use to make a leaf spring; how it would have to perform? I think it'll do the job. Besides, I'm going to test it. Each leaf spring has a series of plates stacked on top of each other and the closer you get to the top of the stack, the smaller those plates get. The topmost plate is very small; damned near useless for armoring the truck. I'll take that piece to the range and put some rounds into it before we devote too much time to this and see how it holds up."

"Anything else?" Amanda asked.

"Yeah, I think I can make a kind of bullet stop to hang off the back of the trailer, too."

Jake's eyebrows rose. "Oh? Do you have enough leaf spring for that?"

"No, but that's not what I want to use. I think I can make a barrier that will absorb a bullet's energy and basically stop it; kind of a soft target. Only thing is that I need you guys to clear me running out to the home improvement store."

"What do you need?" asked Jake.

"Ceramic tile, epoxy, and fiberglass fabric. Probably some metal sheeting and plywood as well."

"What the hell are you going to do with that?" asked Wang.

"I think I can make something that functions like a Kevlar plate carrier," I said. "I'll start with a sheet of plywood, smear some epoxy over it, and then cover it in ceramic tile. Then some more epoxy, a couple of layers of fiberglass, a couple of layers of metal sheets, and then another sheet of plywood; basically make a big goddamn s'more. Clamp the hell out of it with a bunch of weight (we'll basically stack a lot of heavy shit on it) and wait for it to dry. Once it does, you should have something that'll either stop bullets or slow them way down, provided the bullets don't hit a seam between the tiles."

"And you want to make one big enough to span the back of the trailer?" asked Amanda, looking dubious.

"Yeah," I agreed. "We'll just stand it up against that ramp gate in the rear and secure it with strap ties."

"How well would something like that work," George asked. "Is it worth all that effort?"

"I believe it would stop at least a couple of 5.56 rounds to the same, exact location. More than that or higher caliber and we might have some problems. But I believe if there's a chance it stops only a single bullet we should do it."

"Agreed," Jake said. "I don't care if it holds you here past a week. Let's risk the timeline to see that done. Divert both Fred and Oscar to help. Anyone else you need as well. Keep me up to date on progress, please."

"Rah," I said, almost by reflex, and double-timed it out of the cabin.

"Well, what do you think?"

I looked over to my right to see Fred, standing a few feet off from me and staring down range at the little hunk of metal that we'd balanced on a wooden stand. He idly wiped axle grease from his hands with an old rag before tucking it into his back pocket. That Darth Vader voice of his had floated out to me all muffled due to the ear protection I was wearing. He had a set as well, which looked almost comically small wrapped around that bucket head of his.

"One way to find out, I guess," I said, and pulled the HK to my shoulder. I exhaled and squeezed, feeling it chug against my shoulder in time with the crack of the bullet, made almost apologetic by the earmuffs.

Off in the distance (I'd paced out about fifty yards), the little hunk of steel from the leaf spring pinged and tumbled into the air. It landed unceremoniously in the dirt a few feet away. I set my fire selector to safe and repositioned my earmuffs around my neck. From my peripheral vision, I saw Fred do the same.

"Well, let's head over and see how it looks," I said, praying that we didn't just waste two and a half hours' worth of time under that fucking bus.

As we approached, I noted that there wasn't a hole anywhere in the wooden stand. Taking that as encouragement, I stooped to pick the plate up from the ground. There was a black smudge just left of center where the round impacted.

"That looks pretty good," I muttered, rubbing my thumb over it.

"Did it deform at all?" Fred asked from behind me.

"Not by much. I can't see it with my eyes, but if you rub your finger over it, I think you can just feel where it dimpled. I might be imagining it, actually."

He took it from me and rubbed his thumb over the smudge. His eyes unfocused as he concentrated on detecting any imperfection in the surface, after which a slow, satisfied smile spread over his face. Looking down at me, he said, "I think we got something, here."

"Can you drill that?" I asked.

"I'll have to see what Jake has in the shop," he said, turning the plate over in his hands. "If not, we have that torch. I can always cut a hole through. Be janky as hell, but it'll work."

We were collectively able to put such a focus on the Weaponized Ford project that my team was ready to go only four days after Jake originally announced the trip; that's counting the modifications I ended up making to the ceramic armor we attached to the rear ramp of the trailer.

These modifications occurred (you might say they were "suggested") when I was initially laying out all of the layers that would compose the armor sheet to plan how I was going to get the whole thing put together. I'd gotten my hands on several buckets of this two-part Scotch-Weld stuff that was supposed to have a ninety-minute work life, which sounds like plenty of time, but I was still concerned about how much area I had to cover. The folding gate off the rear was seven foot wide by five foot high. For you math whizzes, that meant I had to cover thirty-five square feet in two sheets of plywood, a bunch of ceramic tiles, a whole shit ton of fiberglass, and a few layers of sheet metal. The sheet metal itself wasn't all that thick, honestly; it was thin enough to cut with tin snips. I just wanted it there to add a little heft and to try to spread the shock out just a little bit more along the ceramic underlayer.

I was just getting ready to crack the first epoxy bucket when Jake strolled up to see how I was getting along.

"How's it going, Gibs?" he asked.

"We're in good shape. Fred's just about finished mounting the frame to the truck, and the spring plates will go on after that. I'm getting ready to put this whole mess together." I gestured at the various piles of material in the dirt.

"Will the frame hold, do you think?"

"You saw it, huh?"

Jake smiled and said, "Yeah. You have to admit it's a bit ugly."

"Well, Fred mentioned that the right way to do it would have been welded square tubing, but we don't have an arc welder, so he had to make due. Considering he just had the grinder, nuts, and bolts, I think it came out pretty well. You sure can't flex it in any direction."

"That's good," he said. "I didn't have a chance to tug on it; I only saw it from a distance as I was coming over."

"All that fugly will be hidden once the spring plates are mounted, anyway. It'll look better."

He had begun to walk among the different supplies as I spoke; stopping over the boxes of tile I laid out. "What size are these?"

"Something like twelve by twelve. I figured the big ones would be easier to arrange. Why?"

He scratched his chin before answering. "Do you think a large or a small tile would do better in spreading out the shock from a bullet impact?"

I looked down at the box and scratched my ass absentmindedly, feeling slightly shocked at his question. "Well... fuck, I don't know, man. I'm just making this shit up as I go."

"Well, do you think it would hurt to have a layer of both?"

Forcing back frustration, I asked, "Do we have a large selection of smaller tile lying around, Jake?"

"No."

"Well, then yes, it would hurt my fucking feelings quite a bit to have to go back into Jackson and get a few more boxes of the tile."

Jake raised his hands and said, "Okay, okay. Don't get worked up. I was just asking. If you're comfortable that this will be enough, I trust your judgment." He put his hands in his pockets and ambled back up the path to the garage, presumably to piss in Fred's ear, while I stood there fuming.

I looked at the first plywood sheet, followed by the epoxy, and finally the boxes of tile, trying to convince myself I was good with it. I almost succeeded before that deep, nagging, little bitch voice inside my head spoke up and said, "Another layer will only make it more effective, you know…"

"Goddamned, cock sucking, shit eating, smarmy little taint chewing, bent legged, knuckle dragging, dog fucking, Democrat, ball fondling…" is just a selection of the philosophical musings that spilled from my mouth as I walked up the hill to retrieve the keys to the Dodge as well as my rifle and rig.

Davidson happened by at the time, face fresh and completely pink from having just been shaved, which was a practice I'd noticed him observing with far greater frequency ever since his little dance with Rebecca; there were little patches of toilet paper stuck to his chin from where he'd cut himself. Seeing me lugging my gear, he said, "Hey, Gibs! Where you off to? I thought you were working the trailer this morning?"

"Damn it, Davidson, did you shave your face with a dick? There's white everywhere!"

"I… what?" he asked. The poor kid had come to a dead stop and, I suspected, was in the process of mentally rebooting.

I sighed and wrestled myself back under control. "What I meant to say was to grab your shit. We have an unexpected shopping trip to make."

"More tiles, huh?" he asked.

"What? How the hell did you know that?"

"I heard Jake mention something about it earlier. Said he'd ask you to thicken things… uh, are you okay?"

Realizing I'd been played like a fiddle, I went back to my philosophical musings as I resumed my walk to the truck.

Perhaps miraculously, we finished constructing the sheet that evening. Once completed, it consisted of a three quarter sheet of plywood, a double layer of fiberglass cloth, a layer of large tiles, another double layer of fiberglass cloth, followed by a layer of the small tiles, then (you guessed it) more fiberglass cloth, and finally a few layers of sheet metal and another three quarter sheet of plywood. Each layer was completely smeared in big, sweeping gobs of epoxy before the following layer was applied and, when it was all finally assembled, we clamped the whole thing down by stacking bag after bag of concrete on top of it and just left the thing out overnight to cure.

On the following morning, which was the fourth day, we returned as the sun came up and began to remove the concrete bags. What we saw after the bags were removed was essentially a giant shit sandwich of construction materials with frozen strands of epoxy squeeze-out pooling around the edges. Oscar reached out and tapped one of the squeeze-out puddles with the end of his pocket knife, which resulted in an audible clicking noise.

"That looks pretty good," he said.

"Great. How the hell are you going to get that up on the trailer?" Edgar asked.

"I think we'll have to lower the gate of the trailer and just slide this over it," said Jake. "We can secure it in place while it's still down and then lift it all up together to lock it into position."

I crouched down, worked my fingers under a corner of the sheet, and lifted. It moved a few inches and then completely stopped. "Jesus…" I muttered before bracing myself and pulling harder. It came up a little bit more before my lower back began to send signals to my brain that said, "Hey, asshole, what the fuck are you doing? Stop it. Stop it!"

"I may have miscalculated severely," I said, looking up at the others.

"Heavy, huh?" Fred asked.

"We're gonna need everyone under fifty to take an edge on

this thing when we try to lift it up. Either that or we run the risk of someone projectile-shitting a kidney across the valley. I'm not even exaggerating; this thing is a prolapse begging to happen."

We did eventually get the thing lifted into place and, as predicted, it did take just about every able-bodied back that we had to safely lift the son of a bitch up into a vertical position. It became pretty easy once we got the gate past a certain angle; maybe seventy degrees. Before that, though, I felt like we were more likely to push the planet away than we were to get the gate up. As soon as we had it at ninety degrees, Ben jumped into the back of the trailer, set the gate's arm braces into the side rails wrapping around the trailer's length, and locked it all in place.

We all let go and stepped back gingerly, afraid it might come crashing back down. Without warning, Jake came up from the side and slammed his open palm into the gate, then grabbed the frame with both hands to jolt it violently in all sorts of directions. He shoved and pulled at it so hard that the trailer itself wobbled around on its tires and the whole thing rattled angrily at its mistreatment. When nothing happened, he let go and dusted his hands off. "I think it'll hold. Don't lay it back down again to load it; you'll never get the gate back up again."

"Oh, gee, do you think?" asked an annoyed Wang.

"Do you think we should make the sides higher?" Jake wondered.

"No, damn it! It's good!" I barked.

"Very well," said Jake. His face was completely expression-less, but I swear to Christ I could see a smile behind those eyes. Asshole.

We soon realized that after the trailer's rear gate was shielded there wasn't much left to do but load up the truck and be on our way. Everyone came out to see us off that morning; Barbara had wanted to make us a big breakfast before we left, but I think we all agreed that we just wanted to get out on the road. We instead loaded the Ford's cab up with food that would travel well and be easy to eat on the road without stopping, so basically a lot of stuff that we could choke down cold. We had some crackers and such as well, along with enough water to get us through a week in case we were delayed for any reason.

We stood out by the truck; two groups already feeling separated, with me, Wang, Davidson, and Greg on one side and all of the rest of our people on the other. I stood by my friends looking across at the rest, people that I believe I was beginning to think of as family by that point (I certainly think of them so now) and considered what we had ahead of us. It was a melancholy feeling, looking at them all across that perceived gulf. I felt like we'd already left; like we were out on the road and I was just looking at some sort of afterimage. I saw hope and good wishes in their eyes. Knowing that their survival depended on our success, I sucked in a deep breath and mastered my doubts.

"We'd better get rolling," I said to no one specific.

Jake stepped towards me and extended his hand, which I took. "I like this truck," he said. "Try to bring it back in one piece, huh?"

I laughed and said, "We'll see what we can do."

His face went deathly serious. Well, his expression was as flat as ever, but there was real fire just behind his eyes. The skin around his eyebrows had gone tight, and his shoulders were all balled up like he was carrying some vast, invisible weight.

"You bring yourselves back in one piece," he commanded.

He nodded to the others in my team and stepped back to rejoin the group. Amanda came next. I extended my hand to her as I had to Jake, which she batted aside before throwing her arms around me. I hadn't expected this from her at all and stood frozen with my hands at my side for a brief moment before returning the hug. As we stood there, she lifted up onto her toes, straining to put her mouth next to my ear, and whispered, "If you see anyone out there on the side of the road, keep driving. Understand? I don't care if it's a woman screaming for help or anything else. You keep driving. Got me?"

I looked at Jake, who appeared oblivious to the whole exchange, and wondered if he knew what she was whispering to me. I gave a tight nod to let her know I understood, determining that I would use my own best judgment should such a situation present itself, regardless of whatever the hell anyone said.

Rebecca and Alish approached next, the former wrapping herself around Davidson, which made me smile, and the latter wrapping her arms around Greg and holding on for a few beats longer than would have seemed reasonable, which made me curious.

Finally, Fred Moses approached Wang but stopped just shy of closing the total distance. He held up a bottle of tequila and said, "This is supposed to be the good stuff. I guess it used to go for several hundred a bottle when money was a thing. Never been opened. You and I are gonna crack this baby when you come back, okay?"

Wang smiled happily at him, all past transgressions either forgiven or forgotten, and said, "Are you sure you can deal with a skinny kid half your size drinking you under the table?"

Fred erupted into booming laughter and said, "Deal with it? Hell, I want to see it!"

"You keep safe, Wang," Monica said, pulling Rose tighter into her side. "I want to see that skinny behind of yours back here in three days. Any more than that and we're gonna have words."

"I mean, you don't have to wait three days to see it if it's that important to you..." said Wang. He waved awkwardly and climbed into the passenger side of the truck, barking out a "Shotgun!" to anyone that happened to give a shit.

"Come on, guys, we'd better hit it," I said, and walked around to the driver's side. Greg and Davidson piled into the rear seat as I fired up the engine. Waving to our assembled group of friends, I pulled a wide U-turn and began the long drive out of the valley.

"How's it feel," asked Wang. "Is it handling funny with all that weight on the back?"

I pumped the gas a little just to dig the tires in and push us forward a bit. "Honestly, I can't even tell. The torque on this thing is ridiculous."

"Nice," he said.

"Hey, let me ask you something. Were you flirting with Monica back there?"

"Oh, shit! Wang's goin' for some of that dark chocolate!" laughed Greg from the back seat.

"Dark chocolate? Good God, I can't decide if I should be offended or just embarrassed," said Wang in mild disgust.

"What," asked Greg. "Is that offensive? I wasn't trying to be, man."

"You might as well say 'Yellow Fever,' dude," Wang replied.

I saw Greg screw his face up in the rearview mirror. "Aw, shit, man. Well, I didn't mean that at all. Sorry."

"Being fair," I said, "she does have really lovely skin. Then again, I've always had a hell of a weakness for the black girls…"

"Good lord…" Wang muttered.

26

INTERLOPER

Amanda

It was either two or three days after Gibs and the boys left for Utah that we learned about Jeff; I'm not totally sure anymore after all the time that's gone by. Jake, Lizzy, and I have been here around two years now, and this all came about relatively soon after Gibs's people came to live with us. Jake sometimes refers to them as "the first wave."

Jeff Durand: quiet and unassuming, always helpful, not much for fighting but always there to pitch in on housekeeping. Jeff, who was so good with the kids.

It was Rose that finally told us what he'd been up to.

Or, at any rate, Rose told her mother, Monica, owing to the fact that Rose was fourteen and knew better than to keep quiet about such things. I think the other children (Ben, Maria, and Lizzy) were young enough that the fear of what might happen if they told would somehow be worse than the reality of what was happening. After it was all over, I had been near to shouting at Elizabeth for not coming to me to say anything; it was Jake who had kept me under control and thank God for him, honestly. I would have been wrong. I had to remember that to my little girl, the forces pulling at her to tell would have been at war with Maria begging her to stay quiet. Elizabeth was only eight at the time. She's such a smart kid that I forget her age sometimes.

I wasn't present for what happened initially. We all compared notes a day later and pieced things together. After Rose told her mother, Monica went directly to Oscar, which I honestly can't say was the right or wrong thing to do. After everything we'd all been through, either on our own or together; the Flare, all of the millions of people we lost to it, the Plague, and the presumed billions of people it took… well, this was just something that never would have occurred to any of us in a hundred years. I don't know if there was any perfect way to handle it.

I became involved just as Oscar was preparing to finish Jeff. I had been out on one of my walks, just trying to get a little space between myself and everything else. It's probably the only thing that saved Jeff, too; I'd been sporadic about wearing my sidearm around the immediate area but still carried religiously when I went for my walks, especially since those walks had been pushing further and further out.

I returned to echoed shouting, a cascade of garbled words and moving bodies. I pulled my Glock reflexively before I saw Oscar dragging Jeff across the common ground by the neck towards the site of my future cabin, where many of the tools were located at the time. Several of our people were trailing behind them, some of them shouting while others walked silently. Without knowing exactly what was going on, I could tell things were serious and broke into a run.

As I closed the distance, I watched in horror as Oscar pinned Jeff back against a log and lifted a hammer up into the air. George hobbled towards them and called out to me, saying, "You'd better hurry!" The children were out there, too, separated from the murder that was about to happen by a small ring of adults, including Rebecca and Samantha, who held them back. They were sobbing, with the exception of Ben and Rose, who only looked terrified.

Oscar was spitting a long, unbroken string of obscenities in Spanish, of which I understood only a small portion, and the hand holding the hammer trembled in the air. I was running up from behind him; as I came closer, I could see that Jeff's face was a pulped and bloody mess. I put the barrel of my pistol into the base of Oscar's skull where it joined the neck, and he froze instantly. A few voices from behind me called out either in anger or shock, I'm not sure which.

"Oscar, I need you to put that hammer down and let him go. Right now," I said. I was secretly relieved when my voice didn't shake.

Rather than arguing or trying to plead his case, he complied immediately and backed away a few steps, leaving a panting, sobbing Jeff in a heap up against the small stack of logs that we'd managed to collect for my cabin so far. I lowered my pistol as soon as he moved back but did not holster it; his eyes were drawn to it in my hand, and he understood.

"Ain't like you think, Amanda," Fred rumbled in a cold voice.

"Just hang on, please, Fred. Oscar, I need you to tell me what the hell is going on."

He jerked his chin at Jeff, who only lay there on his side panting heavily, face pointed down at the dirt. "Ask Jeff. Have him tell you what this is all about."

"I will, Oscar. I will. But I'm asking you first right now."

His face screwed up and, amazingly, I saw his lower lip quiver as he said in a breaking voice, "He been putting hands on Maria."

Something like an icicle formed in the pit of my stomach and spread out rapidly through my body. I looked down at Jeff for several seconds, trying to comprehend what Oscar had just told me. I looked over my shoulder at the group of children and locked eyes on Elizabeth. Briefly, I heard what sounded like rushing water, which then muted as though I was moved away from a fast-moving stream at impossible speed; the sound tightened down to a high-frequency whine stabbing through my ear, into the base of my neck, and down my spine.

"Rebecca… Samantha," I said, "please take the kids away. Stay with them."

"Come on, you guys," Rebecca urged immediately, enfolding her arms around them all like a mother swan collecting her nestlings to her breast, and moved them as a whole towards Oscar's home. Samantha looked back at me as they walked away, mouth working. I turned away.

I looked from face to face, trying to determine what should happen next.

…putting hands on Maria…

In my head, I saw Elizabeth's hand closing around the king on a chess board. A small, soft hand with perfect, even nails.

A hand reached out to me, and I heard George say, "Amanda… we can't just…" He either said no more or I didn't hear him.

I realized I had my finger on the trigger of my Glock; a thing I was never to do unless I was ready to use it, according to Gibs. I didn't remember putting it there. I removed it and, making a point to not look at Jeff, I approached Oscar and asked, "Did you see?"

"What?" he asked in a surprised voice.

"Did… you… see?"

"I… no."

"Rose told me," Monica offered.

"And you told Oscar?" I asked, taking great care to keep any possible hint of accusation from my voice.

"Yes, that's right."

I nodded. "Come here, please, Monica."

As she approached, I held my pistol out to her, which she

slowly took in both hands.

"Where's Jake?" I asked.

"I was just with him an hour or so ago," Barbara offered. "He should still be in the house, as far as I know."

"Why the hell didn't he come out?" blurted Fred. "There was enough shouting to pull people from a mile off."

Ignoring the question, I said to Monica, "Nothing happens until I get back. Everyone needs to be involved in this." She nodded her understanding, and I left to get Jake.

Inside the cabin, I stood a moment in the entryway and listened to see if I could hear Jake moving around anywhere while also struggling to bring my racing mind under control. Seemingly on its own, my brain was playing scenario after scenario in my head, each ending in a grisly, broken state. An irrational part of me scrambled to figure out some way to get back to how things were only a short while ago, though such a thing was now impossible. I realized that I didn't want to deal with the situation; also that I didn't want to deal with the very strong desire to take Jeff to some hidden place and solve the problem.

I put the thought out of my mind, or at least tried, deciding that it was best to be sure. Could it be a misunderstanding? Probably not; things wouldn't have gotten as far as they had if this had been a simple miscommunication. What, then? Rose was lying… or Maria? Could Maria accuse Jeff of such a horrible thing out of some desire to gain attention? My head went around in circles, chasing its own tail, as I struggled to find some way to know the truth.

Jake was almost always in the Library if he was in the house during the day, so I went back there first. I called his name as I approached down the hallway to avoid startling him when I entered. Moving quickly, I stopped just long enough to poke my head around the doorjamb to scan the room and confirm his absence. I pulled back and returned to the front of the house, trotting now, as I continued to call for him, and searched the rest of the common areas. He was nowhere to be seen on the bottom floor. Could he be sleeping? I knew he got headaches from reading sometimes and couldn't get rid of them without laying down in the dark for a few hours.

I ran upstairs to his bedroom and tapped on the door before opening it. The room was dark, with the wooden shutters pulled tight. It smelled of Jake, whose scent tended to change occasionally based on whatever soap we happened to find or, when there was no soap to be had, and bathing happened only with water, might deepen into a combined musk of old leather, denim, and some underlying, indescribable *thing* that always made me think of cedar. The bed was empty.

"Fuck me," I moaned, backing out of the room. I stood at the door a moment, trying to decide where he might be. I could feel the opposing door of my old bedroom behind me like a physical presence, pressing into my back, and wondered. I didn't think he'd be in there; he'd never gone in there without me being there as well. I turned to open it, hand stopping short of touching the knob. No, he wouldn't be in there. I turned away.

I returned to the landing and began to descend, so deep into my own head that I didn't see him waiting for me at the bottom until I'd gone three steps down. As usual, my heart leaped into my throat.

"What's the matter, Amanda?"

He looked small at the bottom of the stairs, enough of a distance away from me that it was hard to make out the flattened mass of his nose. His too long hair fell into his eyes, making him appear almost boyish, which was offset by the fact that both his shirts and pants would soon need to be replaced if he was going to insist on always trying to lift more weight with that barbell set.

"What the hell?" I shouted. "I was calling for you!"

He was up the stairs before I knew what was happening, the

backs of his fingers pressed against my cheek and looking at me intently.

"Are you alright?" he asked. "You're sweating. What's happened, are you hurt?"

"I… I need you," I said lamely. I corrected: "I need you outside right now."

It took far less time than I would have thought to explain the situation once Jake was outside. Such an earth-shattering thing, so horrifying, summed up in a simple declaration.

"I guess he was doing more than teaching the kids," Oscar said in a shaking voice. "He was messing with my girl. Touching on her. I'm gonna kill him if I can."

Jeff cringed deeper into himself as Oscar spoke and whimpered, "It's not true."

"I see," Jake said after a moment's consideration. His face was unreadable, which told me everything I needed to know.

He crouched down in front of Jeff, placed two fingers against his chin, and lifted up the ruin of his face to get a clear look. There were several cuts bleeding freely, and the left eye had swollen shut completely.

"Let's get him in the small camper, please. Monica, would you go with him? Clean him up a bit?"

"Why?" she asked, surprising me.

"Because you're strong enough that most men here can't overpower you and you have experience in this sort of thing. I trust you to hold off judgment until we know for sure."

That simple reminder of her past life working in the penitentiary, a job she still avoids talking about, seemed to snap her into action. She straightened up immediately, closing the distance to Jeff and pulling him up to his feet with her free hand, the other holding my Glock. "Well, come on," she said quietly as she pulled him away.

"I need to speak with Maria, please," said Jake. "Alone."

27

KEEP DRIVING

Gibs

Three days later, we were driving north up the 15, having left Las Vegas behind in a cloud of dust and middle fingers; all of us as giddy as soccer moms at a bachelorette party drinking fruity cocktails and playing with a bunch of penis-themed party favors. Our trip had gone better than any of us could have reasonably hoped and it was a true exercise in personal restraint for me to keep from stapling the gas pedal to the floor. The truck bed was loaded down with enough food to carry us into the first thaw of next year, and the trailer was packed with enough hardware to outfit everyone four times over. I suffered an intense, jittering compulsion to get it all home where it would be safe as fast as possible; however, the fuel economy readout of the Ford suggested doing so was a really bad idea.

Through a bit of experimentation, we'd determined that the best we could do was about twelve miles to the gallon at around fifty-five miles per hour or so; we could do a little better at higher speeds if we were rolling downhill. When we tried to push faster, our fuel economy started to take a hit, which was bad because all of the fuel calculations we'd made back in the valley assumed a twelve mile per gallon ratio based on what we'd seen of the truck's performance in day to day activities. If we fell very far below twelve, I didn't know if we'd have enough fuel to get home and couldn't calculate it because there wasn't any kind of fancy meter on the reserve tank to tell us how much was left.

It took us forever to figure out what was happening. I couldn't understand at all why the fuel economy was so shitty on our trip. It's not like the guzzling Ford was standard equipment for the modern Eco-warrior or anything, but we could usually maintain twelve mpg back home well over the speeds we were forced to limit ourselves to on the trip out to Vegas. Wang eventually figured out the most likely cause; we were hauling a metric ass-ton of supplies behind us, and the thirty-five square foot armored sheet that we'd hung off the back of the trailer was acting like a drag chute, forcing our engine to work harder the faster we went.

Once I understood what was going on, I nearly pulled over to the side of the road to ditch the damned thing, reasoning that the extra time we'd have to spend driving translated to elevated risk. I ultimately decided against doing so on the grounds that having a bulletproof ass was a good idea no matter how fat it made you. Additionally, I'll admit I wasn't interested in swallowing a ration of shit over having unloaded the thing after I'd devoted such time and energy to creating it in the first place.

So, I set the cruise control at fifty-five and concentrated on not squirming in the driver's seat as the scenery rolled by at a painfully slow pace.

We'd been driving continuously for the past few days as planned, stopping only to pillage a site or relieve ourselves on the side of the road. Each of us had taken a turn at the wheel by this point but, as luck would have it, we were back in the original positions we'd occupied when we left the commune; with Wang in the passenger seat and Davidson and Greg in the back. There was one significant point of difference between the time we left and the time we were on our way home, though: each of us now had in his possession high-end ballistic armor and helmets capable of stopping multiple high powered rifle rounds. No shit, Jake's little find in Vegas had been a LEO supplier, and we'd walked through the rows of shelving in that warehouse like it was Christmas. There was much more in the trailer as well, if we could just get the damned things home before Christmas actually happened. There were quite a few other interesting things we'd found as well; things that I very much wanted to get home and get comfortable with.

Thus it was that I was in a fairly happy mood, despite our grandfatherly progress up the road, when Wang asked me to pull over to the side of the road so he could recycle a little water. I did so, and he cracked his door to get out; it was nearly yanked from his hand by a nasty gust blowing east across the desert.

"Crap, man, how the hell am I gonna go in this?" Wang complained. "It'll get everywhere. Shit, I don't know if I can hold out until we pass a building or something."

"Just don't walk away from the truck," I said. "Stand right here and just piss into the dirt between the truck frame and the bottom of the door. The door itself should block you from the worst of the wind."

Wang looked at me dubiously and said, "That's a little less privacy than I'd like…"

I snorted laughter and asked, "What, are you afraid I'm gonna see your pecker? Don't worry. None of us are Peter-gazers. Well, Davidson might be."

"Fuck off, Gibs," Davidson laughed from the back seat.

When he didn't move, I sighed and turned to look out the other window. "Hurry up, Wang. Just get it done and let's get going."

Now, you're probably going to say I'm an asshole for what

happens next, but I don't care. It was worth it. Also, that's affirmed: I'm a proud asshole.

I waited to hear Wang's pants unzip, held my breath, and waited a few more seconds before I heard the telltale patter of drops hitting dirt (which wasn't easy due to the sound of the gusting wind, by the way). It didn't take much. I just pulled my foot off the brake, and the idling engine did the rest, causing the truck to roll forward a few feet, exposing Wang to the wind and all the havoc it could cause.

"Son of a… *asshole*, Gibs! You're a giant asshole, man!"

I tried to answer him, but the sound of combined laughter coming from the inside of the truck cab made it difficult. In the meantime, Wang was shuffle-stepping along to get back into the protective shelter of the door.

Through gasps of laughter, I managed to say, "I'm… oh, Jesus, I'm sorry man, I just couldn't help it. Is it really bad?"

"Uh, yeah! I got piss all over my hands and sprinkled the shit out of my jeans, you di—*stop rolling*, you colossal bastard! What the fuck!"

I was doubled up and laughing so hard that my foot had slipped off the brake pedal. I stomped it back down and threw the truck into park until I could get control of myself.

"I'm sorry, man," I gasped. "That wasn't on purpose. Or, the first time it was but the second one was my fuck-up all the way."

"Well, it's not like it matters," Wang said angrily. "I'm done now, anyway."

Greg and Davidson were still bawling uncontrollably in the back seat, groaning and laughing by turns; wheezing and complaining about their sore ribs.

"Yeah, you all keep laughing back there, too," Wang called back at them. "Next time I drive you're all screwed."

"Hey, come on, I'm sorry. Here…" I threw a package of wet

wipes at him. "Clean yourself off, put your wang away, and let's get rolling."

"And he follows it up with a dig at the name," Wang said to no one in particular as he climbed back up into the cab. "There's that twelve-year-old sense of humor we all know and love."

"Hey," I said. "I take exception to that. I'm operating at least at a fourteen-year-old's capacity."

"And the intelligence to match, obviously."

"Damned touchy little pissant, ain'tcha?" I said. "If you're feeling cranky over missing your nap time, I can certainly give you something to suck on."

"You kiss your sister with that mouth?" he grumbled.

"Never had a sister," I said. "Had to make do with smearing peanut butter on my balls and chasing the cat around."

"Wait, cats eat peanut butter?" Davidson asked from the back seat in clear disbelief.

The truck cab erupted into another bout of panicked laughter even louder than before as three of us attempted, and failed, to come to grips with Davidson's thought process.

"What? What the hell? I didn't think they'd eat peanut butter!"

"Stop, dude! Just… stop!" Greg grunted through stuttering coughs.

Eventually, it all died down to a dull roar, with a few random coughs and sniffles breaking up the new silence. My cheeks hurt from so much smiling; the last time I could remember going through something like that was…

"I haven't laughed that hard since Blucifer," Wang chuckled quietly.

I grunted and said, "Hey, I'm sorry, man. It was fucking dumb. Are we cool?"

He shot me an amused look, "What, back there? I'm over that, man. Mostly I was just having fun winding you up."

I was too exhausted to laugh anymore. The sound that escaped my mouth was more of a "*Hunf.*" "Wiseass," I said.

We drove on for a few minutes in silence before a dusty, old memory surfaced in my mind; a rusted, unused thing that I hadn't thought of in years.

"You know, I knew a guy who got it a lot worse than you," I said to Wang. "This was years and years ago—"

"You've been doing this shit to people for years and years?" Wang asked.

"No, damn it, just listen to me. This was years ago when I was still in the Corps; I'd just made E5, in fact. My Staff Sergeant and a few of us Sergeants had to hitch a ride on a Phrog (that's a CH-46 helicopter) to get from A to B… don't even ask me where. I can't remember where we were going anymore, they shipped us around so damned much.

Anyway, it so happened that a Flight Surgeon had to tag along with us to log his required hours-"

"Flight Surgeon?" asked Wang. "You mean like a doctor that has to hang around on an aircraft? Are they fixing up guys who get shot on the helicopter mid-flight or something?"

"No, nothing like that," I said. "They were basically just doctors who'd been trained to serve as physicians to our pilots and flight crew. Military pilots have to meet higher health and physical standards than your average grunt, so you need a doctor trained to watch out for that kind of thing. Also, different types of flying will affect your physiology differently, so Flight Surgeons have to be familiar with those effects and be able to treat them as well."

"Uh, okay, but you said he had to get some required hours. I'm assuming that's flight time? Why do they have to fly if they're just doctors working in some office or something?"

I nodded and said, "Part tradition, part morale, really. They have to serve a certain amount of time as flight crew because they need to be cognizant of what a flight crew goes through. Additionally, the thinking was that it was good for them to work alongside the guys they had to treat just to build up some level of camaraderie."

"Well, that sounds pretty smart," Davidson said from the back.

"Or so you'd hope," I said. "The one that came along with us was a complete tool. Nobody liked this guy, apparently. I'd never met him before that point, but the flight crew sure knew him."

"What was his deal?" Wang asked, becoming engrossed in the story.

"From what I saw that day, I'd say he was probably an arrogant prick with an undeservedly high opinion of himself. So anyway, there we all were, airborne, and this flight doc leans over to the Crew Chief and says something. I couldn't hear what they were saying, you understand; as part of the flight crew, they were all hooked into ICS—basically the onboard radio. I had to get filled in later by the Crew Chief... what the fuck was his name again? Brandt, that's right! Sergeant Brandt. We all laughed our asses off when he explained what happened."

With a smile creeping slowly across his face, Wang asked, "Well, what did happen?"

"Turns out the flight doc had to take a leak pretty bad, and he was worried about his ability to make it all the way to landing. I suppose it was the first time he'd encountered such a thing. Guy figures he can't be the only one this has ever happened to, so he asks the Crew Chief, 'Hey, what do I do?' you know? Those Phrogs didn't come equipped with bathrooms."

"Shit, that's right," Davidson said, mildly surprised. "What would you do?"

"So, I'm not sure if you guys know what a CH-46 looks like, but it's a dual rotorcraft, one up front and one in the rear, right?"

"Oh, you mean like a Chinook?" Davidson asked.

"Exactly," I said, raising a thumbs-up to him. "A Chinook is really just the larger version; that was the CH-47, see? But among the many things the 46 and 47 had in common was a large loading ramp that dropped out its ass. The whole rear of the thing just opened up wide so you could load whatever you wanted or so you could jump out and get moving really quick; that kind of thing.

"So, Sergeant Brandt the Crew Chief says to the guy, 'Look, it's not a big deal. Just go piss on the ramp. We do it all the time.' The Flight Surgeon looks back and forth between the rear of the plane and the Crew Chief a few times, shrugs, and thinks to himself, 'Eh, fuck it. Could be worse.'

"My buddies, Brandt, and I then watched as this guy unhooks his helmet from ICS, straps into a lanyard, strides to the rear, opens up the goddamned ramp, and proceeds… to piss… to piss off the edge." I had begun laughing at the end, unable to contain myself as the memory played back in my mind.

"I don't get it," Wang said. "What's the deal?"

After my laughter calmed down a bit, I said, "Remember what happened to you just now when you got exposed to a little wind?"

"Yeah?"

"We were in flight, man. The wind that came back and hit him while he stood on that ramp was ten times worse than what you just caught."

"Oo-oh no," Greg laughed from the rear seat.

"This guy covered himself in his own piss!" I said, bawling laughter again. "He turned around to face us, and his fucking visor was completely misted like a car windshield in a rainstorm!"

"That's rather unfortunate," Wang laughed. "None of you guys tried to warn him?"

"That's the thing; the Crew Chief absolutely did try, but the Doc had disconnected his radio to walk aft of the plane; the cable wouldn't stretch that far. So Brandt's back there waving his arms and calling out to him the minute the ramp starts to go down, but the guy can't hear. The wind hit almost immediately, so I think Brandt figured the guy would realize how badly it would go if he persisted. Evidently, he didn't."

"But the guy… uh, Brandt, told him to do that," Wang said. "I'm confused; wouldn't he have known—"

"No, he didn't tell him that at all," I interrupted. "He didn't say to piss *off* the ramp. What the Flight Surgeon was supposed to do was piss on the ramp while it was still closed and then open it up after he was finished to clean it off. Christ, they even kept a water bucket in the back for that very reason."

"Oh, God," said Davidson. "Man, that really sucks."

"So now this guy is fucking enraged and screaming back at Brandt. None of us needed a radio at that point; we could all hear what he was screaming. He was wiping his dripping face off after he'd closed the ramp back up and was just going on about it. 'You planned that. I'm going to talk to your CO and have you NJP'd until your fucking head caves in, blah, blah, blah'."

"NJP?" asked Wang.

"Non-judicial punishment," I explained. "The younger guys called it a Ninja Punch. It's basically what they do to you if you've fucked up, but the fuck-up wasn't bad enough for a court-martial. They can suck a little or a lot. Usually a lot."

"So what did this guy Brandt say?" Greg asked.

"This was the best part," I laughed. "Now, you have to picture this: Sergeant Brandt was a little fucker. Like, he was all of five-foot-seven or so. And on top of that, the Flight Surgeon was an officer; that outranks a Sergeant, see? Regardless of that, if he thought you were an asshole or that you'd done something stupid… and if you'd managed to piss him off enough, Sergeant Brandt absolutely would lay into you, and no threat of punishment or personal injury could stop him. While still laughing, he points right at the guy's dripping face and screams, 'You stupid motherfucker! I told you to piss on the ramp not off it! How the fuck are you even a doctor? How is it even possible that you didn't realize what would happen if you pissed into that kind of wind? Jesus Christ, you're so fucking dumb if you fell into a barrel of tits, you'd still come out sucking your thumb!"

The rest of the guys in the truck laughed along with me at the mental image; your average, working-class Marine too amused by a horrible situation to have even the slightest concern over any possible repercussions that might have awaited him on landing, finger extended and screaming in glee.

"So did he get in trouble?" Wang asked.

"No," I sighed, finally coming back under control. "I think the Doc must have realized how much of a douche he would have looked like if he'd followed through on his threat. I think he also knew that me and the guys would have spread the story far and wide in retaliation, too. We all liked that Crew Chief; he was a good guy."

"So you kept it under wraps, then," Davidson said.

"Oh, hell no, fuck that guy," I said. "We told everyone who'd listen. It was too good to keep to ourselves."

"Oh, geez…" Wang laughed. "Nice."

"What?" I asked in my most aggrieved voice.

"Hey," Greg interrupted. "Do you guys see that up there? On the side of the road?"

"Huh?" I grunted and focused my attention ahead. Maybe a half mile ahead was a person on the side of the road standing in front of the hulk of a burned out wreck. Whoever it was, he (or she) was waving frantically.

"What do you think that's about?" asked Wang.

Biting my lip, I said nothing in response. I gazed far out into the distance, willing my old eyes to take in any kind of detail around the wreckage. There appeared to be some sort of debris around the person, knee high and nondescript; maybe boxes or bags.

"Looks pretty worked up," Davidson said quietly from behind me.

I tore my eyes off the person in the distance and looked around in all directions, seeing only desert stretching on for miles with rolling hills in the distance behind us. There were no buildings for as far as I could see and the road was mostly clear, but for that one blemish ahead of us.

"What the hell?" I whispered.

It was a woman, jumping in place and flailing her hand around. She was dressed in clothes falling nearly to tatters; her other hand was clutched to her chest, holding a bundle. With her free hand, she reached down to the bundle at her chest, struggled with it a moment, and finally pulled a tiny, pink fist into view. She continued to jump and scream as she did so, then dropped the little hand back into the bundle and resumed waving her hand high in the air.

"Holy shit," Wang whined. "Are we stopping for her? We're gonna stop for her, right?"

I don't care if it's a woman screaming for help or anything else. You keep driving. Got me?

Amanda's voice had come uninvited to my mind, and I shook my head violently to knock it away. My hands clenched on the wheel as I tried to decide what the fuck I was going to do. A woman screaming for help, I thought. How the Christ had Amanda known to say that? Intuition? Goddamned Spider Sense?

"Gibs?" Wang prodded.

"Hey, Gibs, we need to stop, okay?" Greg insisted from the back.

The woman walked out into the road as we approached, screaming and waving like we were her last hope.

I thought of the people back home waiting for us; depending on us for their survival. *Don't stop driving. Work in shifts. Get back, no matter what. Keep... Driving!*

"Gibs!" Wang cried.

"No," I said calmly and pulled the wheel to the right to veer around her.

The others shouted out in anger and dismay, slapping the dashboard, wanting to know what in the hell was wrong with me. I looked out the side view mirror (as the armor plating we'd installed over the back window rendered the rear view mirror totally useless) and said, "Shut up! What the fuck's she doing back there?"

Everyone leaned forward and peered into the side view mirrors now. In the distance behind us, we saw the miniature image of the woman throw the bundle in her arms to the pavement, which bounced unnaturally and rolled away.

"No shit?" asked Greg. "It was a doll—"

From her waistband, she extracted what appeared to be a pistol, but instead of pointing it at us she elevated the barrel high into the air and pulled the trigger. A flare launched high up into the sky and exploded into a small, bright red flame that began to descend slowly back to the ground.

"What the fuck?" muttered Wang.

I knew what was coming next, of course. I put the gas down and started pulling on my vest and helmet with one hand even as the others squawked at my blatant disregard for fuel economy.

"Yo, Gibs, what's the deal, man?" Davidson asked, sounding panicked.

Instead of answering him, I returned to scanning the horizon. There were no hills or mountains out ahead of us or to the side, but there were plenty behind, stretching forwards toward us from the rear as we drove. Looking in the side mirror, I saw a large dust cloud begin to emerge from behind a low stretch of foothills. My gut clenched involuntarily as I hissed, "Fu-uck…"

"What is that?" Wang asked in a flat voice.

Before I had the chance to answer, a black line of vehicles of all shapes and sizes spilled out from behind the hills, kicking up an ungodly dust cloud as they came. I couldn't count their number at that distance, but I could see several cars, trucks, and motorcycles coming from behind that hill; and they just kept coming, stretching out in a long, mechanized serpent. The tip of the convoy reached the 15 before the tail had come out from behind the hillside.

The mass of vehicles turned north up the highway to pursue us.

THE TRIAL

Amanda

J ake emerged from the cabin with Maria in tow some time later. All the rest of us loitered around outside, sitting around on the porch or leaning on the rails, silently. A few of us sat around Oscar, just trying to keep him sane by means of being physically close.

They came through the front door without comment, Maria hiding just a little bit behind Jake's leg. From his seated position on the front steps, Oscar had to look back over his shoulder to see them. He whimpered, "Maria? Baby?"

Jake leaned down to speak quietly into her ear, hand rested feather-light on her shoulder. She nodded and threw her arms around his waist in a fierce hug, which he slowly returned after appearing to recover from some amount of shock. She released him and ran into her father's arms.

"Take her home, Oscar," said Jake in a hollow, far away voice.

"What abou—"

"Let me worry about it for now," Jake interrupted. "No decision will be made without you but, for right now, she needs you more than you need this."

Holding onto his daughter, running his hands through her hair and kneading her back anxiously, Oscar swallowed hard before nodding silently. Tears had begun to roll down his cheeks unchecked. He looked down and said, "Come on, Mija. Let's go," before gently leading her away.

None of the rest of us said anything at all. The others watched them as they departed towards the container home; all of them watched except me. I watched Jake. He also kept his eyes on Oscar's retreating back, waiting patiently immobile, until father and daughter disappeared around the corner of the building. As Oscar got further away, the worried concern melted slowly from Jake's face to be replaced by… nothing at all. Not anger nor rage, disgust, dismay, or sadness. There was only the void; the Jake Persona I first met all those months ago in Utah, when he'd handed me a knife and told me he'd understand. It had been a while since he wore this face. Knowing what it meant, I wondered if our community would survive what would likely follow.

Without removing his eyes from Oscar's little home, Jake said, "Bring me Jeff."

Jake sat across from Jeff in the library of the cabin, both of them occupying the low-backed armchairs in the center of the floor. To Jake's left was the large executive desk and, to his right, the leather couch on which I sat to serve as a witness to the discussion at Jake's request. Jeff had his back to the door, which was closed. He held a wet washcloth against his swollen eye to soothe the pain.

Jake winced in sympathy as Jeff recoiled from the cloth's

touch and said, "I'm sorry, that looks bad. Is there anything I can get you?"

Jeff shook his head, unwilling to look up to meet Jake's gaze. Instead of accepting the lack of an answer, Jake snapped his fingers and pointed. "Tylenol at least!" He jumped up from his chair, calling out to us as he exited, "Just a moment, please. I know I have a bottle in the medicine cabinet…" The rapid *creak-bang* of a wall cabinet reached us from the hallway shortly before Jake bustled back into the room. Sitting back down in his chair, he opened the little container and shook a couple of capsules into his hand. He then glanced up at Jeff, who only looked on suspiciously with darting eyes; Jake shrugged and shook out two more pills. He put the bottle aside and reached out across the floor to offer the Tylenol to Jeff.

Jeff reached out timidly but pulled his hand back, now finally looking up to meet Jake's eyes. Jake extended his hand further still and said, "Please. You must be in a lot of pain."

The change that came over Jeff was sudden and would have been heartbreaking if not for the situation. His shoulders sagged as he reached out to take the offered medicine, all tension releasing from his body. Here, at least, was a friend, he must have thought.

Jake twisted in his chair to reach behind himself to a table that held an assortment of bottled waters. Grabbing one, he turned back and held it out to the other man.

"Here," he said softly.

"Thank you," Jeff murmured through a swollen lip and used it to swallow his pills. He cringed silently as the rim of the bottle touched his mouth.

Jake waited patiently for Jeff to get the pills down, sitting in his chair with his legs crossed and hands folded over his knees as if he were conducting an interview, before continuing.

"Okay?" Jake asked. Jeff heaved a deep sigh and nodded. Jake continued: "This is such a horrible situation. I don't even know what to say. I'm hoping you'll be patient with me in providing your side of the story. I really want to put all of this behind us as quickly as possible, but we have to make sure we proceed carefully. There can be no doubts once this is all settled, wouldn't you agree?"

Jeff nodded, appearing more at ease in his situation the longer Jake talked.

"Excellent," Jake said while leaning back and smiling. "Now, if you please..."

Jeff raised his eyebrows. "I'm sorry?"

Spreading his hands, Jake said, "Please share your side of the story, Jeff."

"Oh, right." He shifted in his chair and took another painful sip of water. "Honestly, there isn't all that much to say. Maria and I had become close friends over the last few weeks, and she had begun to confide in me over the loss of her mother... I don't think you know the details behind that, do you?"

"I don't," agreed Jake, "but let's not discuss that now, if she told you in confidence. I'm content with this part of your explanation. Please go on." He leaned his elbow on the armrest and cupped his chin, expression intent. His eyes were understanding and kind.

"Okay, that probably is best," Jeff continued. "Well... I mean... that's really all there is. She had some stuff she needed to get off her chest, and I happened to be there for her."

Jake nodded. His eyes flickered to me for an instant, so fast I don't even think Jeff noticed. "Why do you think Rose would have told her mother that you were behaving inappropriately with Maria, Jeff?"

Jeff spread his arms wide and shook his head, face animated, and said, "I have no frigging idea, Jake. Honest to God. You'd have to ask her."

"I may, I may… if it comes to that. I don't think it will, though, really."

Jeff laughed softly, showing clear relief. He took another sip from a shaking hand.

"Had you had any problems with Rose in the past?"

Jeff's head shook side to side.

"Was she having any trouble absorbing the material you were trying to teach her? Did you perhaps chastise her at some point for inattentiveness?"

"Hell no," Jeff insisted.

"Your relationship with her was fine, then? There was no indication at all that she had any sort of problem with you?"

Jeff dropped his gaze towards the floor as his eyes narrowed, which I'm sure he intended to be a thoughtful expression but only looked sly and calculating to me.

"No, there was never any such indication… but…"

"Yes?"

He looked back up and glanced between us both. "Well, Rose enjoys attention. She's easier to work with one on one than in groups because she ends up competing less with the other kids for face time. If she thinks she's being ignored, she's shown a tendency to act out."

"I see," said Jake. "And you suppose this could just be her acting out of a desire to bring attention to herself?"

"I can't say for sure," Jeff said, getting into the discussion (he leaned forward in his chair). "But things around here are always so hectic, with all the gathering and stuff. I think it's fair to say that all the kids may be feeling ignored."

Jake nodded again, expression thoughtful, and said, "This is a very good point." He tapped a cheek with his index finger and looked at me. "This is just a lousy situation. The accusation has been leveled and cannot now be retracted. We have to discover some way to get beyond reasonable doubt or this little group of ours will remain fractured."

I held my breath, not knowing where he was going with this, yet also knowing that there was indeed some hidden plan.

"I'll do whatever it takes to put everyone at ease, Jake," said Jeff, sitting on the edge of his chair. "Whatever it takes."

Jake's head rotated suddenly to lock onto Jeff, and I saw a flicker behind his eyes as they settled into place; it reminded me of some small creature frozen under a spotlight.

"I'm glad," Jake said quietly. "I'm glad. You may begin by unbuttoning your pants."

"What!" Jeff barked. He leaned back in his chair, head whipping over to look at me with a horrified, unspoken question hanging on his lips.

"I'm terribly, terribly sorry for this," Jake apologized. "It really is the only way to be sure."

Unable to restrain myself, I finally asked, "What is this about, Jake?"

"Maria described a birthmark on Jeff's person, close enough to his genitalia that she couldn't possibly have seen it without also seeing his genitals. You see where this is going, of course…"

"You… you can't be serious," Jeff whispered. His face had gone white, and sweat was breaking out over his forehead. "I'm not going to expose myself here… in front of her!"

He wrapped a shaking hand around his wrist and began to spin the silvery bracelet he wore, winding it around and around in nervous jerks. The bright metal flashed and shined in the light spilling through the windows as it darted under his fingers, then back out again. It fluttered and weaved under his hand, reminding me of noon sunlight flashing off the surface of running water. The reflection crossed the path of my eyes, so bright that it caused me to squint.

"You needn't worry," Jake said in gentle, calming tones.

"Amanda won't see anything; I'll ask her to go stand behind you. But I must insist, I'm afraid. It's really nothing, isn't it? Just a quick peek, and this is all over. I'll be able to take this news back to the others and clear your name."

I got up from the couch and positioned myself behind Jeff as Jake had suggested, balancing lightly on the balls of my feet in case things got aggressive.

"This… this is fucking crazy!" Jeff shouted. "You can't do this to people! You can't make them do this! What the hell happened to basic rights?"

Jake hung his head and sighed. "Jeff… look. I'm doing my level best to give you every opportunity to redeem yourself." He looked up again. "I'm inclined to believe you. I want to believe you, don't you understand that? But I have to be certain. You must understand."

I saw the back of Jeff's head jerking left and right silently as Jake rose ponderously from his seat to take a step forward. In response, Jeff sprung from his chair, knocking it backward into the wall with his legs, and attempted to step away from the other man.

Jake's left hand shot out so fast that I didn't even have time to flinch or anticipate the shot to Jeff's face. It took me a moment to realize that he hadn't actually struck Jeff at all; he'd only wrapped his hand around the man's throat to hold him steady. Jeff squawked, wrapped both of his hands around Jake's wrist, and began to struggle.

All of the warmth and understanding had washed completely from Jake's face by now. He was that Thing again, that killer I'd seen stand over a half-conscious woman to offer a simple, offhand remark before shooting her through the face; his own face now as smooth as a porcelain mask, as it had been then. Eyes wide and passively intent, muscles rippled and flapped briefly over the bones in his arm as his hand clamped down. The wide, square fingers buried into the sides of Jeff's neck, plunging into the skin so deeply that I nearly expected them to puncture the surface and bury under the muscle. A horrified, strangled gagging sound began to pour from his mouth without end; I thought of a gazelle being eaten alive, throat torn out completely as it kicked wildly in a futile attempt to run away.

Jake stood that way, motionless, for what seemed a very long time but what was probably only five seconds, and just stared into Jeff's eyes, all the while those panicked gurgling sounds continued to trickle through the room. Finally, his head rotated down to Jeff's midsection. Jake's hand reached out, and I saw his right elbow began to jerk and twitch as he undid the front of Jeff's pants. A few seconds more, and he'd exposed the groin area; his elbow rotated and twitched further as he prodded at Jeff's penis. His left arm remained rigid and motionless as iron; the skin of Jeff's neck began to purple around the trauma being inflicted.

Jake looked back up to meet Jeff's eyes and, without lessening the pressure in the slightest, said, "What would have been your excuse for this, I wonder? She happened upon you while you were urinating into a bush, I suspect. Only, this mark is so faint; no one would even notice it unless... unless they were close, would they?" Jake drew Jeff in, the smaller man's feet tiptoeing, and then partially skidding across the rug. He stopped when their noses nearly touched. "Close like this, yes?"

Abruptly, Jake released his throat and lightly pushed him back, causing him to fall heavily into the chair. Jeff began coughing spasmodically while his shaking hands groped clumsily to cover his crotch. He began to sob uncontrollably as he coughed, which I think remains as one of the absolute worst things I've ever heard to this day.

"Amanda, would you please see him back to the trailer?" asked Jake in a calm, polite voice. "We'll need to decide what comes next."

It wasn't very long after Jeff's interrogation that we all stood together around the front porch of the house, with the exception of Jeff himself, who was confined to the trailer, and the children, who had all been sent to Oscar's place to be together. Jake sat quietly on the top step of the porch, looking deflated as he brought everyone up to speed.

"It's not good, but it could have been a lot worse," he said as he ran a hand back through his hair. "Having spoken to Maria, it looks like he only progressed as far as petting and it seems… Oscar? Are you holding up?"

Oscar stood opposite Jake in the patch of dirt before the steps, surrounded on either side by the rest of us. He held his left arm across his chest with his right elbow propped on top of it; a clenched, trembling fist obscured his mouth. His eyes flicked up from their focal point on the ground to glance at Jake, and he jerked his head in an abrupt nod.

"Fair enough," Jake continued. "As I was saying, it doesn't seem as though he's gone after any of the other kids, but that's strictly from Maria's point of view. I suppose it's possible she just doesn't know. There are two paths we can take at this point. We may choose to question the other children regarding their interaction with Jeff or, knowing what we know now, we can focus on dealing with this problem."

Oscar coughed into his hand and said, "I already know enough, but I'll wait on the other parents if they feel like they need it. I know where he is. It's enough right now."

Faces turned to shift between Otis, Monica, and me. Shortly after that, Otis and Monica shared a glance, and then they looked in my direction as well, more or less lacking the will to add to any decision. I realized it was down to me, so I said what was in my heart.

"You have to cut out the cancer before you can start healing," I murmured. Then louder, "Let's… deal with Jeff right now."

"Right," Oscar said, "gimme a gun."

"Whoa, whoa, hang on!" Edgar yelped. "We're just going straight to murder, here? We don't want to talk this over?"

"Murder, nothin'," Oscar growled. "I'm puttin' a dog to sleep. That ain't murder."

"Now just wait a goddamned minute," George said, thumping his cane into a floorboard. "Edgar's right. This isn't good. We can't just—"

"Maria's not your daughter, old man!" Oscar shouted. "You got no position, here!"

Some of the people in the circle gasped at the venom carried in Oscar's voice; I believe he scared some of the other women, but his reaction seemed reasonable to me, honestly.

"That's a hell of a thing to say, Oscar," George shot back. "We all live here together; every one of us has a stake in this. And your daughter means as much to me as my own children did, damn you."

The fire behind Oscar's eyes died down a little at that remark, but he didn't apologize or retract his statement. Instead, he addressed the rest of us, saying, "I'm not arguing over this. I shouldn't have to. He needs to be handled. There at least needs to be justice."

Edgar said, "From whom, Oscar? You? That's just vengeance." He held up his hands at the black look from Oscar and said, "Hey, I understand how you feel. If I'm honest with everyone, I could go either way on this. But we want to think really hard about what we're considering here. This is big. It's going to change what's normal around here. Is everyone completely comfortable going down this road?"

"I'm good with it," Alish said in a matter of fact tone. "A pig like that… I've seen such as him. What are our other options? Let him go? We would only be inflicting him on the next child he encounters."

"Are we actually taking votes on a murder now?" George asked in dismay.

"Vote all you want," Oscar said. "This all ends up the same way, irregardless."

"No, Oscar," Jake said. "The group may decide that execution is warranted and if it does, the group will decide the best way in which to carry that out. But we will decide as a group."

"But if we go there, should Oscar be the one?" Fred asked, drawing a scandalized look from the other man. He looked in Oscar's direction and said, "Sorry, man, but just hear me out. They used to do this with firing squads, you know? One man got a real bullet, and everyone else got blanks so they wouldn't know who'd actually killed the criminal. If folks're worried about being vengeful, maybe we do something like that? Might make it easier to stomach."

"I'll do it," I said, pulling attention back my way. "No one else has to be involved. I'll drive him out a ways and shoot him in the back of the head. He won't even feel it, and we can be done with the whole thing."

Barbara drew in a shaking breath and said, "Oh, no, Amanda... for God's sake..."

"Don't give me that, Barbara. You don't know where I've been or what I've done."

Tears spilled over her eyes as she whispered, "You don't have to keep doing it, Honey."

I felt a burning in my eyes as I heard Elizabeth's small voice in my mind: *I wish I could kill someone...*

"Barbara," I whispered, "shut up."

George leaned forward towards Jake and said, "Jake... you can't allow—"

"Can't allow what, George?" Jake asked suddenly, standing

up. "What will I tell these people? Huh? That I forbid this? That they must not? What good is that, if I force the decision on them?"

All of us had gone silent at this point. Jake was clearly agitated, eyes widened and searching.

"You people are going to have to decide what you'll allow, now," he said, looking out among us all. He stopped himself a moment, took a deep breath, and slowly pulled himself back into line. In a calm voice, he said, "Listen, all of you. Killing isn't the dangerous thing anymore. Most of us have killed people by now, haven't we?" He looked from face to face, and when no one responded, he emphasized, "Well, haven't we?"

There were several nods; no one was willing to speak.

Jake nodded in return. "We have. This is normal now, in this world. It's an easy thing to do… easy as breathing. And, one must admit, problems do get solved in the act."

He descended the steps slowly and came to a stop in the dirt patch in the center of the circle we had formed but neglected to look at any of us as he continued.

"Certain of us have solved problems in this way. It's without consequence, we say. The police won't come and take you away anymore. There are no repercussions anymore, certainly. Only, that's not entirely true."

He took a few more steps away from the cabin until he stood outside of our circle and turned around to face us. His eyes were exhausted but unblinking.

"Every time you kill someone, you pay a price. At first, you might kill someone that's trying to kill you, which is fair. Nobody would fault you for that, would they? They'd have to be nuts. And after that, maybe you kill someone who's beating a friend of yours, and you can't get them to stop. Again: reasonable, yes?"

He looked from face to face, sighed, and said, "Maybe later still you kill someone for their food. You feel bad about it, but you were starving, of course. You were either going to get that food or die. And, when weighed against your own survival... or your family's, you do what you must do, don't you? And after that? Someone out there in the world, some stranger, has an item that you want. It's... it's not that far a stretch, really."

None of us spoke, hanging instead on every word he said. Oscar, who now had his back to me because he was facing Jake, slumped visibly. A deep anger rose up in my heart as I listened; anger at the possibility that Jake might be right.

"We've all lost so much since the world died but honestly, not everything left behind has to be something that hurts. It doesn't all have to be bad." He pointed a finger at the ground. "This is where we rebuild; it's the whole idea behind what we're trying to do, here in the valley. Or at least, it's what I had in mind that day when I called out to Gibs. I know I took a chance on him. I was rewarded for it, though."

Jake pushed his hair out of his eyes impatiently and looked away from us towards the teardrop camper that held Jeff. His face smoothed over momentarily, just a brief flash before his brow furrowed again. Still looking away, he said, "There's a chance here. Everything is a chance... or a choice, I guess, is a better word. You all have a choice here. You get to decide what you want your world to be. There's no one else coming in from the outside to tell us how to be anymore, so it's all up to us now. Rebuild the world in our own image."

He looked back toward us, eyes on fire. "Part of that choice is whether life will be cheap or precious. Do you want killing to be hard or do you want it to get easy? What kind of world do you want to make? What kind of world do you want Ben, Elizabeth, Rose, Maria, and-"

He coughed and looked away. Glancing down, he shook his head abruptly and continued, "What kind of world do you want them growing up in? Because here's the problem, see; the real challenge." He extended a finger to point at all of us and said, "If life is going to be precious, you all have to decide that it will be so. Everyone has to agree to uphold that ideal. Together."

The vision of Jake standing out in front of us blurred momentarily; I reached up to wipe my eyes. Never in our time together had I felt closer to him than I did at that moment, never did I feel that I knew him better. I thought of Lizzy and knew that he was right… and was ashamed.

"The concept of a precious life is a fragile thing," Jake said quietly; so quiet in fact, that we had to strain to hear him. I felt as though he was talking to himself now instead of to us. "Everyone has to agree for that to work, but it takes only one person to decide that life will be cheap. One person to make that decision for everyone else and there's nothing that can be done to stop it. Because once you cheapen one person's life, you cheapen all life. When your friend sees you kill a man easily, without hesitation or remorse, your friend knows how easily that malice can be redirected. It becomes so, so easy for everyone to assume a reality of kill or be killed. Kill first… just in case."

He was quiet a long time then, standing before us, unnaturally still, as we all struggled to return his gaze. Finally, when I felt as though someone must speak if only to break the silence, Jake relented and said, "One person makes the decision for all. Who among us will accept that responsibility?"

Jake turned away and, wearing only his flannel, jeans, and boots, walked alone out of the valley.

APOCALYPTIC ROAD PIRATES

Gibs

Unwilling to take my eyes off the road ahead of us, I asked, "What are they doing now?"

"Same thing, Gibs. Just hanging back there," Greg said.

"Well, are they closer since the last time I asked?"

"Uh, it's really hard to say for sure but... I think so?"

I grunted. "Close enough to shoot?"

The rear window rolled down, and I heard the sound of rushing wind agitated by a large obstruction. Unable to help myself, I glanced over my shoulder and saw that the kid was hanging his head out the window to look back behind us. A few seconds later, he retreated back into the cab and rolled his window back up.

"I don't think so," he said. "It's still hard to count individual vehicles; the bikers look like dots."

I looked down and the instrument panel. I had the speed pinned at ninety, but the fuel economy had plummeted to a depressing seven. I ground my teeth while wracking my brain for ideas. I could push the truck a little faster, but that shield in back wasn't doing us any favors. Besides, the Ford's engine was built for towing power not winning drag races. I couldn't tell what kinds of vehicles were pursuing us outside of being able to say "trucks, cars, and bikes" in a general sense, but I knew that it didn't take a rare motorcycle to ride circles around us; any average crotch rocket would be able to blow our doors off.

I gnawed my lip and thought furiously, breathing deep to keep my shit together. Can't outrun them and, if we try, we probably burn through all of our fuel long before we get home. Can't stop and fight them, though; too damn many.

"Wang, get that map open. Show me where we are."

He complied, filling the whole passenger side of the cab with fold-out paper that just seemed to keep coming. He pulled the right side up the window to keep the edge out of my area. "We should be coming up on Mesquite next in... uh, looks like twenty-five or thirty miles."

I did some quick math in my head, determining that thirty miles would take about twenty minutes at our current rate.

"Can you tell how far it is from Mesquite to that mountain pass we hit in Arizona?"

Wang cursed and began winding the map back up, not even bothering to try to fold it neatly. I realized he'd have to pull out the Thomas Guide to get a map of Arizona; we only had detailed state maps of Nevada and Utah. Then, even when he did get the Thomas Guide out, it was only going to show him roads, not terrain.

"Relax," I said, waving him off. "Doesn't matter."

Twenty minutes or so to Mesquite then call it maybe another twenty or so to that little mountain pass for shits and giggles. I glanced into my side mirror to look at the blot of people gaining on us; outliers to either side of their column traveled along the soft shoulder, kicking up one hell of a dust cloud.

I began to tally our assets: semi-armored vehicle, enough firepower to supply a small-time warlord, and enough diesel to swim in. It occurred to me suddenly that our pursuers would be running out of gas a lot sooner than we would. Even if we ran our tank down to empty, we could refuel without stopping. We just had to pop the cap and activate the built-in electrical pump. Of course, someone would have to be out there in the truck bed to do it…

I glanced around the cab at the others. "Gear on. Everyone. Helmets too; let's go."

They all responded instantly, shrugging into their new vests and strapping the black ballistic helmets down over their heads. I began to ease off the gas slowly as they did so.

"What's the plan?" Davidson asked. "Why are we slowing down?"

"We need enough fuel to get home," I said, "and we're simply not outrunning these guys. We'll have to slow down and beat them back when and if they get too close to us. They're gonna run out of fuel before we do, but the trick is I gotta have you guys out there to run the reserve line to the truck's tank when we get low. And, I need to get you guys out there now, while those assholes are still out of range."

As I spoke, the other three all became very businesslike and started grabbing their rifles.

"Not you, Greg," I said over my shoulder. "You think you can drive this rig?"

In the rearview mirror, I saw an irate pair of seventeen-year-old eyes flash back at me. Greg said, "Hey, fuck that, dude. I am not sitting up here while the rest of you guys get shot at."

"Greg? Hey, *Greg*!" I shouted, but it was too late. Before I could even respond, he'd slung his rifle, shoved open his door, and stepped out onto the side runner. As I sat there screaming at him, he reached up behind the cab to grab the armor plating that Fred had installed and swung himself up into the truck bed, graceful as a gymnast, slamming his door shut behind him.

"Mother*fucking* shit head!" I yelled out, slamming the dashboard with my fist. "Diso-fucking-bedient little brat!"

"You raise them up to be good little children but, at some point, they always find a way to piss you off in the end..." Wang said.

"Goddamnit, Wang... *not helping*."

"Sorry."

I took a few breaths to bring my blood pressure back down, and then grabbed one of the two team radios we'd brought along with us and handed it back to Davidson.

"Get out there with him and cover up behind that armor wall on the trailer. You guys each take a side. If any of those assholes on our tail comes up alongside of us, light them the fuck up; they'll be trying to shoot our tires out. Keep at it until they drop back behind us. Don't shoot at anyone directly behind us; I want them to think that's a safe area back there. Now, what'd I say?"

"Only shoot the assholes coming up on our side!" Davidson rattled off.

"Outstanding. And don't be shy about rocking that 40 Mike-Mike. That worked out well for us in Colorado. If they're on motorcycles, aim for the seat. If they're in a car or a truck, try to put the grenade into or just under the grill; you could take out the radiator or a piece of the engine and disable the vehicle. A disabled vehicle is just as good as a kill."

"Understood!" shouted Davidson over the roar of the wind; he'd shoved his door open as soon as I'd finished speaking. It slammed shut shortly after, and the truck cab was thrown back into relative silence.

I looked back down at the gauges. Sixty miles per hour and twelve miles per gallon. I flexed my hands on the wheel and tried to keep calm; the hairs on the back of my neck stood up as I could almost feel our pursuit crawling right up my ass.

"They're going to be on us in no time at this speed," Wang said nervously.

"I know, but I'm hoping we only have to hold them off until Arizona."

"What happens in Arizona?"

"You remember that little mountain pass we drove through on the way down here?" I asked.

"Sure."

"Okay. You ever hear of the battle of Thermopylae?"

"Of course. Everyone has," Wang said. "After that stupid movie came out…"

I rolled my eyes. Right; war rhinoceroses and sword-wielding goblin orcs. Totally accurate film.

"Well, that was actually a real goddamned thing that happened, once upon a time," I growled. "A small force of men were able to successfully detain the overwhelming might of the Persian army through the use of superior terrain. Just like we're going to do."

"Did the Spartans survive in real life? They all died in the movie."

"Well… no."

"No?" Wang yelped.

"Relax. The Spartans were constrained in that they weren't able to displace. We are, but we'll be able to slow to a crawl in there and light the fuckers up like it's the Fourth of July. Plus, I'm pretty sure they'll run out of bullets before we do. I think we can take away their will to fight in there. I think we can back them off."

I looked into my side mirror and saw that the column was noticeably closer now. I tried to get a look at Greg and Davidson as well, but the angles were all wrong. I hit my radio and said, "Davidson, how copy?"

"Loud and clear," he came back. "What's up?"

"How're you doing back there? You guys in position?"

"It's about as comfortable as butt sex in a Volkswagen, but we're all set."

I grunted a laugh despite the situation and said, "Nice. It looks like we have a little time yet. See if you can re-stack some of that shit further up, so you don't end up breaking things while shifting around."

"Roger that," he said.

We drove on a while in tense silence, eyes flicking back and forth between the road ahead and our side mirrors, noting that the column had come closer every time we looked back. I glanced down at the speedometer and noticed that it had crept back up to seventy-five. I cursed, pulled it back to sixty-five, and locked in the cruise control to take my twitchy foot out of the equation. I looked into the side mirror again; they were close enough that I could make out the silhouettes of heads inside vehicles. From what I could tell, they had slowed down to match our speed, maintaining a static distance.

"What the fuck are you up to now?" I muttered in a low voice.

"Maybe they just want to talk?" asked a hopeful Wang.

I scoffed. "Yeah, they want to talk us out of our shit. You saw that woman back there; she was bait. Carjackers used to do shit like that."

I rubbed my chin and checked the road ahead of us again.

"My guess is they're wondering why we're not trying to get away. They may be wondering if this is some kind of a trap. Of course, there may be some sort of trap ahead of us, in which case we're fu—"

A high-pitched clank rang out directly behind my head, causing me to duck low behind the wheel and shout, "Gee-zus *Christ!*"

A few seconds after that, two more clanks rattled off, and

Davidson's voice came through over the radio. "That's it! Here they come!"

The cab of the truck erupted with the rapid-paced clanging of rung metal, rattling all up and down the bands of spring steel behind us. It came so fast and heavy that it sounded like we were caught in an epic hailstorm from Hell. I broke out into an instant sweat all over as I resigned myself to just take the punishment for moment, trying not to flinch at every impact; each bullet strike was a physical thing that I could feel in my back, making my muscles twitch and jump.

I hit the transmit button on the radio and shouted, "Davidson! How're you guys holding up? Is that shield working?"

"So far so good," he called back. His voice came through muted by a hail of gunfire. "I don't know how long this will hold, though. It sounds like a drum solo out… oh, shit. Stand by!"

The sound of more rifle fire erupted behind us, this time incredibly close. I looked out my mirrors and saw that a few motorcycles had swung out on either side of us, scouting ahead. Greg and Davidson had begun spraying rifle fire in their direction; Davidson's M4 was clearly set to auto as it spat 5.56 rounds in rapid succession. I saw bike riders begin to go down into the dirt and disappear behind us.

"So far so good," I repeated through grinding teeth.

The rear window exploded into the back seat, showering both of us in little, blocky nubs of safety glass. At the same instant, a tiny hole bloomed in our windshield with cracks webbing out in all directions. Whatever had caused the hole, it had just missed Wang's head by a few inches.

"Holy shit," Wang's voice quivered. He began to brush glass shards off with shaking hands.

"That one nearly had your name on it," I said.

"I can't believe they got one through," he laughed in a thin, weak voice. "Those gaps are tiny!"

"I hadn't planned on them standing up to such volume," I said.

"It's heating up back here, guys!" Davidson shouted over the radio. "Some holes are starting to show up in our barrier back here!"

I jerked my head over to look at my mirror again. A truck with a bunch of guys in the bed swung out to the side and began to pull up alongside of us; some of the men in the bed of the truck appeared to have hands that were on fire.

"Molotovs!" I yelled into the radio.

In a display of rapid threat assessment that made me proud (made me proud later, at least, when all this shit was over), Davidson rolled over onto his side and unloaded a magazine into the whole group, causing the men to drop their improvised explosives in the bed, which broke and engulfed them up to their wastes in flames. Without hesitating, he re-aimed and fired a grenade from his M203 into the passenger window of the truck, where it detonated and blew out all the windows. I had just enough time to see the truck lose speed and begin to roll off into the desert before my side mirror just simply disappeared, having been vaporized by a rifle round.

"*Fuck this*!" I screamed. "Wang, get your ass over here and take this wheel!"

He jerked his head at me, face white with panic, and shouted, "Say what!"

"You heard me; get the fuck over here! Move!" I popped his seatbelt with a jab from my finger, grabbed him by the drag handle of his vest, and yanked him over into my lap. Once he was positioned, I threw my feet over to the right, rammed my palm into his hip, and shoved myself out from under him.

"What the hell?" he shouted as I slapped my radio into his hands.

"Put this on!" I yelled. "I'm getting back in that fight! Do not take your eyes off the road ahead. Be on the lookout for road-blocks and ambushes, do you copy?"

Wang rattled his head up and down like a dashboard bobblehead.

"And take it the fuck off cruise control! I don't know what the hell I was thinking; slowing down was wronger than two boys fucking in the back of a church! Get this piece of shit moving! *Now*!"

I reached across the cab and yanked the earpiece and mic off of Wang's head, hit the button, and yelled, "Davidson, how copy!"

The sound of rapid-fire erupted in the speaker as Davidson's small sounding voice shouted, "Yeah, here!"

"I want you guys to count to five, then stand up from behind that wall and spray the ever-living fuck out of the whole horizon. Over!"

His voice came back immediately. "Copy all! Five seconds starting now!"

I threw the sling of my HK around my neck, braced at the door momentarily, and then rammed it open with my shoulder.

"Don't die!" Wang shouted from behind me.

He timed his acceleration such that we were picking up speed again before I'd swung myself out onto the side runner, which I appreciated the hell out of. Reaching up to grab the steel tubing of the frame Fred had constructed for the armor plating (which wrapped over the roof of the cab), I began to shimmy backward to the rear. As I went, I leaned my head back to look behind us and saw a fat line of vehicles in close pursuit stretching far back enough that I couldn't see the end of them; they were stacked up so thick that they were running off the sides of the road, which I assumed was to maximize the firepower of their front line. Davidson and Greg were standing up in the trailer with their rifle barrels held over the top of the shield wall, shooting at everything they could. It seemed to be helping; the constant rattle of bullet impacts had dropped off considerably.

Just as I closed the gap with the truck bed but before I'd managed to swing a leg up to climb in, I heard the frequency of our gunfire cut in half. I felt a flash of panic and jerked my head to see what had happened. Davidson was crouched low and fumbling with his receiver, either trying to clear a jam or swapping a mag; I couldn't tell which. The return fire picked up again almost immediately. I saw an entire line of muzzle flashes over the tops of pursuing truck cabs and out the sides of car windows in the distance.

I swung my left leg into the truck bed and nearly lost my grip to fall away as something that felt like the size of a softball yet hard as a rock slammed into the back of my right leg, knocking it from the runner and out into open space. I screamed through clenched teeth and pulled myself up over the edge of the bed, using nothing but my left leg and a single hand. Falling into the giant pile of food, I lay there a moment panting. I reached down to feel behind my leg and encountered searing pain, as though a red hot charcoal had been dropped into my pants. I put my other hand back there as well and began to probe around, finding both entry and exit wounds.

"Motherfuckers…" I hissed. I pulled my hand back to look at it; saw that it was covered in blood and… something else. Something brownish-yellow.

"What the fu—" I gasped, trying to figure out what part of the body might produce a goo that color. Intestines? Down in my fucking leg? Had I shat myself?

I pulled my hand closer and smelled it, anticipating the aroma before it hit. I was shocked when it smelled the exact opposite of what I'd suspected.

"Er… curry?" Realization dawned on me immediately. "Fu-uck me!"

I rolled over to look beneath me; several of the MRE packages were perforated by bullets, the contents spilled throughout the bed.

"You cock suckers!" I screamed. Pain forgotten, I heaved to my knees and swam the rest of the distance to the rear of the bed before launching myself bodily into the trailer, bruising several parts of myself painfully on the more jagged edges of ammo crates and boxes that were contained there. Stumbling across the pile of weaponry while fighting with my rifle to keep from tripping up over it, I eventually positioned myself between Davidson and Greg at the back wall. I noted in mixed horror and anger that several holes had punched through over the entire surface.

"I feel as though we've been here before," Davidson shouted.

"Yeah, yeah, shit happens," I shouted back. "How's it look back there? Are they falling back?"

"Uh…" Davidson poked his head around the side and yanked it back immediately. "Negative. They're matching speed."

"Okay, get on the radio and tell Wang to floor it."

As Davidson shouted into his mic, I began to search through the various boxes, bags, and crates at my feet. I grunted and screamed freely as I worked; the hamstrings in the back of my leg ignited in furious pain at the slightest muscle twitch. I began to throw shit around angrily. I'd known where it was when we loaded it up—I'd purposefully made a mental note so I could grab it out and play with it as soon as we got home. Everything had been shifted around now, and I was having a bitch of a time finding it.

"Hey, dude," Greg shouted between taking shots around the side of the wall. "You want to get in on this, or what?"

"Just hang on a minute, damn it."

I saw it then, lying under a pile of vests; a black, hard-shell case only a few feet away. I grabbed it and yanked it over into my lap, popping the latches immediately and throwing the lid open.

Laying inside, just begging to be rotated into the fight, was a Desert Tech SRS-A1 chambered in .338 Lapua Magnum, one of the nastier high powered, long-range sniper rounds ever conceived. With zero hesitation, I yanked it into my lap and kicked the case away, dropped the mag, and dove into the pile of shit in front of me to search for a box of the deadly ammunition. After a few short moments, I hit pay dirt and began thumbing the big, meaty bullets into the five round magazine.

"Greg," I shouted, "get down in this mess and find me a scope. A big one!"

He rotated and dove into the pile like an Olympic swimmer. While he did that, I slapped the magazine home, pulled on the clownishly oversized operating lever, and cycled a round into the pipe.

I turned to face to the rear and, using my one good leg, popped my head over the barrier to see who was back there. They'd fallen back a bit, yet they were still close enough that I could hit them without the need of a sight, of which the rifle currently had none.

"Okay, Davidson, have Wang hit the brakes to kill some of that speed, and then tell him to jam the gas down again."

"Hit the brakes?" he screamed. "Are you—"

"Just do it, already! I want 'em close enough that I can smell their pussies!"

Davidson grimaced and mouthed the word "Jesus" before relaying the message back to Wang. After a bit of argument between them, Wang did as instructed, and we all braced ourselves as our weight was thrown towards the front of the truck. I heard a grunt from my side as Greg rolled over onto his shoulder.

Three seconds later, we were thrown in the other direction as the Ford began to haul some real ass. I took that as my cue and popped up over the wall. I selected my target instantly, a big-ass gray Bronco that was close enough that I could see the paint scratches in the hood, and pulled the trigger.

The rifle butt slammed into my shoulder, nearly knocking me back on my ass due to the fact that I only had the one leg to stand on.

"You missed!" Davidson shouted in disbelief.

"The fuck I did!"

I suppose he'd expected me to disintegrate the driver's head, which I must admit would have been nice, but I'd chosen instead to kill the Bronco, drilling a round straight into the grill. The truck was already bleeding off speed noticeably as smoke erupted from under the hood, creating a barrier that the other vehicles had to swerve around.

I crouched behind the wall to work the bolt on the rifle as Davidson said, "You wanted to shoot out his radiator?"

"Man, I wouldn't be surprised if I punched a hole through his block. That truck is done forever."

I stood up and administered the same treatment to another vehicle; a Mercedes of all things.

"Shit, Gibs! You're shot!" Greg shouted from behind me.

"I am," I agreed. "It sucks but we can't deal with that just yet." I took another shot, murdering a pickup truck. "We have to win the fight first. Always win the fight first! Where's that scope?"

"I've got it here!"

I spun and dropped back down to my ass and took a long cardboard box out of the kid's hands.

"Leupold. Good taste!"

Despite the situation, Greg laughed and said, "What?"

"Nothing. Get back up there and start shooting."

"Right on!" he shouted and did just that.

I ripped the scope from its packaging and confirmed, thank fuck, that it would mount to the rifle's rail. Torquing down the mount's thumb screws, I yelled, "How do they look, Davidson? They falling back?"

"Yeah, they've fallen way back! They're still in range to shoot at us, though. Maybe a few hundred yards?"

"Bet your ass they fell back," I grumbled under my breath. "Show 'em a little tooth and just watch their dicks shrivel up and fall off…"

I didn't have the requisite Allen wrench to secure the Scope's mount to the rifle rail, so I had to content myself with using the pliers on my multi-tool to twist the screws down, scuffing the shit out of everything and not giving one good goddamn. Dropping the scope into its mount, I pulled the Phillip's head screwdriver out of the tool and tightened everything down.

I shouldered the rifle to see how I'd done and found the picture to be about the jankiest thing I'd ever slapped together. The crosshair was all lopsided, making any adjustments for windage or elevation absolutely pointless. I was just going to have to figure out where to hold on target and pray for the best.

Digging out a pair of binoculars, I turned and wrestled myself one-legged back into a standing position. I held them out to Greg and said, "I'm gonna need you to walk me on."

"Say what?" he asked.

I pointed at the rifle. "I just slapped this piece of shit on here. It's not zeroed or anything; I'd be surprised if it even gets close to where I'm aiming. I need you to sight where I hit and tell me how far off I am."

"Oh, holy shit," he groaned, grabbing the binoculars. He put them to his eyes and moaned, "Proceed…"

I took aim and, just before I could squeeze the trigger, a bullet impacted into the wood below my chin, shooting splinters up into the air and stinging the shit out of my face.

"Yeah, they're still in range, I said," an annoyed Davidson shouted.

"Well, why the fuck aren't you suppressing, man! Turn up the heat on them! Jesus Christ!"

He grumbled a bunch of shit under his breath while swapping in a new magazine. He slapped his bolt release, pivoted, and had three-round bursts going down range almost before his muzzle was in place.

"Okay, where was I?" I whispered and took the first shot. "Where'd I hit, Greg?"

"I didn't see it."

"You didn't… were you looking?"

"Oh, no, Gibs, you're right. I was over here downloading porn to my iPhone and twiddling with my dick!"

"Well, put it away and peel your damned eyes, son! You're looking for puffs of debris on the pavement, okay?"

"Got it," Greg said. "Go again."

I took another shot. "Anything?"

"Nothing. I didn't see a damned thing."

"Well, shit," I said and pulled the mag out. "Start shooting back at them, Greg, while I get this hog reloaded."

Davidson suddenly fell on his ass beside me and shouted, "God *damn it*!"

"What! What happened?"

He was alternating between slapping at his chest frantically and holding his hands up in front of his face.

"Davidson, what? Calm the fuck down! What is it!"

"Figure it the hell out soon, will yah?" Greg shouted.

"Tom!" I shouted, grabbing him by the front of his vest and giving him one hard shake. "What the hell, man?"

Relief poured over his face in a wave as he let his head drop back and he began to laugh. "Son of a bitch. I took a hit right to the chest. I thought I'd had it. Felt like a fucking truck!"

I laughed along with him, relieved that he was okay. Lightly slapping his plate carrier, I said, "Glad you're not dead. Now quit skating and get back in this fight."

"Yes please!" Greg yelled, dropping behind the wall to swap in a fresh magazine. With all three of us down, the return fire intensified considerably.

I finished reloading and groaned as I turned to stand up again, accepting Davidson's offered hand. Settling the barrel down on a one-time shield wall that now looked a lot more like Swiss cheese, I glanced at Greg on my left and shouted, "Ready?"

He put the binoculars to his eyes and gave a thumbs-up.

"Alright. Red sedan in the center. See it?"

"Yeah, go!" Greg yelled.

"Davidson, try not to shake the shield, okay?"

He stopped firing long enough to say, "Roger. Sorry."

"Okay," I whispered quietly. "Let's… see…" The rifle crashed, slamming back into my shoulder.

"Got it!" Greg shouted, slapping the barrier with his hand. "You were low and to the left!"

"How far?"

"About a couple of feet left and three down."

"Jesus, that's way off. Okay, how about now?" Another crash. I thought about how shitty my shoulder would feel the next day… assuming I lived that long.

"Nothing that time," Greg said, binoculars glued to his face.

"Maybe too high…" Davidson suggested.

"Yeah, that's what I was thinking," I said. "Okay, here we go. Red sedan…" I exhaled and squeezed.

Have you ever played basketball or maybe just been out on the court shooting hoops with some friends? Sometimes you take a shot, maybe from the three-point line, and you know… you just know that it's going into that hoop. The shot feels so good that you know the ball is going home as soon as it slips off your fingers. Yeah. That's how that shot felt.

"Boom, motherfucker!" yelled Greg. "Right through the hood!"

"That's it. That's where I hold." I smiled and cycled the bolt. "Okay, shit bags. Let's see how well you drive without engines."

I blew out three more vehicles in rapid succession after that. Just… one after the other; bang, bang, bang—like that, before they figured out what was going on and fell back even further.

"Think that's it," Davidson said, pulling his rifle back. "I don't think I can hit them anymore. You guys?"

"Not me," said Greg.

"I'm out too," I said. "This little baby could hit them if I had the scope set better, but I don't know where to hold it on them anymore. I don't want to waste any more rounds trying to find my mark again. Let 'em hang back there for now."

I turned and sank down to my ass, groaning as I gingerly stretched my right leg out in front of me. The entry and exit both seemed fairly clean to me; it wasn't even bleeding as bad as it could have. It hurt so bad I could barely stand on it but outside of that, I seemed to have gotten off easily. I opened up my blowout kit, dug out an Israeli Battle Dressing, and began irrigating the wounds with a bottle of water. "Davidson, get Wang on the radio and tell him to slow it down. Let's not eat that fuel up if those assholes are hanging back. Oh, and let him know we're gonna top off the fuel, so he doesn't freak out when he sees a bunch of lights flash on his console."

As Davidson relayed my message up front, I told Greg, "Hey, *very carefully*, head up to the front and top our tank off, will yah?"

"Uh… can we do that? While we're driving, I mean?"

"Sure. Of course," I said. "It ain't like gasoline. Go for it, kid. Just feed that hose into the pipe and turn the reserve's pump on."

"Oh, okay. I'm on it," he smiled and began to stumble his way across the trailer towards the tailgate.

WANG'S A BADASS?

Gibs

We'd been coasting along at an easy speed while the asshole brigade continued to follow along at a safe distance; about a mile as far as I could estimate. They weren't creeping up on us, but they certainly weren't breaking the chase off either. I was fine with it. As long as they were back there, I didn't have to worry about hot lead drilling up my ass.

The other guys, Davidson and Greg, stayed in the trailer with me while I fiddled around with the scope mounting on the SRS. I figured there was no way I'd get the thing to zero on a moving truck, but I could get the crosshairs aligned properly, which would allow me to at least use the elevation and windage markers on the crosshair to better estimate where to hold my aim. Before, when the orientation made it look more like an X than a cross, I was basically down to holding my finger up in the air and making a wild-ass guess before pulling the trigger.

"Hey, Wang's asking what comes next!" Davidson shouted suddenly from my side, fighting to be heard over the rushing wind.

"What comes next? Tell him to keep driving. Just take us home."

"Well, what about these dicks behind us?"

"What about them?" I yelled.

"Aren't they just gonna follow us all the way back to Jackson?" Greg asked.

"I'm betting on them running out of gas before we get there. And if they have to stop to refuel, we'll just leave them behind."

Davidson was muttering into his mic as he relayed my answer up to Wang. Greg pressed the point by asking, "Are you sure they'll run out of gas, though?"

"Pretty sure," I yelled. "We have to drive through the whole state of Utah before we get to Wyoming. Let 'em keep following us if they're so damned stupid. They'll be coughing on fumes halfway through the state, and we can just bend over and slap our ass cheeks at them as we sail off into the sunset."

Davidson repeated everything I said into the mic verbatim, paused a few moments, and then said, "I'll ask him." He looked at me and shouted, "Wang wants to know what happens if they make another move."

"Hah, Gibs'll just kill their cars," Greg laughed.

"No, he has a point," I said. "This rifle only holds five rounds at a time before it needs a reload. If they rush us, they can get on top of us. Then the long reach of the SRS won't mean a damned thing."

We rode along silently for a few moments, all of us uneasy about the prospect of that entire column coming down on us all at once. Three men with rifles would likely be overwhelmed in no time at all.

"Grab that roll of duct tape," I said, pointing to the edge of the trailer bed. "Let's start hanging that spare Kevlar on the wall, here, while there's still a wall to use. Let's make sure they're all carrying armor plates…"

We spent the next several minutes trying to cover every square inch of perforated board with ballistic body armor, strapping it all down with copious amounts of 100 mph tape. I did my best to help the guys, but with my gimp leg, I spent more time just trying to keep from falling off the trailer than doing anything else and had to settle for holding vests in place for the others while they secured it all.

"You think this'll do it?" Davidson shouted at me.

"Better than what we had before," I said. "Pass me those binos," I said to Greg.

He handed them up to me, and I put my eyes on the column following behind.

"How's it look?" Greg asked from below me. He had his back propped up against the wall with his rifle in his lap.

"Messy," I answered. "There's an awful damned lot of them back there… one, two, three, four… seven… shit, they're moving all over the place, but I'd guess thirty different vehicles of all types, including the motorcycles. Two or three people to a vehicle, more in the truck beds. I guess there could be fifty people back there? A hundred? Hard to tell the way they're moving around all over the place."

"Shit on me," Davidson moaned. "I wasn't even sure there were a hundred people left anymore!"

"Oh, they're out there," I said. "People are gonna draw together over time, just like we are." I spit off the back of the trailer into the wind. "Just like they are."

"Hey, message from Wang," Davidson interrupted. "Says we're hitting Mesquite in five."

"Well, thank God for that!" I shouted. "It's gotta be only ten or fifteen miles from there to the mountain pass. That crowd back there will bottleneck like a son of a bitch. That's our best chance to get some distance on them. Once we get on the other side of the mountains, we'll pull off the road into Atkinville and hide out among the houses there."

"Hang on, hang on," Davidson waved at me. He held the mic up to his mouth and relayed everything I'd said to Wang. After he finished, he looked in my direction, but his eyes remained unfocused, clearly listening to Wang's response. A moment later, his eyes refocused onto mine, and he asked, "Won't we just run into them again if they pass us? When we get back on the road to go through Utah?"

I nodded and said, "We'll camp out a couple of days and then take an alternate route… some road that parallels the 15."

"But the fuel! Won't we run out of—"

"I don't know, okay? Holy mother of the falafel eating Christ, can we just first extract that detachment of Mad Max rejects from our assholes, please? Son of a bitch, we've made it across country without a guaranteed supply of fuel before. We'll do it again."

They both looked down at the deck, uncertain and clearly worried. They looked like a couple of scared kids.

"Hey," I shouted, pulling their attention back to me. I hooked a thumb over my shoulder and said, "Fuck those guys, alright? Only reason they're such a pain in our asses is because there're so many of 'em. One on one, they're jack shit, right?"

Davidson's eyes pulled away from mine, looking straight behind us. They widened, and he shouted, "They're making a move!"

I spun in place, nearly fell over when my bandaged leg screamed in fury and pulled myself back into position using the edge of the barrier and Greg's shoulder.

They had clearly accelerated, bearing down on us hard, and four trucks as well as a handful of motorcycles pulled out ahead of the group and began to swerve haphazardly across the road.

"What the fuck are they doing?" Davidson shouted.

"They're driving evasively, of course," I answered. "They're trying to nullify my ability to murder their engines."

Davidson laughed hysterically. "Those morons!"

"Yeah, no, it actually works," I said. He looked at me in horror, and I shrugged. Pointing at the SRS, I said, "That scope is so far off it might as well be held onto the rifle with bubblegum. I figured out where to hold my aim when they were static at a set distance. With what they're doing now, I'd be better off just throwing the bullets at them. I can wait for them to get closer, of course, but they'll be able to shoot back at that point."

Davidson only stared at me, mouth working silently. Finally, he said, "Well, shit!" and hefted his rifle.

"Here they come!" shouted Greg.

We watched as they came flying toward us, carving wide, sweeping arcs through the dirt, then over the paved road, then back into the dirt on the opposite side. At the last moment, just before I pulled the trigger on my HK, the trucks broke in opposite directions, swinging out to either side of us, while the motorcycles stayed back and peppered the trailer with bullets. The three of us dropped behind the wall and aimed out to the sides of the trailer to try and shoot the trucks as they pulled up alongside, which would have worked great except for the fact that the trucks didn't pull up alongside; they blasted forward, presenting a brief, multicolored blur as they plowed through our field of view. A fraction of a second later and they were lost from sight, somewhere on the road up ahead of us.

I clawed for the radio clipped over Davidson's ear to scream at Wang to get the hell out of the way, but it was unnecessary. The Ford slowed down hard, throwing us all a few feet forward before Wang swerved us off the side of the road. At our high rate of speed, the truck pitched up and down violently like a breaching whale, whipping the trailer behind it. The three of us could only hold on for dear life, nearly being thrown from the vehicle as it bucked like an enraged bull.

As Wang pulled us off to the right, the four trucks that had positioned themselves ahead of us came into my field of view to the left; they slowly repositioned so that the collection of men in the back could shoot at us broadside. Fumbling around with the radio earpiece, I finally gave up and just put my mouth as close to the mic as I could get it, close enough that I could smell Davidson's panicked sweat, hit transmit, and shouted, "Get us back alongside them! Get as close to them as you can! They can shoot our tires out if you put distance between us!"

The truck jigged back onto the road like a bronco, throwing us all into the air again, and slammed hard into a Silverado holding a trio of shitheads with shotguns. We didn't even have to shoot at those guys; the brutal force of the Ford slamming into its side launched the Chevy off the road into the ditch, sending the men in the bed into the air screaming, only to land several meters away. They quickly became unrecognizable as the abrasive dirt and pavement turned them into ex-human meat waffles. The Chevy followed soon after, rolling several times before ramming into a guardrail, which catapulted the vehicle high into the air and back down into the gulch where it finally came to a rest, pulverized entirely.

Before I could say anything else, Wang punched the gas and pulled us up along the next truck in line with a whole new collection of assholes for us to contend with. They pulled their weapons up to bear on us and, I swear to God, I could see a gleeful grin on at least one of their faces.

"Look ou—" I began to shout.

Wang's hand thrust out of the driver's side window holding a brand new 1911 and began to light them the fuck up with round after round of .45 ACP, pulling on the trigger until the weapon clicked. His hand disappeared momentarily inside the truck and immediately thrust forth again with the only thing better than the 1911 he'd just emptied: a second fully loaded 1911. He shot that one empty as well, dumping the whole magazine into the passenger side window of the opposing truck, which swerved frantically across the road; several of the men in the truck bed (who were dead anyway) went tumbling out onto the road like a pile of human speed bumps.

Wang's hand disappeared into the cab again to set his pistol down and then thrust out through the window a final time, middle finger extended towards the retreating truck.

"*Fuck yea, Wang!*" I screamed at the top of my lungs. "*Get some!*"

"Holy shit, Wang's a badass!" Greg said excitedly.

The men in the bed of the third truck were ready for us as we swerved and pulled up on its right. Their rifles were down and firing before any of us had a chance to get a bead on them. Rather than trying to shoot any of us in the trailer, these men unloaded into the side of the cab where the vehicle was soft and unarmored. Wang immediately swerved into the bed of the opposing truck in response, fish-tailing the vehicle, which spun to the right in front of the grill of our Ford, hung there for a moment as we plowed it up the highway sideways, and then slowly slid further to the right where it reversed directions and began to slip by us. Greg was ready for them when they came, shooting into the windshield as they inched by and certainly killing everyone inside. Davidson and I dealt with the men in the bed, who could only hang on as their truck swerved and sloshed around under them.

As they passed behind us, the old, familiar rattling of bullet impacts started up again on the armor wall I was leaning up against, interleaved from time to time with the muted *thup, thup* of slugs hitting the Kevlar vests.

"Well, our friends are back," Davidson said needlessly.

I ignored him. The Ford was hitching underneath us, sputtering forward and then falling back, alarming the shit out of me. "Get Wang! Ask him if they killed the truck!"

A few seconds later Davidson said, "Negative. The truck is fine. Wang took a bullet."

"Fuck me," I growled. "Where at?"

"Where at?" Silence a moment, then, "The hip! Says it hurts so bad he can barely see straight!"

"Fuck, fuck, fuck!" I shouted. "Somebody needs to get up there and relieve him! Davidson, you stay back with that launcher. Greg: go!"

He nodded and climbed to his feet, just as the fourth and final truck swung into view and fell back next to us, close enough that the men in the bed could have boarded us like a collection of apocalyptic road pirates.

Greg looked back at me, and we locked eyes. Time froze down to a single, motionless instant as he and I shared complete understanding. As he stared at me, half a smile hanging on his lips while a collection of men stood behind him holding pistols, shotguns, and rifles, I knew beyond the shadow of a doubt that he was going to jump across to that other truck in an attempt to kill every last one of those bastards or at least die trying. I knew it like I knew the sky was blue and I felt my balls draw up into my stomach in panic.

He gave me the slightest of nods, turned on the spot, gathered his legs under himself, and leaped… and had his momentum arrested immediately as I grabbed his dumb ass by the drag handle of his vest and slammed him into the trailer on his back. My leg ignited into flaming, outraged fury at this action and I fell down on top of him screaming in agony.

Davidson, in the meantime, unloaded everything he had into the bed of the other truck, thoroughly fucking up their entire universe.

"Jesus Fucking Christ, Greg, what the hell were you doing?

Did your mother drink Drano throughout her pregnancy?" I dragged him out from under me and slapped him on the back of his helmet. "I did not give you permission to die, you bent-dick, little puke! Wang needs relief, goddamnit! Get your underfed, boney ass up there and relieve him!"

Face full of confusion, panic, or both, Greg rolled over onto all fours and began to crawl clumsily towards the truck bed. Instead of waiting to watch the climax of his ponderous journey, I set my HK aside and retrieved the SRS. "Okay, sweethearts," I said, "we'll see if you all remember my good friend Mr. Lapua…"

I lunged forward into the shield wall, dragging myself up with a hand and a snarl. Davidson was alternating between diving undercover and popping up just long enough to lob another volley downrange.

I poked my head over the wall and suffered a moment of shock when I saw the long array of cars, buggies, motorcycles, and trucks stacked right up on our asses. I began to consider the very real possibility that we weren't going to make it through this. The mountain pass was so close, but they were already on top of us, and we had just lost Greg's firepower to keep the truck moving.

I confronted the possibility of failure; the idea that the people back home (who were depending on us to save them from starving) would go right on waiting for a bailout that would never come. Winter would come through the area in full force, snow them in, and they would all run out of food. Thinking back to the pulverized MRES in the truck bed, I realized that I didn't even know how much of the food we'd collected was still intact; it was entirely possible that we'd still failed even if we managed to get away.

I looked up at Davidson, who stared back at me wide-eyed, and shouted, "Not another one of those twats gets ahead of us, do you read me? I don't care if we're taking bullets to the face. I don't care if we fuckin' die back here. This truck makes it home, no matter the cost. Clear?"

He swallowed hard and shook his head in a jarring nod.

"Gimme that radio," I yelled, and he did. Bullet impacts rattled behind me, drumming a rapid percussion beat into my body by way of my spine. Davidson stood overhead, shooting and screaming equally, and I couldn't tell if it was his voice drowning out the gunfire or the other way around.

"Wang! How copy?"

"It's Greg! Wang's too fucked up to talk! I couldn't even move him; I'm driving from the center in here!"

"Fine!" I shouted. "Listen to me: pin that peddle into the floorboard, do you copy? I don't care if the engine explodes and the transmission is shat out the back end! You get me every bit of speed out of this bitch that you can find!"

"Understood!" he shouted back, though his voice sounded small in the earpiece, and the truck lurched forward under us again.

I dropped the SRS in favor of the H&K, pawed at Davidson's shoulder to haul myself back into position, and put my muzzle back over the wall. I heard the snap of bullets passing by in the air; saw the pursuit behind us falling back due to our unanticipated surge forward. They were falling back, but then that increase in distance began to slow as they fought to keep up with us. There was shooting in the air all around us, shield wall rattling against our chests like a living, aggravated animal.

I went to work, then, and a blood lust came on me the likes of which I'd never before experienced and have not encountered since. The rifle came alive under my hands, and the world went black around the edges of my vision as I shot at everything that moved before me. I suspect a lot of it was the adrenaline, which had surged up again in response to my exposure.

James Mattis, the patron saint of all Marines, once said, "There is nothing better than getting shot at and missed." Well, I'm here to tell you that wasn't a bunch of machismo bullshit on his part; anyone that's come out of a firefight alive will tell you the same thing. There is no feeling, not even sex, that's as sweet as coming face to face with Death and cheating that son of a bitch. When you're in a fight and the enemy's missing, when the bullets are sliding off of you, and your buddies are standing beside you alive and angry…

There are two circumstances under which you'll ever feel invincible in a gunfight: you're either dominating the battlespace, and everything is going your way, or all means of retreat have been closed to you. When the choices are either to prevail or die, and you're maybe unsure about which way it's likely to go, but you're okay with either outcome.

I don't know which it was for me at that exact moment; don't know if I was kill drunk because things were starting to look good again or because it didn't matter how they looked at all. I remember how hard I screamed—just this long, endless outpouring of rage and frustration. I screamed to drown out the rushing wind and the revving engines and the constant rumble of gunfire. I wanted the ones I was shooting at to hear me howl; to know that I was going to keep on killing them for as long as they'd let me and that I loved them for letting me do so. I was grateful to them for being there to receive what I had to offer.

I don't remember what Davidson was up to by that point; only remember that I could still feel his presence next to me, that I still felt the percussion of his weapon firing at all angles. My vision blurred and I blinked angrily, squirting tears from both sides of my eyes, and I don't know if those tears were from wind or fury. I quit yelling at them only when I had to change out magazines; all I got for a breath was that little window before I was hollering and shooting again, as though my screaming were a requirement to the weapon's function.

We stood like that, Davidson and me, and I killed more people in the space of a few minutes than all the other days of my life combined. For that instant, when the concept of "five minutes later" didn't even feel like a remote possibility, I was fine with it.

GATES OF FIRE

Gibs

The mountain wall rose up out of the ground before us on the right after not too long, and we quickly closed the distance. Our pursuit was fighting to make up some distance again; one last push before we plunged into the safety of the Hot Gates. They'd had a hell of a time keeping up as Davidson, and I had killed enough drivers and engines that vehicles had either rolled to a stop or crashed into those adjacent, peppering the length of the highway with pile-ups and jumbled bodies. I'd taken some rounds to the chest in the confusion of it all, the wall beginning to truly fail despite our best efforts to keep it serviceable.

At one point I looked over at Davidson, who had been laughing, to see that the bottom half of his left ear was gone with a sheet of blood running down his neck. There was a big, grey scrape running up the middle of his helmet accompanied by a visible crack that threatened to make me feel queasy if I spent too long thinking about what caused it.

Before I knew what was happening, the shadow of the desert-brown mountain walls loomed up on either side of us, abrupt as a thundercloud passing in front of the sun, and we plunged into the narrow pass that cut through the Virgin Mountains. The 15 was reduced to two lanes in either direction through these parts, divided in the center by a gorgeous concrete wall. Those bastards could get on the wrong side, sure, but they couldn't get back over at us after they did.

"Greg… copy?" I shouted into my mic.

"Yeah?" he came back.

"How we doing up there, kid?"

He tried to respond, but the signal was broken up by interference. I cursed the piece of shit civilian radio and fiddled around with the display to confirm I was still on the right channel.

"Repeat your last, Greg!"

"I said Wang is seriously fucked up, man! I got a sweater crammed up against his ass, but it's soaked throu—"

More static in the earpiece.

"—pale! We gotta get away from these guys and fix him up!"

"Okay, okay, copy all!" I lied. "Listen: slow us down again!"

"The fuck, man? I just said—"

"I know what you said. Slow us down anyway. We've got to stop these cocksuckers now, or there'll be no fixing up Wang ever."

The column rounded the bend into the cleft behind us and began to gain again; we were crawling along at something like thirty miles per hour. They came at us three abreast, unable to spread out any wider than that in the cleft, each row composed of a couple of vehicles on the road and one on the soft shoulder. Every so often, the passage narrowed enough that the ones on the shoulder had to merge back onto the pavement. Surprisingly (or perhaps not surprisingly; the number of vehicles behind us had been reduced significantly over the last little while), they slowed down as soon as they saw us, once again hanging back to see what we would do.

"What's our play if they don't come at us?" asked Davidson.

Instead of answering, I asked, "How many of those grenades do you have left?"

"Eight."

"Mmm," I nodded. "Crouch down behind that wall where our friends can't see and line us up a few more rifles. Get them all set with full mags, then start refilling all the other empty mags on the floor. Shit, fill a couple of those Mossbergs with slugs as well."

"You got it," he said and dropped to his knees to get busy. He was at it for several minutes while that whole army of cowards hung back behind us, my contempt for them growing the whole time. It seemed they'd been stung enough by then that they were more interested in waiting us out than having another go. When he was done, there were several loaded rifles at our feet, a couple of shotguns, the pouches on both of our rigs were filled near to bursting, and there was a 40 mm grenade waiting in the M203.

"You ready to make an end of this?" I asked.

Davidson reclaimed his position next to me and said, "Hell yes." He knew what was coming next, I think; he had his rifle pressed up against the wall with his knee and hung empty hands out in the open where they'd be visible.

I nodded. I took a deep breath and said, "You would have been an outstanding Marine, Tom." He said nothing back. I didn't know if such a sentiment even meant anything to him anymore; realized I didn't care. It still meant something to me.

"Greg," I said into the radio, quieter now because we weren't hauling ass up the road and the wind was down. "Stop the truck."

He didn't even bother asking what I was thinking that time. The truck just came to a stop.

I bent down painfully and dug an old, white t-shirt out of the pile of shit we were standing on; something we had used to wrap up a few handguns to keep them from slamming against each other in one of the boxes. I held it up high in the air and waved it back and forth.

Given the distance we were at, I could see a number of the men and women still standing in the remaining truck beds look about each other uncertainly. I smiled to myself and said, "That's right. We got no more fight left in us. Come and get your prize."

We hung out like that in the middle of the road for several minutes, walled in between a concrete divider on one side and a jagged mountainside on the other, and I waved until my arm felt like it would fall off. The shirt fluttered overhead, and Greg's voice came again over the radio: "I hope to fuck you know what you're doing, man."

Some more static crackled over the radio and, buried just underneath it, an unfamiliar voice that said unrecognizable things. I put it out of my mind; whatever it was, it sure wasn't going to contribute to the current situation.

Out in the distance, a man slapped the top of a truck cab, and they all started rolling forward again, slowly. It was just trucks and cars at that point; the folks on two wheels hadn't done so well in the last skirmish. A few people jumped from truck beds to walk along on foot, rifles at the ready.

"They're gonna be pissed," I said quietly to Davidson. "They probably won't shoot us outright. They'll want to get close, get us under control. They'll want to do us up close…"

"Okay," he said. His voice was steady like iron.

"…so let 'em get close," I concluded.

We did. At a distance of two hundred feet, give or take, I dropped the shirt and said, "Get some."

The M203 let off a *POONT*! from my right, followed immediately after by the crump of an explosion in the very center of the closest truck's windshield. I joined in with my rifle, taking my time and putting rounds into the center mass of anyone or anything stupid enough to be visible. Davidson continued with the

M203, firing grenades off into the mass of vehicles as fast as he could load them until there were none left and he had to be content with normal bullets.

Screaming had erupted as soon as we'd begun firing, only this time it was theirs. A few of them who were still alive after our initial volley attempted to reverse out of there in a hurry, but the space was so limited that they only jammed into each other and bound themselves in place. There was return fire in our direction but only sporadic, now. When we abandoned diving behind cover before, it was out of a general desperation and disregard for our own safety. Now, we didn't bother with cover out of a general disregard for our enemy's anemic response.

There was no yelling from us this time, no gnashing of teeth or cursing. We proceeded about our business purposefully, methodically. Before, it had been hellfire. This was just surgery. I shot my rifle empty and, rather than taking the time necessary to swap the mag, I just let it hang and picked up one of the others that Davidson had leaned against the wall. I shot that one empty, too.

Davidson did the same, picking his targets carefully and taking his time on them, every slug assigned a special purpose. Cars and trucks slammed into each other only a short distance away; tires spun in place and belched great clouds of white smoke into the air. Not long after, the excess rubber that had been laid onto the road ignited in several places from the heat and bright flames licked up to consume the vehicles' undersides. A few people ignited as well and made to run off in all directions. I shot them when I could but put most of my focus on those that were still fighting.

Despite the fires, many of the vehicles were still quivering back and forth as the drivers attempted to escape. In answer, I dropped my second rifle, retrieved the SRS, and put a .338 round through every engine to which I had a clear line of sight. After a few moments, there were fewer tires spinning. The white smoke rising into the air began to darken over to black.

We both emptied several more magazines between us. After that, I picked up one of the shotguns and started shooting out every window I could see with one-ounce slugs. In some cases, the spray of glass was accompanied by the jerking of a human body, but that was coming less often now. The movement across from us tapered off; then stopped entirely.

We stopped firing and waited. The low idle of a few surviving engines floated out to us through the smoke. We listened for shouts or gunfire but heard neither.

I thumbed my radio and said, "Take us out of here, Greg."

When we emerged from the other side of the pass, the radio came to life, and I heard a voice at once foreign yet totally familiar. It said, "Unknown station, this is Buzzard 1. Please identify, over."

Davidson took note of the expression on my face and shouted, "What? What the hell is it? Wang?"

I sat there and blinked like a dumbass. The radio squawked again in my ear. "I say again: unknown station, this is Buzzard 1. Please identify, over."

Greg's voice came on: "What the fuck?"

I jammed the button and responded, "Buzzard 1, this is Casanova Actual, over."

Davidson pulled a scandalized expression and mouthed, "*Casanova?*"

I waved a hand at him and concentrated on what I was hearing.

"Good to meet you, Casanova. What's your status, over?"

"Traveling north along the 15 freeway just outside of the

Virgin Mountains, approximately sixteen klicks away from the Utah border. Two casualties, one critical, over."

"Roger that. Continue on current route, and we'll come out to meet you, over."

I looked at Davidson and swallowed. "Buzzard 1, define '*we*,' over."

"United States Army, 101st Combat Aviation Brigade, Casanova. Just keep coming. We'll meet you en route. Buzzard 1 out."

Fifteen minutes later, we were pulled off the road facing a recently landed Black Hawk, the gusting wind of the rotor wreaking havoc on anything not tied down. The door gunner came running over to meet us.

In a daze, I saw the screaming eagle of the 101st Airborne riding on his shoulder. Without even stopping to introduce himself, he shouted, "Where's your critical?"

"I… in the cab. He took a round to the hip. I think his pelvis is shattered."

The man (his name tape said Jeffries) winced and started speaking into his team radio. Two more soldiers came running over to the truck with a stretcher.

"You're wounded too, sir." He had a lazy hillbilly drawl like he'd come tumbling out of the Appalachians.

"Huh?" I looked down at my leg. "Oh. Fuck it. It's fine for now. Our friend with the hip is the one who's in trouble."

He nodded and said, "Understood."

"I didn't think you guys were out there anymore," I said like an idiot.

The two soldiers ran Wang out on the stretcher, loading him efficiently into the aircraft.

"We have a base with an FST not too far away," Jeffries said. "My buddies are going to take him out there right now to treat him. How are you set for fuel? Can I ride with you in the truck..." he looked towards the Ford, a battered, brutalized shell of its former self, shook his head, and asked, "Uh, will that vehicle even start up, sir?"

"Yeah, it's good," I said in a daze. "A lot of that will buff right out."

He laughed and said, "Very good, sir. May I ride with you? I'll direct you back to our base where we can wait for your friend to recover."

The Black Hawk lifted up and away, rendering the soldier's question rather a moot point.

"Yeah, sure, hop in," I said. "But listen, we can't stay with you guys for too long." I hooked a thumb at the truck. "We're hauling supplies back to our people up in Wyoming. They're just about out of food, and I've got to get this all back to them before the snows really hit and fuck the roads."

"No worries, sir, I completely understand. Your friend prob-ably won't be able to travel for a while, but he can recover with us in the meantime." He offered his shoulder to me as I began to hobble back to the truck, which I accepted gratefully. "You can come back for him after the roads open up again. I may be able to get him an escort back to you guys but don't hold me to that. Diesel's pretty low."

"It's Jeffries, isn't it?" I asked as I limped towards the passenger seat of the truck."

"Yessir."

"Call me Gibs."

EPILOGUE

Amanda

None of them really had the stomach to kill Jeff, when it came down to it. What Jake had said to us before he disappeared had hit home, and they decided, in the end, that exile was the best solution. It was actually Oscar who made the final decision; even as Jake was walking away, they all made a good show of trying to talk it out, like they were just wrapping up the discussion even though few of them really had any more to say. It's hard to feel as though you can speak with authority so soon after you've been shamed.

It was an unspoken acknowledgment between us that Oscar would have been the one person allowed to disregard Jake's words out of hand. None of the rest of us wanted to even imagine being in his place and, being ignorant of the suffering experienced by both him and Maria, we awaited his decision to see what would come next. Even after hearing Jake, after his words had calmed my heart, I was prepared to let Oscar have Jeff. I would have even helped him discard the remains.

Here's the thing: certain people will tell you that such things solve nothing. They'll tell you that they don't actually make you feel better. Well, speaking from experience, I can say that, in some ways, certain people are right but, in other ways, certain people are very, very wrong.

Oscar shut it all down, though. As we stood around him, waiting to see what he would do, bracing ourselves, he only remained motionless for a time before shaking his head sadly and saying, "He's right."

Several people sighed audibly, bodies shifting as the tension bled out. He raised his head and glanced from person to person. "I'm not gonna make that decision for you guys. It's not…" He sighed. "Ain't my place," he finally said, and left it at that.

Alish and a few others wanted to know what could be done to protect future children from Jeff, given that we were essentially going to vomit him back out into the world; giving him over as a problem for some stranger to deal with.

"Where I grew up," Alish said, "Jeff's actions would have fallen under the classification of *hadd* crimes… but we've already decided that he won't be executed so that no longer applies." She looked at Oscar, eyes flashing as the rest of us hung on her words. "My family came here to escape such practices, and I tend to agree, but sometimes… just sometimes, the old ways seem right to me." She looked towards the silent camper and rubbed her arms as though she fought down goosebumps.

"We had the tradition of *Tazir*, which allowed for punishment for those crimes not covered under *hadd*, meted out at the discretion of the *qadi*. This could be such a crime."

She turned in my direction, fixing her gaze onto mine, and said, "Let him be marked in such a way that cannot be undone or hidden; in such a way that it will be obvious to all he encounters."

I probably don't need to go into how uncomfortable this made everyone else feel, given that she was essentially suggesting that we brand Jeff before sending him out. Some people cried "torture" and "barbarism," which silenced Alish almost immediately, causing her to retreat back into herself. Honestly, it clarified to me why she kept to herself so much; she and her family had indeed fled to a country that afforded them greater personal freedom— she clearly understood that the everyday realities of her native country were brutal; prone to misuse and corruption. And yet, as she had said, sometimes the old ways are best. We were all living in a brutal world now, with no police, government, or jail system to keep us all well behaved and civilized. A part of me (my American self, I suppose I'd call it) struggled with the idea, foreign and ugly as it was. A deeper part of me, a personal, up-close part, thought specifically of Jeff Durand and had no reservations at all.

I did it myself, after sending the others away, with a few ink pens, a lighter, and an X-acto knife. It wasn't anything you could consider to be artful or clean, and yet the word that I'd partially carved/partially tattooed into his forehead was legible at least. Permanent and inescapable.

PEDOPHILE.

Let him be marked, indeed.

I bound his hands, threw him in the Jeep, and drove him out to the boundary of our territory, dumping him on the 191. Cutting him loose, I said, "If you're seen in these hills, you'll be killed. If you're seen in Jackson, you'll be killed. If I hear you're anywhere out here, I'll hunt you down myself. Is that understood?"

He nodded without looking up at me; when I went to cut his hands loose, he cringed away from me.

"Where… where can I go?" he asked.

"Away."

He coughed and looked down the length of the highway as it disappeared into the distance.

"Can I get some food?"

"You can fucking starve as far as I'm concerned," I said. I climbed into my Jeep and drove home.

Jake returned to us a few days later, a little dirtier than when we'd last seen him, with no explanation or comment. He fell back in among us as though nothing had happened and, slowly, we all found a way back to our routine.

I think the incident with Jeff left my friend marked permanently, though. He began to walk off and disappear for a few days at a time, here and there, just as he'd done that first time he simply walked out of the valley, leaving us to wonder if he'd ever return. I sometimes tried to go see him at night, when all of the work was done, and problems solved, standing outside his door but not daring to turn the knob. The remembered words of my mother, about mistakes better left behind, always stopped me. When we finally finished my cabin (much later, this was), it became less of a problem.

The first snow of the season came, blanketing the floor of the valley in white fluff. Gibs returned to us a few days later with Davidson, Greg, a truck that looked as though it had been bombarded with bazooka fire, and a couple of military vehicles trailing behind him. He stumbled out of the truck on a stiff leg and a single crutch, waving his hands frantically over his head while yelling, "This is okay! All of this is okay! Wang is alive! Nobody shoot a goddamned thing!"

Several of us ran over to help him, though he shrugged us off and began to hobble aggressively towards the cabin, holding onto the crutch with both hands. It sunk into the ground here and there, and he ended up hopping a lot on one foot out of impatience.

"Where's Jake?" he barked. "I need to see him."

"He's in his cabin; we can get him now. Who… who are those guys?" I asked, pointing back at the line of very military-ish looking people climbing out of tan and olive drab trucks to stretch their legs and backs.

"Drinking buddies. You'll like 'em."

"Um, okay. Where's Wang?"

"Long story. Jake first; I don't want to repeat myself. We have a lot of shit to talk about."

I looked back over my shoulder at Gibs's drinking buddies, all of them conspicuously unarmed, all of them very conspicuously at pains to keep their hands visible, and said, "Well, yeah. I guess we do."

Gibs hobbled a few steps further towards the cabin, nearly losing balance as the greedy earth pulled at the crutch. I pulled on his arm to stop him and said, "Quit it; you're going to hurt yourself. Just wait here. I'll run and get him."

He nodded curtly as I brushed past, thundered up the steps of the porch, and let myself into the cabin.

"Jake! Gibs is back!" I called as I plunged down the side hallway towards the library. I rounded the corner into the room and found him sitting at Billy's desk (now his desk) with his back to me.

He was nearly reclined in the leather rolling chair, framed in the window behind him, and I could just see the top of his head over the high back. His right elbow was propped up on the armrest, and he held his hand in front of his face, as though he were inspecting his fingernails. In the cupped center of his palm and shrouded by the roof of his fingers, a bright, white light flashed in the low rays of the sun as they cut through the un-shuttered window, brilliant enough that I had to squint and shield my eyes. With my hand held out in front of me, the glare hurt less; he dropped his arm out of sight, and the sun filled the void it left, now unhindered by his hand, forcing me to close my eyes completely.

Through my closed lids, I felt the brilliance of the light pass; a sense of darkening fell across my face. I opened my eyes again and saw that he had turned in his chair to face me.

His hands were clenched together on the desk in front of him, his face a mask devoid of all expression.

FROM THE PUBLISHER

Thank you so much for reading *Commune Book Two* by Joshua Gayou. We hope you enjoyed it as much as we enjoyed bringing it to you. We just wanted to take a moment to encourage you to review the book on Amazon and Goodreads. Every review helps further the author's reach and, ultimately, helps them continue writing fantastic books for us all to enjoy.

If you liked *Commune Book Two*, check out the rest of our catalogue at www.aethonbooks.com. To sign up to receive updates regarding all new releases, visit www.aethonbooks.com/sign-up

J OSHUA GAYOU lives in Southern California with his wife Jennifer and son Anthony.

When he isn't writing, he divides his time between being a senior engineer at a prominent In Flight Entertainment (IFE) company, accomplishing tasks around the house as assigned by his wife (The Boss), building stuff out in his wood shop, playing board games with his kid, and whatever else his twisted little mind takes an interest in.

Visit joshuagayouauthor.com